THE ANCIENT ONES

THE ANCIENT ONES

CASSANDRA L. THOMPSON

Quill & Crow Publishing House

CLEVELAND

THE ANCIENT ONES BY CASSANDRA L. THOMPSON.
PUBLISHED BY QUILL & CROW PUBLISHING COMPANY, LLC.

Cover Design by Lauren Hellekson

Printed in the United States of America.

Cataloging-in-Publication Data is on file with the Library of Congress.

ISBN 978-1-7356863-2-5
ISBN 978-1-7356863-1-8 (ebook)

Author's Website: http://cassandralthompson.carrd.co

For

L.

SHE WAS CRUMPLED AGAINST THE ANCIENT OAK TREE with her head buried in her hands, tufts of raven hair between her fingers.

Although he longed to comfort her, he found he was unable, his own grief squeezing at his chest. Around them, the Upperrealms sighed with melancholia, the turquoise skies cooling to a dreary cobalt as the stars ceased their dance to hold space for their weeping mistress. The animals in the enchanted forest had halted their stirring to watch them, a single crow swooping down to rest on her narrow shoulder.

"You cannot ask this of me," she said as she looked up at him, tears streaming down her face. They pooled at the dip of her collarbones, threatening to spill down her chest. "We just settled in here."

"It is the only way," he said, falling onto the moss beside her. The crow returned to its branch, letting him draw closer. He reached up to tuck a wayward curl behind her ear, amused as it sprang back up in defiance.

"I will tear him apart," she muttered between gritted teeth.

He couldn't help but smile, proud as always of her spirit even in the midst of tragedy. "I have no doubt that you shall," he told her.

She jumped to her feet, her sorrow rapidly replaced by indignation. The skies responded to the shift, lightning cracking through the darkening, thunderous sky. "We created the earth, how can we be ousted from it? Just like the old religion, warped beyond recognition with the Roman gods our replacement. We are no longer wanted."

"The world has grown much bigger than us," he agreed. "Look how many gods now exist. We are but two."

"I know," she sighed. "As I know the earth follows its own rules, like the mothers who created her." She attempted a playful smile but could not free herself completely from her building distress.

He rose to his feet, pulling her hips against him so she was close enough to be kissed. "Humans do not have to remember who we are, but it is still our duty to protect them. That is why we must make this decision. We cannot let him destroy everything they have built."

Her stony exterior dismantled once more, overwhelmed by anguish. "You cannot ask this of me," she repeated. "How can I live here without you?" With her last word, she pushed him away, the skies erupting into a full-fledged storm, as flocks of birds echoed her cries, and the clouds released their downpour.

He pulled her back to him, holding her tightly as he buried his face in her dampening hair. "Do I have to tell you the story of the Lovers, the ancient gods destined to find each other always?" he murmured into her ear.

She closed her eyes, nuzzling into his neck. Her vulnerability was so uncharacteristic, it nearly threatened his resolve. "Please tell me," she said in a small voice.

He shut his eyes, memorizing the press of her body against his, the smoothness of her skin, and the earthy redolence of her hair, like the woods after summer rain. "There are two souls who will continue to find each other until the end of time, the first lovers, whose love for one another transcends all," he began, as folding her hand around the handle of his knife. She let out a sob when she realized what he was doing. They were now drenched in frigid cloudburst, a river gathering where they stood. He gripped her tighter. "They circle the realms throughout different lifetimes, restless and incomplete until they find each other … but find each other, they always will."

"Remember me," she wept.

"Remember me," he whispered, bracing himself.

And with a battle cry laced with the purest despair, she thrust the knife up into his stomach, the realm screeching her pain, crows swooping in to catch her as she fell away from him in unrestrained sobs. He dropped to the ground, picturing her face over and over in his mind, determined never to forget her eyes.

The earth shook, squalls of wind roaring around him as he perished, the Upperrealms incensed by his departure. And then, in the midst of chaos similar to that which he'd been born of, he died, and all the worlds around him faded to black.

LONDON, 1857

O UT OF THE SHADOWS, HE EMERGED.
The chill of approaching autumn nipped at his skin and he pulled the collar of his overcoat up around his ears. The city was smothered in thick September fog, a putrid mixture of factory smoke and the noxious gases that floated up from the River Thames. It hung heavy in the air, reverberating with the laughter of intoxicated streetwalkers in the midst of late-night chicanery. As he moved further into the city, the stench of decay lent its acidity to the unpleasant combination, revealing the presence of wasting bodies packed like spoiling sardines in the alleyways.

As the century turned, overpopulation had rendered London defenseless to an abundance of filth, rotting excess cluttering the streets and rancid water pooling at its crossings. Crime added to its deterioration, and soon, unsolved murder became as common as the thefts heralded in the daily newspapers. London's citizens were either as poor as the dirt they slept in or rich beyond measure. Those blessed with prosperity paid the suffering wretches on the streets no mind, carrying on in willful ignorance as they explored the slums in elegant horse-drawn carriages, hoping to discover some scandalous bit of entertainment before retiring to their grandiose, upper district homes. The stark dichotomy between rich and poor in the city was so commonplace that no one paid it any mind, assuring the lone wanderer that his presence would also go unnoticed.

The combative wind threatened his top hat and he paused to readjust, combing back his rebellious locks with his fingers before tightening it back around his head. He made a habit of keeping his appearance artfully concealed, lest someone notice the peculiar bluish undertone to his skin or the slight edge to his teeth when he smiled. But perhaps his biggest obstacle was his eyes, for if one saw past the odd size of his pupils in the lamplight, they would be transfixed by their abnormally brilliant shade of green, reminiscent of the forest after a spring rain. He preferred to have as little attention on him as possible, comfortable to remain a stranger in the shadows. Though he never offered it, his name was David, and for more centuries than he cared to recall, he'd been what the penny dreadfuls called a vampyre.

The clock tower in the square chimed midnight as he entered the more populated section of town. Lamplighters were finishing their nightly rounds, nodding to him as he passed. The sound of coach wheels churning up water from the previous night's rain floated to his ears, blending pleasantly with the abundance of drunken chatter bellowing out the taverns. He walked towards his favorite, a crowded room tucked inside a rickety old building covered in soot. There was something about the Eastern Pub that had instantly seduced him, causing him to spend long hours there, seated in the back as he observed the colorful characters that passed in and out its doors. Occasionally someone would glance at him, wondering what would draw a gentleman to such a tavern, but more often than not, they were too consumed by their imbibing to give him a second thought.

The lushery boasted its usual pandemonium when he arrived, bursting at the seams with inebriated mirth. Local men and docked sailors, all ruddy with ale, argued amongst each other as a cigarette smog choked the air. Cards were slapped on wood tables as glasses overflowing with cheap ale splashed the perpetually stained floor. David leaned over the bar, meeting the barkeep's eyes. The man faltered for a moment, for as accustomed as he was to seeing David, his appearance never failed to unsettle him. "The usual, sir?" he managed.

"Please." David nodded. He turned as the man fetched his drink, absorbing his surroundings. A stout man with oily hair was seated across the room, helping himself to glass after glass of strong ale as his friends cheered him on. A group of scantily clad prostitutes stood in the corner, whispering as they gazed in his direction. But what caught his attention was a solitary woman of the night sitting nearby, an obvious outcast, her long legs peeking out of her skirts as she swigged her ale. Her haphazardly strung corset struggled to contain her curves, though her build was tall and thin. Hands that ended in dirt-caked fingernails fished about her dress in an attempt to produce a cigarette. Her search proving futile, she looked up to meet David's eyes. They were a listless grey, shadows of terminal illness collected beneath them.

"You got a smoke?" she asked. She didn't bother to adjust her pose nor her expression into the coquettish manner consistent with her occupation, but she was seductive all the same. Her expression was fierce with just a hint of apathy towards the world around her.

He withdrew from where he sat, glass of dark liquor in hand, as the group of women behind them did all but audibly scoff with annoyance.

"Look at this fine gentlemen come to call," she greeted him with an amused smirk. "Overdressed for this place, though up close, you look about as dead as me."

"Perhaps." He mirrored her smile as he seated himself across from her, producing a cigarette case and prizing it open to reveal her desired intoxicant.

"Machine rolled, eh?" She examined the tightly packed tobacco between her fingertips. "Seems an awful bit of work to me." She moistened her lips before lifting it to rest between them.

David studied her as she moved. He surmised she had once been a great beauty, but the imminent death claiming her body had drained her of its promise. She coughed, and he could almost see the pustules of blood clustered throughout her laboring lungs. She wiped her hand across her mouth, upsetting the tendrils of dark hair left carelessly around her face, most of it collected in a piece of fabric at the nape of her neck. He tried not to linger too long on her neck, where nude paste attempted to conceal bruises ending at her protruding collarbones, settling instead on her hands while she smoked. Her fingers were long and thin but calloused, her knuckles swollen and cracked, revealing tiny lines of dried blood in their crevasses.

"What was your profession prior to this?" he asked, curious about her hands.

She chortled at the question, nearly erupting into a fit before she quieted the coughing with a sharp inhalation of cigarette smoke. "I was a gardener by day, evil witch by nightfall."

Flashes of unwelcome memories assaulted David, provoked by her words. He struggled to force them away, looking down at his drink. She noticed the shift in his expression, tilting her head slightly to one side as if she were a confused pup. "I didn't peg you for a religious type. I assure you, I only jest. Though I'm sure I've done my fair share of evil in my lifetime."

David composed himself, taking a careful sip of his drink. Moderation was a practice he'd adopted after the unpleasant discovery that his stomach would recoil at anything that wasn't his main source of nourishment. The revulsion upon consumption faded as quickly as it came, but it was enough to pull him back from the morbid reflection of his past, and he looked up at her with a smile. "I suppose all of us are capable of evil from time to time."

At that, she laughed genuinely, allowing a few more ragged heaves to slip out of her frail body before swilling down the last of her ale and slamming the empty glass back down to the table. "Enough pointless banter. I need to smoke something real." She snuffed out her freshly expired cigarette with emphasis. "Will you be joining me, kind sir?" Her eyes sparkled once they met his, and he realized they were actually a muted shade of blue.

"I would be delighted."

The brisk night air welcomed them as David and his stumbling counterpart descended deeper into the bowels of London's East End. Neither of them hesitated, strolling past the shadowy figures nestled between the looming tenements and the factories narrowing the poorly demarcated streets. She struggled to keep her balance, gripping his arm as the aroma of alcohol, violets, and a hint of decay wafted up from her skin into his nostrils. It occurred to him that as close as she was to him physically, he could not hear her thoughts, something he'd become accustomed to with humans. He surmised she kept them hidden subconsciously, a common practice he'd observed in souls whose lives depended upon secrecy.

The opium dens of Limehouse were perhaps more sordid than its pubs, their congested, smoke-filled rooms teeming with languid bodies sprawled out in various stages of inebriation. The one they entered was no exception. Heavily painted Chinese women moved from guest to guest in a tranquil promenade, silently offering more brown tar for their pipes or removing tools from open palms that had relaxed with the onset of oblivion. This particular den was the best kept secret in London, catering to the elite while remaining cleverly concealed in the slums. Although the décor remained perpetually blurred by thick, brown opium vapors, the walls were papered red, matching the Oriental curtains draped over the windows. Over-occupancy obscured the view of the bedding strewn about the floor for customer comfort, but David knew from experience that it was also covered in the same silk fabric. Soft music trickled out of an unseen room.

A small woman greeted them, wearing a deep-set frown. The black oil paint she'd used for her eyebrows had smeared across her powdered face, giving her an expression of contempt. After offering his companion a look of disapproval, she nodded politely his way. "The usual, sir?"

The woman at his side looked at him, amused. "You've been here before, have you?"

David didn't respond, nodding in the direction of the owner. "Yes, that would be fine. Thank you."

She led them through the congested mass of bodies, a few erupting in disgruntled interjections as the three of them stepped around their sprawling limbs. At the back of the main den was a curtain so large, the owner was forced to awkwardly lift it, revealing a locked door underneath. She retrieved a set of keys from the pocket of her dress, opening it to expose a secret hallway of private rooms. She scuttled down the corridor to the one furthest from the entrance, throwing open its respective door and gesturing them hurriedly inside. "Quickly now. Large crowd to watch tonight."

David pressed more than adequate compensation into her palm, which she wordlessly but gratefully accepted before she hurried away. Although the owner applied the utmost discretion to his occasional visit to the dens, casting a blind eye as he lured patrons quickly approaching self-inflicted expiration into the backrooms, he never wanted her to grow too suspicious, and made a note to monetarily ensure her compliance whenever he could.

His companion flopped down on the cushioned floors in open wonderment of the room. On the table rested an opium pipe brimming with fresh supply, an oil lamp, and matches arranged in a glass bowl. A bottle of rice wine was stationed nearby.

"My luck to have run into you," she murmured, pulling the cork from the bottle to take a celebratory swallow. Her lips pursed in displeasure. "Bloody hell, how do they drink this *shyte?*"

David laughed as he removed his hat, freeing his rusty blond curls.

She admired him from where she lounged. "Ah, so you're Irish, like me."

"Close, but not quite," he responded cryptically. He imitated her reclined position on the floor as he watched her lift the long pipe fashioned out of bamboo. A bowl packed with a fresh opium pellet was secured at its base, which she aimed directly over the flame of the oil lamp. She inhaled as it caught, the murky haze escaping from her mouth as she exhaled. She immediately succumbed to a coughing fit, pounding at her chest with frustration. "My bellows are long past their proper function," she explained between spasms, passing the smoldering pipe his way.

He mirrored her movements, pleasantly surprised at the warmth that soon flooded him. He had never smoked the opium before, only experienced a diluted sensation of pleasure as it flowed through an intoxicated victim's blood into his own.

She took the pipe back from him, the smoke that escaped her lungs filling the room with muddy brown. She sighed with pleasure. "Whatever numbs me and kills me faster."

David was suddenly overwhelmed by her thoughts, flooding him like the euphoric poison now coursing through his veins. She was alone, dying of consumption, without any desire to live on. Her life had become exactly as she briefly revealed, a series of hours spent scouring the earth for anything to anesthetize her final days. But her death was slow and painful, ravaging her body for months with no sign of release. Flashes of her as a cherubic youth with flowing raven hair, dancing freely in the fields of the English countryside. Images of her pulling herbs from the earth with an equally beautiful mother, the knowledge of a bond strengthened through tragedy and solitude.

She peered at him coldly, a sudden sober severity flashing in her eyes. "Now you mustn't do that, doll. It takes all the fun out of it."

David blinked, finding himself at a loss for words.

"Yes, I know what you are and that you can read my thoughts," she offered, her voice suddenly robbed of its playfulness. "Don't think I found you by accident."

He felt the rush of his preservation instinct, prepared to either flee or sink his teeth into her neck until her heart ceased its toil.

"Oh, please, not yet," she said as she sat up to retrieve the bottle of wine. "I've grown weary for good conversation. My life has been without it for quite some time now."

"You know what I am."

"You are a vampyre, are you not?"

David winced. "I suppose that is the word for it now, though I'm not nearly as dashing as Lord Ruthven."

She raised an eyebrow, her eyes sweeping over his crisp suit and the top hat sitting on the table. "Then perhaps you should try not to fit the part," she pointed out with a smile. "Regardless of your preferred title, you are a blood drinker, are you not?"

David sighed. "That I am."

"You probably don't remember the night I first saw you, but I will never forget it. I grew up in the countryside, a novice herbalist and midwife like my mother, who immigrated here when she was very young. The absence of a male in our home immediately cast suspicion upon us, as it always does. So many years after the witch burnings, but still the hatred for independent women remains." She took a generous sip of the rice wine, ending it with another disgusted grimace. "I don't know how she contracted the pox, I can only surmise it was from one of the gentlemen callers who visited her while I was safely tucked away in my warm bed, dreaming a child's dreams. But I witnessed the sickness as it ravaged her later. No concoctions nor any salve we could muster helped. Our most faithful customers drifted away. Whispers trickled throughout our village that she was cursed, a whore, or both. We were forced to leave our countryside home, the home I grew up in, to come to this rotten place. My mother took on the only occupation left for a destitute woman alone in this world. One evening, she left me, as customary, with an older lady of the night turned nanny for the children of the whores. But I knew tonight was different. I knew my mother was ready to die. I followed her into the alleyways, concealing myself in the shadows. And that's when I found her ... and you."

David peered at her as the memory became clear. "You abhor me then."

"I do not, actually," she replied, tucking her long limbs beneath her. It struck him how childlike she appeared; boyish, disheveled, sickly, but lovely, like a once cherished doll that had been tossed into the trash heap. "My mother wanted to die. She begged for it. She never spoke the words aloud, but I knew. I was not only a gifted herbalist, but I inherited her intuition. You relieved her of her pain. I am grateful to you, actually."

David recalled the delicate, sickened woman who had fallen submissively into his embrace, begging him with soft whispers to end her suffering. He hadn't picked up from her thoughts that she would be leaving behind a child. She must have been a clever mystic, even in her final hours. "Is that how you came to follow in her footsteps?" he asked her.

"Aye." She nodded. "There is no place here for healing women like me, and I was too young to flee this dreadful abyss. So I became a part of it. Now here I am, sick and dying, just like her."

David lifted the smoking pipe to her lips. Grateful for the kind gesture, she smiled before she inhaled. This time, her lungs could no longer bear the abuse and she erupted into a coughing fit, her body convulsing with the exertion. Blood spewed from her mouth onto the blankets before her, running down her chin as she halted the hacking with a labored sigh. She paused, fingering her bloodied lips for a moment before seductively lifting them to his.

David closed his eyes, enjoying the tease of her blood. A wave of empathy for her settled over him, and he enjoyed the brief reminder of his long abandoned humanity as her taste sweetened his tongue. "Do you want me to take you?" he asked her, reaching up to caress her face.

She placed her hand on his, shivering at its chill. "Do you hate my company that much?"

"Quite the opposite, in fact," he replied honestly. She was the most intriguing individual he had spoken to in a very long time.

"I've told you my life, now what of yours?" she asked, removing his hand so she could rest her head in the folds of his lap, as a child might her father. Her raven hair blanketed his legs in streams of black. "The night is young and I adore stories."

"I haven't spoken of myself in over a century," he remarked, taken aback by the notion. "I'm afraid my story would be quite a bit longer than yours."

"Then you shouldn't waste any more time," she teased as she looked up at him. "Tell a dying girl one last bedtime story, creature of the night."

"All right, lady of the night. If you insist." David lifted the abandoned pipe to his lips once more, allowing his memories to find their way back into his consciousness. The smoke filled room fell away as he plunged into the worlds of old - accosted by the smells of Ancient Rome as a mortal boy, the feel of warm sun beating down upon him in the peak of the day. He recalled the laborious passage through time, the cold, damp horrors of Wallachia, the Night War, the creatures, the gods. The pain of losing all that he had ever loved. The remembrances became vivid, as if they were happening again, and he closed his eyes as he spoke in the melancholy vein that reminiscence often brings.

CHAPTER ONE

❦ THE BOY ❦

THE ANCIENT WORLD, 58 B.C.

I T WAS THE SIXTH DAY OF THE MOON.
A ring of men stood, the crisp air of approaching autumn rippling their pale robes. A fire roared in the middle of their circle, flames licking the starless sky. The blaze illuminated the figure of an old man who stood prominently amongst them, an elaborate circlet of antlers on his head. His face, weathered by age and the wisdom it brings, arched upwards towards the brilliant half moon, his eyes pressed firmly in concentration, his mouth moving in silent prayer. Shadows danced against the surrounding woods.

Beyond the group of men stood two white bulls bound to an altar made of stone. They were unusually massive, enormous brown horns reaching up out of their skulls towards the heavens. Long, flat stones lay at their feet.

The high priest turned to greet his cloaked tribesmen, continuing his invocation out loud. They echoed his words as the fire grew brighter, throwing ghostly shadows across their bodies. Their chants grew louder and more feverish as a solitary man approached from the forest. His robe was stained deep red, a circlet of tusks barbing at his forehead. He approached the circle, slowly unsheathing a miniature gold sickle from his waist. He lifted it high and brought it down fast, severing a single branch of mistletoe that had been woven around the branches of an ancient oak. Another cloaked man lunged forward to catch the fallen plant, the dark green sprig falling gracefully onto the blanched cloth he held taut in his hands. The man lifted the retrieved branch to the skies and with a sudden howl, the men released their knives.

The bulls roared and twisted in a blur of crimson. The men moved quickly, slaughtering with such uninhibited ferocity that the bulls' cries ceased within moments. Slabs of their flesh materialized on the stones laid out before the altar.

Throughout all of this, he was silent.

His youthful body was concealed easily behind the brush, a child's eyes absorbing the ritual before him, watching as the once mighty beasts were reduced to empty bones landing in the dust. Nothing remained of their majesty, save for the steaming red meat that soured the autumnal air.

He shivered in the wind, the plain cloth he wore useless against it. He was supposed to be resting under heavy furs near a dying fire, but he had left his dwelling in secret. He imagined his mother's disapproving look upon the discovery of her missing son, who had crept away once again to covertly behold their sacred rituals. As much as it displeased her, she had long accepted his powerlessness when it came to the call of the gods, understanding the rites of their people were too enticing for him to forbear.

The boy's father was one of the Druid Elders, a title that filled his son with pride. He yearned to follow the path of his father, the shamanic bloodline that ran through his family very much alive in his veins. As customary, he stayed with his mother, far removed from the High Priest who dwelled with his brethren deep in the northern woods. His tender age forbade him from joining his father to begin his apprenticeship, but the sacrificial violence that followed each ceremony proved far too intriguing. So the perpetual voyeur, he remained.

He had watched the bulls slaughtered as part of Lughnasadh the year before, the ritual initiating the harvest season and the many autumnal celebrations to follow, honoring their god, Lugh. He had also witnessed a wickerwork constructed into the shape of a man, which his people used to imprison those who threatened their tribe. When the prison reached capacity, the wicker man was set ablaze, serving as an offering to the Tuatha De Danann, the gods who protected the Celtic people in their many territories from harm. Great festivity ensued as it burned, resonances of merriment eclipsing the captives' agonizing screams.

Now, the tribal men roasted the tender meat over their great fire in similar joviality, their laughter echoing throughout the forest. They seated themselves along the flat stones, feasting on the charred bull mutton as they passed a jug of spiced wine between them. The woods were alive with their celebration.

The boy withdrew from his hiding place, nothing left for him to see. After he was convinced his movement went unnoticed, he broke into a sprint, his small but sinewy legs easily catching speed. From the distance, his slumbering village appeared, the smoke from dying fires drifting into the air. Its women and children had long retired, resting up for the continued Lughnasadh festivities that would resume at daybreak.

He crept into the dwelling where his mother slept, his hut welcoming him with warmth and the aroma of herbs drying near the hearth. His place on their shared bed, a heap of cloth and furs, remained undisturbed in the corner. He slipped under the coverings, keeping a careful eye on the steady rise and fall of his mother's turned back.

"You snuck out to watch your father again, sweet babe?" her murmur startled him.

He bit his lip, awaiting reprimand.

She turned sleepily to face him, a gentle smile painted across her face. She reached her hand up to stroke his long, fair curls. "Go to sleep, young one. Tomorrow will be long and full of adventure."

He returned her smile, closing his eyes and giving in to slumber.

It was the last memory he would ever have of his mother.

Their clan was destroyed, his people and his home devoured by flame. Powerful men appeared in the night, covered in metal, straddling armored horses. They swarmed the village with roaring torches and menacing swords. They were unlike anything the boy had seen, their metal hats glinting in the moonlight, their faces obscured by the angry diadems. They moved in unrelenting annihilation, shouting to each other in foreign tongues. The few Celtic warriors who called the small Druid village home fought back in desperation, but their meager numbers were no match against an army of soldiers.

He lost his mother as soon as they struck, swept away by torrents of frantic villagers. He barely glimpsed her face, contorted by screams, as her life ended abruptly with the swift lash of a sword. He bolted from the camp in a frenzy of emotion, running as fast as his legs could bear towards the village temple, searching desperately for his father. He reached the mossy enclave where he knew he would be, his heart thumping wildly in his throat, lungs burning for air.

He made his way towards the cave that served as their sacred temple. "Father?" he cried out into the hollow emptiness.

"I am here, son."

He crept deep into its bowels to find his father sitting cross-legged upon the floor, encircled by blazing torches. His lips moved fervently as sweat dripped from his furrowed brow. The boy recognized tools of alchemy spread out around him, his father mixing, grinding, burning herbs, and blending potions at a furious pace. The stench of blood and metal stung his nose, the air around them vibrating with energy.

"Father…can I help you?"

His father shook his head. "Oh, my son," he lamented without pause from his toils, "how I wish I could stay alive to see you flourish."

He lifted both his arm and his athame, severing his flesh deep enough that his blood rained down into the concoction below. "Gods," he cried out, "accept the sacrifice of my flesh at your spear, for I have failed you. Though he is not ready, may you fill him with your power."

The boy recognized the tools his father had laid out before him as the precious relics of the Celtic people. The Daghda's Cauldron, the Spear of Lugh, the Stone of Fal, and the Sword of Nuada were four treasures passed down from their ancestors, the Tuatha de Danann. He had assumed they were myths until now.

His ears picked up the sudden approach of horsemen, drawing closer towards their haven.

"Father, they are coming," he pleaded.

His father lifted a fiery bundle of herbs so that its smoke billowed around the boy's shivering body. "Hush, boy." He fingered the seeping blood from his wound to spread a sigil tenderly on the boy's chest. The intimacy of the moment struck the boy when he realized it was the closest he had been to his father since his birthing celebration, when he was lifted up before the tribe. He had never been close enough to see the lines of his face or notice how light his eyelashes were, stretching almost to the rim of his silvered brows. How bright his eyes were against his weathered, alabaster skin, and how sweet and warm his sage-sweetened breath was as he heaved. For a moment, it was as if the impending calamity had ceased, and he was alone with his father at last. A rising sob threatened the boy's stoic bearing, tears pooling to the surface.

The shrill neigh of horses broke his trance, and he blinked the emotions away.

His father remained unaltered, sprinkling him with dried earth he'd retrieved from a clay bowl that rested on the glowing Stone of Fal. He spoke a few words in the old tongue before telling the boy, "Remember well what you witnessed from afar. Forget not our ways, no matter how the world changes around you."

"Father, are you going to save us?" the boy whispered.

"No," his father replied. "But you will."

The boy cried out as his father grabbed the Cauldron and doused him in its tepid liquid, its vapor assaulting his senses. He choked, momentarily blind as his skin pulsated with heat. He could hear nothing now but hooves galloping directly behind him and his father's desperate voice as he cried out, "Danu, protect your son! The power is now his, may he deliver us from darkness!"

He felt his body being hoisted into the air as they murdered his father, and he thrashed against his captor's grasp. The memory of the bulls twisting in agony came to him, desperate to shed their bounds as their helpless cries pierced the air. He let out his own scream before they lifted a club to his head, and his entire world faded to black.

Pain jarred him from unconsciousness. It stabbed at his head as he struggled to see, squinting in the dim light for any hint to his whereabouts. His body was rocking back and forth against a wall that he quickly discovered he was bound to. He pulled at the chains in vain. "What is happening?" he cried out.

"They are Romans, and we are prisoners on their ship," a woman's gentle voice responded. He faintly made out her silhouette, positioned adjacent to him and also chained to the ship's wall. Her face was concealed by shadows.

"What are Romans?" The stench of the spoiled offal and dried blood that still clung to his clothes from his father's concoction drifted upward towards his nostrils. He quelled the urge to vomit.

"They are a great world power," she replied. "They have already conquered many tribes throughout Gaul. It was only a matter of time until they found us, yet we did not anticipate it would be so soon. We were hopelessly unprepared." She let her head fall back to rest upon the wood of the boat.

"Why are we still alive?"

"They spared us to sell as slaves in their homeland. That is where we are headed now. You have been asleep for quite long."

The boy felt weak, realizing he hadn't eaten or drank for days. Flashes of his burning village and the deaths of his mother and father taunted him, pulling muffled sobs from his chest.

"Shhh, young one," the woman soothed. "I shall sing to you."

Her sweet voice filled his ears, calming him with the songs of their ancestors. He let his throbbing head rest against the ship as tears slipped quietly down his cheeks. Her voice reminded him of his mother's.

The voyage seemed endless, the only glimpse of sun was when it rose in the early hours, filtering through the worn wooden planks above them. They were fed sparingly, either scraps of stale, moldy bread or jerky made from rat meat. The boy's skin wore painfully at his shackled wrists, his muscles seizing with spasms from lack of movement. It was all he could do some nights not to wail in agony. His only consolation was the woman sitting nearby, his constant companion.

All throughout the night, she whispered to him the tales of their people. He surmised there were other prisoners aboard the vessel, but she was the only one close enough for conversation. In the darkness, he imagined that she looked like his mother, with lovely golden hair and bright sapphire eyes that peered out from sun-splotched skin. She had taken to calling him Daghda, the son of the goddess, Danu, and the ancestor king of the Celtic people. Her stories kept his mind from going mad, as she described in vivid detail the great battles that won land for their tribe, far before their expansion and his own clan's migration to Gaul. He enjoyed imagining the warfare and the duels between bloodlines. He envisioned the great king Daghda with his giant club, defending their lands against the Fomorians, a race of grotesque and hideous giants. He saw the brilliant Lugh lunging forward with his spear and Ogma in his lion skin cloak, his bow and arrow poised for attack.

She told him how the gods still lived among them in the Otherworld, watching over them, provided they kept their stories alive. Some nights she sang, explaining that music was its own magic, a great tribute to the gods. The days passed easily with the sound of her voice, giving the boy a reason to live on.

Then late one night, he was jolted awake by a Roman clumsily keying at his locked shackles. The man could barely keep himself upright, reeking of sweat and strong ale. He mumbled in his strange language, grinning at him, the stench of decaying teeth wafting from his mouth. The boy's body stiffened in horror as he realized the man's intentions. He struggled to see the silhouette of the woman, frantically wondering if she was still alive.

"You will not touch him," a low, unfamiliar voice growled in the darkness.

The man looked around him, bewildered.

The boy shared his confusion but was too afraid to react. The palpable sensation that they were no longer alone settled over him.

The lumbering man moved to investigate, and the boy realized his shackles were now loose. He sighed with relief when they fell away from his raw and chaffing skin, but he forced himself to stay still. The man swatted around the cabin, barking in frustration.

His voice was suddenly drowned out by the roar of flapping wings as if the hold had miraculously filled with thousands of birds. The boy raised his arms up to shield himself, watching as the murky darkness shifted and twirled with indiscernible bodies, their screeches piercing his ears. The man shrieked as they attacked him, the sounds of ripping flesh tearing through the hold. They ignored the boy completely, dismembering the man with their tapered beaks as if he was nothing more than discarded carrion.

Then, not long after it started, the calamity ceased. The boy let his arms fall away his eyes, observing the immobile lump that was once a man, collected at the far end of the hold. Gore curdled the air.

The woman was now visible to him in the scant rays of early morning light, her arms still affixed behind her back. She stared at him, calmly. The boy blinked, for he was nearly certain her eyes gleamed a shiny black, blood smearing a mouth that was turned upright into a tight-lipped, maniacal smile. He shivered as the hairs on his arms stood upright.

"He left my hands free," the boy stammered, finding his voice at last.

"Stay seated where you are," she instructed him. "Do not let them know you are unbound. They will be frightened when they see what is left of their fellow soldier."

"What … what happened?"

"Rest now, Daghda. Daylight is fast approaching, and you will need your strength. I shall tell you another story."

The boy nodded, afraid to say anything more.

"Perhaps the most feared of our ancestors was the goddess Morrigan," she began. "Her beauty was legendary, the only descendant of Danu with glorious raven hair. Some say she was a radiant maiden, but others witnessed her as a ghastly crone. On our blessed day of Samhain, when the last of the crops had been harvested and our people prepared for winter's chill, she appeared as a beautiful enchantress to the King Daghda. Naked and bathing in her beloved waters, he happened upon her and when he caught sight of her dark, loosened locks billowing down her snowy skin, he fell instantly in love. Their devotion to each other would prove eternal, the Morrigan joining him in battle to defeat the Fomorian king. Yet as many times as the lovers coupled, the Morrigan could never bear them a child. Legend says that their souls return to earth in an endless cycle to find each other, destined to repeat the dance until at last their union is fruitful and a child is born. It is this child who will ensure that the sons and daughters of Danu live undisturbed for eternity."

The boy relaxed at her words, finally able to recline his aching body across the floor of the hold. His eyes closed, the soft lull of the ship rocking him into submission.

"Morrigan's love for Daghda empowered him, and his for her, her magics growing more powerful as the years passed on. She could appear in all three aspects to enemies: the seductive war goddess, the maiden, or the dreadful crone. Her presence unsettled all who crossed her path, and it was said that one look from her ice blue eyes would cause your legs to buckle beneath you. Her shape-shifting magics soon evolved beyond human form, and stories swirled about her appearing as a horse, a wolf … or a flock of carrion crows …"

The boy found he could no longer fight his impending slumber. He

24

drifted off to the sound of her voice, dreams of lovely black ravens swirling in his head.

He woke abruptly.

The boat had stopped.

Unable to stand, he pulled himself up to the slight opening where the daylight streamed through. Squinting his eyes against its brightness, he peered out into the distance to see what he surmised was true. They had reached land.

"We have arrived," he called down to the woman.

She did not respond.

He fell back from the roof to discover she had vanished. A pair of empty rusted shackles rested against the hull, but nothing else remained. The hold was completely empty, save for the heap of bloody pulp which the ship rats had picked clean. He hurried back to his shackles, clasping them around his wrists just as the Romans appeared to collect him.

His heart hammered in his chest when they noticed the carcass, but after exchanging words accompanied by confused glances in his direction, the matter was overlooked. It was as if they knew the boy couldn't have possibly done such damage, and the man's death was not worth further investigation.

A soldier with short black curls that grazed reddish skin approached him, unlocking his shackles. He lifted the boy over his shoulders, climbing with him out of the hold. The boy clenched his eyes shut against the blinding sunlight, helpless as he was tossed to the ground. Dizziness overwhelmed him from the long weeks aboard a rocking ship, and he tried to calm his nausea as he struggled to find his bearings.

Another man barked orders at him, but he was unable to follow his commands. He kicked him in frustration, the boy unable to hold back his vomit. The man who had lifted him from his prison snapped at the abuser, hoisting the boy up in his arms once more. In them, the boy was able to wrench his eyes open, observing the land that stretched out around them. Their ship had been docked at a port swarming with Romans, some dressed in warrior attire, others clad in tunics similar to those of his own people. His eyes focused on a group of his kin now, moaning pitifully in the sand, their skin split by gaping sores with atrophied limbs unable to erect them. He searched their faces frantically, but they were all unfamiliar. It then occurred to him that they were all men - not one woman nor child had been spared.

Rage boiled inside him. He heard his mother's cries as she was slain, recalling the pain in his father's eyes. Fury reverberated throughout his body, its power strengthening his limbs. He twisted himself free from his startled captor, who had no choice but to drop him onto the sand below. He scrambled to retrieve him before he was halted by the boy's demeanor. The man took a careful step back, fear streaked across his face. The boy reveled in the newfound intensity overtaking his body, his hands suddenly pulsating with heat. He reached up to the sky, words coming from somewhere he could not place as he screamed up to the heavens, "I summon you, Morrigan, the Nemain! I summon you to this horrid place! Avenge the murder of your sisters, show them your fury, for it is my will and so it shall be!"

The sky acquiesced immediately to his cries, blackening out the clear brilliance of morning, wrathful thunder bellowing in the distance. Ominous storm clouds blotted out the sun as the Romans who stood on the shoreline darted for shelter. The eyes of the boy's captor widened as he stared at the sinister sky, the raucous thunder rolling closer.

A screech pierced the air, men clamping their hands over their ears. The soldier turned his terrified gaze back towards the boy, who was breathlessly observing the scene that unfolded before him. "You…"

The boy tried to scramble to his feet in the sand but found he could only scuttle backwards from the shore. The ocean had transformed into a churning cesspool of waves, tossing the docked ships with violent ease. They crashed into each other with such force that they split apart like kindling. The skies parted to reveal a colossal creature coming towards them, black and hideously misshapen. The shrieking grew louder, men falling to their knees in horror.

"The Morrigan," the boy whispered in awe.

He watched as the great shape shattered into thousands of carrion crows. They swooped down to attack, tearing at the flesh of the petrified Romans as they screamed.

The boy watched, motionless, able to witness a second coming of the butchery that had transpired within the hold of the ship. He continued to scoot himself backwards until he reached a cove that obstructed him from open view. The man who had offered him aid died quickly, unlike the other soldiers who were slowly torn apart by the voracious birds. The scene before him was horrific, yet the boy could not contain his amazement. She was magnificent.

He could have watched her for hours, but soon the ravens ceased their slaughter, coming together again. Their slender black bodies danced in a spiral before merging back into a familiar amalgamation, the Morrigan standing before him in human form.

He smiled at her, recognizing the woman from the ship.

Her actual features were nothing like his mother's as he'd once hoped, her eyes instead an icy blue, radiating from a lovely face lined with age. Black coils of hair streaked with white tumbled freely down her shoulders, her entire body was smeared in blood. She was ghastly, but undoubtedly resplendent.

She returned his look of recognition with a gentle wave of her fingers before dissolving into her flock of crows. They returned to the skies, parting the dissipating storm clouds before finally disappearing beyond the horizon. The wind and waters grew still.

A pang of sorrow descended upon him as he realized it was her final departure. But he had no time to lament, for he was struck by the magnitude of his exhaustion and he collapsed into the sand, powerless to prevent it.

The next morning, he awoke, discovering that at last, his limbs could move. He decided to explore, hoping to find something to eat. Before setting out, he lifted the least soiled garment from one of the expired bodies onshore, fitting it as best he could about his famished body. The tunic shifted uncomfortably around him as he walked, the heat from the sweltering sun pouring down on him from above.

The boy had never seen anything quite like the civilization that he soon reached. People hurried about in clean white robes, their bare feet protected by curiously fashioned straps of leather. Their hair was kept short and neat in tight ebony curls that barely fell past their tan foreheads. Giant structures of smooth, polished stone stretched above him in every direction, as metal harnessed horses strolled past, pulling carts on iron wheels. The ground beneath his bare feet was also smooth, laid entirely with flat rocks. He saw no sign of greenery, for he realized the city was devoid of any natural landscape, save for the granite fountains positioned at every street corner that sputtered out fresh water.

A wave of lightheadedness washed over him, but he tried to remain steady on his feet. He looked around for anything he could use for nourishment, acutely aware he was in some sort of marketplace. Romans exchanged hurried words around him, handing over metal coins so they could fill their baskets with food. The aroma of fresh bread and salted meat reached his nose, rendering him completely ravenous. He searched frantically for an unattended cart to steal from, almost colliding with a burly man who snapped at him in surprise. He dodged him, weaving through the horde of people until at last he found a cart with no vendor in sight, lined with flat discs of bread. He crept up to it, reaching out to snatch what he could.

A hand clasped around his wrist.

He looked up to see a young girl, not much older than he, with frantic eyes. She hissed words at him that he could not understand. From behind her, the burly man he had run into reappeared. He scowled, pointing at the boy with a fat, accusatory finger.

The boy was helpless as the girl rose to his defense, offering an explanation while pressing several coins into the man's palm. He glowered at them both, but accepted the payment, placing three bread discs into her basket. She nodded gratefully, grabbing the boy by his arm and swiftly leading him away.

When they were safely out of sight, she stopped, releasing his arm. She frowned, placing her free hand at her hips. The boy was immediately struck by the beauty of her pale, delicate features. Freckles dusted her narrow nose and rounded cheeks, her eyes a soft and earthy green. Golden hair with a hint of rose fell around shoulders that held up a simply cut tunic, draped loosely over her. He knew she demanded something from him, but he could not understand her words.

He stared wistfully at the bread in her basket. "Please," he whispered. "I am so hungry."

She stiffened in surprise, her moss colored eyes widening. "You speak the old tongue?" she whispered back in words he could understand.

Relief flooded over him. "Yes! Yes … oh please, I am almost faint with hunger."

She snapped out of her shock, handing over the food.

He grabbed a disc from her, shoveling it into his mouth unapologetically. She looked around nervously before leading him to a covered bench, an area that offered them a little privacy from the busy market. She handed him another, that he devoured as quickly as the first. She waited for him to finish the final piece of bread before she procured a small clay drinking bowl from a nearby fountain, filling it to the brim with water. Appreciative, he swallowed it down, the shock of nourishment both nauseating and satiating him in paradoxical unison.

Finally, she spoke. "How did you come to be here?"

He was still breathless from his hurried feeding, his now full stomach spasming with confusion. He took a deep breath and wiped the crumbs away from his lips before replying, "They brought me here. My village was destroyed."

She nodded solemnly, her eyes soft. "Mine was as well. Have you already been sold?"

The boy shook his head. "They destroyed my people, so I destroyed them."

A tiny gasp of realization escaped from her lips. "It was you - the massacre yesterday morning. We thought it was a message from the gods. No one has been brave enough yet to move all the bodies. They say the corpses have been picked clean." She lowered her voice to a whisper. "You did that?"

He cast his eyes down, ashamed. "I do not know how, but I believe so."

"The old gods protect us still," she said, surprising him with her understanding. She looked down at her empty basket. "I need to find a way to replenish this food. I work for a man named Eridus, who sent me here to gather bread for this evening's supper. I still have much more to purchase."

"I – I am sorry," the boy offered.

She shook her head. "No, please do not apologize. What kind of soul would I be if I let one of my own people starve to death in the streets? They would have killed you had you been caught stealing. You should come with me. Traveling alone would not be wise right now, especially in light of yesterday's events. We shall pretend you are a fellow slave of Eridus's. When we are finished, I will figure out how to provide you shelter. Come." She stood, offering him her hand, her long and slender limbs giving her a statuesque appearance. Again, he was struck by her beauty, a sensation that caused him to feel hopelessly small and inadequate.

Nevertheless, he followed her through the market, grateful that the citizens of Rome paid him little mind. He helped her gather food he had never seen before, things she called olives, goat cheese, and unleavened bread. His hunger pains had subsided, yet he could not help but crave a taste of the brightly assorted goods throughout the marketplace. He tried to focus on the little sprite before him as she navigated through it, skillfully haggling with vendors until her basket grew full.

She conversed with him throughout their excursion, catching herself as she drifted between the language of the Romans, Latin, and their own native tongue. He learned that her village was not far from his, yet closer to the river than the lush forests the Druids called home.

"I have lived with Eridus for many seasons. I am lucky, for he is kind and just, unlike many patrons here," she explained. "Most of us labor in the vineyards, gathering the grapes to be washed, or in the press room, pressing the fruit into juice so it will ferment in the cellars. He considers me his personal servant, for he is secretly a eunuch, without a wife nor children, and I act as his companion when he goes out in public. I am also responsible for maintaining the slave quarters and alerting him to any of their needs. On occasion, I even assist with his business affairs."

"You do a lot," the boy remarked.

She laughed. "We all do. I consider my position fortunate. Many slave owners do not treat their female slaves with such kindness."

The sun reached its peak in the midday sky, and the boy's clothes were soon completely drenched in sweat, his skin burning to the touch.

"You should come with me to the villa," she suggested, noticing his reddening flesh. "The boy who worked our stables recently fell ill and died - I can tell Eridus that I found you as his replacement. I will explain that I was able to purchase you from the slave market for an alarmingly low price, which will account for the money I spent on the bread you ate. He might grow cross with me for making such a decision without him, but his anger usually subsides quickly. Especially when he realizes keeping you will be much to his benefit." She paused, studying his expression. "So, will you come?"

He nodded immediately, for although he didn't have many options, he already knew he never wanted to leave her side.

She brightened at his response. "Wonderful! Follow me."

She led him down the stone laden streets out of the marketplace, in the opposite direction of the harbor. After a short distance, the overage of stone buildings fell away, plant life coming into view. The boy observed trees dull compared to those of his home, as if years of overbearing sun had bleached any trace of emerald away. They grew in inelegant, awkward shapes, vastly different from the enormous conifers and broad oaks native to his land. He felt a sharp pang of longing settling in his chest.

They walked on until nothing was left but a dirt path that stretched between miles of flat green landscape. The air was calm, but still seasoned with a hint of salt from the distant sea. Sweat continued to pour down his back, his misshapen tunic sticking to his skin. His feet were caked with dust, clinging uncomfortably to the moisture. He wondered how much further they had yet to travel.

"Our villa is just ahead," she responded pleasantly as if he'd spoken the words aloud.

As arid and strange as this new land was, he truly enjoyed her company, their stroll the only lovely experience he'd had in months. She seemed at ease around him as well, her rose gold locks bouncing around her face with each animated word. He noticed the freckles that dusted her face also grazed the back of her shoulders, earned by long hours in the sun.

She entertained him with stories of life at the villa while they walked, including what he could expect as a winemaker's slave. After reaching the top of a large hilltop, a beautiful stucco building finally came into view. From where they stood, the boy could see miles of lush foliage stretching behind it. Her trot quickened, and he hurried to keep up with her. "Come," she beckoned.

The structure grew larger as they approached. Like the city, it was built with the same smooth, flat stone, its facade boasting columns larger than the elder trees of his homeland. They held up sloping, red rooftops that stretched out on either side, creating a massive geometric construct that towered over them as they approached. Rows of smaller columns flanked both sides, covered in vines, grand fountains at each base. Its porches were broad and open, offering a glimpse of the bustling bodies beyond its walls.

"Eridus is the richest winemaker in Rome," she explained as he took in his surroundings. "He built the most magnificent countryside villa to boast this fact. The vineyard you see beyond it stretches for miles, the largest in the territory."

She guided him past the impressive front architecture towards the rear building, which she referred to as "the slaves' quarters." That area and the main portion of the house were separated by an open garden that housed a long wading pool, surrounded by marble statues and flowers in bursts of reds, oranges, pinks, purples, and blues. The grandiosity subsided only modestly for the second building, for although it lacked vivid flora and sculptures, it was still far more remarkable than the crude temples of home. The hall they entered was swarming with people, dressed in simple, clean tunics like her, their limbs stained vinous red. After closer inspection, the boy realized it was not blood, as he originally gathered, but the juice from the fruit they carried in their rounded baskets.

A few of them nodded to her in greeting, one exchanging quick words with her before relieving her of her market bounty. Arms now freed, she tenderly grabbed his, directing him further into the quarters. A long hallway stretched out before them, revealing several empty rooms. She ducked into one of them and pulled him in after her.

The room was bare, save for several linen sheets piled neatly over a bed of straw. A water basin rested on a small wooden table, catching the light that streamed in from an open window. Beside that was a small pile of clean rags. She grabbed them, moistening one with water from the bowl. She scrubbed at his skin with it while he winced, sore from the afternoon sun. She murmured an apology, and gingerly resumed her task. He instructed himself to relax, comforted by the nurturing gesture after months of agonizing captivity. She startled at the sight of his wrists as he exposed them upwards, patting the broken skin before wrapping them in clean scraps of cloth. He watched as a few drops of his blood raised to the surface, tarnishing the immaculate whiteness. Visions of the crow ravaged pulp came to his mind.

"My, what a hard journey you have had," she whispered, her voice pulling him away from his morbid thoughts.

At the doorway, another girl appeared.

The boy stiffened in alarm.

Yet she who bandaged him placed her hand on his shoulder in reassurance before rising to greet the arrival.

"I have the tunic you requested," the girl explained. He recognized her from the main room, surprised that she also spoke in his native tongue.

"Thank you, Moira." She took the pile from her arms. "Now remember, not a word of this until after I have spoken to him."

"Your secret is safe with me, Gaia," she replied, sneaking a shy glance at the boy, her beady grey eyes poking out from underneath a fringe of auburn hair. "Hello."

"Hello," he replied.

She erupted into a fit of giggles before scurrying away.

Gaia frowned. "Please pay her no mind. She is a peculiar girl."

"They call you Gaia? Is that a Roman name?" he asked her.

"In a sense," she replied, resuming her task of cleaning him. "The Roman gods are borrowed from the Greeks, the gods of Olympus. They are very different from the gods of our people, mischievous, fickle deities less concerned with war and ancestry than they are self-seeking relationships with humans. Roman walls are filled with frescoes of them, hundreds of statues erected in their honor. I am named after the earth goddess, Gaia, since I have been told I have a maternal way with all the slaves. Eridus's choosing, of course."

"It suits you," he offered.

She met his eyes, suddenly appearing flustered. She stood, tossing him the tunic. "Here, dress yourself in this. I shall turn away for your discretion." She spun around, letting him finally peel away his soiled tunic and crawl into the one she had produced for him. It fit snuggly, the fabric comfortable against his tender skin. She turned back when he was finished and grinned, proudly.

"Now you look like one of the gods," she decided.

He looked down, instantly bashful.

"Well, now that you know my name, what shall I call you? I need a name to explain your presence to Eridus with."

"I was known only as Son of Semias, or Son, before my father died. He was a great Druid Elder, so tradition requires that he be called by the name of the very first Druid of our clan. I would have taken his name after my apprenticeship and his passing. Then I was nicknamed Daghda by a woman…" he trailed off, remembering the Morrigan.

Gaia frowned, hands settled on her hips in a now signature gesture. "Well, that will not do. The Romans are not exactly accepting of the customs of conquered territories. Especially a name of significance." She thought for a moment. "I shall call you Davius. It is as Roman of a name that I can muster."

Davius. He paused to consider it before giving her a firm nod.

"Then Davius I shall be."

She smiled. "Welcome to Rome, Davius. This will be your new room. Please rest, and I will be back to fetch you as soon as I have spoken to our master."

He frowned when he heard the word, master, disliking it immediately, but his eyes caught sight of the bed, which beckoned his weak and weary limbs.

"Rest," she insisted, before drawing up to him, bending her knees to compensate for her height, and kissing his cheek. His heart fluttered in response. She beamed and without another word, she withdrew, leaving him alone to finally rest in peace.

LONDON, 1857

SHE STARED AT HIM IN AWE. "You have lived through centuries."
David met her eyes in silent affirmation.

The night had stretched into the early hours of morning. Their tar had long run out, yet the owner of the den knew better than to disturb them, even to inquire if they needed more. His companion was seated upright, listening to his story with the rapt attention of a child, any trace of intoxication absent from her pale eyes. "But when did you become what you are?" she asked. "Did it happen at the villa?"

"It would be several years before I would change. The years with her, as a young man, were some of the happiest I've ever known. I guess that's why my story begins with her."

"You loved her."

"We were inseparable." He nodded. "She was my first romance, that sort of naive and dreamlike experience only few are fortunate to have before the harsh realities of life take hold." He slowly rose to his feet. "We should leave this place. The hours grow into morning."

"But you've only told me the beginning!" she objected, nearly sending herself into another fit of heaves.

He lifted his hand to silence her protests. "I would be honored if you'd join me at my home," he offered, surprising himself. "I will make sure your companionship is compensated for," he added for good measure.

She delighted, jumping up before realizing the unsteadiness of her gait. He reached out to stabilize her, waiting until she had regained her bearings before he gently took her arm and linked it around his own. Her eyes met his in silent gratitude. Without further ado, they withdrew together from the stale room.

They brushed past the openly shocked woman from earlier, not allowing her the opportunity to make a comment, and pushed open the front door of the den, releasing a hazy cloud of smoke into the night air. The scent of foreboding daylight reached David's nostrils, a silent warning to find refuge soon. Not a soul roamed the streets at this hour, save for those involved in racketing and chicanery, and his personal coachman who, as per their evening ritual, had been patiently patrolling the area to collect him.

"Good evening, Jacob. Or shall I say good morning?" he greeted him.

"Sir," the older man nodded back, peering at him beneath the rim of his hat. "Good evening and good morning to ya, sir."

Jacob had been a remarkably loyal manservant over the years, content with minding his own affairs while residing in the gatehouse of David's manor. He acted as groundskeeper, coachman, or personal servant, depending upon request. He never questioned his employer, satisfied with the generous payments left each week under his shabby doormat and the free, commodious lodging.

Now he pried open the coach doors, politely averting his eyes past David's companion as he gestured her inside. She gathered up her plentiful skirts before hoisting herself in, settling into the plush, cushioned seats as David climbed in after her. The carriage lurched forward as she admired the richness of the fabric, the horses springing rapidly to trot.

She pointed excitedly out the small carriage window as they rode, thoroughly enjoying the view of the rolling landscape as they traveled out of the city. He left her to her excitement, leaning comfortably against the seat. He felt a few stubborn hunger pangs, but the malaise that had settled over him was less about needing to feed as it was daybreak fatigue. He sighed, letting his body rest as the last of the opium worked its way out of his pores. His mind drifted back to his story. It had been so many decades since he had thought of her, his lovely Gaia. He closed his eyes, trying to remember the sweet floral smell of her skin and the feel of the warm Italian sun on his face.

Ancient Rome, 49 B.C.

"Davius!"

From far beyond where he could see, her voice called to him. The marketplace was spun with chaos, the bustle of frantic Romans preparing for the Festival of Neptunalia drowning out the sound. Yet her arm branched out from the throng of bodies, waving for him to come.

Although Davius had adjusted to the brutal Roman sun, the summer months proved almost unbearable. He was not alone in his vexations; because of the scorching temperatures, food vendors only kept their carts open until midafternoon, forcing citizens who desired fresh fruit or meat for their evening supper to come at daybreak. This only added to the frenzy of today's feast day preparations, bodies pressing him at all sides. Gaia finally pushed her way through them, her cheeks pink from the exertion.

As the years passed, he had grown fiercely in love with her. Like him, she had been transformed by adulthood, the age difference between them now hardly apparent. Her rose golden hair still bounced around her narrow shoulders when she spoke, but most of it was now kept fastened behind her head in a delicate gold clip, the rest falling beyond her rounded breasts and settling into the small of her back. Her hips had grown generous as she aged, offering ample room for legs that were long enough to drive the hem of her tunic up around her thighs. Gone was the spritely girl who had met him in the marketplace, her replacement a voluptuous Roman goddess.

It had been nearly a decade since Davius first arrived in Rome and into the care of Gaia, becoming another personal slave to Eridus Acacallis

Aganus, the winemaker. The wealthy patron took a liking to him immediately, eventually treating him like he did his closest slaves. His only household duty was to tend to the stables, but it was a task he enjoyed rather than toiled at.

He learned the new language easily, his accent gradually diminishing as he acclimated to his new home. He had also grown accustomed to Roman culture, even embracing the religious practices they upheld. Eridus allowed him to visit the Forum when time permitted, and it was there that his mind blossomed as he spent hours listening to the musings of the great philosophers who orated from behind stone pedestals. He broke away only to explore the surrounding temples dedicated to various Roman gods, finding solace and inspiration within their walls. It was there that he discovered his calling, enthralled by art in its various forms, gliding his fingers over the marble sculptures and across the heavily painted frescoes that covered the walls. His obsession soon evolved into passion, inspiring him to create art of his own. He concocted his own paint by smashing bits of fruit or insect shells into paste, adding them to drops of leftover olive oil. He experimented with other materials, such as resin for black and cinnabar for red, until the entire spectrum was represented. He would then spread the colors on flat stones he found in the woods or on scraps of old cloth, painting everything from images of deities, old and new, to scenes from nature, to that which he cherished most, his Gaia.

He moved towards her now, pushing a wooden cart heavy with loaves of bread, jugs of honey and poppy seeds, and baskets of figs. He had yet to purchase the requested pork and bird, but the heat prevented him from doing so until the final moment before their departure. Not only was today a Roman feast day, but it was the day of Eridus's birth, and he had sent him to fetch as many delicacies and seasonings as he could carry for a lavish banquet to be held that evening. He sent Gaia to accompany him, her task to barter with Vaticus Marcaoneus, a rival winemaker, to trade some of his fine wine for a jug of Eridus's best. She held a jug of it now in her dewy arms, the afternoon heat wilting away her countenance. "The forum is unbearable today," she remarked.

"Hopefully all this worship of Neptune will bring rain," he agreed. "Let us head to the meat market so we can return home."

She nodded, adjusting the wine jug into a more comfortable position in her arms.

The meat market was easy to find, its telltale stench radiating from the far end of the forum. Although it was purposefully shaded, butchers were still forced to take desperate measures to keep the meat fresh, trickling continuous cool water over the slabs while warding off tenacious flies with traps of honey. Davius and Gaia weaved through the crowd towards it, conversing excitedly about the approaching events. Feast nights offered them rare moments of freedom; Eridus had the habit of growing far too drunk on his own wine, his excessive merriment extending out to his slaves. He allowed them to celebrate after all his guests had either left or fallen out from over-indulgence, often joining them in their quarters, lest he be forced to end the celebration entirely. Gaia loved to regale the other slaves with the story of how she found him one morning, face down in the middle of the atrium, snoring, still clothed and spotted with food.

They passed the main body of the forum where Davius often frequented, the amount of lounging Romans as excessive in number as in the marketplace. A group of patrons stood crowded together, their conversation animated by wild gestures and raised voices. Davius recognized the elder who stood in the center, aware that he was not only a respected Senator, but regarded as one of the greatest philosophers of the forum. "They found her on the shore," the man recounted, "the wound on her neck so deep that it nearly severed her head from her body. I have never seen anything so tragic. It is truly a warning from the gods."

"Neptune would never allow it. Not on his feast day," one of the younger men scoffed.

"But it is true, young man. She was found this morning."

"This is truly the work of the gods!" another man interjected. "We must make sacrifices to Pluto and repent! We have not served him enough! He enacts his vengeance upon us!"

The crowd erupted in fearful banter.

Davius felt cold horror wash over him, prying its fingers into the bowels of his stomach. He had not thought about the day of his arrival for many years. Could it be...?

Gaia slipped her fingers into his hand instinctively, giving it a firm squeeze. "No," she whispered. "This was not you. Old men love to hear themselves talk. Let us go."

Grateful to be freed from overhearing more of their troubling words, he obeyed.

They reached the butchery where Gaia produced her pouch of coins to purchase quail, dormice, snails, and pork. Davius helped her stack the cuts neatly on the cart, then covered them with a straw mat to ward off the flies. "We have only moments before it starts to spoil," she reminded him. "Let us hurry."

Davius nodded absently, still unable to meet her eyes.

"It was not you," she repeated firmly, pushing her face near his so he was forced to look into them.

"It was not me," he echoed.

They took turns pushing the cart until their villa came into view. Already the smoke from culinary fires billowed up from the kitchen, the commotion coming from behind its walls audible from the outside. They burst through the door, immediately assaulted by the clamor of frantic preparation, the cooks shouting at each other over the noise of chopping knives and clanging pots and pans. Davius felt as if the wind had been sucked from his lungs, the temperature of the kitchen far exceeding the outdoors, its open windows no match for the oven's giant flames. The cooking slaves paid the oppressive heat no mind, dancing from pot to stove to butcher's block dressed only in meager strips of tunic cloth which were soaked with sweat and discolored by grime.

"I brought more!" Davius called over the racket, setting down his cart. They immediately attacked the spoils, reminding him of ants swarming over freshly dropped fruit.

Davius and Gaia withdrew from the inferno into the shade of the villa, its coolness kissing the heat from their skin. They moved down the stretch of hall that separated the slave quarters from the main residence to meet Eridus, who was already pacing feverishly up and down the length of his peristyle. It was decorated to project magnificence, ornate columns and fine marble statues overcrowding each room. They were currently adorned in Neptune's colors, draped in sea green and sky blue, ornamented with glistening silver. The colors complimented the intricate frescoes covering each wall, creating the atmosphere of an underwater palace fit for a sea god.

"You." Eridus's baritone voice cut through Davius's thoughtful observations. "You were able to get everything that I asked for?"

"Yes, sir," Davius replied.

Only a hint of relief softened the man's stern, ruddy face. Eridus was a corpulent man, the huge swell of his stomach obscuring the belt of his robes, his fleshy face a constant shade of overexertion. The color spread to the bald spot atop his head, surrounded by patches of grey, wiry hair that clung to his skull in desperation. His tree trunk legs were in constant motion, pacing back and forth when he grew apprehensive, which tended to be far more often than he was calm.

"And the wine?"

"Yes," Gaia assured him. "Marcus and the kitchen slaves have already begun preparing the feast, and Urtus is filling the carafes. I was able to make an even trade today, and Vaticus Marcaoneus sends his regrets."

Eridus waved his hand, dismissively. "No one will miss that old bastard anyway. He can barely handle his wine." He turned his back to resume his anxious march as Davius caught Gaia stifling a laugh.

"Gaia, go retrieve Moira," he ordered as he came back around to face them. "She will help you dress for tonight. As you may have expected, I will need to be the main servant. She purchased robes for you earlier this morning. I need you to look your finest."

Gaia lifted herself up to the tips of her toes to give him a gentle kiss on the cheek, not unlike the way a daughter would her father. "As always, Master Eridus, you have my heartfelt gratitude," she said warmly. "I shall not disappoint."

Davius observed his face flush, his sour mood faintly sweetened by the gesture. "Ah, yes," he stammered. "Go on now, she waits for you in your chambers."

Gaia offered a good-natured bow to him before she withdrew, sneaking Davius a wink before she disappeared down the hall to her rooms.

Eridus turned back towards him, inching closer to where he stood. "Now, Davius," he said in a low mumble, "your job will be to keep a watchful eye on all who arrive. Make sure they keep their distance from my cherished possessions. A man can trust no one, even the Roman elite. I may ask you to bring in wine from time to time, however..." He faltered suddenly, hesitant with his words. "Well...I do not need to warn you of the lustful advances of a drunken Roman on a young slave boy..."

Davius quickly nodded in understanding, alleviating the man's discomfort. "Of course."

He clapped his hands together, pleased. "Excellent. Hurry along now, the hour of festivities is upon us!"

Davius nodded, leaving him to his nervous stride as he headed down the corridor that led to his room. He often fantasized that someday he would be as rich as Eridus with a multitude of servants at his disposal and Gaia as his wife. His daydreams helped to pass the long hours he spent working in the stables, imagining what it would be like to finally press his lips against hers, running his hands around her soft curves. He loved her completely; he spent each day yearning for the moments they would be together. Sometimes he thought of their children, picturing their bright green eyes and cherubic faces, confident they could have no better mother than his patient, nurturing Gaia.

He entered his room, smiling as he imagined small, golden haired babes running into her arms. He pulled a freshly laundered tunic over his head, the fabric pulling at a frame that had recently peaked in masculinity. He would need larger clothing soon, he thought to himself, as he ran a comb through his tousled hair. His coppery blond locks were much longer than the fashion, but Davius had been taught long ago that a full head of hair and a strong beard were the achievements of manhood. Although he embraced Roman culture, it was one Celtic tradition he wasn't willing to part with.

Since his arrival, there had been no sign of the tempestuous deity who had protected him on his fateful journey. Gaia never again spoke of that morning, and for that, Davius was grateful. She left her village too soon to have learned the old ways, and he didn't want to risk upsetting her with bloody tales of gods that had no place in this land. He kept them buried inside, honoring them when he could, feeling their presence with the turn of each season, in the smell of fresh blood wafting from the butchery, in the crackle of bonfires. The old gods remained alive, but quietly, hidden away in the recesses of his heart.

He headed towards the dining quarters to assist where needed. The setting of the long, elegant dining table was nearly complete, large decanters of wine, drinking glasses, and polished silver place settings obscuring the cerulean tablecloth. Similarly, colored cloth was draped over the lounging couches, the smiling ivory sculptures of Bacchus and his nymphs that were etched into their sides peeking out from underneath their new blankets. Slaves buzzed around him as he adjusted one of the wayward pillows, sneaking a grape from one of the fruit platters near him. The action led him to notice an absent olive oil carafe, which he knew should accompany the bread plate. He turned towards the kitchen to retrieve it, colliding into another slave. "Forgive me—" he began before his words were snatched from him.

Gaia was a vision of divine enchantment. Her curves were wrapped in sanguine robes trimmed with gold, with jewels of ruby and gold sparkling at her ears and throat. Her skin had been powdered into an iridescent sheen, delicate gold bracelets winding up her shapely arms. Dark kohl outlined eyes which shone like polished emeralds in the glow of the setting sun.

She observed his speechlessness with amusement. "What, did you not believe I could look refined?"

He laughed, broken away from her spell. "You look perfect."

She beamed, despite herself, nervously casting her eyes on the floor. "Well, thank you."

The aroma of her jasmine perfume wafted up from her skin. He suddenly felt the urge to take her into his arms.

"Davius!" a voice bellowed from afar, startling him.

He turned and began to jog down the hall towards the sound of Eridus's voice. "I will see you tonight!" he called back to her, playfully using their old Gaulish tongue.

She smiled and echoed the language, "Tonight."

The banquet continued well into the late hours of night, the laughter of inebriated Romans echoing throughout the halls. Davius had retired to his room after several hours of servitude, stretching his limbs out across his bedding as he listened to the belches and upheavals customary to a proper Roman feast. The guests had already worked their way through all seven courses, sating themselves now with copious amounts of wine and leftover olives. Sleep availed him, his apprehension over Gaia's presence around the drunken dinner guests proving a bit too much for him to bear.

He withdrew from his bed to the open window, the cool summer breeze running its fingers through his hair. He inhaled, letting its gentle greeting calm his nerves. He enjoyed the peace for a few moments before hoisting himself up and wriggling his body through the narrow aperture. He latched onto the terra-cotta tiles with his fingers, pulling up on the roof with all his strength until he catapulted onto his desired destination. His landing was graceful, but he still made sure to establish balance before maneuvering to his usual spot where an old tattered blanket waited for him. He smoothed it out and settled himself across it, tucking his hands behind his head as he reclined. He let out a sigh, drinking in the sparkling stars above, radiant orbs freckling the dark, infinite skies.

He had memorized the constellations long ago, tracing them now with an extended finger. The fireball of Venus outshined the waxing moon, illuminating her neighboring constellation of Pegasus, his pointed wings perfectly visible to the naked eye. Davius found solace in the knowledge that the stars he gazed at now were the same as when he was a young boy laying in the fields of Gaul. He imagined the tribes left standing after the Romans' plunder, congregating under the same moon he beheld above.

He inhaled once more, letting his heavy eyes close to the celestial splendor above, content to let them swirl in his memories.

"Davius?"

He jolted out of his trance, nearly toppling off the roof.

"Davius, where are you?"

He let his head hang down over the edge so that it appeared upside down in the window. "Here," he called.

Gaia startled. "What are you doing on the roof?"

He laughed, admiring once more how lovely she looked, even with his vision askew. "I am gazing at the skies. Will you join me?" He noticed she was holding a half-filled carafe in her arms.

She looked skeptical. "How am I to get up there?"

"I will pull you up. Come." He gestured her forward.

She laughed at the absurdity of it, handing him the carafe first before she lifted her skirts and hoisted herself up through the window. "Please do not let me fall," she begged as he grounded his feet and pulled her up the rest of the way.

It was a success; she faltered only for a moment before gaining her footing. He led her to his makeshift perch, where she sat, pulling the carafe near her to uncork it. "This took much guile on my part to sneak away unnoticed," she teased, taking a sip before handing it to him.

He sat down next to her, putting the opening to his lips. "Was the dinner terrible?" he asked, pleasantly surprised by the robust flavor as its heat descended into his stomach. The slave wine they usually drank was watered down and almost rank, but tonight she managed to procure that which was saved for honored guests.

"Not too terrible," she replied as she took it back for another swig. "It was the usual exchange of forced pleasantries, boasting of personal successes, lamenting over politics. Eridus invited that terrible Nirus, so he kept my summoning to the table as infrequent as possible."

Davius shuddered. Nirus was the most nefarious slave owner in Rome, stories of his merciless abuse well-known among its citizens. Since he was a prominent war hero and belonged to one of the wealthiest families in the Empire, his misdeeds frequently went ignored. He was also adored by the slave traders, his constant demand for new bodies keeping their pockets full. "I would have killed him if he touched you," he muttered.

She smiled. "I know. I feel safe knowing you are here."

The warmth of the wine and her words flushed his face, and he lay back to return his gaze to the skies.

She followed suit, gasping immediately at the sight of them. "My gods, how beautiful. Do you come up here every night?"

"When sleep escapes me. The skies calm me and remind me of home."

She frowned. "Do you miss it still?"

He turned towards her, his nose assaulted once more by sweet smelling jasmine. "Sometimes," he replied honestly. "I love my life here, but I do long for crisp air and majestic trees."

"I do not remember much from home. My mother told me stories of it though, how the people were one with the forest, not cultivated and detached from it like in Rome."

"You have never spoken to me about your mother before." Davius took another large swallow of wine.

"I came here with her and worked by her side for many years," she explained. "She died one day, mysteriously in the fields. Alone I was prey for ruthless slave traders, but Eridus found me before it was too late. I guess it hurts to speak of her still." Gaia lifted the carafe to her lips as if to dismiss her words.

"I am sorry," he offered, sincerely.

"Please do not be. My only regret is that I know nothing of my heritage - our heritage." A thought occurred to her, causing her to brighten. "You can teach me! Will you tell me of our gods?"

Davius considered her request. Memories tucked away in the corners of his mind began to surface. He thought of the Morrigan and her wicked, triumphant smile as she stood, surrounded by human carrion. Reluctantly, he agreed.

"Wonderful," she beamed. "I will be the most apt of students."

Davius couldn't help but laugh.

"I will," she protested, batting at him playfully. She took another drink. "It has suddenly occurred to me that I am going to soon be very drunk and climbing down this rooftop will present quite a challenge."

Davius grabbed the carafe, taking another generous sip for himself. "Then we shall lay here until morning, and I will climb down the wall with you on my back."

She laughed. "And what if Eridus finds us?"

"He is already well past the ability to climb a rooftop," he pointed out.

"Now that is certain," she agreed as she retrieved the nearly empty bottle, draining the last of it. She handed it back to him, reaching back to unclasp the pins that held her hair, releasing ringlets of reddish gold cascading down her back.

"I could never be a wealthy woman," she declared. "I could not imagine waking every morning to have slaves push these torturous pins into my head."

"So when I become a wealthy artist, and you are my wife, you will never wear your hair in plaits?" Davius teased, before he could stop himself.

Her eyes widened in surprise. "We could never be married," she sputtered. "I am years older than you and we are both slaves!"

He shook his head. "You are not too old for me, and I will buy our freedom from Eridus."

"With your paintings on the sides of stones and your carvings in tree trunks? No one would pay a slave for his services, even if you did manage to display your work for the public to see."

He turned away, wounded by her words.

She immediately softened, placing her hand on his arm. "I am sorry, Davius. I am dizzy with wine - I did not mean what I said. I know you will be a great artist someday. I just...I hate that we are not free. Dreaming of it seems futile, a waste of time."

Davius turned back to her, their faces inches apart. "But if I do sell my work and can afford our freedom, will you marry me?" he pressed, imploring her eyes with his own.

Gaia sighed, smiling despite herself. "Of course I would."

Before she could say anything further, he kissed her, her lips soft against his. He pulled her tightly against him and she momentarily submitted, their bodies melting seamlessly together in embrace. She pulled herself away, alarmed by their passion. "Suddenly, I am very tired," she managed.

"Sleep then," he gently suggested. "I can hold you under the stars."

She acquiesced gratefully, nestling her body next to his. Her curves fit into him as if they were made to, and he gazed at her until she closed her eyes, listening to her breathing steady. Assured she was comfortably asleep, he turned back up his eyes, letting the celestial dance of the heavens carry him away to dreamland.

CHAPTER TWO

🎄 THE MAN 🎄

His breath caught in his throat, panic clenching his lungs with frantic fingers. Darkness surrounded him, save for the creature trudging towards him, its eyes ablaze. Its limbs were gnarled and taloned, charred skeletal bones jutting out of its scaly black skin. He wanted nothing more than to flee, but found he was frozen where he stood. The pressure of heavy liquid was smothering him, choking him with its syrupy aroma. He raised his hands to wipe free his nostrils only to realize he was dripping with rich crimson blood, his mouth assaulted by its smoky metallic taste. Horrified, he looked up to see the being now stood directly before him, its black leathery wings whipping the air around them like an angry tempest. The creature was holding the body of a young woman in its arms, its loathsome dragon-like face twisted up into a grin. He caught its burning eyes with his own before the realization dawned on him.

The creature was him.

Instantly, his perspective shifted so that he saw out of the creature's eyes, his mouth tingling with the taste of the woman's blood as if he'd been feeding on her. She offered no resistance, hanging limply in its taloned claws. He didn't want to see her face, trying not to move his eyes past the gaping wound at her neck, that poured its gore down the plane of her freckled skin, staining her strawberry blonde hair.

He could hear the creature's laughter echoing in his ears as his human self finally screamed, the eyes of his love staring lifelessly ahead...

Davius sprang from slumber, drenched in sweat. He pitched himself up fast enough to vomit out his bedroom window, the sharp bile burning his throat. He paused there, gasping for air. The mild breeze of early morning tickled his damp forehead, lovingly attempting to soothe his distress.

The sun peeked out from above the trees, its rays bringing brilliance to the cloudless skies. He realized he had slept well into the morning. Reality slowly came back to him. It was only a dream.

He threw his blanket off him, jumping up from his bed. It had been only two days since he had fallen asleep with Gaia by his side. He smiled as he recalled her soft skin against his, her warm breath on his face. The terror of his nightmare faded away.

He dressed quickly, exiting his room in equal haste. The temperature of the countryside had already begun its balmy ascent, the morning stirring with wildlife. He traveled down the familiar dirt path that stretched beyond the vineyards to the stables where he worked. They were filled to capacity with Eridus's prized horses, an array of heavily muscular bodies and sturdy legs, slapping their long tails against biting flies. He didn't mind the routine of feeding them, greeted each morning with the sweet and sour smell of clean straw and pungent waste. The day was hotter than Davius expected, and he let his tunic fall around his hips to expose his chest. He pushed the dream far from his head, deciding to worship the beauty of morning instead.

The horses whinnied happily at the sight of him. He smiled, gliding his fingers down their smooth bodies as he filled their troughs with meal. His work consumed what was left of the morning into the afternoon, ceasing only after the straw was fresh, the drinking trough refilled, and the horses' coats gleamed. He filled his own drinking pouch with water before heading back towards the vineyards. Slaves toiled diligently, plucking juicy grapes from their vines and collecting them in barrels for the grape-crushing shack. He once enjoyed such a task when he first arrived at the villa, before he earned Eridus's trust, and he fondly recalled the sensation of pulp squishing between his toes.

Down past the vineyards was the property's vast lake, where a couple slave girls took turns bathing in its cool waters as they laundered loads of the household's soiled clothing. Their soaked tunics clung to their bodies as they slapped the linen on the rocks, ridding them of excess water before setting them out to dry in the sun. He snuck past them, continuing his journey further into the forest where he maneuvered cautiously around the brush and fallen trees. After he'd traveled quite a distance, he paused to wipe his brow, taking a generous sip of water.

Suddenly, he heard a rustle in the trees, and went still. He heard the squirrel nibbling, mere footsteps from where he stood. He focused on the sound as he slowly slipped the tunic off his waist. He paused, naked, pulling the cloth taut in his hands. The squirrel sensed him and prepared to flee, but without hesitation, Davius lunged.

Tiny claws ripped at his skin as the squirrel screeched and struggled, frantically trying to free itself. He doubled the tunic cloth around it tightly, preventing any opportunity for escape. He continued on into the heart of the forest, stopping only when he reached a fallen tree with symbols carved alongside its broad trunk. Its dead branches varied enough in size to create a thicket, hidden from plain sight. He pushed a few of them aside, revealing a cleared space which he stepped into without hesitation.

His altar greeted him, the stone slab stained maroon from his last sacrifice. Rocks surrounded the makeshift table in a circle, garnished with various flowers and herbs. He moved towards it, holding the ensnared squirrel in one hand. With the other, he unsheathed the handmade knife he wore strapped to his thigh. The marble shard glinted in the light that streamed down through the canopy of trees. He knelt, placing the squirming squirrel on the altar. He bowed his head, Druid prayers he hadn't forgotten spilling from his lips. He let the words move him as the sounds of the forest chimed in unison. He imagined the Tuatha De Danann drumming in the distance as a circle of Druids spun around fires built in their honor. He recalled the sweet herbal scent of his mother's skin, the sight of his father's stern face, the damp earth beneath his feet. He pictured Gaia moving freely amongst his tribe as they celebrated, his way of asking the gods to bless their future union.

He continued his chant in ascending fervor, freeing the squirrel from the bundled tunic. Its black eyes bore into his, an equal mix of fear and hatred. Davius thanked it for its service, and swiftly brought the knife down to sever its tiny throat. The squirrel had no time to register pain, its body jerking with finality as its blood pooled beneath it. Davius thanked the gods and rose to his feet, when suddenly, it hit him. He doubled forward, the knife falling from his hand. Heart hammering in his chest, he struggled to collect himself, but his vision had blurred. All he could see was an ocean of red, as if the blood from his dream now swam in his mind, obscuring all else. He clawed at his eyes in panic, the forest around him melting away. He could taste the metallic horror in his mouth again, feel the waves of revulsion.

The vision vanished as quickly as it had come. He realized he was panting.

He looked down. The squirrel hadn't stirred, its wound clotted in death. He grabbed his knife from the forest floor and dumped out his water onto the altar, washing the carnage away. He gathered the rest of his things, withdrawing from his copse with haste.

The warm sun welcomed him back into its kind light, and he closed his eyes briefly to savor it. His mind drifted to the Morrigan. Was it she who haunted him now? Whatever it was, it felt different than her, as if these visions were coming from somewhere other than his gods. Could it be Pluto, the Roman god of the Underworld? The night goddess Nyx? He shivered, although the air around him was pleasantly tepid.

He longed to see Gaia.

Eridus's villa appeared in the distance, which he gratefully entered.

"Davius!"

Relief flooded him as he recognized her voice. He disregarded his usual apprehension of onlookers, scooping her into his arms. She batted him away, but the act was half-hearted. "Where have you been? You are lucky Eridus left early this morning. We are having more guests tomorrow, he told me. Apparently, his dinner was such a success that more patrons wish to do business with the winery. Which is horrendously timed, because I am beside myself with exhaustion."

As she spoke, he noticed the lack of sparkle in her eyes and the gray shadows that collected underneath them, contrasting against an unusual pallor. "What is the matter?" he asked with concern.

Gaia lowered her voice to a whisper. "Last night, one of the slaves fell ill after being wounded - it was Moira. I have never seen anything like it. Her face is sallow, and she trembles without cease. When she is not moaning in agony, she mutters strange words over and over as if she were in some sort of trance. I cannot help but worry that it is more than a simple sickness. Yet her agonies are not enough to convince Eridus to postpone his dinner plans," she added, wryly.

"What does she say?"

"I think she speaks in the old language, but I cannot decipher it. You should see her, Davius, maybe you can translate her words. I have never witnessed a person in such a state, let alone someone so close to us."

"For you, I will," he promised, taking her hands in his.

She kissed his cheek gratefully. They lingered together for a moment before he reluctantly let her slip away, watching as she disappeared in a blur of rose gold.

The subsequent dinner party was not as raucous as the night before, the house unusually subdued. The evening had brought a gentle summer rain which tapped softly at the rooftop, muffling Davius's footsteps as he crept to the guest quarters where Moira lay. The household was pre-occupied, allowing him to enter the room unnoticed.

The sight of her immediately troubled him. It looked like she was starving, though she had only been sick a few days, her body motionless on the bed with rib bones protruding out of her stomach. Her skin had taken on a ghostly shade, marred by clusters of violet bruises. She struggled to breathe, emitting a croaking wheeze with each labored effort.

"Moira?" he whispered.

She gave no sign that she noticed his presence. Her thin fingers were folded at her chest as if they had already prepared her body for the funeral pyre.

He bent down next to her, placing his hand on hers to observe it was cool to the touch. He noticed her neck was wrapped in bandages, tarnished by rust colored splotches from her wound. Curious, he unraveled them, grateful that she remained still as he gingerly lifted away each soiled layer. He hesitated with the last piece, steadying himself before pulling up the damp cloth to reveal what lay beneath.

He jumped to his feet in alarm. A chunk of flesh had been torn out of her neck as if she had been attacked by a ravenous animal. The glistening wound pulsated, her weakened heart pumping out the last few gasps of her life force. He forced himself to rewrap the bandages with shaking hands, images of his nightmare threatening to surface.

A cold hand suddenly clamped down on his arm.

Moira's eyes bore into his, entirely black as if the pupil stretched beyond its iris. It made her look inhuman, her auburn hair wild around her ghastly face. Her mouth opened with the slow creak of a corroded iron box, her throat croaking out a voice that was not hers, speaking in perfect Gaulish, her words ending in reptilian hiss, "House of the Lost Godsssss…"

David flew from the room in horror.

Memories from his first few months as a slave assailed his mind as he tore down the corridor, the old abandoned town house, tucked behind the dilapidated buildings left ignored in the less desirable part of Rome. He had been exploring the streets only to discover he was lost, immediately drawn to the crumbling architecture that stood out among its skeletal counterparts. Upon closer inspection, the open windows revealed fading frescoes hidden within its walls. Intrigued, he found a way in, discovering a myriad of illustrations, telling tales of gods worshipped long before the advent of Greek religion. Much of the paint had chipped away, the walls in various stages of decomposition. He later learned that the temple, and the buildings clustered around it, had been built before the advancement of stone masonry and left to decompose. It smelled of old earth, aging moss crawling up its walls, unapologetically obscuring patches of artwork, nature reclaiming what was meant to be hers.

Young Davius ran his fingers over the moldering images, enthralled by the pictorial tales of blood and violence, sex and love, life and death. He paused at the image of a half man/half beast, towering over frightened peasants with a bleeding corpse in his jaws. Warriors stood at its taloned feet, their bows and arrows aimed up at him as the surrounding flames threatened to devour them all.

It was dusk before he pulled himself away, racing back to the villa before his absence was noticed. For years, he wanted to return, but was never able to find the mysterious, perishing temple again. In his mind, he called it the House of the Lost Gods, a name he breathed to no one, and like so many events in his life, the memory of it had faded with time.

Yet the beast from the temple had come to life, nestling itself in his dreams, taunting him.

Davius stopped running to stand in the rain, letting it cleanse his mind, the cool, melodic tapping on his skin helping him gather his thoughts. He was being haunted by a god he had no knowledge of, a god older than the gods of Olympus. It was now living among them, Moira the first of what could be many victims. Or perhaps the second, if he believed the news reported by the old philosopher days prior. What would stop it from destroying all who he cared for? In the shower of rainfall, he decided he would seek the creature out and see to its ruin. He had faith that his gods were stronger than any beast this new world could summon.

"Tuatha De Danann," he whispered up to the pouring heavens. "Hear me. I call upon the great Daghda, he who lives in the storms, to strengthen me now. Show me the path I must follow. In the name of the goddess Danu, accept my humble plea."

Thunder bellowed in response, followed by a crackle of lightning.

Renewed, he returned to the dry warmth of the villa, shaking the rain from his hair. He was immediately struck by the strong aroma of incense, its dense vapor wafting throughout the residence. He realized the dinner guests had left, the hallways now cluttered with pacing slaves. A few wept, consoling each other with murmurs of kindness and gentle displays of affection. Priests from the Pantheon hurried past them, herbal smoke billowing from their censors.

Davius knew instantly that she was gone.

No sooner did the presentiment occur to him did a young slave boy appear from around the bend, tears streaking his sullied face. He wrung his hands, looking up at the surrounding faces with mournful eyes. "She has passed," he informed them as he trembled.

Open displays of lamentation echoed throughout the halls. Davius searched frantically for Gaia, but she was absent from the crowd.

"Pluto has cursed this home," he overheard a woman sob in fear.

He pushed past them, alarmed that he could not find her. The hallways leading to the guest quarters seemed to stretch endlessly before him as he hastened around their twists and turns. His pace slowed when he finally reached Moira's doorway, where a group of weeping slaves stood, wrapped in each other's arms.

The room was aglow with slender, waning candles, casting thin shadows across the walls. Eridus was seated at her bedside, his customary pacing absent, his head resting in his hands. Robed priests surrounded Moira's body, singing soft hymns as they blessed her body with herbal essence, preparing her for her journey to the Underworld. She was covered up to the neck with light material, which rolled gently in the wind. Two gold coins rested on her eyes, a kind gesture from a slave master, assuring she would have the payment required so the ferryman Charon would give her safe passage across the river Styx.

The wound at her neck no longer bled, her body finally drained of life. Davius pictured her alive, the innocent cherubic beauty with warm brown eyes who giggled when young slave boys brought her flowers, wearing them proudly in her auburn hair.

Davius pulled his gaze away from her, scanning the room for Gaia. Eridus caught his eyes. His face was soaked with tears, his body completely succumbed to lachrymose. "She is looking for you," he managed, the whites of his eyes shot through with blood from weeping.

Davius nodded, grateful to withdraw from the mourning room. He exited the guest halls to greet solitude, where he paused. He closed his eyes, steadying his breath, letting his intuition guide him.

He found her in his room, crumpled on his bed. She lifted her head as he entered, her sweet face damp and corrupted by sorrow. "She died in my arms."

He tenderly took her into his. "You did everything you could," he assured her.

"My gift is to nurture and care for those I love, I feel as though I have failed her," she sobbed. "Her death was unlike anything I have ever seen before…maybe we are cursed."

He swallowed, afraid to divulge his recent revelations. "Eridus is a kind and just slave master," he reminded her. "He treats us better than any patron in Rome. His business dealings are fair, his close associates humble. There is no reason for this house to be cursed."

"The gods are not always fair."

"My gods are," he muttered, before he could stop himself.

She sniffed, lifting her face from his chest. "You never speak of your gods. Our gods, I suppose."

"There was never reason to. The gods of Olympus have served us well in this life. Moira's death was unnaturally soon, that I will not argue. One day its nature will be revealed, but I am certain it will have nothing to do with this house and its morality."

"Thank you for saying that." She wiped the tears from her face, her hand still streaked with Moira's blood.

He grabbed the water basin near his bedside, taking her hand in his and dabbing it softly with a cloth. The gesture made him smile. "Remember when you bathed me once, not so long ago?"

She returned the smile, a tiny spark coming back into her eyes. "It seems like an eternity has passed since that day."

"I think I wanted to marry you from that moment."

"I think I may actually accept your tender words today." She leaned over to kiss his cheek, but he swerved to catch her mouth. He managed to pull himself away, placing the water basin back on its table.

"Can I stay here with you tonight?" she asked.

Davius was torn. "I would love nothing more. But Eridus…"

"He will not retire to his room tonight. This happened years before you came, when another slave girl died. I was too young to remember the details of her death, but I remember he did not leave her side until the funeral pyre. He stayed awake throughout the entire evening, soothing himself with wine. I have no doubt he will be the same tonight."

"Another slave girl…" Davius frowned, disturbed by the revelation.

Yet Gaia was lost to her own thoughts. "I do not understand what kind of creature would do that to her. It could not have been a human, but there are no beasts capable of such wounds so close to the city. It must have been a monster of some sort, a lower god."

Davius didn't respond, silently hoping she wouldn't recall the morning of his first arrival, nor connect Moira's death with the news they'd heard in the forum on Neptunalia.

"Nevertheless," she continued, "I cannot sleep alone …I am not feeling very strong right now."

He took her face in his hands, lifted it so that her eyes met his. "You are a strong woman, Gaia," he said firmly. "We are allowed moments of weakness. You loved Moira, so of course your emotions are heavy at her passing. You would not be the beautiful person I know you to be if you did not feel sorrow over her loss. But do not fret, I will humbly be your anchor until you feel strong again."

Her eyes glistened with gratitude. "I love you."

He kissed her once more, briefly on her lips. "And I love you. Now please, sleep. I will watch over you tonight."

His words relaxed her finally. She sunk down into the softness of his bedding, curling into the bundles of blankets. He aligned his body with hers, inhaling the sweet floral perfume of her skin as he sifted through her hair with his fingers. She was asleep within moments, tiny snores escaping from her mouth as her breathing steadied.

His thoughts floated back to Moira and the creature in his dreams. He decided he would leave the following evening while the house slept and return to the temple to search for clues that would reveal the creature's whereabouts. He promised himself he would not rest until he'd put an end to its existence.

Gaia stirred.

"...house of the lost gods..."

Every hair on the surface of his skin erected. He stared at her, with eyes wide and his breath in his throat, but she continued her steady, slumbering respire as if she hadn't uttered a word.

He carefully pulled his arm out from beneath her head and withdrew, freshly determined for this to end. He pulled his cloak over his shoulders, swooping down to kiss her on the cheek. With his finger, he signed over her head the same sigil his father once traced on his own chest. "Nothing shall harm her this night," he firmly petitioned the gods. He reached under his bedside table for his knife, securing it tightly to his thigh. Then without another moment's hesitation, he slipped into the torchless hallway. He passed the darkened rooms of his fellow slaves, all asleep before the fast-approaching dawn. He crept down the corridor, resolved not to wake a soul, when his ears suddenly caught the sound of shuffling. "Who is there?" he whispered harshly into the void.

There was no response.

He squinted into the shadows, as the few lone torches that still burned ineffectively availed him sight.

The hallway remained silent.

He continued his muted pace back towards the guest chambers, near where Moira's remains lay. It was the easiest way to pass unnoticed out of the villa, the only route free from the watchful eyes of the guards stationed around the villa's perimeter. Davius observed that although the priests had long departed, the aroma of precious spices still lingered in the air. A white sheet had been draped over the doorway to her room, and it now rippled in the evening breeze.

The rustling sound came once more, this time from inside the room. Davius unsheathed his knife, his nerves moistening the handle as he tightened his fist around it. He saw no sign of Eridus behind the curtain but didn't want to chance frightening a man in mourning. He approached the doorway cautiously, waiting until the wind lifted the curtain enough to reveal what it concealed.

A brief flicker exposed a bulky shadow hunched over Moira's body.

Davius tore the sheet from the doorway, startling a creature who moved effortlessly despite its great size. It turned to behold the intruder, its eyes glowing fiery red. Black clouds of smoke swirled about its form, obscuring its face completely, save for fangs that glinted menacingly in the dim candlelight.

It hissed at him. *You have come to disturb me, Great One?* It did not speak aloud, rather its voice echoed in his mind.

Davius stared, unable to respond.

It snorted. *I do not see what makes you so great. You reek of human weakness. The girl is already dead, do you intend to use that knife to protect her?* It laughed, thoroughly amused with its joke.

"Leave this place," Davius demanded, finally able to find resolve.

As you wish, O Great One. See you soon. The shapeless mass threw itself out the window, disappearing into the night, a billowing cloud of smoke trailing behind it.

Moira's body had been left undisturbed, but her expression was twisted into a tight grimace. Davius went over to her, swathing her in her fallen dressings as he gathered his wits about him.

"For you...for Gaia," he whispered to her before he lunged out of the window, landing onto the dewy grass below. He tore after the creature, his muscular limbs easily catching speed. The waxing moon cast its glow down on him as he ran, illuminating his path. The cool summer air bit his lungs, but he welcomed it, letting her winds revive him, empower him. He reached the city within moments.

The dead hour of morning had left the forum barren. It looked oddly exposed and skeletal, deprived of the hundreds of vendor carts that regularly congested its streets. A few torches were sparingly ignited, offering meager lighting to drunkards, thieves, and other night crawlers. Davius avoided them by keeping off the main road, skillfully cutting through the alleys. Although he had not been able to find the temple before, it called to him now, guiding him past Rome's magnificent edifices into the desolate part of town.

At last, the mysterious building appeared, nestled behind two derelict structures that were no longer able to maintain shape. The ascending moss of the temple had finally claimed its prize, barely a patch of stone visible from where he stood. A dim light smouldered from within, betraying any attempt at secret occupancy.

He swallowed down his last residual bit of fear, preparing himself for battle. He slipped passed the once impressive façade of Ionic pillars to the rear, his heart drumming relentlessly in his ears. Upon closer inspection, he saw several candles were lit inside, the windows barred with planks of wood and draped with heavy curtains. The arrangement was undoubtedly human, his disbelief mounting as he discovered graceful statues and furnished couches leaning against the temple's frescoed walls.

He frowned, uncertain what to do next.

"May I help you?" a voice startled him.

It was a man, hidden in the darkness.

"Forgive me," Davius stammered. "Forgive me - I did not -"

"Would you like to come in?" The figure pulled open a makeshift wooden door, gesturing him inside. "Please. Do come in."

Davius found he could do nothing else but follow.

The inside of the temple greeted him with warmth. Scented oil lamps perfumed the air as a small fire crackled inside an old fireplace. The majority of the plant growth had been scrubbed away from the inner walls, the dirt floors laid with fresh planks of pine and covered with ornate rugs. The faded images painted on the walls appeared otherworldly in the flickering firelight.

"You seem familiar with this place." The man's face was clearer now, yet carefully obscured by shadow. Davius made out pale skin against long black curls that cascaded down his back. He wore a luxuriously crafted toga which swallowed his very tall, thin frame in fabric. He gave him a warm smile, his teeth unusually bright. "I am Lucius," he offered, neglecting any other customary Roman titles.

"Davius," he managed. "I was looking for a - I am dreadfully sorry, I am nothing more than a common slave. I belong to a man named Eridus and I really must be going back now..."

"A slave?" The man who called himself Lucius sat down on one of his couches, as if he knew Davius would inevitably join him. Davius was struck by how he walked, his movements fluid and graceful, almost serpentine. "The way you look at the walls of my home, one would think you were an artist," he remarked.

Davius was taken aback by the words, nearly laughing at the absurdity of how accurate the stranger's intuition was. "I assure you, kind sir,

I am merely a slave. I really must return to my master." He moved back towards the door.

"What brings you to my humble dwelling?" Lucius asked, unwilling to accept his polite departure.

Davius blinked away the image of the inky creature huddled over Moira's body. "It was an honest mistake, truly…"

"Were you hunting?" He tilted his head towards the knife still clenched in Davius's hand.

He lost his words once more, unable to construct a passable lie.

Lucius laughed, softly. "Do not fear me, young one. I am a soothseer of sorts. I know why you have come, but I cannot help you find the beast you search for."

Davius squinted to make out his features. He distrusted this strange man, but found he was profoundly intrigued. The exotic beauty of his decor revealed that he was a traveler of foreign lands, yet his disposition was comfortably Roman, his words lacking any unusual accent. He'd heard of soothsayers from his visits to the forum; the most noted being the advisor to Caesar, whom he kept housed away from commoners at his personal dwellings. Save for him, the word usually carried a disconcerting stigma and wasn't used freely.

"I have made you uncomfortable," Lucius observed. "Please, sit down. I promise you are welcome here, regardless of your status." An elongated arm that ended with narrow fingers gestured towards a nearby couch.

Reluctant, Davius sat.

"I do apologize if I have frightened you. As you might guess, I have grown accustomed to solitude. A late-night visitor does provoke inquiry, but I am sure you were not prepared to discuss the mythological so quickly." He reached behind him, procuring a decanter and an opaque goblet. "May I offer you some wine?"

As much as Davius could have used an elixir to steady his nerves, he respectfully declined.

The strange man nodded, filling his own chalice to the brim before settling back into his seat. Davius observed the lack of slaves in his home; it seemed this man really did live entirely alone.

"So you know of this beast?" Davius asked him, carefully.

"I do," he replied, taking a generous sip of wine. "It has plagued me since my arrival."

"Do you know what it is?"

Lucius sighed. "Where do I begin?" He looked down at his cup. "From the beginning of time, man has been haunted by the unknown. He has scrambled to make sense of it, composing elaborate stories to explain the inexplicable. These things, whether the uneducated Roman believes they are punishments from the gods, or the philosopher believes them to be the fancies of the disturbed mind, creatures exist for reasons we may never know. What you saw was a *daemon*, a lower being who feasts on human energy, either from the living or from the departed souls on route to the Underworld. These beings only move by nightfall, and being a nocturnal person myself, I have witnessed this particular creature's rampant cavorting many an evening. I suffer from a plague of the skin, which prevents me from enjoying the sunlight," he explained.

"How do you know of these things?"

"I am a traveler," he replied easily. "I was born in Greece to a wealthy family who all died when I was quite young. Since I was a child, I yearned to sail across every sea, to investigate every unknown land. I have spent most of my life in active exploration. My greatest passion is the quest for knowledge, the only true power in this life. You may conquer the world like Caesar, but you will never hold the truest command. Look at how many advisors he surrounds himself with. Only the man who unlocks the mysteries of the mind can truly master the world." He paused, as if preventing himself from rambling.

"To answer your question directly, I learned of *daemons* during these travels. Each civilization, from the Egyptians to the Chinese, calls them something different, yet the creatures are all the same. Some cultures argue their authenticity, but I can attest that they are very real. I suppose I do not have to convince you of this, however."

Davius was quiet for a moment, pondering his words. "Do they speak?" he asked.

Lucius looked thoughtful. "I suppose if they could, they would."

"Do they...cause visions?"

"That, my friend, is another conversation all on its own." The man's concealed eyes seemed to scintillate behind their shadowy veil.

Davius tore his eyes away from his gaze, settling his attention on the paintings that surrounded them. He now understood what the strange, illustrated creatures depicted in fresco paint were. He briefly wondered who the original artist was, and what it would be like to bring the once so vivid images back to their former glory.

"Would you paint them for me?" Lucius asked, as if he had read his thoughts.

"Sorry?" Davius blinked, openly caught by surprise.

"Paint, my dear boy, paint." Laughter twinkled in his voice. "I have renovated my home in all other aspects. I briefly considered chipping off what is left of these frescoes, but I could not bring myself to do it. I recently discovered that the artist was a mad priest who inhabited this place, feverishly painting his religious hallucinations until he descended into a lunacy he could not come back from. How could I possibly scrape them away after learning such things? I would be forever indebted to you for your help. You have the delicate hands of an artist. Besides, my intuition never fails me...and it screams that you are a gifted painter."

Davius ached to accept his offer, but life at the villa surfaced in his mind. "I am but a slave, sir. If you wish to purchase my services, you will have to speak to my master," he said, sullenly.

"In Roman custom, yes. Fortunately, you and I are not true Romans. Besides, does your master give you this?" Lucius tossed him a satchel, which Davius scrambled to catch. He opened it to reveal dozens of gold coins that sparkled in the candlelight.

Davius thought of Gaia, and his dreams of what their life could be. Money like this could be used to purchase their freedom and secure their place as citizens of the countryside.

"One last thing before you make your decision," Lucius's voice interrupted his musings. "I would not be able to forgive myself if I did not impart one last piece of information. Daemons prefer to prey on slaves, since they have learned of their worthlessness in Roman society. Their absence rarely causes distress, their deaths seldom examined. This allows them to feed undisturbed. I am sure you have noticed the unusual disappearances of some in your employ. It would be a wise choice for you to earn your way to freedom, along with whomever you may be close with."

Davius was silent.

"You can come at nightfall as your master slumbers," he pressed. "He will not notice anything amiss. I will pay you a piece of gold for every night you can sneak out to visit me." He stood before him, removing the bag of coins from Davius's hands and exchanging it with a single gold piece, which he pressed into his palm. The metal was warm and wonderfully alluring.

"Shall we begin tonight?"

Exhaustion had taken its toll on Davius.

Since Moira's death, Gaia's demeanor had shifted from warm and lively to dejected and melancholy. It was unbearable for him to see her suffer, his efforts to lift her from depression were in vain. It was as if the entire villa had succumbed to despondency, the usual cheerful chatter that accompanied their daily labor absent for weeks. Eridus no longer paced, instead wandering aimlessly about his home, unkempt in a depressive stupor, bottle of wine at hand. Rumors circulated that Eridus loved the girl more than was blatant, and it was a lover's heart that was shattered by her passing.

It took all for Davius to muster the will to continue his work in the stables, as he eagerly awaited sunset. He kept vigil over Gaia each evening, whose initial stay in his bed had evolved into a nightly occurrence. He comforted her the best he could before she fell asleep, leaving her each night with a kiss before slipping off into the darkness. He came to cherish his evenings with Lucius, his tribulations falling away as he listened to the man's endless chatter, his brush alive with each deliberate stroke. Lucius had purchased for him the finest oil paints in Rome, horsehair brushes, and rare charcoal pencils. Davius was mystified by how easily they applied to the concrete walls, entranced by the rich pigments as he tenderly caressed the faded artwork back to life.

Lucius's stories added to his pleasant dissociative state, regaling him with tales of his adventures overseas. He was a masterful storyteller, describing in vivid detail places beyond the conquest of Caesar, where people of odd shapes and colors, with equally strange customs, dwelled. His riches had enabled him to hire the most skilled shipbuilder in all of Greece, who availed him a vessel more impressive than the Roman fleet. It was luck that prevented any shipwreck, only one great storm had threatened to end his voyages. Davius remained skeptical of the accuracy of his tales, but enjoyed them all the same, accepting the budding friendship with this strange man who kept to the shadows, goblet in hand.

Days passed without the opportunity to sleep, and he often succumbed to dozing in secret in the warm, clean straw of the stables. These brief rests remained sound and unburdened by nightmares, until one evening when they unexpectedly returned.

He had accidentally fallen asleep next to Gaia, whose warmth seduced him into lucid sedation. He planned to visit Lucius that evening, as usual, but the melodic rhythm of her breathing had craftily lulled him into an unintentional slumber.

He was immediately submerged once more into the ocean of blood, landing on a flat surface as flashes of misshapen *daemons* hailed him from below. He realized he stood on a great precipice in Tartarus, the realm beneath the Underworld where evil doers were banished. Their tortured wails echoed all around him, the heat of the realm's fiery Phlegethon River scalding the air. The creatures looked up at him with grotesquely distorted faces, their leathery skin torn by protruding skeletal wings, small versions of the original beast from his dreams. Their voices permeated his mind like burrowing worms in his skull, *Great David! You are home!* They took turns bowing to him, their bones loudly popping and creaking with exertion. Their clawed hands and feet slipped on the blood-soaked floor beneath them. One approached from behind the crowd, dragging a heavy mass behind it.

An offering! it chirped, fixing its bulging eyes on him excitedly before tossing its cache at his feet.

Davius recoiled but forced himself to look, observing the body of a woman, whose identity he already knew.

Drink! Drink! the creatures sang, happily, and to his horror, he was struck with the overwhelming desire to follow their commands. He reached down to scoop up his subdued, but still alive lover into his arms, brushing back a fallen lock of her rose tinted hair.

She looked up at him, sleepily. *Where is Davius?*

I am Davius, he replied helplessly, overcome with the maddening desire to puncture the lovely, throbbing vein housed within her neck, releasing the sticky warmth that flowed inside. He could barely focus on her face, her flesh beckoning to him, begging him to taste her. The *daemons'* laughter surrounded him, and he closed his eyes in submission, bending forward and plunging his teeth deep into her, releasing into his body the sweet throb of ecstasy...

"Blood dreams."

Lucius pondered the words, absently fingering the rim of his cup. His long frame was stretched out across a dining couch, the remnants of his barely touched supper summoning the occasional fly. Davius had yet to see the man eat, but he always made sure to have his table set in anticipation of Davius's nightly arrival. He spared little expense, heaping servings of roasted parrot and pickled jellyfish regularly accompanying the customary bread, olives, and cheese he never neglected to provide.

Davius sat adjacent to him, unable to sample anything from the feast set out before him. He found he was unable to paint as well, his pallet of fresh pigment gradually hardening from lack of use.

"It is the only way I know how to describe them," he admitted. "I feel as if I am going mad."

"Every man is mad, it is only a matter to what degree," Lucius declared.

"Then what could they mean?" Davius pressed, a note of despair hanging from his voice.

Lucius rose from the table, his unusually long black robes rustling behind him. He peered through a crack in his boarded window, a habit that had become customary when he was deep in thought. "I believe I will need some time to consider this," he finally decided. "Please. Will yourself to paint. You inspire my mind when you do so."

Disappointed, Davius nodded, moving towards his pallet listlessly. Yet it wasn't too long before he found his flow, grateful for his friend's gentle nudge. His latest focus was a pair of lovers, swirls of peach and golden yellow creating their intertwined bodies. Without realizing it, Davius had given the man sand colored hair, the woman, a lovely reddish gold, the forest and sage greens of their irises radiating from the white of their eyes. He had painted himself and Gaia, captured forever in a lovers' embrace.

"Marvelous," Lucius breathed from behind him.

Davius paused, studying his work.

"The man is you," Lucius noted. "Is the lover real or a fantasy woman?"

Davius sighed. "Oh, she is very real. She is a slave, like me."

"She is exquisite. Now I understand your desire for wages," he said from behind a knowing smile.

Davius nodded. "I wish to earn enough to buy our freedom. It is my dream that one day we will be married, escaping to the countryside to raise our children. It will not be the same as our homeland, but I long to live in the woods once more."

"I see."

"She...she is in the blood dreams."

Lucius was silent for a moment. "Do you know of Stoicism, Davius?"

Davius turned towards him, noticing for the first time that his eyes shone a magnificent ochre, like gold coins glinting in the sunlight. He nodded. "Yes, it is a branch of philosophy. I used to spend my free time in the forum, listening to the trending theories and latest arguments of its philosophers. Stoicism was a favorite topic among the old sages."

"I am impressed," Lucius remarked. "To the Stoic, nothing passes unexplained. The death of a loved one, the eruption of a volcano, the thunderstorm crashing through the sky. They believe that everything has a purpose and a reason in Nature, for Nature itself is god manifested into a material form. Therefore, everything that happens in Nature is the will of the Divine.

"The Greek and Roman gods also reveal themselves through nature. A great crash of thunder is Jupiter's rage. An overturned ship is the curse of Neptune. A Stoic, however, would say that the reason it thundered was not simply because Jupiter is throwing a tantrum, but because it is a sign that something else significant will occur. Do you understand me so far?"

Davius nodded. It was not the first time Lucius had embarked on a long tirade of philosophical musings, nor the first time he'd shared his learnings of world religions. He relaxed, gliding his paintbrush seamlessly along the wall.

"Stoics also believe that there is a driving force within them, the soul," Lucius continued. "Divinity is to Nature as the soul is to man. They believe that the human's soul is preordained by destiny and controls a human's decisions, further illustrating their theory that nothing passes unexplained. This soul is said to come from an even greater soul, a sort of collective consciousness, if you will. Although every human is different in appearance and personality, every soul still holds ties to its original form."

Davius paused, a shiver running along his skin.

Lucius set his goblet down. "I think we should resume our conversation tomorrow. There is too much to discuss regarding this matter and morning approaches. Come at nightfall as usual, but tonight, be dressed in your best tunic. We should sit down together for a formal meal, no painting. I will pay you regardless. Do we have an accord?"

"Absolutely," Davius replied, curious to know what more would be revealed.

"Good," Lucius nodded, slipping his lithe form back into the folds of shadow, gesturing towards Davius's unfinished work. "Now, back to the Lovers."

Davius languidly shuffled home, watching as the stars and moon that had shone so brightly in the evening sky submitted to the now rising sun. Sapphire and turquoise splashed across the sky, interrupted by a faint rising pink, clouds pirouetting in their gentle dance of dawn. Although his body ached with exhaustion, he considered capturing the glory of the morning sky in paint. He envisioned mixing the perfect blend of vermillion and yellow ochre to create the orange, white and red lead for pink. He continued to muse as he walked, trying to ignore the throbbing ache of his limbs, when he heard a branch snap from the woods that flanked the path.

He tensed, squinting into the darkness. It was the curious hour where both day and nocturnal creatures slept, and the forest was eerily still. He saw nothing in its dense shadows that revealed the source of the sound, nevertheless, he quickened his pace. It was after a louder rustle interrupted his walk once more that he turned to see what stalked him, jumping back in alarm at what stood before him.

It was an enormous boar, doubling him in size, with two elongated husks protruding from a quivering snout that dripped with saliva. Davius snatched the knife from his thigh, carefully maneuvering backwards as he braced himself for the attack.

Yet the boar did not charge, its beady eyes gleaming through tufts of copper fur that seemed metallic in the moonlight, one eye interrupted by an angry scar that rendered it milky white. Davius realized the creature was not of this earth, but from beyond the physical realm. "Are you another *daemon*?" he whispered.

I am unlike that which you have seen before, the creature replied. *I come to you as an ally, to warn you of what is to come.*

Davius frowned. "Then what are you?"

There are so many questions, but time prevents me from answering them all. I come to you in disguise, one I cannot maintain for too long. I am being hunted as we speak. The boar paced around him, its one good eye piercing into his. Its muscular legs flexed slowly as it moved, causing ripples of brown and ecru fur. *You must cease your visits with he who calls himself Lucius. Your visions are not dreams; they foretell of what may become.*

"I am not a monster," Davius snapped, surprised at the ease by which his ferocity came.

But you will be. He wishes to corrupt you, to use you for his own purpose. He is not what he says he is, and he cannot be allowed to continue his plans. He is powerful in this realm, yet he has no power over you. You must stay far away from him or your fate will be compromised.

"What are you?" Davius demanded once more. "How do you know Lucius? You must be a *daemon*."

I am quite the opposite, coming to you in a form that will fool both him and his minions. There is much more to this world than you know, Davius. There is a Great War that wages as we speak. Not all can be revealed to you at this time, but you must heed my request. See the beast who calls himself Lucius no more.

As if startled by something unseen, the boar retreated.

"What war do you speak of?" Davius cried. "My dreams - what do they mean? Where are you going?" He panicked as the boar retreated back into the forest. "Come back here! What am I supposed to do?"

But it disappeared, the night silent once more.

Davius slumped down to his knees from where he stood, scooping breath back into his lungs. He was dizzy from the encounter, his palm raw from clutching his weapon. He sheathed it, attempting to gather his thoughts. The sun had started to rise, reminding him to return home.

Bracing himself, he found his legs.

"It was another dream, perhaps," he murmured to himself. "You have not slept, your brain is not at its best." It seemed to be the only logical explanation. He had not slept well in weeks, he must be suffering hallucinations.

Convinced, he pushed his tired body towards the villa. He crawled through the open window of his room, which had not yet seen the sunrise. The cool darkness welcomed him as he slipped into his bed, eager to rest. Gaia's warm body welcomed him as he snuggled her close, draping an arm around the bend of her waist. She rolled over to face him, a sliver of faint sunlight revealing swollen, reddened eyes. He realized she'd been crying.

"What is wrong?" he asked, alarmed.

"I was dreaming of Moira," she replied.

"Forgive me, my love. I could not sleep so I crept onto the rooftop. I did not want to disturb you." He felt a pang of guilt tear at his stomach as the lie spilled from his lips.

She accepted his excuse, wiping at her moistened face. "I am glad you are back," she said, trying to give him a smile.

Davius gathered her into his arms, placing a kiss on her warm shoulder. "It pains me to see you suffer so."

"Davius, do you remember what you said to me the night I joined you on the roof?" she asked. "That you wanted to marry me, to take care of me until the end of our days?"

He pulled her away from his chest so that he faced her. "Yes."

"I want you to marry me. You must get me out of this place. I cannot bear it any longer. I want to be free - I want to be married and bear our children. I cannot remain a prisoner in this miserable home any longer. I want it to be you and I, for eternity."

Davius gazed at her, her words pulling such emotion from him that a tear drifted slowly down his cheek. He kissed her softly on her forehead. "It will be, Gaia. I promise."

The smile that lit up her face was genuine, and she lay back, pulling him towards her to cradle his head against her chest. Her fingers trailed through his hair as he listened to her heart pumping a soothing rhythm against his cheek. He suddenly noticed one of her breasts had fallen free from her tunic, and on impulse, he lifted his head, sliding his tongue up its curve. She stirred, but did not stop him, and his lips continued to caress the flesh that was now freely exposed. "Davius…" she hesitated, her face fearful but flushed with desire. He grasped it in his hands, allowing his eyes to pour into hers. "I have loved you from the minute I laid eyes upon you," he whispered in their old Gaulish tongue.

Another tear trickled down her cheek, but it was not of sadness. She echoed the language, her lips gliding gently with the whisper, "And I have always loved you."

He said nothing more, for his mouth found hers. He could no longer control his hands, undressing her so that his fingers could roam her bare skin, his lips and tongue trailing over every curve and crevice he could find. She groaned with pleasure, her body twisting underneath him as he tore off his own clothing, their naked bodies soon moving together in perfect unison. The wind sighed all around them, the sounds of awakening birds sweetly singing their praises. It felt as if the world had paused and it was only them, trapped in each other's sweaty embrace. Afterwards, she ran her fingers up and down his back, sending shivers along his skin as they lay in wordless relief, the sound of their breathing keeping rhythm with the songs of dawn.

"Davius," she finally whispered, her fingers in his hair.

"Gaia," he answered.

"I do love you."

He smiled, lifting himself up to kiss her one last time before the heavy press of fatigue demanded compliance. He fell back, pulling her close to him. She nestled her nose into the crook of his neck as they both obeyed slumber's demands. All thoughts of mythical beasts and nightmares drifted away from him, his mind finally at peace.

CHAPTER THREE

🙚 THE MONSTER 🙚

HE'D BARELY SLEPT MORE THAN A FEW HOURS, nevertheless, he greeted the morning refreshed and renewed, the taste of Gaia still lingering on his lips. The summer heat had mercifully cooled, the vineyard shady and pleasant as he strolled through it. Streaks of shadows crossed over him as he passed through hundreds of meandering vines curling around their wooden posts. He avoided the barrels of harvested grapes that cluttered the walkway, searching the aisles for Eridus.

"Good Morning, Lavida. Have you seen Master Eridus?" he asked a woman who had paused to wipe the sweat from her brow.

"I believe he is preparing to go to the races today," she replied, wiping her hands on her stained apron. "I last saw him in the press room."

Davius nodded his thanks and headed back towards the villa. The press room was a large cylinder structure standing just beyond the vineyards, closest to the slaves' quarters. It reeked of fermentation, housing a gigantic iron vat at its center, surrounded by dozens of small wooden barrels that drained into reservoirs underneath the floors. The vat was able to fit a dozen pressers at a time, the fruit easily smashed to pulp before it was collected in the lower barrels for a second press. These could only fit one man, who both pressed and sifted until only the extract of the grape remained. These barrels overflowed constantly at harvest, slaves scrambling between the press floor and the cellars below where the juice was collected for fermentation.

He pushed open the door, choking even though he'd anticipated the wickedly pungent aroma. Eridus stood amongst a cluster of slaves, gesturing emphatically with his instructions. Standing next to him was none other than Gaia. His face flushed immediately upon sight of her. She turned, brightening as she noticed him.

Before he could greet her, Eridus also took note of his arrival, a grin stretching across his fleshy face. Davius tried not to expose his surprise at the man's disposition, for it was the happiest he'd seen him in months.

"My boy!" he greeted him with a hearty slap on his back. "I am going to the Circus Maximus today and you will be joining me."

Davius could no longer hold in his surprise. "Me?"

"Yes! Great things have come to pass. Gaia will fill you in with the details. I'll need you to suitably dress. We will head towards the city within the hour." He turned, resuming his conversation.

Gaia shyly inched closer to Davius, a coquettish smirk dancing on her lips. "Hello, Davius."

"Hello, Gaia," he grinned. "What has him in such a mood?"

The two headed back to their villa. "Caesar has returned from his conquests and wishes to throw a celebration," she explained, hesitantly.

Davius stiffened at the man's name. He had long discovered it was Julius Caesar who waged the Gallic War campaign responsible for the destruction of his home. It was something he'd accepted - men wage war and conquer other men. But it was not something he'd ever forget.

"He has requested barrels of Eridus's wine for the feast," Gaia continued when he did not interject. "In a great coincidence, Tiberus Gallaenus, the athlete, is interested in purchasing one of Eridus's horses. They will be discussing the terms today at the race."

"Well, it is about time he has had some good news," Davius remarked. "I have not seen him so spirited since before she passed."

Gaia agreed. "He knows I grow bored at sporting events, but he still desires a companion. Lucky you," she jested, playfully.

Davius waited until they were safely behind the walls of the slaves' quarters before he grabbed her, kissing her deeply. Her body caved into his without resistance. "Will you come to me again tonight?" he whispered when he was finally able to wrench himself free.

"You know it will be dangerous now that Eridus is out of mourning," she reminded him breathlessly, her cheeks flushed. "Though I wish for nothing more."

"Well, then I will just have to make sure our dear master is thoroughly drunk tonight," Davius decided, grinning.

Gaia laughed. "Lucky for you, that will not be too hard a feat to accomplish."

The back door suddenly burst open, revealing the bulky shape of Eridus behind it. They decoupled just in time.

"So Gaia has informed you of our plans?" Eridus asked. He didn't wait for a response. "Come, you will need fresh sandals and a tunic that actually fits." He put an arm around his shoulders, leading him away.

Gaia waved delicate fingers at him before turning back to the main residence.

In a whirlwind, he was dressed and prepared for the expedition. They mounted two of Eridus's best horses, a pair of majestic Arabians Davius had grown fond of over the years. Behind them trotted a collection of Eridus's personal guards, only a few of whom Davius knew by name. An excited apprehension gripped him as the city edged closer into view, the steady hum of faraway voices elevating in volume as they approached.

Rome was overwhelmingly crowded for the afternoon hour, the revered event causing many to brave the scorching temperatures of the midday sun. Citizens were dressed sparingly, carrying water in *utres* strapped to their waists. Eridus led them through the throng of bodies and slave drawn litters, several patricians nodding to him respectfully while the plebeians merely stared. The winemaker had wasted no effort in his appearance, the copious number of jewels adorning his attire dripping pomposity. For a moment, Davius considered what it would be like to be wealthy and respected, his thoughts drifting to the purse of gold coins that was nestled under his sleeping cot. He doubted the reality of such a prospect, but soon enough, at least he would be free.

Their entourage reached the grandiose Circus Maximus, which swarmed with spectators like ants on the hive. They clustered the entrance and lined the front booths, where citizens placed bets on the chariot they were sure would win. Children ran about in hats made from cheap bronze, fashioned to imitate the elaborate headdresses worn by the charioteers. They laughed as they chased after each other, darting around the legs of their conversing parents. Eridus led them to the stables where a man helped them dismount before taking their reins. Eridus exchanged a few words with him, placing a hefty coin purse in his hand. The man nodded gratefully and called for their horses to be well cared for.

Eridus leaned in towards Davius. "He best honor his word. It would be an insult to both me and their caretaker."

Davius beamed in spite of himself as Eridus gestured him inside the arena.

The Circus was shaped like a giant horseshoe, the best seats in the arena closest to the end of each *spina*, or row, where each of the four chariots grabbed their markers before doubling back towards the starting line. Eridus wove through the crowd towards them, assured their seats were reserved.

"Eridus!" a man called as they found their places.

"Marcus! How good to see you!" The men embraced. "Davius, this is Marcus Barraceus Similus. He is part of the Senate, and a dear friend of mine."

Davius bowed his head respectfully.

"This is Davius, one of my best and most trusted slaves," Eridus explained to his friend.

The man was short, with brown eyes and hair frosted by gray. He was neatly groomed, his hair tightly clipped to his head and a clean pressed toga decorated in the colors of his charioteer. "Good to meet you. Where is Gaia on this fine day?"

"Oh, she detests these sorts of things. She is currently playing steward to the winery in my absence. Have you heard the news?" He turned away from Davius, as the two men engaged in private conversation.

Davius sat down on the stone benches, taking in his surroundings. He watched the event hosts below rush back and forth, barking orders as they paused only to wipe the sweat from their frantic faces. A few slaves swept away any rogue sand out of the spinas, which were each lavishly ornamented with sculptures, water basins, and fountains, all decorated in the color of their team. Their flags rippled in the arid wind, like a sea made of red, white, blue, and green.

He suddenly thought of Gaia, smiling at the memory of their encounter. He imagined convincing her to join him at the races, sitting together on one of the upper benches as they wrangled their brood of strawberry blonde children, all waving their flags in excitement.

A bellowing voice pulled him from his daydream. His eyes scanned the crowd until he found the owner, a man seated several rows back with wiry hair and a large, crooked nose that did little to distract from his prognathous jaw. He was shouting at the woman seated next to him, whose fine dress did little to mask her malnourishment and exhaustion. Her mournful eyes were cast downwards as she nodded, rising weakly to her feet before heading towards the refreshment tent. A giggling young girl with a mess of curly brown hair was seated at his other side, oblivious to the plight of the slave girl. The man turned his attention towards her to share in the laughter, his open admiration revealing the girl was his child. Although the scene before him projected a tender moment between father and daughter, the icy edge to their snickering sent a chill along his skin.

"That is Nirus Octarius," Eridus informed him, appearing from behind. He seated himself next to Davius, handing him the metal cup of chilled wine he had been served as he spoke to his friend. Davius sipped it, gratefully. "He was once an integral part of Caesar's army, one of the greatest but bloodiest war heroes of all time. Caesar kept him nearby during every battle."

Once more, Davius felt ill at the mention of Caesar's name. He understood the nature of conquest and was aware of the tendency for betrayal between Celtic clans, especially for those hungry for political advancement, but he would never be comfortable with Caesar's growing power. Yet he made sure his face showed no change in emotion. "He seems upset," he commented neutrally, referring to the war general.

Eridus nodded with an air of indifference. "He only bore one child through a slave woman, a daughter, who he kept and spoiled. He banished the mistress when he realized she would bear him no sons. He tries with a new mistress every so often but has never again bore a child. It is rumored that he abuses his slave girls, but I am no gossip," he sniffed. "I have sold him wayward slaves of mine in the past and he does not harm them. He is simply strict where I am not."

Davius tried not to appear troubled by his words, reminded of the reality of his position. Eridus might have been kinder than most, but he was still a slave owner, Davius just a slave. He had power over them, regardless of their peaceable interactions.

"Ah, the games are about to begin."

Davius shifted his attention back towards the arena as the chariots were released into their starting boxes. The crowd roared with excitement, waving their colored flags wildly against the pale blue sky. The charioteers took off, steering their horses with careful precision, lest they tip over to their deaths. Davius fed off the energy of the spectators, finding himself cheering for the sportsman he had no real preference for prior. He was drawn towards the red team, watching as they spun like tornados of gold, gaining speed. After a few close calls, they flew past the finish line, nearly colliding into the crowd as they pummeled back into its starting box. The Circus erupted in a swarm of crimson.

The crowd settled as the intermission began. Davius noticed Julius Caesar sitting several rows below him, surrounded by members of the Senate. Eridus did as well. "If you will excuse me, boy, I am going to take this opportunity to talk with some members of the Senate. Caesar himself has requested several barrels of our wine - and doing business with him means I can easily work my way up to a seat in the Senate. Between that and my marriage to Gaia, I cannot believe what good fortune is descending upon our household."

Davius felt the blood drain from his face. "Your marriage to whom?"

Eridus blinked, then laughed, clapping him on the back. "How could I have forgotten? I suppose in the excitement I forgot - but on this very evening, upon the moment of our return, I will be asking for Gaia's hand in marriage. She has been a loyal slave of mine for many years and she can run the household like no other. I trust her completely, and it is high time I increase her status in Roman society."

Davius couldn't speak, the clamor around him starting to spin at a nauseating tempo. Sweat beaded his forehead as he fought the urge to faint.

"Are you well, boy?" Eridus squinted at him, perplexed. "The sun is quite harsh today, I would imagine even more so for those with non-Roman pallor. Perhaps you should visit the refreshment tent while I speak with the Senators?"

"Yes, sir, thank you, sir..." Davius managed, fighting his way out of the spectators' seats as black spots threatened his vision.

He barely made it to the refreshment area before he retched, drawing several disgusted glances but thankfully no further attention. He spat, his chest struggling for enough breath to calm his growing hysteria.

His Gaia, his wife. What was he going to do?

The brisk evening air proved inadequate to comfort him as he maneu-vered through the darkened streets of Rome. He was grateful to be released from Eridus's company, the slave owner sending him home with one of his guards, assuming he suffered from heat stroke.

He hadn't looked for Gaia, quietly gathering his things before escaping out his bedroom window and heading towards Lucius's home. His stomach was still sick with sorrow, his mind a whirlwind of frantic thoughts. He knew the meager earnings amassed from Lucius would not be enough to purchase their freedom, but he couldn't bear the thought of Gaia dressed in bridal robes, her bare feet crushing the customary rose petals as she walked down the temple aisle to meet Eridus at the altar. Although he knew the man couldn't consummate the marriage traditionally, nausea churned in his stomach when he envisioned Eridus's meaty hands caressing her skin, his alcohol ripened mouth grazing lips that had been forcibly pledged to him.

He tried to rid himself of the loathsome images, sullenly entering Lucius's home. His friend didn't notice his temperament, greeting him with a joyous grin. "Davius, welcome! Your feast awaits." He was wrapped in dark, ornate robes, trimmed with delicate patterns of gold that matched his eyes. The tiny flickers of candlelight revealed they were an aubergine shade so deep they appeared black. His equally dark hair blanketed his shoulders in thick curls, his aurous eyes gleaming with anticipation.

So apparent was his friend's excitement, that Davius couldn't bear to let him see him downcast. He willed it away, forcing a gracious smile. "Hello, Lucius."

"Come, come." Lucius's cold hands took his, pulling him towards his dining room. Davius was struck once more by the fluidity of his movement, as if he drifted across the ground instead of walked, a strange attribute for a man so tall. Oddly, it was in that moment that he recalled the monstrous boar he met the night before. His moments with Gaia, the Circus, and now Eridus's revelation had distracted him so much that it felt as if an eternity passed since the strange appearition. A wave of panic coursed through him as he realized that if what the boar told him about Lucius proved true, he would soon be left with no one.

He stopped mid-stride. "Lucius, I must share something with you. Another *daemon* came to me … not long after I left your dwelling at daybreak."

Lucius waved his hand in dismissal. "Let us not speak of such things now, there will be plenty of time for conversation later. The presentation of the meal is half the pleasure - you must allow me this moment." He commenced pulling Davius to the dining chambers, the doorway of which was concealed by a decorative curtain. He grinned before lifting it with dramatic flourish.

Davius gasped despite himself. Piles of food were stacked upon the table, garnished with exotic flowers and brightly colored fruit. Varieties of meat surrounded baskets stuffed with bread, ranging from stuffed bird to seasoned fish to cooked snails. Platters of fruits and vegetables towered amidst carafes of herb-infused oils and curious sauces, while rich cheeses and black olives complimented every dish. An enormous decanter of wine sat beside the place setting he assumed was his. The hunger he had been ignoring throughout the day resurfaced with a low growl in his stomach. He turned to Lucius, his mood brightened. "You have outdone yourself," he complimented him.

Lucius grinned. "Tonight is a celebration! Please sit and feast!"

Davius eagerly complied, seating himself along the couch that Lucius gestured him towards. From the shadows, a woman appeared. He startled briefly, for he had never seen a slave before at Lucius's home.

"I hired her for tonight," Lucius explained, noticing his expression. "I am paying her as I do you. Slave labor has never appealed to me."

Davius nodded, allowing the frail woman to fill his plate. His eyes lingered on her for a moment, noticing her meager appearance and the unusual scarf draped about her neck before he set about devouring the food before him. He savored the unusual flavors, forgetting for a moment the painful circumstances that currently surrounded him.

Lucius watched him, quite pleased. "At this rate, you will not be able to have the conversation you insisted upon having!"

Davius gave him a close-lipped smile, his mouth brimming with food.

He watched Lucius tap his cup, which the girl immediately filled with a separate carafe that she fetched from afar. Her face was impassive, her movements slow and methodical. Lucius graciously thanked her, taking a full swallow from his refreshed goblet. His plate remained barren and untouched.

Davius reached to pour himself a cup from the bottle stationed nearby, when Lucius halted him. "Please, try some of mine tonight, Davius, for the sake of occasion." He motioned once more to the slave girl.

Davius accepted the offer with a nod. As the girl approached, it suddenly struck him how vaguely familiar she appeared. Perhaps he had seen her at the marketplace, he surmised, watching as she filled his cup and set it down before him. Her skin was grey, several faint bruises clustering at her wrists and dotting her chest. His thoughts drifted to Gaia, thinking about the sort of life she had narrowly escaped before Eridus's rescue. Although it pained him to consider it, her life with him was infinitely better than what could have been. He lifted the rim of the cup to his lips, eager to drown out his harrowing contemplations. The wine was thick, its aroma rich and robust. He drank, pleasantly surprised by the decadent gustatory sensation.

He looked up to see Lucius studying him joyously. "Do you approve?" he asked.

Davius agreed emphatically, taking another generous swallow. "How could I not? No wonder you are never without a full glass."

Lucius roared with laughter. "I do enjoy your company so."

"As do I," he said. "It may become short lived, however," he added dismally.

"Whatever do you mean?" Lucius retorted. "Your work here is nowhere near finished."

Davius cast his eyes downward. "My life has taken an unexpected turn. Do you remember the woman that I spoke of last? My master has decided to marry her. He told me this morning. If he succeeds, I will not be able to remain there. I cannot bear the thought, let alone be able to witness their union."

Lucius was appalled. "Well, then we will not allow it to happen!"

"What can I do? As grateful as I am for the payment you provide me, I cannot afford to purchase both our freedoms."

Lucius grew quiet with contemplation. "Then I shall pay you in advance," he decided. "I will give you the entire amount tonight, which you can take to your master in the morning. Then you both can stay with me, under my protection, until your task is complete. Then you can be off to marry your love and retreat in bliss to wherever you wish!" He leaned back on his couch, pleased with himself.

Davius was at a loss for words. "You would do that for me?" he whispered.

"Of course I will. I need my artist to be happy, do I not? I could not bear it if you left without finishing these walls. Besides," he added softly. "I have not had a friend in very many years."

Emotion washed over Davius. "Thank you, Lucius. Truly, thank you."

"A toast!" Lucius declared, summoning the girl once more. "Refill his glass. Now there truly is a reason to celebrate!"

The girl lumbered over to him, carafe in hand. She leaned forward, the scarf slipping slightly away from its coil around her neck. His eyes caught a brutal gash that had split open her skin, the wound still gaping and horribly putrid. He jumped, knocking over his cup, the contents sloshing out onto the table. The thick liquid moved like honey, coating his plate with rusty scarlet. Realization dawned on him.

Horrified, he looked up to see Lucius, whose golden eyes burned with excitement.

"What was in my cup?" he demanded.

"You enjoyed my concoction."

"Lucius, what was in my cup?"

He sighed, shrugging his narrow shoulders in defeat. "It was blood."

Davius spat, furiously. Waves of nausea threatened his resolve. "What is the meaning of this? How could you do such a thing? Is this some cruel jest after I intimated to you the nature of my dreams?"

Lucius rose from his couch, approaching him carefully. "It is no jest, my friend. Please, sit down. I will explain everything."

Davius felt ill. His world tilted and spun as he struggled to maintain his composure. His arms flailed in an attempt to keep balance, sending dishes of food flying across the room. He caught sight of the girl, who had remained motionless throughout the entire endeavor, finally recognizing her identity. Moira's reanimated corpse was staring blankly ahead of him.

His blood visions assaulted him for the first time fully awake, the pace at which they came overwhelming his senses. He cried out, falling to his knees as he gripped his head as if to shield it from their merciless onslaught. He heard Lucius shouting at him to breathe, but they were coming too fast, violent, gruesome images that now felt like memories from a time long passed. He heard the shrill cries of ravens and visions of his father in midslaughter, praising gods who had no names. He clawed at his eyes, trying to force them away as he crashed helplessly to the floor, his world fading to black.

He awoke, screaming.

The dank, earthy smell of decay reached his nose before his eyes adjusted to the darkness. He bolted upright from where he lay, learning that it was upon a slab of concrete caked with layers of dust. He looked around him, observing walls constructed of moldy, crumbling limestone, tangles of spiderwebs obscuring every visible corner. Human bones scattered the dirt floor, rats startling them briefly before scurrying back into hiding. He realized he was in a crypt that hadn't been used in many years.

His eyesight adjusted, revealing two slender candles burning before him, Lucius seated upright on a sarcophagus between them. He was watching him patiently, his signature goblet resting between his folded legs. "Good morning, my friend," he said softly.

Davius wiped the crust from his eyes. "What have you done to me?"

"You fainted from shock. I brought you down here so we could talk in peace."

"What is this place? The Romans do not bury their dead."

"We are underneath my home. A great temple had once been erected next to the mad priest's residence, with catacombs dug beneath both. He was a foreigner, bringing his customs with him. I come down here often, to relax and reflect." He looked around, affectionately. "When the priest first began his downward spiral into insanity, he made this place his chambers. The bones you see are undoubtedly his, though I gather he is accompanied by more than a few unsuspecting victims."

Davius shuddered. "What is it that you want from me?"

Lucius rose, waving his hand so the torches that lined the walls suddenly burst into flame, illuminating the sepulchral chamber. Lucius delighted at Davius's open surprise. "Just a trick," he smiled. "Unfortunately, I am bound to many of the same laws that you are in this realm." He came closer, gliding across the dusty floor.

For the first time, Davius was able to view him in vivid detail. His face glowed an iridescent white, his eyes sparkling amber and gold, swirling together like pools of ink. His hair fell in rivers of shining black, edging his handsomely sculpted face. His smile revealed straight polished teeth, save for two perfectly sharpened canines that reminded him of a wolf's terrible grimace. Although David was tall in his own right, he appeared to tower over him.

He tried to move, but Lucius held up his hand to stop him. "Please sit. I want to answer all of your questions."

Davius acquiesced, his curiosity stronger than his repulsion.

Lucius paced around the undercroft, as he often did when he spoke, taking careful sips of his drink. Davius nauseated with the newfound knowledge of its contents. "I am one of the oldest deities in the world, before the concept of deities, actually," Lucius began. "I was an idea, the shadow that light creates, that evolved as humanity flourished, as their simplistic brains progressed into minds that could create and conspire. They gave me form with their words, the ultimate explanation for all of their woes. Eventually, humans would build civilizations, and their simple stories would expound into grandiose tales with intricate pantheons of gods and goddesses. The names changed, but I had already become, evolving along with them."

"You are evil," Davius whispered.

Lucius laughed, pleasantly. "Good and evil are human concepts. I am far older than that. I am simply the darkness. All other qualities have been attributed to me over time by man. I accept them all, however, regardless of their accuracy."

"Then you are a god."

"You could call me that if it makes it easier for you to understand. I once loved humans, their abhorrence of me giving me purpose, an intoxicating feeling of empowerment. I have taken on so many different names and faces, through each civilization, each tribe. I have been called Aži Dahāka, Hades, Leviathan, Set. I have even been associated with your Morrigan, who I happen to adore."

Davius was shocked. "You converse with my gods?"

"Do you not converse with them yourself?" he pointed out. "Gods exist when they are called into existence by the minds of men. We are given power and meaning by those who worship and fear us. The lush hills of Gaul have always been captivating to me, as are the Tuatha De Danann, who your people, the Celts, conceived. All the gods coexist together in outer realms unable to be penetrated by the human eye, unless one knows where and how to look. Your father knew all this. So did our poor priest who met his demise within these walls - it was the knowledge of it that inevitably drove him to madness."

Davius paled at the mention of his father.

Lucius looked down at the bones that lay at his feet, watching as a brave rat wove through them. Lucius snatched it with lightning speed, crushing it instantly in his hand. Blood poured from the animal's crushed body, which he drained into his cup before tossing the corpse aside. Davius looked away in revulsion.

"Does this sicken you? How different is it than your sacrifices in the woods?

"Yes, I have been watching you for quite some time," he answered, before Davius could speak. "It pleases me that you have kept up with your traditions. Your father knew the power in sacrifice. He made a pact with me far before your mother bore you that for every sacrifice made in my honor, his son would be given power beyond human restrictions. He was a great magus, your father. He knew precisely how to bend all of the gods to his will." He returned to his seat on the sarcophagus, crossing his long legs in front of him. "He did, however, pay for it with his life. You survived of course, delivered to me without harm, your destiny fulfilled."

"So you are to give me power," Davius stated flatly.

"For a price," he replied casually. "My purpose in creating the pact with your father was selfish. For centuries I existed, adoring humanity from afar, obsessed with their ambitions and earthly desires. I longed to be one of you. It was a sorceress who finally summoned me into mortal form, but her magic was not strong enough and I am flawed. I have strength and immortality, but the light of the sun scorches my flesh. I do not require food nor drink, yet my body demands the blood of animals to thrive. I once lusted for such earthly delights, but I see now that those pleasures are necessities required by lesser beings. Blood ensures my unending survival, blood earned only through the sublime experience that is the hunt."

"What is it that you want?" Davius pressed once more.

"What do all ambitious men want? Power! I did not choose to come into the world in this form, I wanted to be human. But now I have realized that this is the true power - I am stronger than any man alive. I am a god among them, and one day I will be hailed for it! And you will help me achieve this.

"This life has served me well. I am capable of enough magic to propel my journeys to foreign lands. I have scoured the world, seeking knowledge, absorbing cultures, witnessing the beauty of an earth I can finally see, and smell, and touch. But I am lonely, Davius. I have had trysts with human women, yet they have never been able to truly satisfy. Then one evening, it occured to me that I should make more creatures like me, to walk alongside me in this life. Yet every time I have tried to bring another into this world, I have failed. You will be an exception."

"Why me?" Davius murmured.

"Because you were offered to me, and you are the only one strong enough to bear these gifts."

Rattling bones suddenly shattered the silence of the tomb, the door wrenching open and slamming shut with a thunderous clang. Davius was running, so fast that his legs burned within moments, his lungs squeezing for breath. He heard Lucius's frustrated cries echoing behind him. "You run now, but you will be back - you will! This is your destiny!"

Davius burst out of the house, the cold air slapping him like an open fist. He sped faster and faster, thinking only of Gaia. They would flee Rome tonight, he decided, whatever the consequence. He raced down the stone street, his bare feet tearing painfully from exertion. He sprinted towards the villa, not registering that it was alive with torchlight, a rare occurrence so early in the morning. He ran faster, fearful Lucius had stolen all his time.

"You!"

Davius had almost crossed the threshold when three of Eridus's guards blocked his path. Startled, he tried to come up with an explanation for his whereabouts. "I—I was…" he stammered.

A fierce blow shot into his stomach, causing him to double over, a foot landing hard in his ribs as he gasped for breath. He had expected reprimand, but nothing like this. He fell to the ground, watching a spittle of blood from his mouth darken the dirt below. A guard lifted him roughly by his neck, tossing him into the atrium. He looked up to see Eridus looming above him.

"Get up," he growled. His face was a mask of blotched red fury.

"Please let me explain—"

"Get up!"

A foot lodged itself into his back, forcing him to rise.

Eridus's large frame towered over him, surrounded by dozens of armed guards. He caught Gaia out of the corner of his eye, her arms held behind her. Her head was down and her eyes averted, concealing the details of her face.

Confused, he looked up at Eridus, meeting wide and blazing eyes. "You," he spat. "I trusted you." His words were short, dripping with venom. "I treated you like a human being - I gave you everything!"

Two guards flanked him at Eridus's command, one delivering a cruel blow to the soft of his back. Davius fell to his knees once more in anguish. His vision trembled as he tried desperately to see Gaia, who he could hear crying in response to his beating. She hung helplessly at the mercy of her captors, tears streaking down her face and collecting at a swollen lip that was caked with her blood.

And then, it dawned on him.

Eridus knew.

"I treated you better than you deserved, and you betrayed me!" the man roared, continuing his beastly display of rage. "You have taken what was intended to be mine!"

Davius hung his head.

He was too late.

"Gaia will be sold tomorrow," Eridus confirmed. "You will remain chained in the stables until I can find someone who will purchase you as well. Why end your life when I can profit from your sale." And with that, he stormed away, gesturing curtly at his guards. Blows assailed him from all sides, leaving him no other option than to curl himself into a ball. Pain seared through every angle of his body, his head pounding with each strike.

It felt like hours before the onslaught ceased and they hoisted him into the air. He thought immediately of his childhood, and the tormenting powerlessness that is captivity. He was a child once more, helpless in their hands. They tossed him in the stables like a butchered piece of meat, chaining his arm tightly to one of the posts. His joints screamed with pain. The horses whinnied in alarm, kicking their legs in confused agitation.

He could do nothing to comfort them, listening to their cries as he hung against his bounds in misery, his battered chest heaving with sobs.

He wrenched open a single eyelid, the other swollen beyond proper function. Blood throbbed throughout his battered body, prickling at the spots where his skin was torn. He licked arid lips, revealing a single vicious split that separated what was once a neatly sloping Cupid's bow. The events of earlier resurfaced, as he shamefully recalled his inability to save his lover. He had to find her. He attempted to move, realizing he was no longer bound to the stables, but resting in a warm bed, swathed in blankets.

He pulled himself up in surprise, grimacing as his body excruciatingly rebelled at the effort. He succumbed to its protests, resting on his elbows so he could examine his surroundings.

"Ah, you are awake."

Sitting before him was none other than Lucius.

"I found you in the stables, near death," he explained. "I was already out searching for you. I could not let you leave so upset after our last parting. You are fortunate that I found you when I did. I believe your master's fury had rendered him ruthlessly apathetic to your wellbeing."

"How long have I been unconscious?"

Lucius approached the bedside. As much as it bothered him to admit it, Davius was relieved to see him. "I let you rest for several days, changing your bandages and administering oil treatments I learned from abroad," he replied. "I also took care of your slave master. Ending his life proved most satisfactory for me. While I can empathize with crimes of passion, nearly killing someone who is close to me is unforgivable."

Davius was quiet, letting his words sink in. He expected to be more shocked and dismayed to learn of Eridus's death, but he was not. "And Gaia?"

Lucius sighed. "I have yet to find her. I heard rumors that she was sold immediately to a man they call Nirus."

Enraged, Davius attempted to move once more, but his attempts were futile.

"So you have heard of him," Lucius remarked. "Davius, you must let your body heal. You are of no use to anyone in this state. Nirus keeps his residence fortified like a crazed emperor, possessed by suspicion. Penetrating his fortifications will require skill." He moved away from his side. "While you were unconscious, I did some research on the man. I discovered that his authority lies within his relationship with Caesar. The two were comrades for many years during his conquests until a sudden brain fever rendered Nirus impotent as a soldier and quite insane. I believe this is the reason behind his barbarous behavior."

Lucius ignited the oil lamp resting on the bedside table. The room was flooded with light, revealing Egyptian hieroglyphs etched into the walls, stretching from the heavily draped ceilings to the polished marble floors. Gold plated sculptures littered every corner, their gems sparkling in the lamplight. "Is this your bedchamber?" Davius asked.

Lucius nodded. "You needed somewhere comfortable to convalesce. My body does not require much rest, it is more of a pleasant luxury to pass the time," he explained.

He moved across the room, his long robes sweeping the floor. "Apparently this Nirus has never taken a wife," he resumed his delineation. "However, he does have a daughter through one of his slaves, whom he spoils excessively."

Davius recalled the giggling, brown eyed girl at the Circus.

"His slaves are not so lucky," Lucius continued. "He occasionally keeps male workers, but prefers a steady flow of women, who all end up dying prematurely, either directly by his hand or by starvation."

Davius stiffened.

"Women are rarely as weak as men would paint them, Davius," Lucius soothed, noticing his stricken face. "I have witnessed human women overcome far greater trials than this in my lifetime. They have mastered an inner strength that can defeat any enemy when physical force proves inadequate."

"I wish I was there," Davius murmured despairingly. From outside Lucius's heavily veiled windows, he heard the distant crooning of a crow.

Inspiration suddenly struck him. "Lucius. I need you to call one of my gods, the goddess Danu."

"I am bound by this realm now, Davius," he reminded him. "I cannot commune with your gods any differently than you can."

"Then I will need you to gather me some items." He threw off his blankets, wincing as he hoisted himself up into a seated position on the bed.

Lucius nodded, intrigued.

"I will need a knife, a bowl, and several eggs. Do you have eggs here?"

Lucius withdrew to the dining room, returning with a clay bowl of rotting eggs and Davius's marble knife. "I found your dagger in the stables and recognized it immediately. These pigeon eggs are from our feast days ago. I haven't had the heart to clear the table away quite yet. Will they do?"

Davius nodded emphatically, accepting the items with gratitude. He promptly smashed the eggs into the bowl, ignoring the rancid stench that soon choked the room.

Lucius seated himself across from him, observing his preparations curiously.

Davius inhaled, centering his mind and calming his breath. He focused on the cacophony of cicadas in the distance, the strident music of the night. He started to feel power building inside him. "Mother Danu," he called out. "Hear me now! Protect she who needs you, your daughter. Be her strength where I cannot."

He pressed the knife into his arm, spilling his blood into the bowl so that it swirled gruesomely with the spoiled embryo. Lucius's eyes sparkled with excitement. "Accept my sacrifice, Mother Goddess," Davius cried, his heart racing with exhilaration. "Protect your daughter!"

The curtains suddenly whipped up in fury, a tempestuous wind tumbling in from outside. It howled throughout the chambers, as Davius struggled to keep his concentration. Power now hummed throughout his body, the room responding in a tornado of chaos. Statues toppled over, curtains were ripped from their fastenings and sent flailing. The oil lamp crashed to the ground which Lucius hurriedly snuffed out with his foot. His black curls thrashed around his face like snakes. "Davius!" he called. "Your invocation is not working as you intended - it is you who becomes strong!"

Davius looked down to see that Lucius was right, his wounds were fading away from his skin as if they were water evaporating into an arid sky. The building windstorm had no patience for this revelation, sending one of Lucius's statues soaring across the room. It landed with a violent crash, shattering into pieces.

"Go, now!" Lucius yelled over its roar.

Davius threw off his bedding, startled by his newfound strength. He bolted from Lucius's chambers into the heart of the raging storm. Branches and rocks lashed at him, gusts pummeling his skin as he sprinted towards the House of Nirus. The city was in a state of pandemonium, Romans racing for shelter from the viciously forceful gales. Citizens slammed closed their shutters, securing their loose possessions and bolting their doors.

Beyond the congested stacks of insulae apartments and their frantic occupants, the house suddenly appeared, a massive architectural fortification ominous against the turbulent sky. The storm had forced its guards inside, allowing him to reach the windows easily, their wooden shutters recklessly open and flailing.

He peered inside them with caution, sheltered from the storm by the sloping roof. He observed a feast in progress, easily picking out Nirus's lopsided frame amongst a dozen jovial soldiers, all in various stages of gluttony. Several emaciated slave girls pressed themselves against the surrounding walls, fear painted across their gaunt faces and shining in their eyes.

The mere sight of the man enraged Davius. His pointed features and splotched, gray skin gave him the appearance of an overgrown rat, his eyes black and beady. His progressing disease not only ravaged his face but had caused the muscles of his legs and arms to atrophy, several fingers missing from a hand wrapped awkwardly around his glass.

"Quite the storm raging outside," one of the men commented, his voice barely audible over the celebration.

Nirus snorted. "We feast until daybreak."

"Nirus! We are running low on drink," one called to him over the table.

"Bitch! Come to me now!" he shouted behind his shoulder.

Davius stared in horror as Gaia emerged. Her lovely curves had already deflated, her once supple skin hanging waxen off an alarmingly narrow frame. She was barely clothed, only her breasts and her womanhood shrouded in thin purple fabric. Wrapped in her arms was a swollen decanter of wine.

Davius nearly leapt from where he was perched, fury threatening to choke the sanity from his mind, but something outside of himself willed him to pause.

One of the soldiers lunged at her, but Nirus slammed his fist down upon the table, toppling over several half-filled glasses. "There are plenty of girls here for your satisfaction, but this one is mine. I just bought her from Eridus the Winemaker, one of his prized possessions. She has proven very difficult to break, which intrigues me." He reached up to pinch her cheek in mock affection.

Gaia's face was stone, her eyes burning with hatred. "As long as you are intrigued," she said flatly.

Nirus bellowed with laughter. "She really is something, is she not?" he asked the crowd. "Fill up everyone's glasses now before I lose my patience."

She started around the table, sloshing wine into every open cup. The soldiers continued to eye her longingly, one so visibly frustrated that he grabbed one of the other girls leaning against the wall. He pushed up her tunic, forcing her to bend against the table. His comrades roared with laughter. The poor girl cried in fear as her assailant reached clumsily beneath his toga.

Suddenly, Gaia whipped around, overturning the decanter and, with unusual strength, smashed it against the soldier's head, sending wine and glass spraying. Stunned, the man fell, blood pouring from his wound. The room exploded with chaos.

On cue, Davius dove through the window, wielding his knife with unrestrained savagery. The stupefied soldiers had little time to grab their weapons before he found a neglected sword to brandish. It moved easily in his hands, the power he had inadvertently invoked still coursing through him as he connected with every target. Furious squalls of wind tore the room apart, as gore sputtered from the wounds of rapidly falling soldiers. Davius slashed without mercy, a perfect vessel of carnage, the reincarnation of warriors come before him. He abandoned himself completely, his body dodging their swords as he tore through each one of them with cold, unrelenting calculation.

"Davius!"

Her voice broke him out of his battle trance as he narrowly avoided a blade that came down from behind him. Gaia shrieked with anger, bearing down with her own pilfered sword, cleanly severing his attacker's head from his body. Davius froze, breathless, staring awestruck at her wild expression as blood sprayed up into her face.

"Davius, I am wounded, please..." she mouthed, shifting her left arm to reveal a vicious wound gaping at her stomach.

Davius shook out of his brief stupor, gathering her into his arms. He scanned the room for Nirus but was unable to pick him out amongst the carnage of bodies. "I will kill you one day, you coward!" he called out to him. "I shall return for you!"

He hoisted Gaia against his chest, tearing away from the house and back into the restorative night air. The wind embraced him, fueling his trek as he streaked towards the forest, the only haven he could think of. Her frail body folded against him, silent as he hurdled over scores of fallen branches to his private copse.

He pulled away the branches and hurried inside, the thicket offering them shelter under its dense brush. He laid her delicately atop a pile of fallen leaves, pulling back her arm to study the wound. Alarmed by its severity, he ripped a piece off his tunic, pressing the fabric against it in an attempt to stop the bleeding. Gaia shivered uncontrollably, the moon casting its light across her trembling lips. He pulled her next to him, hoping the warmth of his body would quell her tremulous state. He gazed down at her, brushing her hair back from her dampened forehead.

Tears glistened around her eyes as she reached up to caress his face. "Forgive me," she whispered, "that I could not survive."

"Stop," he said in panic, the truth of their predicament suddenly becoming clear. "They are just wounds, they will heal."

"I am dying, sweet Davius," she negated gently. "It is my time." He was struck by how hallowed her face had become since he'd last seen her, its fullness lost under ashen skin. Her eyes had yellowed, her alluring olive irises dimmed to a murky brown.

He succumbed to the impending heartbreak, unable to stop a barrage of heavy tears from spilling down his cheeks. "Please," he begged her. "Please just hold on."

She offered him a small smile as her eyes closed. "I have seen our gods, Davius," she murmured. "I have seen the Otherworld … it is beautiful, like eternal springtime."

Davius sobbed, squeezing her tightly as if to will it away.

"Do not cry for me, my love. I have made peace with death. Danu will guide me home." Her voice wavered as she spoke, gradually growing weaker. The gushing wound at her side soon blanketed them both in copious ichor. He let it flow, understanding there was nothing more he could do to stop its heartrending intention.

"She told me secrets," she continued, her dry lips cracking with the effort. "About your destiny."

He hovered over her, so their faces were inches apart, taking her hand tightly in his. "How can I live without you?" he whispered.

Her eyes opened. "You will, and one day, you will become extraordinary. Do not let my death be your downfall, use it as your strength. I have seen so much…" Her words were interrupted by a violent cough, blood sputtering from her mouth. "Follow the gods always, Davius. They will not fail you. You will see me again, I promise. For the stars have declared you my husband and our souls will never part."

And then, too quickly, she took a final breath and was gone.

A deep melancholy settled over the forest. The wind had ceased, the earth was still. He rested his head against her motionless chest, allowing himself time to weep. She had been his everything, his friend, his mother, his sister, his lover. He would never see her give birth to his children, never experience freedom together.

After some time, he lifted his moistened face away from her gradually cooling skin. She looked the perfect earth goddess in repose, her body engulfed by the clusters of plant life that surrounded her, welcoming their daughter home.

He decided to leave her where she lay, in his sacred copse, in the arms of her goddess namesake. He draped her with his robe, scattering over her body the herbs from his makeshift apothecary and flowers collected from the wood. He circled her body with stones so that he might find her again, etching one with the words: beatae memoriae, of blessed memory. He stammered through a eulogy in Gaulish, pausing at the end. He produced his knife, reopening the wound that had summoned his strength, letting the fresh droplets perforate her shroud. "I vow before all the gods, old and new, I will avenge this death, lest I never rest until I do."

He swiftly brought the dagger down into the dirt, sealing the oath. He kissed her lips through the fabric, one final time. "Goodbye, my love."

He withdrew in silence.

It was cold, as if the sweltering heat of summer collapsed into autumn chill overnight, his tattered tunic useless against it. He was unaffected, however, the smoldering embers of hatred keeping him warm. His grief was overpowered by the rawness of his fury, pushing his battered body onward. The borrowed strength from earlier had left him, his limbs now sore and muscles aching. The magic he had worked was not enough to finish his task, and he knew he needed more to carry on.

He moved back through the city, observing the remains of the storm, fallen branches and shards of broken sculptures cluttering the roads. An overturned water fountain gushed out its contents. The citizens of Rome were still welled up in their homes, quiet in the late hour.

The abandoned temple that Lucius called home resurfaced ahead. He barely reached the entrance when its owner appeared in the doorway. His eyes were brightly burning saucers. "Did you find her?"

Davius couldn't respond. He suddenly felt exhausted beyond restoration.

"Come, come," Lucius took him by the shoulder, guiding him inside.

He had cleaned up the shattered vestiges of Davius's tempest, the atrium now oddly barren. Lucius pulled him to one of his couches, forcing him gently into its folds. He seated himself directly across from him, his smooth, unblemished face marked with concern. Davius realized how beautiful a creature he was exposed under direct lamplight, a man frozen in time.

"Is she dead?" he asked.

Davius nodded, his voice wavering as he spoke. "And I am physically powerless to avenge her."

"What happened?"

Davius wearily disclosed the evening's events. "I could not get to the loathsome rodent in time. He ran away, a true coward."

Lucius, who had been listening to his story with rapt attention, finally moved to cross his legs and lean back into his seat. "You cannot go for him tonight, Davius. If you murdered that many soldiers, you are now being hunted. And once they learn of Eridus's murder… Nirus's dwelling will be swarming with guards. Besides, you are far too weak to do anything now."

"I will empower myself once more," Davius argued, indignant.

"It is true, I have never seen magic worked that impressively before. You were absolutely prodigious. But I fear it will not work so perfectly again."

"What do you mean?"

"Magic in this realm works for a price, Davius. It cannot be used lightly. While you are obviously an extremely adept sorcerer, which I would assume was inherited from your father, you cannot borrow from a well that has run dry. To demand the powers that be to vitalize you twice so quickly is simply unreasonable." He rose to his feet. "In fact, I am not even certain who or what you invoked this evening."

"The gods, of course," Davius retorted.

Lucius sighed. "Davius, gods are only given power through worship, through the masses that have faith in them. The Tuatha De Danann inhabit the Otherworld in Gaul and the other Celtic lands. While there were plenty of Celtic slaves who brought their gods to Rome, the majority of them adjusted to life here, eventually absorbing the Greek religion as their own. And without being worshiped, what is the point of staying in a foreign land? So the gods move on, back from whence they came."

Davius frowned, absorbing his words. "When I came to Rome as a slave boy, I was protected by the Morrigan. She stayed in human form throughout my long voyage here, presenting herself as a woman from my clan. She protected me, cared for me. Then she transformed when we arrived, massacring the entire Roman harbor in a swarm of carrion crows."

Lucius was mystified. "Amazing," he breathed. "Have you seen any signs of her since?"

"No," he admitted. "She left as quickly as she came."

Lucius nodded. "That does reflect her temperament. I am astonished she chose to protect you, revealing her powers in such a way. I have tried to communicate with her before on this land but could never reach her."

Davius sat quietly, his brow furrowed in contemplation. Finally, he spoke, his words careful and composed. "Lucius, I have made my decision. I want to be as you are."

Lucius stared at him, trying to contain the elation bubbling beneath his composed exterior. "Do you mean this? Truly?"

Davius felt a sudden wave of calm, as if by speaking the words out loud, the fates aligned with his choice and offered him their blessing. His haunting visions felt like a distant memory, a new sense of determination and finality settled over him. His rage was transformed into purpose, his lust now only for vengeance. He realized he was willing to do whatever was required of him to accomplish it. He stood, firmly replying, "Yes."

Lucius did not waste another moment. He flew up to him in an instant, a serpent striking its prey, sinking his teeth deep down into the flesh of his neck. Davius instinctively tried to resist, but a strange euphoria crept over him, rendering him useless. His knees weakened as his body was drained of life, yet his sire held him tightly, even as darkness swam over his eyes, threatening to collapse him. The pain in his throat was both excruciating and orgasmic, a dichotomous paradox, as his body fought to live with involuntary spasms.

His mind raced with images, memories of his past, nightmares of lives lived before this one. He saw his father's face flushed with religious ecstasy, smelled the sweetness of his mother's skin. Everything seemed to make sense yet was frustratingly incomprehensible. He was dying, and the realms between his and the next swirled with maddening disarray. His soul was drifting, his mind in panic as his body realized how wonderful it was to be released of mortal bondage.

And then, as the antilogy his consciousness was experiencing grew unbearable, Lucius dropped him. Davius writhed on the floor, unable to do anything else.

Lucius gasped, apparent that he too felt the intensity of what transpired. Blood ran down his chin as he spoke. "I fed you my blood at our feast, and now I have drunk yours. This is how you become like me - an exchange of vital essence. You will feel your body perish, but your soul will remain constant, though it is now altered forever."

Davius didn't need his warning. He knew his body was dying, his thoughts consumed by the agony of his muscles collapsing, the frightening spasms of his organs ceasing their tedious exertion and the horrific sensation of his wastes letting themselves go. His soul floated above his motionless body as unearthly cries surrounded him, beckoning him to follow them. He looked down to see the crimson that ran from his gaping neck wound turn an inky black. The wound then closed itself, the skin fastening together seamlessly, ending the flow of liquid with a halt. Suddenly, he was struck with the sensation of falling - pummeling actually - until he landed with a painful jolt. He was whole.

And then he stood.

Energy pulsed through him, alien and new. His nose was overwhelmed with scent, realizing he could smell everything from the young slave girl Lucius had stashed away in the house to a couple who hurried down the street blocks away. He smelled the woman's excitement, the drops of perspiration running down her back, the man's intoxication and the heated pheromones of his lust.

His eyes darted across the room as he tried to absorb surroundings that were familiar, but now seemed new. Colors were blindingly vivid, the paintings on the walls pulsating with pigment. He moved to touch them, to inspect his dried paint with new fingers, when he realized he had moved with such speed that he upset the few tapestries that still hung on the wall. He stared at them in amazement, for he could see every intricate detail of every waxen strand from where he stood, several feet away. Every shadow that cast itself upon the floor seemed like sunbeams, and he could count the hairs upon the spider that scuttled up the wall.

"What ... am I?" His voice was barely a murmur.

Lucius stood before him, and Davius looked upon him for what seemed to be the first time. He was a vision to behold, his skin aglow, his eyes burning golden fire. He smiled adoringly at his new creation, his teeth blindingly bright and severe. "You are an immortal!" he exalted.

Davius looked down at his hands. His skin was so transparent that he could make out maps of veins pulsating black blood, coursing up and down his fingers. His nails were now sharp, almost like claws, and they glinted in the candlelight. He moved his arms, feeling a fluid sort of power in them, effortless in their movement. He looked at Lucius again in wonder before a deep hunger pain jolted his stomach, as if he hadn't eaten or drank in days.

"The hunger you feel is natural," Lucius responded to his silent amazement. "It has now become a part of you, the price you pay for perfect strength and immortality."

Suddenly, Davius vomited, violently dispelling the last remnants of humanity from his body. He wiped his mouth, staring at his maker. "I am so thirsty," he moaned.

"You will drink. But first, I must teach you. Moira, come to me," Lucius called. His voice seemed to dance in Davius's head, a medley of beautiful tones and pitches. He again became so entranced by the vibrancy of his world that he was able to put aside the hunger gnawing at his stomach.

Moira appeared, yet this time Davius felt no sorrow for her. He sensed she was like they were, but her eyes did not glisten like Lucius's. She appeared weak, as if the last scraps of humanity still clung to her like the rotten bark of a dying tree.

"She is also like us, just a lower form," Lucius explained. "She is stronger than a human and can hunt for herself, but her mind is mush, malleable and compliant like a service animal."

He went up to her, lifting her face for Davius to see. Her eyes remained cast downwards, dully staring at the floor. "She is a revenant, a creature unable to have an intelligent thought on their own, though she is immortal, just the same as you or I. Her kind is created when one tries to turn a human after death has already occurred. Her soul has completely moved on, but her corpse still remains, animated by my blood."

"A *daemon* attempted to take her soul," Davius remembered. "I interrupted it."

"I fed upon her initially, but was interrupted and she managed to escape," Lucius explained. "The daemon sensed she was between worlds and went to collect her soul, which you interrupted. I went for her after, curious to see what would happen to a human drained without my blood as replacement. Would she still turn? Would she heal? I had to know. I stole her body before the pyre and drizzled my blood into her mouth until her limbs moved once again. Yet since her soul was already gone, a revenant, she became."

Davius was initially shocked by his admission, then struck with confusion over his apathy, realizing his countenance was cold and emotionless, a far cry from who he was. "I no longer feel pity for her, Lucius. I do not care that she is weak, nor that she died at your hands. I feel … nothing."

Lucius laughed. "You are an immortal now, Davius! You need not be bothered by such trivial things such as human emotion. Some feelings will linger, but pity is one far too primitive for you to hold on to."

"Will she live forever with us?" he asked.

"Ah!" Lucius clasped his hands together. "Here is your first lesson. As I told you before, the witch who brought me into the earthly realm was not as proficient as I had hoped. We are bound by earthly laws, which include ways to reach an untimely demise. Without violence, we will live forever. However, there are two things that will bring about our end. The first is the sun. We are forever nocturnal. Our skin cannot bear sunlight and too much time spent under its rays will incinerate us into non-existence. Man-made fire will turn our bodies into charred remains, but we will not fully die. Although I can wield the power of fire with my hands, there may one day come a time where I am caught unaware, and I shudder to think of a scenario I cannot control. So fire we shall always evade. The second is silver."

From his robes, he produced a stiletto knife, its handle bearing a single obsidian stone. Without warning, he thrust it into Moira's breastplate with a sharp crack, piercing her heart with the blade. She gasped, eyes wide as she tried to remove the implanted dagger, only to dissolve into a cloud of black dust. The ashes fell to the floor, the dagger landing with a sharp clank. Moira was no more.

Lucius retrieved the knife from the ground, shaking it free of the residual fragments. "Beware of silver, Davius. I do not know why it kills us, perhaps because of some ancient sorcerers with daft notions of good. Regardless, it is to be avoided and the truth of its power kept a secret at all costs." He slid the knife back into its sheath.

"So we can die at the hands of humans," Davius remarked.

"She was no more than a walking corpse with a few drops of immortal blood. She died by a simple knife, but for you and I, it will not be so easy. We equally share my powerful blood, and it will take an entire day in the sun or the purest silver to bring us to our end. Even then, godly death has yet to be seen." He smiled with an air of impudence.

Davius nodded, letting the knowledge sink in as he fell into one of Lucius's upholstered couches. He wasn't tired, but his legs were still enervated by shock.

Lucius approached him, placing his hand on his shoulder. "You feel beleaguered by all this, I understand. Some human thoughts and feelings will linger until you have fully grown into your new existence. You are like a newborn - everything is fresh and titillating but overwhelming just the same. You may rest now if you would like, and we can finish our lessons later."

"No." Davius rose to his feet. "I must avenge Gaia."

Lucius sighed, visibly disappointed. "And the frivolous feeling of love still remains." He came up to face him, tenderly taking his hand in his own, his eyes pleading. "I appreciate your lust for revenge, my dear brother, but it is not the time. There is still much more to learn before you can attempt such a feat. Most importantly, you have to feed."

Hunger pangs let themselves be vociferously known in Davius's stomach. "Yes, I should feed. Please."

Lucius smiled. "Follow me."

LONDON, 1857

THE NIGHT SKY HAD CRACKED OPEN, revealing an angry orange at its horizon, spilling the vibrant hue onto the clouds as the sun threatened its ascent. The air through the open window of the carriage was crisp but heavy with moisture, and although the brilliant swirl of color teased daybreak, David knew rain would soon interrupt its plans. Nevertheless, he retrieved a pair of tinted eyeglasses from his breast pocket, tucking the frames behind his ears. The immediate reprieve from brightness was soothing to his tired eyes.

The initial thrill of the carriage ride had subsided for his companion, her long frame now stretched back into the seat as she sporadically emitted tiny yawns. She tried her best to hide her building lassitude, encouraging him to continue his story with strategically placed sounds of astonishment and genuine gasps of awe.

He had paused moments earlier, aware that they would soon be approaching his place of residence. "You will see it right over the hill," he explained.

For most of his life, he had wandered, briefly inhabiting hotels or renting townhomes in whatever city he found himself. Yet London had charmed him immediately, its perpetual choking fog and congested populace allowing him the undisturbed seclusion he so desired. Housing had also greatly improved with the turn of the century, and David found himself enamored by the spacious manors that affluent mortals erected for themselves. How many rooms and stories a man could fit into one household was a mark of stature, the grotesque expense of the undertaking, a reflection of his greatness. Many remained within the city borders, satisfied with elegant townhomes, but a select few cherished not only the capaciousness of a residence, but the accumulation of land. These folks ventured out into the English countryside in an action reminiscent of the Ancient Romans, snatching up vast amounts of acreage before there would be no more land left to purchase. Intrigued, David had followed suit, and soon discovered what would be his manor, the Estate of Lardone.

The impressive building appeared in the distance, nestled away by acres of countryside. The articulated iron fence that surrounded it kept it strategically obscured from potential onlookers, its twin spiraling towers the only parts visible from the road. He had chosen his home first for its beauty, a gargantuan edifice hidden by hills, stretching three stories high and two wings in length. But the discovery of its history is what kept his interest.

"It was once a church used by the wealthy," he explained to his inquisitive companion, "the exact year of construction unknown. It served as a welcome departure from the harsh city streets, aristocrats traveling for miles to worship in a place surrounded by lush landscape and warm sunshine. It remained in operation for quite some time until the advent of the railroads breathed new life into the city and officials began to renovate the districts of the West End, adding fancy hotels and attractive taverns. With the newly revamped lodgings came the desire for local places to worship, and soon a new chapel was erected nearby, replacing several dilapidated buildings that were eagerly torn down.

"The patronage of the countryside church dwindled steadily until it was forced one day to close its doors forever. It was then purchased by Charles Lardone, a wealthy steel tycoon who had moved to London with his family during the peak of railroad construction. They transformed the simple church into a magnificent estate, adding wings with spiraling towers filled with rooms, gardens, and a carriage house. They left the windows of colored glass and the tall cathedral rooftops intact during construction, which only served to add to its grandiosity. When the manor was finished, it was truly a sight to behold.

"The wretched Lardone Family, however, only lasted a few months in their new home before petty rivalries between the brothers destroyed the entire family in one act of vicious bloodshed. It remained abandoned for years before I found it, most Londoners far too superstitious to purchase it for themselves. As you might guess, I don't suffer from these trepidations."

"I didn't expect you would." His companion smiled.

As they drew closer, she pushed her head out of the small carriage window. "Bloody hell," she exclaimed. "It's even more beautiful than you described."

David smiled.

Jacob slowed the horses to a complete stop as they reached the towering gates, then carefully maneuvered himself down from the driver's seat. David heard the jingle of his keys as he turned them in the massive lock, and his grunt as he heaved open the iron gate doors. Within moments, they were moving forward again, and he tried to envision what his companion saw from her clear vantage point; stone ashen with time, coils of ivy crawling up towards the skies as if begging for divine redemption. The Greek revival inspired buttresses with carved pinnacles, the meticulously tiled roofs, the elaborate glazed windows on the upper side walls. He was particularly fond of the use of tracery around the building, the elaborate geometric shapes and patterns allowing the revamped cathedral to safely boast architectural splendor.

He wondered if she had been able to tear her eyes away from the manor itself to notice the graveyard laid obliquely to the house, the final resting place of the tragic family. Dilapidated stones jutted out from the earth in an awkward pattern, forever inferior to their neighbor, a giant marble crypt boasting the name Lardone. The graveyard was his most cherished attribute, an open sanctum he used frequently to pass the hours.

"You may want to tuck your head in, miss, the skies look like rain," Jacob's voice came from above. As if on cue, thunder rolled in the distance.

She pulled her head back into the carriage, breathless, eyes widened by amazement. The carriage halted with a sharp jolt and the horses whinnied in response. Jacob wrenched open the carriage doors as another crackle of thunder shook the ground. "Best hurry, sir, the rain is starting," he suggested.

No sooner had he spoken did the heavens part, letting down a torrent of frigid water. She let out a startled cry, hurrying towards the great front doors that were hastily opened for her.

When they were safely inside, Jacob gathered their effects from them, water droplets falling to the marble floors as he tenderly hung each coat upon the rack situated near the wall. He then quickened his movement, igniting the numerous sconces along the walls to deliver them from the dark.

In the meantime, his companion stared about in silent wonder, absorbing the great house with innocent marvel as it came to life under the lamplight.

David wondered what it would be like to see the inside of his home through the eyes of another, taking in the dual staircases that climbed up each side of the massive foyer, the chandeliers that were once magnificent but were now tarnished and caked with cobwebs, the somber curtains that choked any light from the rooms, save for the dozens of stained glass windows hovering near the ceiling. Left completely intact, the glorious masterpieces depicted Christ's agonizing journey to the cross, the overtly religious tone ironic when considering the Lardone Family and their sinful affairs. David enjoyed the aesthetic beauty they provided, allowing just enough filtered sunlight for the rich hues to sparkle across the halls without causing his eyes to strain.

"You chose a home that was once a church, just like Lucius did," his companion interrupted his thoughts, following his eyes to the macabre depictions of a half-clad man bearing his great affliction.

David blinked, realizing the connection for the first time. "You're right. I suppose I am still entranced by religious art."

"It's difficult not to be," she offered dreamily as she ascended the stairs, her wide eyes continuing to drink in the splendor around her.

"Jacob, if you would, please fetch some provisions for our guest before you retire," David murmured to his manservant before following her up the stairwell.

The old man nodded, politely tipping his hat as he disappeared into the labyrinth of halls. If he was surprised that David had brought a guest into his home after so many years of solitude, he didn't betray it in the slightest.

David caught up to her, gently guiding her back down the stairs into the parlor, the room where he spent the majority of his waking hours. He moved towards the granite fireplace to stoke the glowing embers into combustion, the enkindled flames soon illuminating the room, revealing stately furniture with silk upholstery, several bookcases, and an extravagant grand piano. The room was painted in reds, with deep crimson wallpaper stretching from ceiling to floor, the latter covered by rich carmine rugs.

"Many of these furnishings came along with the house," David explained with a chuckle, noticing her befuddlement at the pretentious instrument. "I myself have never played."

He lit a match to ignite the candelabra perched atop it, the burst of light revealing weathered yellow keys that had almost been masked by the piano's distractingly shiny paint. Satisfied that the room was now warm and inviting, he gestured her towards the loveseat, and after noticing the chattering of her teeth, offered her a blanket that was folded over an adjacent chair. She burrowed under it gratefully, removing her hat and letting the damp spirals of her dark hair fall around her neck.

He removed his sack coat and hung it near the fireplace before taking the chair, reclining so that his long legs stretched out before him, letting the growing heat of the fire dry his clothing.

"You look so young without your top hat and coat," she remarked, admiring him.

"Well, I haven't aged in centuries," he pointed out, good-naturedly.

"How strange to remain frozen in time," she remarked.

"I agree," he replied softly, his eyes drawn to the crackling fire.

"May I have a cigarette?"

He gestured towards a small pine box on the table near where she sat. Grateful, she opened it and fiddled for a moment before lighting her prize with a satisfied flourish. She fought against the subsequent coughing, wiping a bit of escaped spittle from her lips with the back of her hand. "So what happened next, after you transformed?" she asked, bringing them back to the task at hand. "Does Lucius live here in this house with you?"

David nearly choked in surprise. "Oh, heavens no." He found himself stumbling for words. "Lucius has not walked this earth for quite some time. In fact, it was I who killed him."

Old Man Jacob interrupted them, entering the room with a hobble, the thin silver tray of sandwiches and tea he held rattling as he moved. He set the tray down on the nearest table, pouring David's companion a cup of tea from an elegant china teapot and placing it, along with a craftily prepared finger sandwich, in front of her. David was surprised at his efficiency, realizing he must have acquired the impromptu meal from his own kitchen, as David's own remained perpetually empty.

"Why thank you, sir, I am positively ravenous." She nodded to him, shoveling the food into her mouth without the slightest regard for manners.

David grinned sheepishly at Jacob's mystified face before waving him away. "Thank you, Jacob. You may retire for the evening."

"Yes, sir. Please ring if you need me." The old man bowed his head, taking one final peek at the strange woman devouring food in his employer's sitting room, before shuffling off.

Once he left, David's companion set down her sandwich and met his eyes. "Did you bring me here to kill me?" she bluntly asked.

David frowned and looked away, watching the flames dance in the fireplace. "You cannot imagine the loneliness I have felt over these centuries. To have someone to speak openly to, who knows what I am…" he trailed off, unnerved by his open vulnerability. "I brought you here for that reason alone."

She nodded, satisfied with his answer. "Then you must continue."

David continued to stare, transfixed by the fire, as he opened his mouth to comply.

CHAPTER FOUR

🎗 The Immortals 🎗

Ancient Greece, 44 BC

THE EVENING WAS TRANQUIL, the surface of the Mediterranean smooth
and black, interrupted only by the hull of a ship as it slid through
the water with the ease of a lover. Davius stood motionless on its deck,
the soft wind caressing his hair with gentle fingers. The slumbering city
appeared in the distance, the torches that burned at its borders flickering
in the darkness like summer fireflies.

"We are nearly there."

From behind him, Lucius appeared, joining his gaze towards the
approaching land. The two stood comfortably in silence, Davius enjoying the rhythmic lull of the water lapping against the sides of the ship.

Rome had recently descended into chaos. Conspiracy and revenge
ripped apart the sturdy fabric of the empire, sending its citizens into
a sheer panic. Attempting to restore the Roman Republic, and fearing
the absolute power of one man, several powerful senators ambushed
Julius Caesar, brutally stabbing him to death. What these few idealistic
aristocrats hadn't anticipated was the reaction to the beloved dictator's
assassination, the common citizens of Rome wasting no time in setting

the forum and its surrounding structures ablaze in ferocious rebellion. The anarchy frightened Lucius, who argued that the instability of Rome was quite possibly the worst setting for two unusually wealthy, very secretive blood drinkers.

Davius agreed, and they abandoned their home to find haven in Greece. Lucius pushed for Athens, claiming that it was the most logical choice, as he owned property there which he could easily reclaim. Davius speculated otherwise, suspecting Lucius's motives of relocation were more influenced by the recent influx of philosophers to the city, rather than simple repossession of property. Regardless, he concurred, and they left swiftly under the cloak of nightfall with as many possessions as they could manage.

A stream of silver moonlight peeked its way through the heavy clouds of the night sky, casting a sliver of light across the ocean waves. Davius inhaled deeply, letting the cool vernal air caress his lungs, wondering absently if breath was even essential to him anymore.

It had been five years since the night he was transformed.

Life as an immortal blood drinker had come easily to him, embracing the ways by which they fed with ease and unquestionable skill. In the beginning, Lucius kept vigil, an ever present mentor, as Davius found himself entranced by the seductive hunt and conquest of his victims. The power coursing through his body as he latched onto their submissive necks proved itself insatiable, the rush of pleasure as he engorged himself on their essence, intoxicating. He was so enamored by his new life, that it wasn't long before any lingering memories of human life faded, the love between Gaia and the slave boy from Gaul simply an ambiguous recollection.

He also discovered that the thrill of the hunt was only one of the gifts this new life offered, ecstatic the day he realized his remarkable speed. Although inevitably exhausting if pushed for too long, he could now dash across villages in a matter of seconds, his body traveling so fast, it was as if he flew. Lucius never cared much for the power, content with his nightly strolls, yet for Davius, it became another obsession. He found himself giddy as a child as he darted through forests for sport, leaping from tree to tree in an ironic homage to a youth he'd long passed.

Lucius, in the meantime, had busied himself with acquiring material possessions. Delighted at having a new companion, he set to work to ensure that their lives lacked nothing short of the absolute pinnacle of luxury. He spared no expense, indulging in his conspicuous tendencies without hesitation. He renovated their humble temple into a magnificent residence that soon became the envy of Rome. It boasted pools, gardens and elaborate statues, all erected of the finest marble. He imported art from Egypt and Africa, their vestibule becoming a gallery of world treasures. It even piqued the interest of Julius Caesar, who expressed the desire to dine with them before his brutal, untimely demise.

But they had left that all behind now, abandoning Lucius's domestic masterpiece to the mercy of a raging mob.

The ship made its way towards a secluded part of the beach, which offered more privacy than the Athens harbor, the elevated city growing larger and more intimidating as they edged closer to the docks.

It had taken great persuasion on Lucius's part to have them sail at night; the captain threw quite a fit, tossing out accusations and mumbling about superstitions before Lucius threw a bag of gold at his feet. After picking it up and examining one of the polished coins with a crude bite, the man nodded, and arrangements were made. Now Davius could sense the seaman's anticipation upon their arrival, tapping the deck anxiously with his boot as he navigated the ship to harbor.

Lucius remained pleasantly unaffected. His ring laden hands rested neatly on the edge of the ship as the wind picked at his black curls. "Almost home," he remarked softly.

No sooner had they reached the dock when several men appeared. They carried blazing torches that illuminated the swords precariously sheathed at their sides. They numbered at least twenty, their collective stance revealing their intent. "Who are you, strangers, that greet us at so late an hour?" one called out.

"These are wealthy men from Egypt, once Grecian citizens who now wish to return to their homeland," explained the seafarer, nervous sweat dripping down a body misshapen by corpulence. "Egypt's harsh sun has made their skin sensitive to light, so now they can only travel by nightfall."

"We must see proof of this, sirs," the leader of the pack retorted. "Romans wishing to escape persecution have tried to seek refuge here, but the people of Greece want no part in their civil unrest. We remain rightfully suspicious of every new arrival. Please, step down to the docks."

Davius blinked only once before Lucius pounced. The mob of men cried out in unified terror as he tore through them, the sounds of snapping bones and ripping flesh reverberating down the shoreline.

Davius turned to the seaman, who was frozen in shock, and offered him a sad smile. "We appreciate your assistance," he said, not unkindly, before sinking his teeth deep into the man's neck. The blood released into his mouth, assaulting him with the man's final thoughts, the strongest memories of his life. He had shocked even Lucius with the initial discovery of his psychic power, that human blood released its secrets to him in a stream of clairvoyance each time he fed. Lucius was pleasantly surprised, surmising that the ability was inherited through his father's bloodline, dormant until his transformation.

Davius was now assailed by images of a brown-haired boy dancing excitedly on the beach as ships rolled into port, the brackish sea air, the heat of foreign summer sun. He saw the man's family, felt the pain of losing a wife in childbirth, and the agony of years of loneliness, alleviated only by incessant voyages at sea. The man had yearned for death well before Davius's fatal bite. He waited until the man's heart gave one final shudder before he released him, wiping his lips as the cumbersome body fell to the ground with a thud.

"Are you ready, brother?" Lucius called up to him from below, standing the victor amongst a sea of fallen bodies.

"I am," he replied, joining him on the bank. "However, it occurs to me that we killed them before they could unload our belongings," he added, playfully.

Lucius's smile tightened, and he cursed. "I suppose I shall have to travel to our dwelling and retrieve the slaves that are awaiting our arrival. Will you be joining me?"

Davius paused, thoughtfully, beholding glassy waters splashing the shoreline against the cloudless sky. "I would actually like to explore a bit, if you don't mind."

"As you wish." Lucius nodded. "I will not be long." He disappeared seamlessly into the shadows.

Davius left the docks, heading up towards the city. Their arrival and brief massacre had gone unnoticed, the streets empty as he walked. He was struck immediately by the graceful precision in the city's construction. Unlike Rome, Grecians worked with the natural topography to assemble their capital, columns and fortitude climbing up and down the mountainous landscape, all the way to the great Acropolis that loomed miles ahead. Even in the sparse moonlight, he could see tendrils of plants crawling down the smooth marble buildings and sprouting out of magnificent vases that depicted Athena in battle. Statues of the goddess were abundant throughout the streets, her watchful eyes affixed to her namesake city. Intricately designed temples were erected just as plentifully, strong Doric columns holding up terracotta roofs, with decorative acroteria standing at each point of pediment. The city looked strong and foreboding yet reflected the refined intellect of its people. Davius decided he approved of Lucius's recommendation to reside there.

He headed back to the beach, leaving the quiet metropolis behind him. The discarded bodies were still scattered across the rocky sand, the ocean waves that rolled over them threatening to drag them into the depths of her murky abyss. He assisted, lifting them one by one and placing them into the hungry sea. He watched as she swallowed the last of her meal, as a faint memory of water sacrifice surfaced in his mind.

It caused him to pause, realizing it had been long since he'd remembered anything distinctly from his human past. He pushed away the unwelcome thoughts, wondering instead what could be keeping his companion so long.

"Hello, Davius."

Startled, he whipped around to confront the unfamiliar voice, furious to be caught unaware.

What appeared to be a man stood before him, yet Davius could smell, taste, and feel humanity, and this creature was certainly not that. His body was deformed, hunched over as if weighed down by an invisible stone. A pair of coarsely castrated stumps protruded not only from his spiny back, but from his forehead, as if he was once a creature with not only the wings of a bird, but the horns of a goat - both severed simultaneously in a single act of cruelty. He stared at Davius through one perfectly blue eye, the other clouded over by a white film, an angry scar interrupting its almond shape. What might have been soft golden hair now looked like straw, laying unkempt about his shoulders. He looked like a being who had seen many battles, an aged warrior carrying the weight of a lifetime's worth of war.

"Who are you, and how do you know my name?" Davius demanded.

"I have visited you once before, in another one of my guises."

"The boar," Davius remembered, recalling the peculiarity of his eyes.

The creature smiled, revealing a set of sharp teeth similar to Davius, which took him aback. "My name is Libraean," he said, "I help preserve the balance between two worlds. I have much to tell you before your master comes."

Davius laughed at his audacity. "I have no master."

The creature who called himself Libraean apologized with a humble nod. "My intention was not to insult you, Davius. I do not socialize much and often forget the connotations behind words. Please, come, follow me."

He darted off with speed similar to what Davius had grown accustomed to using. Davius considered his request for only a moment before dashing after him. Within minutes, they arrived at a cave nestled in the rugged mountains, its mouth high above the roaring sea where no human being could hope to enter. The waters crashed against the jagged rocks below, sending up a soft spray of salty mist upon their faces.

Libraean gestured him inside.

The womb of the cave was warm and inviting, a low fire still burning between a cozy heap of blankets and a table laden with eating utensils. The walls were bare, the light from the flames casting shadows against the russet colored rock.

Libraean moved to stoke it, and Davius noticed the shabbiness of his tunic underneath his fraying cloak. His feet were wrapped in makeshift boots of winding leather straps that seemed far too bulky for comfort.

"This is your dwelling?" he asked, breaking the silence.

Libraean nodded. "It is quiet here, a comfortable place to pass the time. As you may guess, I do not see much daylight. But I am content to be alone with my books." He gestured to a heap of loose parchment and handcrafted scrolls nestled under the shelf. They lay near a handmade stylus and a small clay jar of writing ink. "I write here, as well," he added.

He hobbled towards his bedding, procuring a pallet of sheepskin. He laid it out next to the fire, across from where he sat. "Please, sit," he invited, settling down onto his heap of blankets.

Davius accepted, his near proximity and the growing flames offering a better view of the unusual creature before him. Besides the peculiarity of his eyes and his blunted horns, he could have passed for human, his weathered face once undeniably handsome. "Why have you brought me here?" he asked him.

Libraean sighed, gazing into the fire. "I warned you once before about Lucius, but you failed to heed my plea. Now that you are one of us, I must elaborate further."

"One of us? You are an immortal?"

"I was once exactly what you are. Now I am simply this creature, the bitter manifestation of my failures." He looked down, unwinding the straps of his boots. He pulled one off, revealing not a human's foot, but a large cloven hoof. "My deformities are my penance in this world."

Davius peered at him curiously. "Who created you?"

"None other than Lucius," he replied, pulling off the other boot and reclining so that his hooves warmed by the crackling fire.

Davius was shocked.

"You were not the first creation as Lucius claims," he continued. "He once told you of his true nature, but he did not divulge everything. Lucius was a dark god as he said, but what he left out was that there is also a god of light, a god who transcended him in power. This humans' preference of this other god infuriated Lucius, who began a campaign to realign the loyalties of an evolving populace back towards him. He created *daemons*, their sole purpose to stalk the earth creating chaos and misery, while compelling mages to wreak havoc in his name. Yet all of Lucius's efforts were in vain. The more fearful their world became, the more humans turned towards the god of light, the exact opposite reaction of what Lucius desired.

"Frustrated by his antics, the god of light banished him from the realm they both shared. The split forced two separate domains to be, one light and one dark, a summerland and an underworld, the latter where Lucius's spirit roamed, resentfully brainstorming a plan to be released. He longed to join the earthly plane, to be close to his cherished humanity. Many years passed before a woman was born with magic so powerful that she could raise his spirit into corporeal form. He came into this world imperfect, a *daemonic*, beastly creature who breathed fire, and it took masterful sorcery to transform him into something that could pass for human. When they finally succeeded, he immediately set out to create others in his image.

"I was his first attempt, but I was deeply flawed. In the beginning I acted just as you do now, Lucius's loyal, doting companion. Yet our era was not as civilized as it is now; I followed him through the blood-soaked battles and the violent massacres that waged between tribes. Lucius found pleasure in war, realizing that no greater thrill could be had by an abominable creature than spilling the blood of men in droves. We were unstoppable warriors, he and I, feared by humans who were forced to honor his name. Yet as time passed, my creation proved to be his ultimate failure.

"As more time lapsed, my nature reversed. Humanity crept back into my body, my soul started to clear. I felt pain, guilt, shame, remorse - human emotions and feelings. I could no longer bear to take innocent lives to fuel my own. I refused to leave our dwelling, fraught with painful memories and guilt over the pain I caused others. Disgusted and furious, Lucius eventually abandoned me.

"I knew I would not die quickly, for I was made so strong that it would take days of painful sunlight to rid the earth of my existence. But I was willing, wrapping myself around the trunk of a tree to await the dawn and my excruciating demise. But what came to me then was not the hellish burn of sunlight, but an angel, a creature that is the opposite of a *daemon*, who brings peace to mankind. They align themselves with the god of light. Where a daemon is shrouded in darkness, often deformed and antlered with the protruding bones of a starving animal, these angels glow with sublime radiance, their only deformity a pair of wings that enables them to soar through the skies like beautiful ethereal birds.

"This particular angel called himself Gabriel, and told me that if I should rebuke Lucius and his ways by working to restore the balance of good and evil upon earth, then I may die a peaceful death and spend eternity in the heavenly realm with the angels." He paused to smile at the memory. "The broken horns and ripped wings remind me of my own constant battle, for as much as the *daemonic* part of my body still yearns for the blood of humans, my soul must stay pure and on the path of goodness and light. They remind me I am part angel, part *daemon* for the rest of my days."

Davius frowned. "Why are you telling me all of this? I have no loyalty to a god of light. Besides, nothing in this world is truly good nor truly evil. So what if Lucius is a dark demigod in human likeness, he has told me all of this before."

"Did he tell you that you are the Daghda reincarnated? One of the most powerful gods in the Celtic pantheon? It is why you were able to manifest weather storms as a human. It is why you were strong enough to bear Lucius's forceful transformation."

"You speak of gods I have long forgotten," Davius murmured. For a moment, he saw the autumnal breeze tossing red and amber leaves around the forest floor, a circle of Druids dancing in celebration of a bountiful harvest.

Libraean nodded. "You have forgotten much in your conversion, but that does not negate the accuracy of my words. Gods reborn as humans do not recall their past lives, it is the curious law of this land. You are now an earthbound blood drinker, but you have the perfect strength of an incarnate god that can withstand the dark power that was given to you. That divine strength creates balance within you, your light combating your dark. You can tip the scales whichever way you decide. If you choose light, you will be the one to restore true balance to this earth, enabling its creatures to survive by sending Lucius back to his degenerate realm. You have a fortitude where I do not."

Davius scowled. "You are wasting your time. I have no desire to harm my friend."

"Did he tell you that you need not take a human life? That you can drink from them enough to satiate you, leaving them so disoriented that when they heal, they will not remember what has transpired?"

Davius blinked before finding his rebuttal. "I have accepted taking the life of humans. I feel no pity for them - they are prey, as the deer is to the wolf. Neither the wolf nor the deer are wrong or right, it is simply the natural cycle of life."

"That does not make it right," Libraean countered. "You are still bound by the same morality as us all."

"You speak to me of morality, yet you are the one who turned against the one who empowered you, who cherished you as his family." Davius snorted.

"I do not expect you to understand my motives, Davius, I only hoped to share with you my story, since we are now connected by blood. I was once plagued by blood dreams, the same one you had. They offered glimpses of Lucius's realm and his hideous denizens – that is not where you and I belong. But I know you are too new of a creature to feel as I do. I have suffered long as a result of my transgressions, for allowing the bloodlust to consume me. My work upon this earth is now to cast *daemons* out from it, restoring this realm's intended balance as best I can. It is the only way for my redemption. I wish to spare you my torment," the creature explained. "My early memories were also dim at first," he added. "But yours will come back, I assure you, and then you will be at a crossroads, as was I."

"How do you survive if you do not feed?" Davius interjected.

"You once saw me in the form that I take to eat. The boar seeks its prey in the form of small animals, not humans, a true part of nature's cycle, as you brought up, and therefore, acceptable. Soon I hope to eat real food again like humans do. That is what I have been promised - as long as I continue to fight the battle against darkness, the less of a creature I will become."

Davius sighed, rising to his feet and dusting himself free of the dirt from the cave floor. "I think I have heard quite enough."

"Please wait, there is more," Libraean pleaded. "Do you remember Gaia, who you loved so deeply as a mortal man?"

Davius froze, a wave of sorrow settling over him like morning frost. It was a foreign sensation to him in this life, an old familiar pain reacquainted. "How do you know of Gaia?"

"My records," the creature replied excitedly, pulling out scrolls from underneath his improvised table and sending the loose sheets of papyrus flying around the cave floor. "Not only do I slay daemons, but I keep extensive records of all that transpires between the earthly and spiritual realms. Every god, every goddess, every cult, every creature. Your coming was foretold to me and I have been watching you for quite some time."

"Rather invasive," Davius remarked.

"I apologize," Libraean faltered, realizing he'd gotten ahead of himself, and he shoved the scrolls back under the table. "My point is you chose to become like Lucius to avenge her death. Yet five years have passed, and her captor still lives. You have the power of an immortal, yet you waste it on gluttony and avarice."

Davius felt his anger rise. "Who are you to judge me on things you cannot possibly understand."

"I do not mean to upset you, Davius, only to beseech you," the creature pleaded, rising up to meet him, awkward on his cloven feet. "You may not feel the same sorrow you did as a human, but you will. And it will be this that will inevitably drive you to madness. You must return to Rome, find Nirus, and avenge the death of the mother of your child. You must, or it will haunt you for eternity."

Davius felt as if he'd been struck by a bolt of lightning. "The mother of my child?" he repeated incredulously.

Libraean's clear eye widened, his face paling with apprehension. "You did not know?"

"What? What did I not know?" Emotion overcame him, raw, visceral sensations he had not felt for a half a decade. He faltered on his feet, fluctuating between sorrow and inundated rage.

Libraean flew to him, taking his hands in his. The kind gesture surprised

Davius, but he gratefully accepted it, the creature's warm touch calming him. His unmarred eye swam with sympathy as he spoke. "Davius, she was with child when she died. It was yours...no other man had a chance to take her."

Davius fell to his knees. His mind raced, distant memories now painfully vivid - he could smell her, taste the sweetness of her skin, see the gentle bounce of her rose golden hair. He recalled his shattered dreams of a lifetime together, children they would never bear frolicking through the countryside, running into his arms. Liquid amassed around his eyes, and when he wiped them, he realized he was not crying tears, but the hideous black blood that now ran through his cadaverous veins. He swept them away in disgust.

"You must avenge her, Davius," Libraean's gentle voice broke through. "It is the only way. I am so sorry to have brought you this pain."

Davius met his eyes, too heavy-hearted to make words.

"There is one last thing I must tell you, for your new companion is the master of lies. He will tell you that only he can create others like you, but you have that same power. You are able to do exactly as he, but do not succumb to the temptation. For creating another blood drinker will only bring more pain and suffering in the end, for not all beings can withstand and bear the metamorphosis like you could. Avenge your love, Davius," he pressed. "Free yourself of his presence."

"I must go," Davius decided. He didn't wish to hear anything else out of the creature's mouth. Libraean tried to protest, but Davius dove from the mouth of the cave, darting over the churning ocean and back to the docks in a single, flying swoop. He fell to his knees as he landed on the sand.

Above he could hear the call of seagulls, a sound that was eerily similar to the screech of crows.

He looked down the beach to see their ship, where dozens of revenant slaves were unloading their belongings. He rose to his feet, heading towards them.

Lucius, who had been quietly supervising, turned to greet him. He frowned at his disheveled appearance. "Davius, whatever is the matter?"

"I am not sure where to begin," he replied with a sigh.

"Come," Lucius beckoned with concern. "Allow me to show you our new dwelling, then we can talk."

Lucius's home was far from what Davius had imagined. It was large, yet not overwhelming, constructed of humble mud brick and topped by a plain stucco roof. Its facade was entirely barren, the smooth exterior concrete interrupted only by a single door and two windows that had been boarded up with pine. It was nestled behind several tall, unused buildings to provide shade during daylight hours.

The inside, however, revealed the uninhibited extravagance he had become accustomed to with his friend. Every tile that lined the floors had been arranged into dizzying patterns, frescoes depicting both the Greek and Egyptian gods covered each wall in fantastically vivid colors, an unusual mix of hieroglyphics and Latin scrawled beneath each depiction. The rooms were filled with empty tables plated with gold, patiently waiting to be adorned by Lucius's extensive pottery collection. The revenants had already unpacked many of their belongings, adding modern flavor to the Grecian finery Lucius had left behind. Davius explored the rooms, noticing that the addition of Roman busts and vases complimented his eclectic miscellany nicely.

His conversation with Libraean and the emotion that it evoked drifted away easily as he moved through the house, the familiar comforts of home bringing him back to his reality. He was calm again, watching the light of a hundred silver wall sconces dance across the ghostly slaves as they gradually pieced the house together. Lucius appeared, handing him a goblet similar to his, brimming with blood infused wine.

Davius sipped it gratefully, for it had been hours since he'd fed.

"Well, what do you think?" Lucius asked him.

"I noticed you took great pains to assure that we would remain hidden," Davius commented.

Lucius frowned, thinking he was disappointed. "Come now," he said, placing a delicate hand on his shoulder. "I know this is not how we lived in Rome, but we must make do. When I lived here many years ago, I wanted to remain hidden. Unfortunately, we must live that way again, lest we bring any unnecessary attention to our presence."

"I know, my dear brother, I was only chiding you." Davius patted his hand reassuringly.

Lucius looked relieved. "Come, let me show off the dining hall. You will love it - it will remind you of Rome."

He led him down the main corridor to a vast chamber lined with couches, creating a rectangular border around a single elongated table. Candelabras set in gold cluttered every corner, draped with deep purple fabric. The table left no room for platters of food but was instead covered with exquisite ivory carvings of *daemonic* creatures and glossy black pottery. Davius lifted a sculpture of a particularly repulsive looking beast, its face a distortion of manic laughter, with a lengthy, protruding tongue flopping out of its mouth and oddly situated, bulging eyes. He laughed at the absurdity of it. "Where on earth did you find something like this?"

"It is from my past, far before we met. Is it not lovely?" He lifted the sculpture out of his hands to admire it himself, before setting it down lovingly amongst the other oddities. "Come, there is more." He gestured for Davius to follow as he maneuvered down the hallway.

Davius complied, surprised that the farther they walked, the larger the home seemed to be. Room after room unfolded until they reached a final hallway that led to a sizable unopened door. Lucius paused before he pushed it open, adding exaggerated flourish as he revealed what was hidden behind it.

Davius gasped despite himself. It was a garden so exquisite that it rivaled any that he could remember in Rome, save for the absence of the customary open atrium that allowed sunlight to stream through. Instead the ceiling was covered with translucent fabric, permitting enough moonlight to filter through to coax the plethora of nocturnal plants below it into blossom. At the center of the garden stretched an enormous pool, tendrils of bougainvillea wrapping its lovely fingers around the granite borders. Bursts of exotic jasmine complimented the two great fountains that flanked the pool, both fashioned after the Greek god Pan, two chubby little nymphs with mischievous smiles and horned foreheads, complete with tiny cloven feet. They poured water into the pool from smooth black vases, the streams catching the speckled starlight that peeked through from above.

Davius couldn't help but grin, recalling a conversation he once had with Lucius, where he made the comment that although they were wealthy enough to partake, they would never be able to use the customary Roman bath houses, lest they burst into flames. How it must have pained Lucius to keep such a secret from him.

"Shall we?" Lucius grinned.

He nodded, and slaves appeared at Lucius's beckoning. They undressed, draping their garments over the outstretched arms of the exsanguinous, vacant-eyed slaves before entering the steaming bath. It was large enough that they could sit across from each other comfortably, the water churning around them pleasantly tepid.

Lucius stretched as one of the revenants retrieved his goblet of blood wine. Tendrils of long black hair slithered in the water around him.

Davius relaxed, enjoying the sensation of warm water against the chill of his skin. Steam soon rose up copiously around them, threatening to smother the inflorescent plants that crowded the room. A single bud of jasmine fell from one of the bushes, becoming a dancing white star as it chased the swirls of moonlight sparkling across the water's surface. Davius caught it in his hand, examining its tender construct as he inhaled its sweet scent. He frowned, the aroma wrenching the memory back into the forefront of his mind, the smell of Gaia's skin, the sound of her twinkling laughter. He threw the flower away from him in frustration.

"Davius, you must tell me what troubles you so," Lucius implored him, observing the shift in his mood.

Davius cast his eyes downward, unsure of how to proceed. He decided upon honesty. "I met Libraean."

Lucius's eyes widened with surprise. "I have not heard that name in many years."

"So what he says is true? That I was not your first successful protege, it was actually him?"

Lucius sighed, setting his goblet on the edge of the pool. "He was not a success."

Davius stared at him wordlessly, an intentional gesture meant for him to continue.

"I told you that I tried to make others like us but could never quite achieve it. Libraean was not a human when I met him; he was a halfling, a beast with the attributes of a man, like a centaur or the god Pan." He gestured to the statues behind them. "He was like that before I transformed him with my blood, and I believe that was a part of my failure."

"He seems to think his disfigurement is a penance for his transgressions."

Lucius snorted in disgust. "He was always carrying on about good and evil, how feeding on humans was the epitome of immorality. There is no stark dichotomy in this realm or any other, those polar oppositions are an inconsistent human construct. If he chooses to live his immortal days as a self-righteous martyr, then that is his business. I have no room in my life for erroneous absolutes." The water around him began to bubble, heat expelling from his skin as he spat out his words. "Did he tell you that he kills *daemons?* That he serves a god of light? I am sure he filled your head with all sorts of nonsense. The god of light is another foolish concept, a being who has never taken corporeal form. The idea of it, apparently, is beneath him. But although he holds himself in such high esteem, he is just as capable of flaws and egotism as any other manmade god. God of light, indeed," he snorted.

"He said that you created *daemons* as a way of punishing humans for worshipping that god, instead of you."

"Utter nonsense! *Daemons* and angels, nymphs and centaurs, dragons and harpies, chimeras and sirens - they are all manifested out of the minds of humans. No god creates an otherworldly creature. They align themselves however they wish. Fortunately, most of them align themselves with me."

"So my creation is not part of some vendetta between you and this god whom you oppose?" Davius pressed.

Lucius's golden eyes smoldered against the dense haze surrounding them. "Absolutely not, I have yet to even meet him. I really wish you would have alerted me to this conversation you were having in my absence."

Davius didn't respond. He retrieved his own goblet from where it stood and sipped it, wincing slightly as he realized it had cooled. "He also told me something about Gaia."

"Oh?" Lucius relaxed, grateful for the change in subject. "You have not spoken of her in years."

Davius swallowed, hoping the human emotions plaguing him earlier would remain buried. He finished his glass, trusting the blood would help him keep his wits about him. "He told me that she was with child when she died...my child."

"Is it true?"

"I do not know. It could very well be. He also mentioned the gods of my youth. He said the reason that I am able to bear the power you have given me is because I am the Daghda, reincarnated."

Lucius looked at him solemnly. "That I believe to be true. It is what your father supposed, which is why he offered you to me so easily. He believed that by me granting you immortality that it would empower your gods, carrying them into many generations to follow, eventually leading to eternal power for your people."

Davius was stunned. "I never felt like a reincarnated god when I was human."

Lucius laughed. "Of course not. Humans have a strange way of ignoring the obvious. Your father did not have time to teach you the secrets of the Druids, but you know sorcery all the same. You bent the weather to your will and invoked the protection of the Morrigan as a child. You have always been powerful, even before I gifted this new power to you."

Davius let the information settle before he offered his thoughts. "I think I would like to avenge Gaia's death," he said finally. "I believe that murdering her assailants will help me to put my human life behind me. I have no interest in anything the halfling said. He seemed misguided by his own wayward bias. Please understand, I have fully embraced this path and believe our life is wonderful, but I do not think I can rest until I have tasted the flesh of that wretch that calls himself Nirus."

Lucius nodded, surprising Davius with his easy persuasion. "Then we shall," he agreed. "But returning to Rome is out of the question. We cannot risk another voyage, Davius."

"I know you do not enjoy the speed by which we can travel on foot, but there may be another way. I have an idea if you would be open to it."

"Of course."

Davius sat forward, sending a wave across the bath. "If what you have told me is true, I have brought the Celtic gods here simply by my presence, since I am a Druid, the most spiritual sect of my people, the truest believers. I should be able to invoke the Morrigan, the shapeshifting goddess, as I did long ago when I arrived in Rome and ask her if she will aid us in our journey."

"Amazing." Lucius was genuinely impressed.

Davius's heart pumped in excitement at the notion, grateful for Lucius's compliance.

"What will we need?"

"We must wait until the Dark Moon, the evening before the moon transitions into her New Phase," he explained. "We will need the blood of our foes, dozens of crow feathers, and as many red and black stained candles as can be found. We can call her here, right in this bath, for water arouses her interest."

"You remember this alchemy from your childhood?" Lucius asked, mystified.

"These rituals, these ideas...they live deep in my mind, as if I have always known them. They never disappeared with my transformation but remain dormant until I have use for them."

Lucius clapped his hands together, the sharp crack echoing throughout the steamy chamber. "Then it is settled! We shall have your ritual, Davius. I do hope it works, I have not seen the Dark Goddess in many eons. I look forward to her presence once more."

"He wakes."

"He is no longer human."

"Disgusting."

"Stop, he will hear you."

Davius opened his eyes to a collection of images distorted by blurred vision. He blinked, realizing his mind was just as muddled, a fog of disarray preventing his senses from grasping his surroundings. A dream? He hadn't dreamt since his transformation.

He realized both his arms and legs were shackled to a post erected at the crux of a giant wheel. Furious, he pulled at his bounds, but his strength, supernatural as it was, failed him. As throes of frustration burned the cobwebs from his mind, his eyes adjusted, and he was able to make out four creatures surrounding him in each direction.

"You are in the astral plane, an intermediary space between the realms," a luminescent man with white wings explained to him, a trace smile at his lips. He held a book lovingly in his arms. The word angel came to mind, Davius recognizing the term from his conversation with Libraean.

"We brought you here to help you," an enlarged eagle to the right of the man continued, staring at him earnestly with warm ochre eyes.

"To offer you the tools you will need for your spell," chimed in a lion to the right of him, his own set of wings stretching out behind his flaxen mane.

"For you invoking the Morrigan's aid is but a part of a greater plan," finished a similarly bewinged bull who brought the circle of extraordinary beings to a close.

An incandescent blue surrounded them all, interrupted only by swirling pearls of clouds, as if they all hovered weightlessly in the zenith of the sky. The wheel at his feet was a smooth, sparkling amethyst reminiscent of polished marble, gilded lettering corrupting its immaculate surface. Davius was unable to decipher the symbols, the language foreign to him. He watched as one of the ideograms moved, coiling itself into the shape of a snake, its thin body rippling as it made its way to where he stood.

"You do not need to understand the words. You are a monster, anyway," it hissed, a tiny bifurcated tongue flitting out towards him with derisive disdain.

"Enough, Typhon," sighed another creature who also seemed to materialize from the symbols etched on the wheel. It moved towards Davius, a box grasped between his hands.

Davius had never seen a creature like it before, presenting the muscular body of a man but with the head of a coal black jackal. Radiant jewels lay on his chest and gold wrapped his arms. "I am Anubis," he offered, holding up the box for Davius to see. "Within this chest holds the power that you were promised, one of the six elements required to manifest ultimate power on the earthly realm. Your father has already endowed you with four. Since you have heeded the advice of the Libraean, we have decided to honor your father's dying request and offer you this."

Davius observed the same glowing script scrawled across the box as the floor, this one in a shape resembling a cross but with a loop replacing the top arm.

"I know we are not the gods you are accustomed to, but our motives are the same." The mouth on the jackal face stretched upwards into a grin, a gesture intended to be friendly, but giving the opposite effect as it revealed acute carnivorous teeth.

"Do not be afraid," the shimmering man said in his soft voice.

"We all work together here," the lion assured him.

Davius was too dumbfounded to struggle as Anubis edged closer. The snake Typhon hissed his displeasure as the jackal man before him slowly pulled the jaws of the box apart. It opened with a wail, black smoke escaping from its prison with gusto before assaulting the creature before it. Davius choked as the piceous vapor forced its way into his lungs through his mouth and nose, smothering him with its invasion. He was powerless to stop it, succumbing to its assault as the creatures and the wheel vanished, and darkness enveloped every one of his senses.

He awakened to see Lucius standing above him, watching him intently. He looked past where he stood, the length of the surrounding candles revealing that it was well into the evening. Davius threw off his silk blankets, an unusual grogginess disorienting him as he tried to move.

"You still dream?" Lucius asked curiously, stepping backwards to offer him room to pull himself together. It appeared that he had been perched over him for quite some time, like a patient bird of prey, his goblet in one hand and a slender candle in the other, dripping wax in tiny pools on the floor. Davius noticed he was oddly well-groomed for the late hour, his curls neatly combed and fastened at the nape of his neck, his rich violet robes pressed and clean, accented by silver hardware.

"I have not dreamt until this night," Davius replied, the events of his strange experience slowly trickling back into his consciousness.

"Interesting." Lucius handed him the goblet that was in his hand, which he gulped down hastily, grateful it still had its warmth. "Are you ready for our ritual?" he asked when he finished, an air of excitement buzzing around him.

Davius remembered their plan. It was the night of the dark moon. He sprang up from his bed, hastily draping around his frame the toga he'd laid out prior. He shook the persistent fogginess from his mind.

"I prepared everything as you instructed," Lucius informed him as the two hurried down the hall. The house was fully illuminated in preparation for their guest, revenant slaves standing idly in each hallway, awaiting instruction. Two had been situated at the entryway to the bathhouse, and they tugged open the giant door at the sight of their approach.

The room scintillated from the flames of dozens of black and crimson candles, set in standing candelabras that surrounded the length of the onyx pool. The flickering light animated the twin Pan fountains, whose playful smiles stretched into manic grins, their marble eyes glittering in wicked delight.

Davius caught the scent of human blood, mixing pleasantly with the aroma of flowering jasmine. It drew his eyes to the forefront of the chamber where an altar had been stationed. It was draped with red fabric and crow feathers, with a silver bowl, knife, and cup resting upon it, patiently awaiting use. Tied to a post near the altar was a trembling man, stripped completely nude.

His terrified eyes caught theirs and his body instinctively recoiled. Davius recognized him immediately. It was one of Nirus's soldiers, the exact one who had stabbed Gaia, years ago. Amazed, he spun around to look at Lucius. "However did you find him?"

"I petitioned a *daemon*," he explained, proud of his guile. "Although their guise is convincing, *daemons* are not corporeal beings; they can dissolve from one place and appear in another. It makes them the perfect tool for transporting desired items."

"Good to know," Davius commented. He laid an affectionate hand on Lucius's narrow shoulder. "Thank you, my friend."

"Please - please let me go," the man interrupted them. "I did not mean to kill all those girls - they were only slaves, I would never hurt a real woman."

"We should silence him," Davius suggested.

Lucius snapped his bony fingers together and one of the slaves moved to gag their cowering captive. He turned back to Davius. "Shall we begin?"

Davius nodded.

He lowered himself to his knees before the altar, memories of past sacrifices surfacing, moments in time surrounded by the hum of nature. Anticipation gripped him as he wondered if he could still invoke his power as he once did so long ago, the happenings of his dream filling him with doubt.

He closed his eyes and inhaled, quieting his racing mind. He sharpened his ears to the muffled pleading of the gagged man, the trickling water fountains, the seasonal locusts singing outside the walls. He imagined the fields of Gaul, the lush and fragrant woods, the cool wet grass beneath his feet. He saw the stars painted across the sky, the shrill call of cicadas, moonbeams, and roasting fires. He saw the burning wickerman, its flames licking the sky, while Druid priests, cloaked in white, chanted in harmony with the circling crows, who cawed in anticipation of fresh carrion.

He was there.

Power reverberated in him more intensely than ever before, extending outwards, air rushing around them as if a tiny storm waged within the chamber. It threatened to extinguish the surrounding flames, but Lucius hurried to keep them lit with his own endowment of fire. The bath water churned, funneling into a massive whirlpool, ripping the flowers off their vines with its intensity, scattering the crow feathers across the room.

"The Morrigan!" Davius called out, the strength of his voice matching the raging wind. "I summon you upon this night. I hail you for your ferocity and beauty, she who destroys her enemies without mercy, come to your humble denizen!" He envisioned her magnificent violence through a child's eyes, standing amongst a beach of shredded corpses, her black dress and raven hair billowing behind her. He recalled her voice, the brilliance of her crystal blue eyes. She smiled in his memory, as crows circled their mother in a perfect spiral dance.

Davius rose to his feet in a trance, calmly taking the cowering prisoner by the neck with one hand. He lifted him high, slicing his throat with the fingernails of the opposite hand. Blood poured from the wound profusely, splattering his altar and gathering in the cup and bowl. "For you, my love," he whispered, tossing the draining corpse into the open mouth of the churning watery vortex.

Suddenly, the bathhouse was alive with hundreds of ravens that seemed to materialize out of nothingness, their sleek obsidian bodies a whirling tornado, blackening out the entire chamber in a flurry of feathers. Davius maintained his composure amongst the turbulence, silently focusing on the dark funnel the water created until it opened to reveal a silhouette that rose out of the swirling mere. The corvids circled in closer, conglomerating into the sinuous shape of a woman.

Then, in an instant, all was silent.

The upended objects which had joined the windstorm fell to the ground, the flowerless plants relaxed, and the pool lay still. Blossoms and feathers slowly drifted downwards from the torn open ceiling.

The Morrigan stood, in her maiden aspect, before them. She presented a stunning figure wrapped in a thin black dress, sharp collarbones exposed, thick waves of raven hair pouring down her shoulders and curling at her breasts. A delicate diadem of corvid bones lay across her forehead, the beak of a crow skull resting between a pair of brilliant azure eyes. Her bare arms were artfully sculpted and wrapped in silver bracelets, thin black tattoos interrupting her creamy alabaster skin. Her face was hard and narrow, high sculpted cheekbones softened only slightly by the radiant sparkle of her eyes and her long black lashes. Her lips were a moist blood red, pursed in annoyance as she spoke. "Yes?" she asked, impatiently.

Davius realized he had been staring rudely, completely transfixed by her image.

"Morrigan," Lucius's voice broke the silence to greet her, moving forward from his stance behind Davius. "Welcome, dark goddess."

"You," she startled upon recognition of him. "You accomplished what could not be."

"I have," he said proudly.

"What is this place?" She looked around her as the rain of feathers finally ceased, a few landing peacefully on the blanket of her hair.

"My home in Greece. The bathhouse, more specifically." Lucius moved closer, keeping steady as his feet slid on the blood smeared marble.

Davius watched her gaze move away from Lucius and lock onto him, her eyes widening in similar astonishment. "And you." A smile slid her swollen lips upwards. "I remember you."

Her bewitching gaze disarmed him, the residual power from his sorcery still twitching throughout his body, his muscles in gentle spasm. "You look different than I remember," he commented, wondering why he had never noticed her allure before.

She laughed, the pitch reminiscent of her beloved crows. "I can shift into many forms, sweet Daghda. I am certain some dormant part of you remembers."

Davius blushed despite himself, still unable to peel his eyes away from her.

"Perhaps we should move somewhere more comfortable," Lucius interrupted, blatantly eager to have her attention back on him.

"Why have you summoned me?" she ignored him, her eyes still fixed upon Davius. "Most do not call upon me unless it is to aid them in battle. There is no war here. I have traveled a long way at your command."

Davius faltered only slightly before finding his words. "We need your help to exact revenge."

"Wonderful," she cooed with satisfaction, approaching him with careful footsteps. Her pale thighs flashed through the open slit of her wrapped dress, her feet bare, absorbing the carmine spillage from the floor.

He could smell her now, the raw scent of heated skin, the autumn woods, and the smoky embers of a dying fire. He felt as if he'd known her long before this lifetime, once kissed her earth-caked lips and caressed her narrow curves.

She reached out to touch his face, her hand warm against the coolness of his skin. "You are not human," she observed.

Lucius interjected once more, visibly dismayed by their interaction. "He is my creation, an immortal human graced with the power of a god. He is like I am, my companion in this world."

"Companion," she echoed, finally tearing her eyes away from Davius, studying Lucius now with equal curiosity. "You have found a way for a god to become flesh, but still maintain our power. Impressive."

Lucius beamed. "Well, there are a few stipulations, but yes, I have. Please, let us be freed from this chamber," he urged. "Let us enjoy the night air."

Morrigan acquiesced, and a raven that had been perched on one of the fountain statues swooped down to land on her shoulder, its intense black eyes affixed on them both.

Lucius led them out into the courtyard, the warm summer air trickling through the garden flora. The absent moon allowed the stars to sparkle brilliantly in the dark sky, freckling the ground with their glow. He gestured for them to sit on engraved stone benches, upholstered with patterned fabric stuffed with wool. A few revenants appeared, lighting the torches around them. One handed Lucius his signature goblet before bowing back into the shadows.

Davius noticed that Morrigan was translucent in the light, not the solid form he had originally understood her to be. He wondered how he had been able to smell her and feel her caress, as if she were physically standing before him.

Regardless of her solidity, she sat gracefully on the bench, her thin legs popping out of her skirt as she crossed them. Her delicate feet were still stained with crimson, and he found himself imagining the act of running his tongue along their slender arches, lapping up the remains. She smiled, noticing his gaze.

"Now to business," Lucius declared, after taking a sip of his brimming cup. "Morrigan, my companion has called upon you to ask if you would aid us in exacting revenge against a man called Nirus. He resides in Rome, many miles away from here by sea. Currently, Rome is a treacherous place for us, so we humbly ask for your guidance regarding shape-shifting, as your abilities transcend any other god among us."

She enjoyed the compliment. "Do you wish to travel as ravens?"

Lucius nodded. "If possible. We need to enter Rome unseen, end the human's life, and leave hastily without arousing suspicion or causing any unneeded disturbance."

She considered his words. "And what exactly are you now? Are you bound by human laws?"

"We are immortal blood drinkers, earthbound gods, if you will," Lucius replied. "We can move with the speed of lightning and our strength exceeds that of ten men. Our only imperfections are that we cannot withstand sunlight and we must feed off the blood of living creatures to survive."

"Fascinating."

Davius observed the slightest hint of color blushing his friend's hollow cheeks.

"I can wield the element of fire at my command," he continued, "while Davius seems to have dominion over the wind."

She nodded, turning towards Davius with adoring appraisal. "Aye, Daghda has always been the master of weather."

"Ah, yes," Lucius cleared his throat, visibly uncomfortable. "So, to answer your question, we do have our select godly powers, but are bound by a few earthly restrictions."

Morrigan shifted in her seat, the raven at her shoulder suddenly flying off to survey their new perch. "You were quite brazen to turn one of ours, Lucius," she remarked, gesturing with her eyes towards Davius. "You are lucky Lugh knows nothing of this."

"He was given to me by one of your shamans, Morrigan. The boy's father."

"But still," she sighed. "And you, Daghda, do you ever speak?"

Davius, who had been perfectly content remaining silent as he observed their exchange, cleared his own throat. "I do."

"Then what do you have to say about what is being proposed?"

"Years ago, I was a mortal man, happily in love," he began. "However, my lover and I were both bound to slavery, and when our affair was discovered by our master, he nearly murdered me and sold her to a vile human being with a lustful penchant for torture. It was in his home that she met her demise and I swore a blood oath over her grave that I would one day have my revenge. As you can probably guess, much has transpired since that night."

She nodded as she listened, her lovely eyes swimming with empathy.

"I regret having called upon you for something so trivial. An immortal soul should not feel lingering human emotion, but I still do. I fear I will never be whole, never able to fully embrace this new life unless I honor the oath I made."

She gave him a gentle smile. "You do not have to apologize to me for matters of the heart, sweet Daghda. I understand these things much more than is known." She turned to face Lucius. "What made you this way, what turned you into earthbound immortals?"

Lucius perked up, grateful to have the focus back on him. "It was a very dear friend of mine, the most powerful spellcaster on earth, long ago in a land that they now call Dacia. She summoned me with her sorcery, and I rose to earth in a beastly guise. It took formidable manifestation on her behalf to deliver me out of that form into one that was human, but she was able. Well, something like a human, anyway."

"And how did she accomplish it?" Morrigan pressed.

Lucius stole a glance at Davius, mindful of his words. "She lured a man into the cave where she kept me hidden, ridding him of his human soul so that mine could enter. And here I am." He made a gesture of satisfaction.

Morrigan looked thoughtful, linking her fingers together at her knee as she weighed her decision. "I will honor your request," she said, finally. "Yet, after it is done, and your vengeance is satisfied, I want to be made into one of you."

Lucius let out a sound of surprise. "Why would you want such a thing?" he asked, incredulously. "You are a perfect goddess, adored by your followers."

Suddenly her face hardened, the slight clench of her jaw increasing the severity of her angular features. "I am summoned to war, yet I am never a part of it. I soar above the battlefields, inhaling the carrion soured air and blood-soaked earth, but never can I touch it. I long to walk amongst them, to feel the true exertion of a violent campaign."

"My dear, you sound very much as I once did," Lucius said adoringly.

"Then you will honor my request."

"We shall," Davius replied firmly for him.

Morrigan's eyes flickered in his direction.

"But we do not have the means to do so," Lucius objected. "My friend has long since passed, and it would take time to trace her bloodline. And even so, it is a gamble whether any of her children developed into a sorceress as powerful as she."

"I will do it," Davius declared. "I can easily work magic, as a human or as an immortal, and if I truly am the reincarnation of a god, then I am far more powerful than any common spellcaster. We will honor the Morrigan's request."

Lucius stared at him, speechless.

Morrigan grinned and rose to her feet, beckoning her crow with a shrill caw. It swooped down to her, landing gracefully on her extended arm. It arched up its wings obediently, allowing her to gently remove two long feathers from its slender shape. She handed them to Lucius, who had been sitting in silence, an expression of defeat painted across his face.

"Upon the night of your vengeance, you will each hold one of my feathers close," she instructed them. "Envision the raven, feel the air pummeling your face as you soar the vast and empty skies. Your body will transform, and you will maintain your new appearance for as long as you wish. But do not lose this feather, for if you do, you will not be able to evoke the magic again to bring you back home."

Davius took one of her hands, her skin still warm, but slippery as it lost its tangibility. "Thank you."

Morrigan smiled as she slowly pulled away. Her apparition was fading, the foliage of the courtyard now visible through her form. "Our lands call to me, Daghda, and I must listen. Remember your promise to me. It is a great honor that I have just gifted you."

"You have my eternal gratitude," he replied earnestly.

The wind picked up around them and she stepped backwards, letting it lift and twirl her skirts and hair until it created a swirling shroud of black around her. Her companion crow shrieked and was joined by the rest of its murder, their piercing calls resounding throughout the court-yard. She left the two creatures with one final smile before her figure dissolved into dozens of tiny black bodies, joining the rest to disappear seamlessly into the night.

"And she is gone once more," Davius commented softly, watching the night sky absorb the corvidian cloud. He turned to look at Lucius.

His expression startled him, his handsome features distorted into a menacing grimace. "You promised her what we cannot give," he snapped.

"I will work the magic," Davius assured him, surprised at his venom.

"You may be powerful, Davius, but your hubris has blinded you. You cannot create immortals as I can. I have told you, they must be human first or terrible things can occur. We cannot just go about making other gods corporeal - it is madness!"

Davius was silent. The events of his dream danced in his mind, creating a tarantella along with the recollection of Libraean's words. Ah, dear brother, but I can create others as you, he thought.

Lucius rose to his feet, angrily sweeping the trails of his robes behind him. His eyes burned a ferocious gold as he glared at him. "This is your mistake. This will be yours to resolve. You can invoke the wrath of the Morrigan by disappointing her all by yourself. I want no part of it." He stormed into the house, slamming the door shut behind him.

Davius sighed. He looked up, noticing the brilliance of the stars had peaked, signaling the approach of dawn. His body was tired, the power that had risen in him earlier now dissipated entirely. He found himself unsettled that Libraean's unsolicited presaging had come true. Although he had no distinct memories of it, if he was a reincarnated god, that meant he was an equal counterpart to Lucius, with the same abilities and power. Lucius was blatantly lying to him. Perhaps the notion of impartiality threatened him, provoking his visceral, furious response. He sighed again, rising to his feet. Daylight approached and his body called for rest.

London, 1857

RAIN HAMMERED ON THE ROOFTOPS, running in streams down the ashen windows of the parlor. Thunder grumbled in the distance, the occasional crack of lightning flashing ominously over the plot of gravestones below. David moved back from the window, crossing over the room to where she sat.

She had finished her meal and was now curled up on the loveseat nearest to the fireplace, completely wrapped in the wool blanket he provided for her earlier. Color had crept back into her face, the narrow slant of her jawline barely visible above the blanket's folds. David was once again struck by her unusual beauty, imprisoned by ravaging sickness. Her expression was fixed with intrigue as she peered up at him with wide, grey-blue eyes. "Did you do it?" she asked. "Did you shapeshift into ravens?"

He nodded, moving towards a glass decanter of scotch situated on the end table, a purposeless arrangement he kept up for appearance's sake. He removed the glass stopper and sniffed it, hoping it hadn't grown rancid with neglect. Satisfied, he drained the amber liquid into a glass and handed it to her.

She accepted it wordlessly, her slender arm snaking out from beneath the thick blanket.

He resumed his seat across from her, his eyes following the swirling floral patterns of the parlor's claret wallpaper. "I cannot find words to accurately describe the sensation of shifting into a body that is not your own," he said honestly, resuming his tale. "It was nearly as painful as my immortal transformation, yet it was a dull and throbbing pain, a sensation very much like being squeezed. Once the process was over, however, Lucius and I soared easily through the skies, our travel only lasting a mere handful of hours. It was both strange and wonderful to see the sun again, to bask in its warmth without fearing the flame. Once we arrived in Rome, we perched and waited until nightfall before returning to our former residence. We found our home much like the rest of the city, in shambles. What little furnishings Lucius had been able to part with when we left had either been stolen or shattered to pieces.

"She was waiting for us when we arrived, draped across a pile of tapestries that our ransacking thieves had apparently deemed invaluable. She collected us lovingly to her chest, whispering incantations until our bodies shifted back into their rightful proportions."

"Morrigan waited for you there?"

"Yes. She neglected to inform us of that part during our conversation. Apparently, she had decided we required supervision. We were grateful for it, for both of us ached from the exertion, Lucius collapsing to the ground, gasping for breath. She waited patiently for us to regain our senses before offering us the clothing she had found around the house. I could still taste the salty air in my mouth, my senses still buzzing with avian intensity."

"My God," she murmured, taking a sip from her glass. A thought occurred to her suddenly. "Do you require rest?"

David smiled. "I don't need much sleep, but I will indulge in it during the daylight hours to pass the time. At the current moment, I have your company for that."

Satisfied with his response, she returned the smile, reaching for the end table to procure one of his rolled cigarettes. "Please continue then."

"Rome, as I mentioned before, was in complete disarray. Weeks of rioting had ruined her aesthetic beauty, the aftermath of Caesar's assassination settling over the city like a malevolent fog that choked its citizens, many of whom stowed away in fear that chaos would erupt again. The Roman Republic was shattered, the furious and grief-stricken lower class now a force to be reckoned with. Roman patricians with no overt political affiliations maintained their daily affairs quietly in the background, those who either criticized or supported Caesar were nowhere to be found. Many, like us, found refuge in Greece, others in Rome's many territories.

"Nirus, an open supporter of Caesar, was hidden in the home of his daughter, Delicia, who usurped him in his weakness as head of his estate. It only took a little digging to discover his whereabouts, for the household still demanded its frequent supply of fresh slave girls from the local trader.

"Although we were surprised at Morrigan's initial appearance, she left us alone to our conspiring, her specter fading in and out over the course of the next few days, playing the part of the perpetual overseer. Even though Delicia's gender rendered many weary, she soon won over most of Rome's affluent society, obstinately throwing dinner parties in the wake of the recent disaster. She chose to inhabit the home of none other than Eridus, whose murder had never been solved. With no heir nor family to claim his estate, the purchase price was reasonable, and Nirus had snatched it up expeditiously in the hopes of running his own lucrative winery. He ended up being unsuccessful, the once lush vineyards a desert of brambles and shriveled vines stretching beyond the desolating property. Upon his spurious disappearance shortly after, Delicia assumed complete authority of the villa, eager to bring to life the rich soil that had once proven so fruitful.

"She called a meeting of investors and the quiet allies of her father to her home, with the promise of a grand Roman feast, the likes of which hadn't been seen for months. It piqued the interest of many an affluent Roman who had grown tired of the perpetual gloom that had settled over the city. It was during this event that we decided to strike."

David stood and headed back to the window. He watched as the onslaught of continuous rain created pools in the consecrated earth below. He envisioned the rats who lived inside the dilapidating Lardone crypt, scurrying frantically as the water rising rapidly around them rendered them immobile. Their beady eyes reminded him of Nirus's, hideous black orbs trapped within a face disfigured by the advanced stages of disease, a disgusting specimen rotting away by his own determination. Although many years had passed, David found himself still shuddering at the thought of him.

ANCIENT ROME, 44 BC

T HE NIGHT FELL LATER THAN USUAL with the approaching vernal equinox, dusk settling around Davius as he dressed for the feast. Its soft orange glow filled chambers which had been haphazardly furnished to accommodate their brief stay.

Davius was unable to place his mood, consumed by a purposeful melancholy that haunted his typical detachment. As the tumultuous events of the past few days settled, he'd succumbed to morbid contemplation. Memories of Gaia were becoming increasingly vivid, the devastation of her loss prying its nimble fingers into his mind. He sat on one of the stone benches, unable to peel his eyes away from the frescoes he had once worked so painstakingly on. The image of the lovers, tangled in each other's arms, seemed to dance in the warm citrus hues of sunset.

He wouldn't let himself believe that Gaia's womb swelled with life as she died. Eternal life had robbed him of the ability to produce offspring, a thought which hadn't occurred to him prior to his transformation. He would never know a paternal bond, never feel a child's tiny hand wrapped around his finger. Lucius had positioned himself as his only family. Even so, Davius questioned his intentions and loyalty. Lucius openly pined for Morrigan, who did not return the sentiment, preening about like a cat when she made her brief appearances. He grew increasingly bothered by her obvious preference for Davius, whom she continued to lovingly refer to as "her Daghda."

The endowment frustrated Davius as well. He was still unable to recall any memories of past lives before his human one, visions of that life consuming his mind. Yet, as discouraged as he was, he allowed their invasion, hoping the fresh taste of agony would transmute itself into the powerful energy he needed, not only to destroy his enemy, but to rebirth their new ally, the Morrigan.

His thoughts were interrupted by the swish of Lucius's robes as he appeared in the doorway. "Well?" he asked. "Do I look the part of an inconspicuous Roman?"

Davius startled at his appearance, realizing he had shorn off his thick, spiraling locks, leaving a patch of black curls clustered at the top of his forehead in a perfect imitation of an authentic Roman hairstyle. The absence of his long mane accentuated his slender frame, exposing his long pale neck and dramatic facial structure. "You look so different," he remarked.

Lucius smiled, the exaggerated size of his teeth dominating his angular face. Davius thought immediately of a snake, its large head beholding slanted eyes and striking teeth. "I know better than to ask if you will do the same," he remarked, wryly.

Davius snorted, a smile creeping across his face as he raked his fingers through his beloved unkempt curls. "Highly unlikely."

"So I assumed." Lucius joined him where he sat, following his eyes towards the image of the embracing lovers. "Soon, my friend. Soon you will have your vengeance and we can move on from this place for good."

As if on cue, Morrigan surfaced from the shadows. Davius could still smell the aroma of wet earth each time she grew near, her scent now filling the room as she approached with one of her birds on her shoulder. Its beady eyes met his in silent greeting; a strange camaraderie had evolved between them ever since he had shifted into corvidian form.

"Why did you cut your hair?" she addressed Lucius in surprise. "I happened to like it."

He reddened, the color creeping up his exposed neck. "It will grow back by tomorrow's nightfall. It is another one of the curious laws we are bound by. Our appearances will never change, no matter the aesthetic alterations."

She frowned. "So I will forever keep the form of the body you find for me?"

Lucius sighed. "I honestly do not know. You are a shapeshifting goddess. You may be allowed to retain your power after you transform. We will only know once you have turned."

She nodded, though her face looked visibly perplexed. Their exchange was interrupted by a loud rapping at the door. Morrigan disappeared as quickly as she came. Davius rose to his feet as Lucius opened it.

The litter they requested had arrived, the decorated wooden plank dressed in luxurious beige fabric. Four shirtless slaves held each corner on their shoulders, patiently awaiting command.

"I will need it back before daybreak," the owner reminded Lucius as he paid him, eyeing them both suspiciously.

"Absolutely, sir, thank you again," Lucius soothed, pressing a few extra coins into his palm to pacify any lingering apprehension.

The man nodded, snapping his fingers at the entourage who immediately fell to their knees so the two of them could enter. The litter was fitted with ornate pillows stuffed with lamb's wool, and both men reclined on the plank comfortably. They were lifted smoothly into the air, the transition barely disturbing the elegant beige drapery that surrounded them on each side. Although they were concealed, Davius found solace in knowing the night was still and they could move through the city undisturbed. Lucius was uncharacteristically quiet, staring off into nothingness, apparently lost in his thoughts.

"Please forgive me for making the promise to Morrigan," Davius broke the silence. "You have not been the same since."

Lucius turned to him. "Humanity seems to be creeping back in you after all."

"I only wish to make peace with you, Lucius," Davius explained. "You are the only family I have in this world." His entreatment was only partially earnest; he was still wary of Lucius's motives, but preferred not to be at odds with his maker.

He sighed, but Davius could tell he was secretly pleased. "This is true. And soon our family will grow by one more as the Morrigan joins us, although one can only speculate how those events might unfold."

Davius shifted in discomfort. "Do you think it will work?"

"I do not know," he replied honestly. "When the spellcaster brought me to life, I was a beast. I shudder to imagine what might transpire when an intense deity such as the Morrigan attempts to possess a human body." He turned towards him, his face hardening as he changed the subject. "You are my protege, Davius. My brother in this life. We embark on this mission of vengeance because I care for you, but this is the last time I will entertain such things. These human inklings have no place in our lives. After tonight, we will return to Greece and plan our travels moving forward. You must allow me that."

"Absolutely," Davius responded, though he was slightly taken aback. "I am grateful for your support," he added.

Lucius resumed his reclined position, satisfied with his answer. "Of course. I do appreciate a good killing anyway."

The litter came to a halt. They exited through curtains that opened to reveal dozens of armed guards poised to greet them. They accepted their arrival without question, leading them through the front door of what was once Eridus's villa. A chill settled over Davius as he re-entered his former home. The interior had been completely transformed, rendering him curiously impressed. Not only did its new occupant restore the villa to its former glory but surpassed it in extravagant decor.

The entire atrium was now laid with imported white marble, the deep reds that once draped every window and chair exchanged for a scale of rich purples and soft lilacs. The masculine busts Eridus once favored were replaced by smooth polished statues of the fiercely independent Diana and the curious triple-faceted Hecate. Each candelabra and lighting fixture was fashioned in bright silver, while intricate tapestries draped the walls and woven rugs lined the floors.

The dining room they soon entered mirrored the entryway in concept. Gone were the dining couches boasting the jolly face of Bacchus, the plain white marble benches that replaced them giving the room a look of sterile elegance. Frescoes depicting tales of the Greek goddesses covered each wall. Davius's eyes pulled immediately towards the front of the room to the scene of Arachne transforming into a spider, her eternal punishment for her hubristic challenge of the goddess Athena. Her shriveling frame cowered beneath the war goddess, who stood fierce and unwavering. Delicia was seated directly underneath the painting, her choice in position a blatant warning to all who might follow in such footsteps.

She was preoccupied by conversation, offering them a distracted nod as they found empty spaces at the long, oversized table. Her apathy towards their presence allowed Davius a few moments to observe her. Although the mousy girl he had once seen at the Roman Circus had grown into a woman, she was still small and delicate, wrapped in a lilac toga with silver adornments, as if strategically matched to her preferred decor. It hung awkwardly against her tiny frame, silver earrings dangling beneath the mousy brown hair piled loosely atop her head. Her slightness offered the illusion of attractiveness, but her face was quite plain. She had inherited her father's beady eyes, though they glimmered a pleasant brown rather than cold ebony. They darted around the room as she feigned interest in those who spoke to her, making it appear as if she hunted rather than entertained.

Davius seated himself, quietly taking in the room. It felt as if an eternity had passed since he'd last witnessed a Roman feast. Delicia spared no expense in spoiling her guests, the spread before them an endless compilation of obscure foods. Along with the customary fresh fruit and bread platters, she had somehow managed to acquire ostrich from Africa's northern boundaries, pickled peacock brain, and a platter of exotic flamingo tongues boiled in red wine. Yet the peculiarity of the victuals was apparently lost on the party; the exotic menu and sophisticated room did little to deter them from their gluttonous imbibing. They thought nothing of slamming around their beverages until they sloshed over the lid onto the floor, spit running down their chins as they licked greasy fingers.

Their host seemed unperturbed as she delicately sipped her drink and picked at her plate, but Davius sensed her vehement displeasure. Her eyes caught his for a moment, revealing a burning intensity carefully concealed behind her stony exterior. He offered her a pleasant, close-mouthed smile, which brought the briefest warmth to her cheeks before she hardened and promptly turned away.

Conversation rolled smoothly throughout the evening, the musicians Delicia had hired drowning out most of the idle chatter from Davius's ears. Lucius was at ease playing the part of a Roman aristocrat, but Davius remained quiet and still, save for when he was forced to laugh when appropriate or when he pretended to swallow bits of food which were secretly discarded into his napkin. He was unprepared for how delectable the scent of so many humans near him would be, grateful that Lucius had brought a flask of blood to pass between them under the table.

The night pressed on mercilessly as Davius struggled to maintain his pleasant facade, when at last someone spoke the words he had been waiting to hear. A voice shouted out over the clamor, "And where is our elusive Nirus tonight?"

Delicia cleared her throat, waving her hand to silence the instrumentals. "My father is not well, as you all know," she replied.

"Bring him out, you are among friends here!" another man called.

Her smooth face offered no emotion, yet Davius once again sensed her growing displeasure. This was her house, her party, and she hadn't intended on sharing the spotlight. After a moment of consideration, she called to one of her slaves, a meager looking young woman with eyes rimmed in charcoal. She whispered in her ear, the girl nodding nervously before disappearing into the folds of the house.

Delicia took a sip of her wine. "I will remind you once again of my father's illness, and the fact that I have taken great pains to keep him hidden from those who would enjoy seeing him jailed for conspiracy," she said. Her voice was soft but strong, with the regal air of a monarch. "His weakened state would see him dead in such conditions. I ask that you remember that I am now head of his estate and the negotiations made tonight are strictly of my own affairs. I am willing to have him join us as a courtesy to you all, an extension of good will in our dealings, but know that his authority here has ended."

The men surrounding the table nodded, murmuring acquiescence, one raising up his glass towards her in a gesture of respect.

Davius was struck by the fierceness of her eyes as the men surrounding her agreed to her terms, an expression similar to that of the Morrigan. He smiled to himself, briefly wondering where their guardian goddess had wandered off to.

And then he appeared.

A gasp floated about the room as a shriveled creature appeared at the doorway, leaning heavily on a slave girl who could barely handle his weight. His right leg was completely mangled, hanging uselessly from his body as he limped forward, favoring his left. His beady black eyes bulged from their sockets, his face a swollen map of purple bruises and oozing sores, sloppily covered with flesh colored oil paints that only enhanced their grotesqueness rather than concealed it. He was completely bald, which magnified the misshapenness of his skull and the hideous absence of his formerly elongated nose. It seemed to have shrunk back into his head, leaving two large nostrils exposed as they pulled at his upper lip to reveal less than a dozen teeth hanging hopelessly to his skull. Even from across the room, he reeked heavily of alcohol and decay.

"Romans! How I have missed you so," he managed through his deformity, spittle flying from his desiccated lips.

The dinner party managed to hide their horrified surprise, cheering his presence with extended glasses.

"How is he still alive?" a man on Davius's left mouthed in an inaudible whisper, one that only an immortal could hear.

Nirus slumped down onto one of the open couches, greedily slugging down the cup of wine before him. "More!" he demanded, slamming it back down on the table, sending his dishes flying.

Delicia looked perfectly mortified.

His personal slave girl hurried to refill his cup. A sense of satisfaction gripped Davius as he watched Nirus struggle to put it back to his lips, both his drunkenness and his disease rendering him utterly pitiful.

"You must listen to my daughter, you fools!" he roared. "I have never been prouder to have her by my side."

Delicia forced a thin smile. "Thank you, father."

"The only child I ever bore! Born to a real cunt of a mother, though, who did not last very long in my employ, if you catch my meaning. I am glad she inherited her brains from me at least." He erupted in laughter, spit and wine flying freely from his rotting mouth.

Delicia's eyes burned with hatred, yet her pleasant countenance was unwavering. "Do you need more drink, father?"

"I need music! I need whores! Come now, I haven't had a proper feast in years."

The party chimed in accord, the music recommencing as the Romans resumed their festivities.

Lucius studied Nirus as he awkwardly chugged another tall cup of wine, letting the roar of the party rise to its original intensity before murmuring to Davius, "He suffers so already. Perhaps there are worse fates than death."

"I made a vow," Davius reminded him.

It was not long before the intoxication of Nirus overshadowed any hopes for constructive talk of business. He fell twice from his dining couch, resituated only to slosh his wine about his place setting like a defiant child. Delicia was now openly furious, her eyes pleading with her father's friends in the hopes someone would help discourage his antics.

Finally, it was Davius who stood, smoothing his robes before approaching the spectacle before him.

Delicia watched him curiously.

"Drink! Bring me more drink!" Nirus slurred as he came up behind him.

"Hello, sir," Davius interrupted, bending at the waist to match his level. "My name is Marcus Athenus, my father fought with you in the wars before his passing."

"Ah, yes." Nirus nodded enthusiastically, feigning recognition.

"I have always been interested in winemaking as a business venture," Davius continued. He gestured towards Lucius, who had decided to follow. "My associate here once owned a successful winery in Greece. We came here tonight in the hopes of making arrangements with your lovely daughter, for our resources are vast. I also hoped you would be willing to let us tour your wine cellars. I am sure you have more than ample provisions stowed away." He winked at him.

Delicia opened her mouth in protest before she realized what he was doing for her. She nodded gratefully. "Yes, Father, I think that would be a wonderful idea. Take him to the eastern cellars, where your wine is stored."

Davius beamed at her. "Wonderful. My associate, Greyus, can speak with you regarding our interests in my absence."

Lucius appeared in the seat next to Delicia, taking her hand in his. "It is wonderful to meet you, Madame."

"Yes - more drink!" Nirus struggled to rise to his feet. "A tour we shall have!"

Davius bent to offer him balance, masking his revulsion at the putrid, slimy skin that rubbed against his own. The stench exuding off him was positively revolting, the scent of his blood similar to that of curdled milk.

Davius struggled to keep him upright as they left the dining room, entering the familiar household. He navigated effortlessly through the hallways towards the press room, where he knew beneath the cellars lie. Nirus did not question him, far too drunk to do anything but allow Davius to carry him down the hall. His besotted state prompted his credulity, easily convinced that Davius's father was once one of his most trusted comrades, even referring to Davius as his brother while clapping his back with joyous intimacy.

Davius maintained the charade as he observed the villa, struck by how still it was, the bustle of slaves he had once lived amongst eerily absent from its halls. Torches still lined each wall, their flames now catching in the silver pottery Delicia had added intermittently below.

"This is not right," Nirus protested, realizing where they were. "We are headed towards the wrong cellar."

"Nonsense," Davius assured him. "Right this way." He ushered him faster, the man helpless against both Davius's immortal strength and the vulnerability of his intoxication. Davius threw open the back door to reveal the neglected west yard, overgrown vines spiraling around the cracked and misplaced stones. The cylinder-shaped building that once served as a press room loomed before them.

"No, please! We cannot go in there!" Nirus panicked.

Davius dragged him towards it, noticing the front door had been barricaded with chains. He tore through them easily, throwing open the door with such force that the wood slapped against the inner wall with an angry thud.

He immediately stopped in his tracks, the reveal of what was behind it taking him utterly by surprise.

Although the room hadn't been used in years, the reek of fermentation still hung heavy in the air, now mixed with the tantalizing aroma of blood. He realized the room had been turned into a makeshift torture chamber, rusted chains hanging from the walls, the floors painted with viscera. There were tables laden with various tools and sharp instruments, and a dresser devoted entirely to knives positioned against the far wall.

Nirus found his footing at last and began to pull away from him. "This is not my room!" he insisted. "I love a good tussle with a slave girl, but she is the one who cuts and drains them! She thinks their blood will preserve her youth and beauty - I tell her it is madness, but she does not listen!"

Davius noticed that the giant iron vat once used for pressing grapes was as equally smeared in crimson as the floorboards, a metal slab suspended by two chains hanging above it. The previously established stairs that led up to its mouth now included a table on its landing where fresh towels had been recently stacked. "She bathes in it," he deduced, incredulous at the thought.

His moment of clarity allowed Nirus the opportunity to wriggle out of his grasp. He slipped around the floors towards the entrance, his attempts to stand useless. Davius did not rush to retrieve him, assured he wouldn't make it to the door. He continued to inspect his grotesque discovery, heading behind the repurposed pressing cauldron.

He noticed a figure hanging limply against the far wall, partially concealed in shadow. The memory of his captivity resurfaced, and he shuddered as he recalled the agony of chains. Alarmed that he hadn't been able to smell a human being in the room, he approached the figure carefully. As he grew closer, he could see the soft blonde hair of a woman and the angles of her emaciated frame. He was mere footsteps away before he realized that despite her protruding skeletal bones, her stomach swelled with child.

He rushed towards Gaia as her sweet face looked up to greet him with relieved elation. He took it in his hands, his body awash with emotion. She was as lovely as he remembered, her olive eyes swimming with adoration as her rose colored lips turned upwards into a smile.

Somewhere inside, he knew she was only a spector, but he embraced her regardless, his nose filling with the aroma of jasmine as her skin warmed his. He wanted to remain eternally in the moment, her fruitful curve pressing against his stomach as he smothered her face in unabating kisses.

"Davius…" her voice came out in a whisper but seemed to fill his head.

"No," he murmured, his lips grazing her cheeks. "Please do not ask me to leave you."

"Davius…"

"No…" he repeated, aware of the hollowness of the word as he reached up to rip down her chains.

Hands now free, she grabbed his face, forcing him to see the fire in her eyes. "Kill him, Davius!" she cried.

The intensity behind her words broke him free of his astonished stupor. He whipped around and lunged at Nirus, who had no chance to register his attack. Davius twisted his head backwards and plunged his teeth deep in his neck, toxic blood surging from the interrupted vein into his mouth. He slurped it down his throat feverishly, regardless of its putrid taste, as he was accosted by visions of the man's vile life: the wails of women he'd beaten and raped, the image of Gaia's face burning with hatred as he loomed above her, whip in hand.

When Davius could not bear to drink any longer, he threw him to the floor, smashing his hideous face with his fist over and over, until his eyes bulged from their sockets and his jaw cracked away from his face, his voice gurgling as it tried to plead for mercy. He stopped only to position the mangled creature onto its back. He lifted his own wrist to his mouth, severing his radial artery and releasing black rivulets of immortal blood down his arms. He mounted the pulp that was Nirus's body, positioning his dripping wrist directly over its gaping mouth.

Gaia appeared next to him. Her hand on his shoulder signaled him to stop and he withdrew obediently, the two watching in silent satisfaction as Nirus writhed on the floor in agony.

"It is done," her apparition said once the body temporarily ceased its struggle.

Davius turned to her, the sight of her beautiful, heart-shaped face with its garden of freckles flooding him with nostalgia. Regret twisted painfully his core as he wiped the taste of rancid blood from his lips. He knew remnants of the gore still streaked his face and neck as she gazed at him. "My love," he whispered, full of shame. "I have become a monster." He hung his head, unable to look into her eyes.

She tenderly lifted his face with her hands, the smell of jasmine so strong that it masked the horrors around them. "For now," she whispered. "Stay the course, my sweet Davius. There is so much more that will be revealed to you."

He felt tears fall from his eyes, horrified to think they would look as decayed as his blood. Yet Gaia was not affected, placing his hand where it could caress her belly while she pressed her lips once more against his.

And then, without another word, she dissipated, the vision of her trickling away like fragments of dust caught in rays of sunlight. He felt her warmth throughout his body as if her soul passed through him. He fought to keep the vision of her fresh in his mind, imagining her returning to the emerald grass of Gaul where she ran joyous and free, keeping pace with a sandy haired bairn who skipped alongside her.

The anguish of her departure settled over him, slowly bringing him back to the present. He looked down at the lifeless creature at his feet. He moved quickly, hoisting it up against the wall and clasping Gaia's former chains around each wrist. He watched as Nirus's soul returned to its new form, its beady eyes wrenching open in violent resurrection.

Davius stood back to observe him, satisfied that the transformation had not relieved him of his disfigurements. His eyes were masked by films of pus as they struggled to take in his surroundings, his jaw still broken and hanging slackly from his noseless face, its blackened tongue lolling pitiably with nothing to restrain it. His complexion had cleared, and his leg seemed sturdy, but his shriveled scalp still boasted no hair and his skeletal frame was still contorted by his human deformity.

"Thirsty," he slurred, his tongue trying unsuccessfully to reposition itself back into his mouth.

Davius smirked. "It is a thirst that will never be quenched for the rest of your miserable days."

"Who are you?" the creature garbled.

"Surely you remember the slave boy who once stormed your feast."

His clouded eyes widened in recognition. "What have you done to me?"

"You will live for endless days, hideous and thirsting, your eternal punishment for the murder of my wife and child," Davius scathingly replied. "You will yearn for death, but it will never come to you for the rest of your wretched days as an immortal on this earth."

Nirus fought his chains, but the attempt was futile, any immortal strength he might earn not yet evolved. "I need drink!" he screeched in desperation.

"What have you done?" a furious voice cut through the room.

Davius turned to see Lucius in blood smeared clothing, his face an equal mix of astonishment and rage. His fist was wrapped around the tiny wrist of Delicia, who wore an equally mortified expression. The scent of a human being in the room set the newly transformed blood drinker into a frenzy, his rattling chains echoing throughout the chamber. His fat wormy tongue protruded towards her as if it were an intelligent appendage, hideous as it lapped pitifully at the air.

"Father," she whimpered, cowering beside Lucius, who kept his hold on her firm. Any ferocity from earlier had left her eyes completely, her frail, folded body giving her the appearance of a wounded gosling more than a ravenous bird of prey. She struggled unproductively against his grasp.

Lucius's eyes, however, were black with anger, his alabaster skin mottled by heat.

"You said it yourself, there are some fates worse than death," Davius offered before he spat, the taste of rancid blood still lingering in his mouth.

"Let my father go!" Delicia begged.

Lucius glared at her. "Oh, please, you detested the man. You should be as angered as I am that my imprudent counterpart decided to prolong his miserable existence."

He turned back to Davius. "And what shall we do with him now? Do you want to be responsible for the care of a decrepit blood drinker whom you despise?"

Davius wiped at his lips with the back of his hand. "We can wall him up, right here in the cellar, where he can live in eternal torment. As you can see, his defects have not been resolved in the transformation."

Lucius deflated minisculely, intrigued by the idea. He let Delicia pull herself free from detainment and fly to the door, where she began to tug at it fruitlessly. He peered at Nirus who had grown incensed with hunger, thrashing in frenzied abandon. "My word, you are right. He still looks the perfect monster."

"Fitting, is it not?"

Lucius tore his curious gaze away to glare at him once more. "Just because you have intrigued me does not mean that I am not irate with your blatant carelessness. You have attempted what only I have done, and you have done it impulsively, without any foresight. We cannot go about this world creating creatures so carelessly - we must protect ourselves! It is bad enough I had to kill every last remaining Roman patrician, even if we are fortunate that it is during a time of civil unrest. You have created a monstrosity that we now have to properly dispose of!"

"I told you, we can seal him up here. It seems our Delicia was quite the little deviant in her own right." Davius gestured around him.

Lucius was taken aback, realizing for the first time where they stood. "My, you are a perfect specimen," he called back to her in bemusement.

She continued to pound at the door, her hopeless screams for rescue reaching a fervent pitch.

"As befitting the notion of locking him away for an eternal life of torment may be, we cannot risk it. What if some day, some year, even centuries in the future, he is released? There is no telling what may occur. We have to end it, and do so properly," Lucius decided.

Davius frowned. "How can a blood drinker suffer in death?"

There was a pause, as they both realized Delicia had stopped screaming.

They turned to see the Morrigan, holding the woman up by one hand clasped tightly around her neck. She struggled powerlessly against her. Morrigan slid towards them with her prize, her glistening eyes expressing her delight.

"Drink!" Nirus begged from his chains.

With a smile, Morrigan complied, tossing his daughter to him like a bone to a pack of wolves. Nirus finally broke free of his bounds, catching his terrified daughter in his arms and shoving his teeth into her neck, blood pouring sloppily from his disjointed mouth as he sucked from her unrestrained.

"I have found my vessel," she explained to the surprised Lucius, who quickly sprang into action. He wrested Delicia away from Nirus, lest he consume the fatal drop, and with a flick of his wrist, caught the wretched being ablaze. He tore about the room in panic, his shrieks reverberating throughout the press chamber. Although he could not see her, Davius could feel the presence of Gaia surrounding him once again, quietly conveying to him her satisfaction. The charred remains finally collapsed in a cloud of black smoke, a few stubborn flames fighting to survive as what was left of Nirus wheezed for breath.

Meanwhile, Lucius had given his blood to Delicia, whose body began to transform. He loomed over her as she ripped at her hair, eyes wide and frantic as her body coiled in pain. He looked at Davius. "You must do it now before the transformation is complete."

Morrigan slid next to him, her smooth skin brushing against his. "Please, Daghda," she pleaded. "Make good on your promise."

Davius nodded, closing his eyes as he pulled her into his arms. He pushed all that had transpired out of his mind, letting the apparition of Gaia slip away from his consciousness. His invocation of wind picked up as his mind cleared, swirling around them and sending their robes flailing. The screams of crows filled his ears as he immersed himself with thoughts of the Morrigan, drinking in her earthy scent, allowing her to consume him. Waves of pleasure rippled through his body as he recalled the first moment he saw her, a memory that was not his, of her bathing in one of the vast rivers of their homeland. He could feel her muscular body sliding against his in the water, the metallic taste of her mouth in his.

"I will always find you," he had whispered to her in the rain, as the last of mother's leaves fell around them, kissing away her tears as he brushed back her raven hair.

His eyes snapped open, for the memories faded and he had returned. He grabbed the moaning body of Delicia off the floor and kissed her, breathing into her body the soul of the Morrigan.

And then, all was still.

Across the room, Nirus's glowing, charred remains crackled and popped.

Lucius stared at Davius in astonishment. "Did it work?" he whispered.

Davius looked down at the limp body draped in his arms. The woman who was once Delicia was still.

Then her eyes burst open to reveal the clearest blue eyes he had ever seen, radiating out from porcelain skin. It was Morrigan. She beamed up at him, her lips pulling back to reveal two neatly pointed teeth.

Davius hadn't the chance to speak before her eyes shifted back to brown, and he was staring again at the mortified Delicia. Surprised, he dropped her, watching as once more, the eyes snapped back to icy blue.

"What is happening?" Lucius demanded.

"She fights me," Morrigan managed to reply, trying to pull herself to her feet before crashing to the ground as if her body was under attack. Delicia pulled at her hair, sending Morrigan back with a howl, only to re-emerge moments later. "Her soul will not leave!" Morrigan cried out in frustration.

Davius stared helplessly at the struggling creature before him. "What should I do?"

"There is nothing to be done," Lucius replied with sudden realization. "Their souls are braiding, forever bound together for as long as their physical body shall live. All we can do is wait until their contention is over."

As if on cue, the body went limp.

Delicia/Morrigan rose to their feet in one eerily fluid motion. They stood for a moment before delicately sweeping the dust from their lavender robes. Their face was Delicia's, but was sculpted by Morrigan's hard beauty, one of the eyes a soft brown, the other perfectly blue. "You may call us Morgana, for we are Delicia, but the Morrigan commands us," she declared.

Lucius flew up to her, taking her hand to give it a kiss. "We are honored to have you join us."

Morgana smiled at him with delight.

Davius felt as if his legs would buckle beneath him, suddenly drained of energy. Morgana noticed immediately, rushing to his side. "Lucius, we must feed. For my new body and for the sake of poor Daghda."

Lucius's mouth twitched in annoyance at the persisting favoritism but nodded. "Let us take our leave of this place. We are no longer bound to Rome - we can feed now before sunrise and leave immediately at the next nightfall."

Morgana laughed. "Nonsense. We fly tonight - dinner will be had at home."

Before he could reply, she shifted into a raven, opening her beak to give them a shrill, beckoning caw. Within moments, the chamber was filled with birds, circling them until their bodies shrunk back into their corvid guise. They ascended into the skies, leaving the tragedy of Rome behind them. Davius hadn't the time to put his thoughts together, nor time to consider what had just transpired, but he knew, as he soared over cities and landscapes, that his life moving forward would never be the same.

CHAPTER FIVE

❧ THE IMPOSTERS ❧

LONDON, 1857

THE LAST DYING EMBERS OF THE FIRE finally extinguished themselves, yet David did not stir to revive them. He watched thin vines of smoke escape from the skeletal remains of the firewood, drifting listlessly up the chimney flue into oblivion. Still no sunlight peeked through the drapes, although the rain had ceased. He lazily retrieved his pocket watch, surprised to learn that the sun would be setting soon. His body ached as if it was early morning.

He finally rose from where he sat, pausing to drape another blanket over his slumbering companion. He wasn't sure when she finally gave in to its inevitable lure, but he had no desire to wake her unnecessarily. He brushed back a lock of hair that interrupted the smooth plane of her cheek, noticing a cluster of bruises below her neckline. Her lungs wheezed with each grueling breath, and he wondered if she would be able to make it through another night.

He removed a cigarette from the almost empty box near where she lay, lighting it with the last match. He drew a sharp inhale before extinguishing the waning candles with a wave of his hand, putting the room to rest.

The ostentatious grandfather clock in the hallway chimed rudely as he walked past. It provoked a smile as he imagined Lucius would have highly approved of the design, had he lived to see the nineteenth century. He realized he hadn't thought of him, nor Morgana, in a great many years, even though for centuries they had been an inseparable triumvirate.

He couldn't recall exactly when he changed, when the fundamental characteristic of being an immortal ceased to stir him, and he drifted into an endless mire of melancholy and regret. When exactly the thrill of the hunt and the lust for blood were replaced by the harsh realities of empathy and guilt. He'd tried to keep their emergence a secret from his friends, pretending to enjoy feeding off humans as much as they did until he could no longer bear the burden of his facade. The particulars were lost to him, the endless centuries bleeding together, distinct memories artfully avoiding capture.

The house was still, Jacob long retired to his gatehouse in anticipation of nightfall. The hall clock kept time with his footsteps as he slipped past the staircase into the foyer, retrieving his coat and a pair of hunting boots that had been resting neatly against the wall. Although his own chambers beckoned him, reminding him of the many days since he'd last slept, he knew his mind was too restless for slumber.

The evening air rejuvenated him as he pushed open the heavy arched doors, the aroma of rain-soaked earth drifting pleasantly towards his nostrils. He was immediately grateful to be wearing boots as he carefully maneuvered his way through copious pits of mud towards the back of his estate. The graveyard materialized ahead of him, its headstones darkened by rainwater, rivulets still running down the flat stones of the boastful mausoleum. He retrieved his keyring from the inner pocket of his coat and selected the passkey most laden with rust, wiggling it into the opening of a padlocked chain wrapped around the entire structure. When it released, he exerted his supernatural strength to heave open two stubborn doors that groaned in protest.

The musty smell of decomposition wafted into his face as he entered, escaping into the night before he slammed shut the cumbersome doors. Five sarcophagi fanned out like playing cards before him, yet he ignored the first dust-laden four, heading towards the fifth one, placed farthest to the right and conspicuously clean. He lifted its lid easily to uncover a staircase hidden beneath. He descended the stairs without hesitation, following their winding path until he reached the vaults they led to.

The first door of the vault was left open, and once he walked through its doorway into the next set of vaults, he was met with the smell of cooking bacon. The chambers were illuminated by candlelight, casting a warm glow onto the sparse living arrangements that interrupted the sterility of the room. As many furnishings as David donated over the years, only the frayed Oriental rugs, broken bookshelves, torn sofa, and desk had survived.

He walked past them into the southern vault, which had been converted into a kitchenette, complete with a coal burning stove with an innovative pipe extending above ground for ventilation. Although eternal life could be monotonous, David had mused when he first saw the invention, it did offer plenty of time for random ingenuity.

"Ah, just in time for breakfast," its chef remarked upon his entrance.

"Good Morning, Libraean," David greeted him, draping his cloak on one of the chairs that surrounded the modest kitchen roundtable.

The creature turned around to squint his way, revealing the addition of a thick pair of eyeglasses which obscured both his one clear blue and his one faulty eye. Like David, his face had not changed much over time. His broken horns were now covered by a weathered bowler hat and his clipped wings concealed by a heavy wool vest. To the unsuspecting onlooker, he looked like a common cripple, his hunchback and awkward hobble only adding to the charade. His hair had gone white, however, and his skin had splotched and wrinkled as if time finally allowed him the gift of senescence, the last stop on the pathway to life's inevitable release.

The creature looked down at the bacon crisping in the skillet. "This might be too well done for you."

"It's quite all right -"

"Nonsense, I have uncooked ham on ice." He hobbled towards a cabinet where he retrieved a slab of raw pork and a bottle of sanguine liquid. "The butcher gave me fresh pigs' blood as well."

"All right then," David acquiesced, touched, as always, by his hospitality.

"I didn't think you'd stop by today. It's been quite a few days since I've last seen you," Libraean commented as he poured the pigs' blood into a tarnished teapot, warming it before carefully drizzling it over the pork as if it were gravy.

"Last night was the first I've been out in over a week," David replied, softly.

"Ah. Falling into one of your melancholy spells?" He poured the rest of the contents of the teapot into two cracked teacups and placed them and two sets of silverware on the table before offering David his prepared plate.

David was silent in reply, retrieving the plate from his extended arm. He waited until Libraean grabbed his own plate and maneuvered to the table before he sliced a piece of the raw meat and lifted it to his lips. It wasn't nearly as fresh as he preferred, but it was still pleasantly edible. He took a careful sip from his teacup, the pig's blood and wine concoction wonderfully tepid. "I was actually hoping to ask your thoughts on a matter."

Libraean met his eyes, the milkiness of his dead one swimming grotesquely as they both moved upwards to peer over the rim of his glasses. "Of course."

David frowned, not quite sure where to begin. "I've been contemplating the events of my life again. I often find myself getting lost in the timeline."

"I've long advocated record keeping," Libraean lectured, taking a bite of his bacon and using the leftover portion to gesture at the volumes of books stacked around them. Not only were the walls of his living room completely lined from ceiling to floor with publications, but the kitchen area also boasted its fair share of overstocked shelves.

"Yes, but why pen my own memoirs when you are so efficient at chronicling?" David asked with a smile.

"Indeed," the creature smiled as he resumed the consumption of his meal. "Ask your question."

"I cannot seem to recall the moment when I changed. I remember clearly the zest for the predator's game and the unquenchable craving for human blood. And then one day, I was different. I began to hear the minds of humans clearly, even before I fed on their blood, and became increasingly plagued by an evolving conscience."

Libraean raised a substantial eyebrow. "As I warned you would happen?"

David sighed, setting down his fork. "Yes, you did warn me." He looked up from his plate. "My point is, I cannot recall precisely when your premonition came to pass."

Libraean sipped at his teacup. He set it down, folding his weathered hands above his now empty plate as he gazed at him. "You really don't remember?"

"I would not ask if I did."

Libraean rose from his seat, scooping David's empty plate under his own and tossing it into a nearby basin of soapy water before shuffling from the kitchen into his living space. David followed, admiring as he often did, how flawlessly Libraean had transformed the Lardone vaults into a place fit for habitation.

The creature struggled to reach the top shelf of one of his numerous bookcases, but David knew better than to ask him if he needed assistance. With an audible grunt, the tips of his fingers clasped the spine of a wilted, red leather volume, sending it downwards towards the floor. A generous bit of dust came along with it, settling around the crumpled tome. He picked it up with another grunt before falling into one of the upholstered couches, the furniture creaking with his weight. He dropped the book on his sofa table with a thud, snapping his fingers to light a nearby candle.

David blinked, surprised. "All these years and you never once used your powers in my presence."

Libraean looked flustered, realizing his mistake. "I generally avoid their use. But my body is not as nimble as it once was, and sometimes the thought of using them to ease my growing discomfort is too strong a temptation for me to fight."

"Understandable," David offered, magnanimously. "I see you have the *Manibus Ignem* like Lucius."

Libraean nodded, opening the book carefully. "I did not lie to you when I said he created me in his image, even passing on to me the hands of fire." The pages crackled as he gingerly leafed through them, the parchment heavy with ink.

"To think, at one point my compendium was written on papyrus," David remarked.

Libraean nodded. "The oldest blood drinker that ever was. And still is." He paused at a page. "Ah. Here you are. Hopefully, this will refresh your memory."

He spun the book around so David could read it. Bold letters at the top spelled out the date:

Jerusalem, 36 Anno Domini.

David closed his eyes as the memories flew back to him. "To think I'd forgotten," he said, softly.

Libraean was quiet, closing the book tenderly. "After you avenged

Gaia's death, your transition occurred slowly, like the crocodiles evolving out of Egypt's Nile. But on this day, you were notably changed forever."

"Thank you, Libraean," David murmured, his voice brimming with emotion.

The creature cleared his throat as if to stifle any of his own emotions from surfacing. He turned his back to David as he replaced the book on the shelf. "I'll see you again soon, then?"

David rose to his feet, understanding the familiar cue. Although their bond had strengthened over time, the only two creatures left in the world, both cherished their respective solitude. "Yes, I will call again soon. Enjoy your evening, Libraean."

"You do the same."

David retrieved his cloak, wrapping it around his frame as he moved through the succession of vaults and back up the stony crypt steps.

The rain had resumed, quickening the pace by which he resecured the mausoleum door and ventured home. Jacob greeted him at the entrance, appearing well rested and groomed. "Good evening, sir. Your friend is awake. She requested Irish whiskey, but I instead brought her bourbon with lemon and honey for her cough."

David smiled at the old man's thoughtfulness. "Thank you, Jacob. I'm on my way to check on her now. I'll call if she will be needing to return to her residence."

Old Man Jacob nodded neutrally.

David moved past the staircase to enter the parlor, which was already warm and bright. His companion was seated comfortably on her couch beneath a fresh stack of blankets. Her face brightened upon sight of him. "There is my handsome abductor." She grinned.

"I do believe you came willingly," David pointed out, though his tone was pleasant.

"I only jest," she assured him.

"I assume Jacob has taken good care of you?" he asked.

"He has been most hospitable." She gestured to the remnants of a toast and jam breakfast next to a short glass half-filled with bourbon.

"Wonderful. I presume you'd like to return home to your residence soon?"

She frowned. "I dozed off after you described the creation of Morgana. Surely that was not the end of your tale."

"I'm afraid you are correct. There is still much more left to tell."

Her lips turned upwards, satisfied with his response. "Then I have to stay for the Second Act."

"Of course. But I must jump ahead in time, for my evolution into the creature you see before you now was a tedious ascension...or descension, depending on whom you're talking to." David walked towards a mahogany bookcase, crammed with uneven volumes and columns of old papers tied with string. Towards the top were rolls of parchment, situated between stacks of scrolls so old they were flattened behind panes of protective glass. The oldest piece was not within view, but as his fingers lingered nearby, he could recall it clearly, singed edges lost forever to the flames which had nearly destroyed it. He closed his eyes, picturing Lucius's narrow silhouette erected amongst walls of fire, palms turned upwards as his rage pulled the old library down around him. He could almost hear his own screams.

He sighed, carefully removing the piece of rolled up parchment that had been laid beside it. He delicately unwound the frayed piece of ribbon that held it together, unrolling it on top of the piano. He smoothed out its creases, securing the top and bottom with candelabras that had been stationed nearby.

"As I changed, so did Lucius," he began, "leaving behind the scholarly creature intrigued by the minds of men and becoming something quite different. He grew bitter, frustrated by the devolution of the world around us, which grew less intriguing to him as time passed. He never had the patience for the fine art that is stalking one's prey, but had always enjoyed the physicality of combat, and as the cultured intellect fell away, the volatile beast inside him grew stronger. He was inexplicably drawn to the wars of men, the complexity of his mind sated as he arranged them like pawns on a chessboard, his participation in battle doing its part to satisfy his bloodlust.

"I originally assumed his renewed love of warfare was heavily influenced by Morgana, for never once did he cease in his longing for her. But his transition was much deeper than that, I'm afraid." David looked back wistfully at the stacks of ancient texts he'd painstakingly preserved.

"I remember clearly the moment I realized I'd lost him forever," he continued. "We had journeyed to Egypt upon his request, to the depreciating city of Alexandria. He had spoken so highly of the city, an intricate maze of architectural splendor established by Alexander the Great long before my human birth. He regaled us with his recollections of its breathtaking temples, a magnificent lighthouse, and a library boasting thousands of scrolls written by true geniuses of men.

"What we discovered upon our arrival was a much different story. Religious wars had destroyed the city, its glorious temples either torn down or hastily converted into Christian churches. What looked to be a once impressive lighthouse was now in desperate need of repair, abandoned, rotting ships cluttering its docks, swinging lifelessly with the waves. Lucius was silent, staring blankly at the crucifix laden buildings and the crumbling watchtower, the faces of the Greek gods it once boasted thoughtlessly removed.

"We hunted separately that evening, Morgana and I eager to abandon the destitute city and the scrutinous eyes of its citizens as soon as we were able. This was after my taste for humans had dwindled, so I waited until she'd abandoned my side before I found sustenance in the bounty absconded from fishing nets near the harbor.

"Covertly maneuvering my way back into town, I noticed a building that had once been quite striking, stretching two stories high and surrounded by coupled marble columns. It seemed to have suffered the same defacement of its statues; inside, busts that could have either been pagan gods or Roman patriarchs had been disfigured beyond recognition.

"The intricately designed bookshelves that lined each wall were minimally filled with scrolls, so many of the compartments empty that, from a distance, the walls seemed to give a toothless grin. The floors were missing their tiles, ruining what must have been handsomely crafted mosaics. The carpets that laid across them were frayed and looked cheap. Yet the inner columns were still etched with hieroglyphs and several paintings of Egyptian gods were still faintly visible on the walls. Intrigued, I began to wander, until I reached the Roman style atrium, where the early morning light filtered through. And that is where I found him, seated right in the center of the room as if awaiting immolation, his face the same expressionless mask he had worn since our arrival. I could tell by the pallor of his skin that he had not fed, that he had most likely been sitting there for hours."

"Lucius," I called out, tentatively. "It is nearly morning."

He didn't respond, which drew me closer.

"Lucius, where you sit, the sun's rays will surely reach you," I reiterated.

"This was once the grandest of libraries," he said, as if he hadn't heard me, the low echo of his voice devoid of emotion. "A haven for edification, coming into fruition by Ptolemy II Philadelphus during his reign, centuries ago. He was a grandiose king by nature, bursting with ideals and aspirations for Egypt, fascinated by the pursuit of knowledge and scientific advancement. Alexandria became the capital for learning, a mecca of innovation and ideas, with its monumental library at its core. Caesar nearly burned it to the ground during the height of his civil war, threatening to swallow mankind's records forever, yet through several donations, from myself included, she was restored to her former glory.

"And now look around you!" he cried out in a sudden burst of vehemence, throwing up his hands in indignation. "She lies in ruins! Humans do not care for the pursuit of knowledge and enlightenment - all they care for is power! This new religion - this Christianity - is disputable! Look for yourself - less than half the ancient scrolls are gone! They are no better than animals," he seethed.

"Now, now. We have conversed at length over these new religions. The Christ's message was a sound one," I reminded him.

"And look how they have twisted it," he spat. "They have completely ignored his actual teachings and warped it to suit their own desires for advancement. They have become exactly who he rebelled against - the idiocy is astounding! They have defiled this entire building, a place where free thinking and philosophy once flourished. It is beyond pathetic."

I could sense his growing distress. "You have said to me many times, Lucius, humans are merely a food source for us," I attempted to appeal to him. "Do not take their actions to heart."

"All I ever wanted was to live amongst them, to study their minds and bear witness to their evolution," he continued his rant, undeterred by my words. "Yes, we feed from lesser creatures, but never once have I forgotten the fascinating complexities of their thoughts, the curious inner workings of their minds. But I now see how clearly I was mistaken."

He flicked both of his wrists, and before I realized what he was doing, the remaining scrolls sequestered in their diagonal homes promptly caught ablaze.

I cried out for him to stop, leaping from shelf to shelf, attempting to grab what I could before they were consumed by the growing flames. From the corner of my eye, I caught a single scroll tucked away the highest of them all, which I snatched just before the shelving succumbed to the inferno.

I seized Lucius as well, pulling both of us to safety as the rooftops collapsed, taking the remains of the greatest library man has ever known along with it.

David blinked, remembering the ashes of a thousand scrolls fluttering down around them like snow. "He did not speak for a full week after," he murmured. "I was glad I salvaged what I did, including the Greek Septuagint, which I've managed to keep in my possession for centuries."

His companion appeared from behind him, her aroma of violets and illness prickling his nose. He could hear her strident lungs rebelling against her movement, her presence carrying him away from the memory. He welcomed her closer with his arm, directing her eyes to the contents of the parchment. "This is a map of Wallachia in the late fifteenth century, the place where we inevitably settled. You might have heard of the Kingdom of Romania?"

She turned to him, mystified. "I've only heard stories from sailors passing through town."

He nodded. "Most Londoners know of the country through trade. I had never heard of such a place until we traveled there, another one of Lucius's cherished territories that he insisted we return to. He visited it centuries prior, when it was known as the Kingdom of Dacia."

He looked down at the map, meticulously traced by his own hand. While he hadn't the heart to scribe his memoirs like Libraean, he found comfort in sketching the many lands where he'd lived. He ran his finger over the assiduous quill ink, remembering the musky aroma of his old study. He closed his eyes, the entire castle blossoming into a clear memory.

She coughed, interrupting his visions and provoking him to guide her back to the couch, regardful of her condition. "Please go on," she urged him, when she was seated and could manage the air to create speech.

"After the burning of the Library of Alexandria in four-twenty-three, Lucius succumbed to self-destruction, becoming more avaricious as each century passed, until nothing was left but a rapacious need for power. A millennium later, we found ourselves in Wallachia, one of three principalities that would one day become the Kingdom of Romania. Both Lucius and Morgana had been drawn to the war-torn land, the constant battles between the citizens of Wallachia, their neighboring territories, and the Ottoman Empire the perfect setting for them to indulge in their calamitous tendencies.

"In fourteen fifty-six, Lucius sought to usurp its prince, Vladislav, claiming to be the true son of Vlad Dracul, the assassinated prince who ruled prior. He succeeded, securing the throne and the vast land of Wallachia for the three of us." He carefully rolled the weathered parchment back up, returning it to its place amongst the other hand drawn maps. "By that point, I'd had shed the name Davius, for I was no longer the bright-eyed Roman boy who fell so deeply in love that he was willing to take on the world in her honor. That boy was dead, his body stolen by a vile creature rendered impotent by a human's conscience that sought to painstakingly devour him whole.

"In fact, I used to frequently travel to Italy during this time and once I happened upon a young artist who moved me, reminding me of that lost boy. I saw him again years later, when I had taken advantage of a cloudy day in Florence to explore the streets. There was an unveiling of an artist's work at the Palazzo della Signoria, and I quickly realized it was the artist I'd met before, whose name was Michelangelo. He stood humbly near his creation, a magnificent sculpture depicting the Biblical David who defeated a giant named Goliath to the delight of the Israelites. But when they pulled back its covering, I saw my own face sculpted in marble. He told the crowd he'd gotten his inspiration from a peculiar stranger he'd met, years ago." He glanced up to see her look of wonderment and felt his cheeks redden. "Anyway, the name David has a lot of meaning for me now, so David I remain."

"Amazing," she breathed. "And what of Morgana during this time?"

David frowned. "Morgana proved to be the consummate blood drinker, relishing in Lucius's newfound vainglory. She soared over the battlefields in her raven form, swooping down to attack our enemies with skillful precision. They carried on in that fashion for decades, feeding off each other's lust for victory while I stayed back, content with my solitude." David suddenly drifted off, choked by an unwelcome wave of regret from memories long forgotten. His eyes caught the outline of a keepsake box, another memento kept high atop the bookcase, one that hadn't been touched for years.

"Until...?" His companion pressed him.

David sighed. "She eventually went mad, unable to reconcile two souls sharing one body. She had an immortal's thirst for blood, a war goddess's thirst for battle, and a madwoman's thirst to inflict pain. It created a frightening culmination that would have rendered her fiercely indomitable had the advancing instability of her mind ceased."

His companion murmured a sympathetic sound of understanding as she waited for him to continue.

WALLACHIA, 1462

THE CORPSES OF A HUNDRED SOULS surrounded the castle, impaled upon iron spikes set in such perfect symmetry, they created a gruesome barricade that repelled all who crept near. The sky above them remained perpetually blackened by avian scavengers, circling their plentiful bounty as they besmirched the air with their shrill cries.

Even without its grim frontage, the castle itself was ominous and severe. Set high in the mountainous region of Wallachia, near the Great Arges River, its angular construct and pitched towers presented a formidable facade as it loomed down from atop its vast pedestal of highland. The colossal height of a castle perched atop a mountain rendered the town below it forever blanketed by shadow, the townspeople knowing nothing but the faintest glimmer of sunlight at the peak of high summer.

Besides living in eternal darkness, so much death surrounded the castle that it kept the villagers in a constant state of fear. They dared not speak ill of the *voivode* who inhabited the castle, nor his subjects, lest they be doomed to share the same fate as the poor souls picked apart each morning by raptorial birds. There was no worry of invasion under the protection of their prince, but that did little to quell their overall apprehension, as whispers circulated about the village that their baron was far from human.

Deep within the hollows of the castle, David was perched at the window, watching as a group hoisted up yet another addition to the stockade of unfortunate souls. A fat vulture sat patiently nearby, eager to fight the circling ravens for the prized meal of freshly expired meat. He sighed, wondering what the man had done to the prince to deserve such a fate.

"Master David," a voice interrupted him.

He looked up to see a meager servant standing at the doorway. "His Majesty wishes to speak with you in the dining hall," he stammered.

"Thank you." David dismissed him, watching the malnourished creature struggle to walk away.

He sighed once more. Never again was Lucius able to create an immortal in the truest sense, but it hadn't stopped him from trying, his court filled with creatures closer to revenants than their demigod sire. These *nemorti* were able to think independently and feed on their own, but their strength and prowess posed no threat to their predecessors. Lucius was pleased by the discovery, realizing that submissive minions served his purpose far better than equals. He kept them comfortably imprisoned, forbidding any departure from the castle, feeding them as one might domesticated hounds, either the prisoners from the dungeons he kept overstocked or the unsuspecting villagers who he sent Hunters out to capture. It served as another method of control, keeping his court slightly underfed to ensure that no one would have the strength to revolt against him.

The *nemorti* lived blissfully unaware of his tactics, content to live out their immortal lives under the dominion of their *voivode*, fighting his wars for him in fervent obedience. The only outlier was David, who spent his hours in the solitary confinement his study provided, reading the endless manuscripts man had penned over the centuries or by sketching intricate maps of the worlds they'd traveled. Cartography was the last surviving piece of Davius, the artist in him buried beneath centuries of sorrows.

The sounds of hammering spikes shook David from his musings, and he realized his shoulders were knotted from lack of movement. He stretched his arms as he stood, wistfully leaving behind his books and drawings to head down the long corridor into the main hall. The vaulted ceilings caused his footsteps to echo as he strode briskly, eager for the conversation to be had and through with.

Lucius's affinity for extravagance served him well in his latest charade, playing the part of royalty in exemplary fashion. Vivid sanguine tapestries bearing Lucius's insignia cluttered the walls in boisterous profligacy. It was a nod to Vlad Dracul's membership in the Order of the Dragon, depicting a black dragon as an ouroboros, its tail wrapped around its neck, and a thin black cross in the background. Crimson rugs interrupted the stone floors, the oak tables that lined the halls painted black to match the onyx candle holders and sculptures Lucius had kept over the centuries. Various weaponry hung on the walls, creating an intimidating pattern with Lucius's prized collection of skulls, the species ranging from elk, to human, to the few unlucky nemorti who had dared to cross him. The entire palace kept the macabre color scheme, down to its baron, who turned to greet him with a swish of his carmine robes. His gold jewelry glittered in the torch light, bringing out the manic glint of his amber eyes.

"David," he greeted him, with a forced warmth that only David could detect.

David smiled, although he easily matched the displeasure, acutely aware of the tension building each time they shared a room. "You called for me?"

He noticed several of Lucius's nemorti servants moving about the room, dressing the five long dining tables in scarlet tablecloths and setting out the silver cups and bowls that were used at every feast. A larger number of revenants worked in the background, languidly securing what appeared to be large iron cauldrons against the southern wall. David couldn't help but feel a mixture of contempt and pity for the lesser creatures, forced to live out their days in blind submission.

"Yes, I did." Lucius led him away from the bustle towards the high table, an elevated structure set far enough away from the others to offer privacy. David noticed there was a recent addition of a painting in Lucius's likeness situated right above his throne. The artist had exquisitely captured his spiraling sable locks and the extravagance of his royal turban, a flamboyant piece of red velvet headwear, lined in pearls and adorned by one large, precious ruby.

"Planning another feast, I presume?" David asked, deciding against mentioning the portrait, lest he be drawn into one of Lucius's magniloquent explanations.

"As you are well aware, we have won the war for the Wallachian throne, ensuring longevity for our kind," Lucius replied. "The last of the Transylvanian Saxons are either dead or rotting in our prisons. It is high time that we have a celebration."

"Of course," David murmured, curious where this was leading.

"I have planned something unlike anything we have seen before, a treat for my court." Though his lips were tight, Lucius's eyes betrayed his excitement, his pupils glittering. They had widened over the centuries, eclipsing his golden irises with intrusive obsidian.

"And you wish for me to be there," David finished, unenthused.

"I would, however, I am well aware of the abhorrence you feel towards my feasts," Lucius replied, an air of annoyance drying out his words.

At the beginning of their lives as Wallachian royalty, Lucius developed a favorite pastime, the feast. Prior to his discovery, a blood drinker's habits were a solitary endeavor, yet with so many newly minted *nemorti* and revenants to feed, Lucius decided to turn the necessity into a social event. He transformed the castle kitchen into a butchery, adhering hooks to the ceiling so cooks could easily drain humans in mass quantities, filling troughs to be drained into decanters and poured into the hundreds of goblets set at the tables. Sometimes the meals included raw meat from various species; a favorite treat amongst the court a recently removed heart. David was present at first, even though he was irked Lucius had robbed them of the pleasures of hunting, a ritual David cherished even with his newfound conscience. But it wasn't until Lucius brought a live human into the hall to serve as entertainment that David found the event more than he could bear.

The moment the man was dragged into the room, David was assaulted by his thoughts, coming to him as clear as any blood clairvoyance he'd received in the past. He froze in dismay, mentally fighting the oppressive visions of the man's life, playing right before his eyes. He was a kind Turkish man with three young daughters who loved him dearly. David could hear their twinkling laughter as he chased them around his humble household, could smell the stew cooking on the fire near an old lady who could only be his mother. The man thought of nothing but his motherless daughters, the delirious refrain playing over and over in his head, "But my daughters, I have to get home to my daughters…"

David had jumped from his seat at the high table, much to the surprise of Lucius and Morgana, fleeing the room before they had a chance to question him. He had not returned to the dining hall since.

"My main concern tonight is Morgana," Lucius interrupted the recollection. He lowered his voice to an audible whisper. "You know how highly she is regarded amongst the court. If they were to catch on to her decline…" For the first time in years, David saw a glimmer of his old friend, his expression crumpling with visible concern for the object of his unrequited love. Yet no sooner had the look surfaced, did he blink and turn back into the cold, grimacing creature he had hardened into.

"I can visit her chambers to assess her wellbeing," David offered hesitantly, unsure of his reaction.

"Excellent. I'd advise you to do so soon. We will convene for dinner within the hour."

David nodded, bowing his head towards him in a good natured gesture, one he'd learned kept their growing tensions at bay.

A group of *nemorti* heaved past them, pushing a massive cart piled with bundles of wooden pikes. "Right this way!" Lucius instructed them upon sight, leaving David's side.

Grateful for his distraction, David strode out of the room, down the winding corridors towards Morgana's chambers which were tucked in the residential keep. The tapestries that hung from these walls were akin to those in the main halls, with the addition of a slender black crow perched behind Lucius's dragon. Silver vases filled with red roses decorated every furnished surface, elaborate headdresses constructed with avian bones nailed to each stone wall. It was eerily quiet as he moved through her hallway, absent of the daily bustle customary to the main castle.

Then the aroma of human blood hit him, precisely at the same moment someone physically collided with him as he turned the corner. Startled, he recognized Morgana as she tumbled into his arms. He struggled to maintain his grasp on her, realizing she was not only nude, but completely slick with cruor.

The eyes that met his, when he finally stabilized them both, were a vacant, dull brown, not unlike the despondent expression of a dying animal. It was a look that was becoming increasingly familiar to him as her episodes grew more frequent, as well as the sudden shudder they gave right before the irises shifted back to vibrant blue. It was after such a transition that he knew he spoke with the Morrigan, untainted by her bodily counterpart. They shifted now as she searched his face with confusion. "Daghda?"

He checked to see if anyone witnessed their encounter, hoisting her fully into his arms and ducking into her bedchamber. He slipped on the floor as he entered, nearly taking both of them to the ground. He steadied himself, observing the entire room was splattered with gore. Both hunger and revolution assaulted him as he pieced together what had occurred. As a human, Delicia had taken great pleasure in draining the bodies of young women to acquire blood to bathe in, convinced of its beautifying properties. Recently the practice had been revived in the weakening amalgamation that was Morgana. The dead servant girl lying motionless in the bathtub, and her lingering thoughts as her soul passed to the Otherworld, was all the evidence he needed.

He set Morrigan carefully on her feet where she remained still, staring blankly at the tub as the liquid streamed from her hair down the curvature of her lithe but muscular body.

David rifled through one of her many wardrobes to produce a chemise. He lifted it over her head and tugged it down around her body, the fabric clinging to the dampness of her skin, revealing nipples erected by the draftiness of the castle. His eyes lingered on them for a moment before he hastily averted them, discomforted that his lust for her had not faded, although their fleeting tryst had never evolved beyond just that.

Thankfully, she didn't seem to notice the color that had crept into his face as he led her to her four-poster bed. He covered her with a few linen blankets before sitting down beside her, dabbing at her moistened forehead with his wrist. It pained him to see her so broken, a mere trace of the fierce creature he once knew, ruined by a faulty vessel unable to house dual souls as it once had.

"Why am I like this?" she asked him, as if she read his thoughts, gazing up at him, crestfallen.

David's heart sank. "I do not know for certain. The only thing I can surmise is that Delicia's fevered brain cannot hold the power that is the Morrigan."

She smiled weakly at his attempt to lift her spirits, turning her gaze out the window at the distant swarm of birds that bespeckled the sky. "I have no real power anymore," she said softly. "Even my crows have left me."

He leaned over to kiss her damp hair. "You will always be powerful," he assured her. "I shall never forgive myself for your condition. It's my fault you have become like this."

"No," she objected, turning back to face him. "It was I. I would not listen to Lucius's warnings, I chose this defective body as my vessel. You only did as you promised me, fulfilling a vow I forced you to make."

David sighed. "Your words do little to alleviate my guilt."

"You and your guilt," she teased. "Perhaps you are as defective as me."

He laughed, pleased to see her mental strength returning.

She glanced over at the woman in her tub, whose soul had finally passed, leaving the shell of her body behind her. "I do not understand how I keep ending up with living women as servants."

"Delicia demands the Hunters fetch them for her," David explained, referring to the only servants Lucius allowed to leave the castle, those sent out weekly to fetch provisions for the court. "She fails to grasp that immortality itself will keep her young and beautiful, without the unnecessary bloodshed."

"Again, your guilt surfaces through your words. Why do you care for mortals so? They are a food source, weak, pathetic creatures, nothing more. The crow does not pity the mouse as he eats it. He is grateful for the nourishment it provides. We are nature's predators, Daghda, gods among men."

"Yes, but they have souls," he argued, before he could catch himself. Her eyes bore into his for only a moment before they slowly rolled back into her head, the lovely azure irises resurfacing a murky brown. The enlargement of her pupils threatened eradication of any pigment, giving her a manic look that was not unlike their mutual sire. "You are pathetic," Delicia jeered.

David sighed, disappointed his conversation with Morrigan had ended so soon.

Delicia threw herself out of bed, tearing off her soiled chemise and rendering herself nude once more. "You are distracting me from getting ready for Lucius's feast. Where is my servant girl?"

"You murdered her, Delicia," David replied flatly. "She lies dead in your tub."

"You will address me as Morgana," she hissed, flying up to where he stood, her combative stance reminiscent of a harpy poised to attack. "The bitch still lives inside me, no matter how desperately she wants to be free."

His face darkened as a storm brewed in his chest. "Careful, Delicia," he warned her through gritted teeth, hackles raised as he matched her stance. Their faces wavered mere inches apart. "You would be nothing without her power."

"How dare you, you impotent excuse for an immortal," she jeered, her cold brown eyes dancing with truculence. "Be gone from my rooms before I tear you apart myself."

David braced himself for attack, just as Lucius entered the room.

"Please, no arguing between brethren," he began. He paused, his eyes sweeping around the room in a similarly confused fashion as David moments earlier, finally settling upon Morgana's naked form. A low growl rumbled from his bowels as his eyes caught sight of David. In an instant, he had him by the throat, slamming him against the wall in untethered rage.

David felt his pharynx crushing under the passion of his fist, unable to correct the misunderstanding as he fruitlessly pried at Lucius's clenched fingers.

"Lucius, no!" Morgana shrieked, mercifully restored to her Morrigan half. She threw herself at the two of them, grabbing Lucius's outstretched arm.

He relented at her touch, as David crumbled to the ground. He shuddered at the pain in his throat as his immortal body worked to heal itself. He was grateful he had instinctively stiffened far before Lucius charged, or he might have spent the evening unconscious from the affliction.

"You let him touch you?" Lucius spat at Morrigan.

Morrigan's face twisted in anger. "Just because you lay with the wench you fused me with does not make me your property," she seethed. "I can barely stand our endeavors as it is."

Lucius's expression melted, giving way to fretful unease. He put his hands on her shoulders. "Surely you don't mean that, my love."

Morrigan threw his hands off her, coming to David's aide. His throat had mercifully restored itself to its proper shape, and with her help, he stood to meet Lucius's level.

Only once had David succumbed to his desire for the Morrigan, long before they came to Wallachia, when they roamed the lands of Gaelic Ireland per her request. And Lucius had never forgotten it.

It was a time when David took part in their many battles, his innate predator relishing the opportunity to utilize its immortal strength. It served him twofold, for not only did war sate the beast inside of him but aligning himself with Celtic tribes similar to his own ancient clan offered him a detached sense of justice.

The world had descended into late autumn, around the festival of Samhain, when the last copper leaves surrendered, amassing in piles around the barren trees. It was a battle like any other, the raven Morgana soaring above the advancing warriors, unleashing her shrill war cry as Lucius led them through the wild grass into combat. David had focused his energy upwards, pooling together a spiraling windstorm that blotted out the sun.

Although disoriented by the tumultuous weather and vicious birds, the enemy fought hard, David utilizing all his strength to clear rows of bodies with the sweep of his hammer. Splattering blood obscured most of his vision, but he caught glimpses of Morgana in human form, her hair a mess of short, wild curls left after she chopped it before each battle, holding her ground not far from where he stood. She moved with the grace and poise of a dancer, bending and twisting around the extended limbs and swords, slashing her double-edged spear with artful precision. He felt compelled to run to her aid only when they surrounded her, covering her tiny frame in a wall of brawn intent on ripping it apart. Yet she shattered their hold as she shot up from the center of them in an eruption of ravens that exploded as soon as it reached the sky, raining down upon them in merciless slaughter.

He stood watching her, in the midst of the chaos around him, transformed into the young boy who watched in awe of the carnage she brought to the Port of Rome.

After the men lay ravaged and motionless in the mud, she was human once again, her chest heaving with the exertion, streaks of dirt and gore covering her scant clothing and the acres of flesh it exposed. She pulled a wayward arrow out of her thigh, casting it aside as the wound released a short stream of obsidian blood and sealed itself as if her skin had never been torn. She noticed him gazing at her and responded with a wild, triumphant smile.

The battle was over, the carnage so great that every man left standing was covered in the splattered remains of the savage butchery that had occurred. They roared cheerful victories over a battle fought hard but won.

The horde made their camp along the nearby Unshin River, the three creatures finding shelter in the nearby caves. Lucius, normally bright eyed and exhilarated by a good fight, instantly fell into a deep slumber, the rarity of such an occurrence revealing he'd gone weeks without rest. Although it had been the same for David, he found he was unable to follow suit, opting to meditate near the rushing river waters instead.

As soon as he reached the tributary behind their caves, her figure came into view, ghostly pale in the moonlight against the sapphire pool where she stood. She was a perfect vision of the Morrigan he once knew, all traces of the madwoman Delicia fallen away, as if the magic of her homeland absolved her of her burdens. She turned towards him, exposing rounded breasts neatly stacked upon rippling rib bones, her ivory skin taut over her stomach and thighs. She reached up to let down the long onyx hair which had grown back at nightfall, letting it tumble down in shimmering waves about her sylphlike curves.

He was in her arms instantly, tearing off his tunic and leathers and letting them fall carelessly into the river with a splash. She proved to be as intoxicating as any conquest, and soon he was lost in a carnal desire he hadn't experienced since he was a young man enthralled by a slave girl named Gaia. He held her easily as she mounted him, her muscular legs gripping his waist as she ground her hips into him. She buried her teeth in his neck as she climaxed, sampling his tarnished essence as her body shuddered in release. Breathlessly, she then tore open a vein from her own wrist, pressing it against his mouth to offer him the same experience. His eyes rolled back in surrender to the exquisite pleasure of being connected to her in every way, her blood whispering her secrets, centuries of life as the great, formidable Morrigan.

When it was finished, they both collapsed into the water, delirious with exhilaration. He lunged for her, eager to begin again, only to realize the water around them had grown unusually warm.

David looked up to see the figure of Lucius standing on the muddy bank, his body tensed in fury, currents of red heat sparking around his body like electric lightning, radiating from his hands in currents of fire. He had created a ring of flames around them, slowly bringing the water to a treacherous boil.

Morrigan immediately drew David into her arms and transformed, pulling him out of the river with her talons. She carried him through the air to the mouth of the cave where they had made camp, shifting back to human as she landed and pulling him inside. David barely managed to pull on a tunic before Lucius arrived and promptly pounced, pinning him to the ground in a chokehold. "Did you forget that I am your sire, *your master?*" he cried, his eyes black and face contorted by violent wrath.

David wrenched his scorching fingers away from his throat as Morrigan grabbed Lucius by the hair, tossing him across the room. In the narrow confines of the cave, the air began to churn into funnels, threatening to intensify.

"Enough," Morrigan commanded, standing firmly between them, "unless you want our lives to end in a fury of wind and fire and crow."

Lucius remained crouched at the farthest nook of the cave, regaining his breath as the angry sparks that wound around his body cooled to a flicker.

David noticed the vision he had seen of Morrigan in the water had faded away, the woman before him restored to the dual deity that was Morgana. Her variant eyes looked compassionately towards his assailant as she moved closer to him. "Please forgive me," she crooned, her voice now flavored by the sopranic pitch of Delicia. "I was under the spell of this land."

David glanced at Lucius, who gazed up at her with pained eyes. It suddenly occurred to him that his sire's lust had evolved into something much more than he had realized. He rose to his feet, brushing the cave debris from his clothes. "Apparently, so was I," he said flatly.

Morgana crouched next to Lucius, holding him to her chest as a mother might soothe her babe, running her fingers through the mess of his dark hair. "I love you both as my family," she declared, looking directly at David. "But Lucius's bed is the only one I will share."

David knew that the creature before him was not the Morrigan, and that even if it were, she could not be contained nor possessed. In fact, he felt no desire to, their brief interaction enough to hold him off, though he could still taste her on his lips. His response was genuine as he told them, "I never meant to come between you. You are both my brethren in this eternal life. How was I to respect something of which I did not know?"

Lucius's face did not soften as he peered at him coldly through the tangle of Morgana's sinewy arms. "Now you are aware."

David felt as if ice poured through his body as Lucius's eyes bore into his. Gone was any trace of the being who once called him brother, David confronted with pure malice, the antithesis of compassion. Chills prickled the flesh of his skin.

He remembered looking away, unable to maintain his gaze.

The same look was painted across Lucius's face now, his mustached lip quivering as it pressed the other into a thin line, his eyes roaring funeral pyres. "This madness must end," he said brusquely through his teeth. "We must find a way to fix her."

Morrigan left them to their current standoff, moving towards her wardrobe to retrieve and pull on another chemise. She turned back to face them, her dried hair flowing wildly from her chiseled face, eerily reminiscent of the Medusa. "You must kill me," she said simply. "It is the only way I can be freed of this torment through which I live."

Lucius softened, his eyebrows unfurling as he pleaded with her. "Morgana, you cannot ask that of us."

David felt similarly in sentiment, sorrowfully observing the fierce resolve behind her words.

Frustrated, she withdrew to the window. "I long to fly free once more," she murmured, gazing out onto the clouded horizon.

David met Lucius's eyes in a fleeting moment of camaraderie. "There must be another way."

Lucius sighed. "There is."

Morrigan whipped around to face him, her jaw tight. "Do not ask Daghda to perform magic," she warned. "You know that both of our powers have left us."

David flinched at her words. The Morrigan had her condition to blame for the disappearance of her shapeshifting abilities, but David's powers had also faded over time, around the same time that his insidious new conscience took hold. Only Lucius had maintained his manipulation of fire, yet he seldom, if ever, found himself in need of its power.

"Neither of you can help," Lucius agreed as he paced, his robes sopping up the contents of the floor. He looked strange without his signature goblet, choosing to clasp his hands behind his waist in its absence. "Long ago, when the spellcaster brought me to life, I made a pact with her that she and her offspring would have unlimited power. She lived in Transylvania, centuries before its name. It might be possible that her lineage survives. If they are as strong as their matriarch once was, they might be the solution to our problem."

Morrigan looked hopeful, the expression softening the severity of her features. "May we try?"

The brief glimpse of her vulnerability brought Lucius to her side. "Of course we will," he assured her, wrapping his arms around her in a comforting embrace.

She allowed him to hold her, flinching only slightly when he rested his cheek against her hair. He continued to glower across the room at David. "David will join us for one last supper before he rides out to Transylvania," he asserted as he kept him trapped in his glare. "Perhaps he will be able to find her daughters and restore you back to health. We know how much he enjoys his nights away from our home, the search should prove satisfying for him."

David frowned, but couldn't disagree. The bulk of his evenings were spent finding any excuse to escape from the castle, whether it was hunting in the nearby woods for game or traveling abroad. He didn't need much persuasion to leave but was moved by the prospect of restoring the Morrigan to her former glory. Even if that meant the resurgence of the Lucius and Morgana battle antics.

Both awaited his response, two otherworldly beings confined by mortal bodies, intertwined in a mess of ebony hair and waxen skin, doused in shades of crimson. A vision of the Lovers he once painted surfaced from memory, the two creatures before him a macabre inversion of the pure connection he'd tried to capture so long ago. Yet, for all their faults, and his growing animosity towards their actions, he still loved them. They were his family, his only companions for centuries.

"Yes," he sighed in defeat. "I will dine with you, then I will depart this evening."

"Wonderful," Lucius said. He released Morrigan so he could face her. "You can dress for dinner, and I will get someone to clean up this mess." He grimaced once he finally realized the extent of the room's desecration, gingerly lifting his sullied robes. He glanced back up at her. "Are you able to dress yourself for tonight, my dear, or shall I find you another lady in waiting?"

"I think I can manage on my own," she replied.

CHAPTER SIX

❧ The Others ❧

The great hall was brimming with nemorti when David entered, his stomach churning with apprehension. He'd dressed hurriedly, securing his olive doublet with a belt that matched his riding boots, which he had donned in preparation for his travels. He shifted uncomfortably in his stockings, which he loathed wearing, never acclimating to the stifling clothing of modern custom. They never seemed to make them roomy enough for his muscular legs.

David could already hear the frantic thoughts of the distressed prisoners below, reminding him that being in a room filled full of dying humans was going to be unbearable. He promptly gathered what Lucius's plans for the evening entailed, large wooden spikes that could hold a man's weight lined the two main walls, empty iron vats waiting at each base. He wondered how long he would be able to withstand witnessing their slow, agonizing deaths, as hundreds of mindless *nemorti* drank to their misfortune.

The sight of the Morrigan calmed him, grateful to see she had yet to slip back into her Delicia aspect. An amused smirk slid across his face as he realized she'd barely wiped the smeared blood off her face, the warrior goddess thoroughly enjoying her war paint, regardless of dining formalities. She also left her hair flowing free without a hat to tame it, her skirts and sleeves poorly matched, and the deep v-neck of her gown revealing the complete lack of underdress. Her blood-streaked breasts threatened to fall from the plunging neckline as she leaned forward to greet him.

His presence drew several curious stares from the court as he moved towards the high table, assuming the place normally left empty in his absence. Morrigan's azure eyes shimmered as he approached, her cheeks flushed with a liveliness he hadn't seen in her for months. "I'm so glad you have decided to join us, Daghda," she purred.

David squeezed her shoulder reassuringly as he slipped past her, taking his place to the right of Lucius's throne.

From his seated position, he was able to observe Lucius's court of animated death conversing amongst each other as they gazed approvingly at the pikes erected around them, eager for the festivities to begin. The women were pallid and rail thin, swallowed by wool gowns with intricate patterns of reds, greens, gold, and black. Their hats dwarfed them, the elongated cone shapes creating a rippling sea of color as their heads bobbed and weaved with animation. Men also wore the traditional colors, draped in layers of robes to hide their malnourishment, vests of fur plumping out their narrow chests. The room was aglow with torches set in sconces around the cavernous hall, causing the smooth, deeply stained wooden beams set in the ceiling above to shine. An ample fire roared in the vast fireplace at the southern end, the aroma of blistering oak flavoring the stale air.

David longed for the meal to be over, eager to be in the dense woods that surrounded the castle, even though he knew his leave was less about pleasure than it was purpose. His eyes flitted impatiently at the doorway, just as Lucius's main servants waltzed through it to announce his presence.

The commotion dulled to a low hum as his subjects took their respective places in front of their chairs. Lucius appeared from behind the two revenants, vainglory incarnate, dripping in gold effects as his thick mane of polished black hair flowed regally behind him. His court hailed him as he entered, murmuring venerations as he proudly peacocked through them to his throne. He mirrored the portrait above him in grandiloquence, his fur lined robes matching the conspicuous red and amber hues of his velvet turban. His thin fingers were dominated by gold rings bearing precious stones, an extravagant garnet situated at his throat. He stood proudly, stretching his arms up and outwards towards the mass of denizens below.

"People of Wallachia!" he addressed them in their language, his voice ringing through the capacious chamber. "We come together tonight in celebration of the Dragon's hold on the Wallachia throne!"

The crowd burst into cheers.

"As your deeply benevolent ruler, I have decided to throw a feast to surpass all who have come before it!"

Acclamation reverberated throughout the hall once more.

Lucius beamed, relishing in the open adulation before raising a slender hand to silence them. "But first, I offer my court a treat unlike any other. Before we dine, we shall enjoy a rare entertainment." He looked down at David, who was inspecting him with an air of confusion. "Do you remember the balatrones of Rome, brother?"

David blanched at the archaic term for court jester. He knew that only tragedy would befall the unfortunate soul Lucius had targeted, quite the opposite of any merriment the title usually invoked. His trepidations were confirmed as the massive hall doors were thrown open once more, revealing a man weighed down by heavy chains. Two *nemorti* soldiers dragged him onward, their stocky arms and sturdy bodies revealing their status as Hunters. David's mouth went dry, the room taking on a nauseating sway.

Although he had spent much time in Lucius's damp and perilous dungeon, the man's face was handsomely chiseled and youthful, even with the strange attribute of a full head and beard of silvered hair. He was both tall and broad, requiring the exerted strength of both his captors to pull him forward, even though he was closely chained and starved. He looked up with wild, dark blue eyes that pierced David's own with their ferocity. It occurred to David that as close as he was to the man, he could not hear his thoughts, something he hadn't encountered since his initial telepathic revelation.

"He has been raving in his cell for weeks, telling fantastical stories of giant wolves and mythical beasts," Lucius elucidated to the *nemorti* who already buzzed with excited anticipation. "I thought we could use a little laughter to begin our meal."

The court offered sounds of approval.

The two soldiers threw the heavily bewhiskered man at the foot of the high table before Lucius, David now able to see the brightly colored fabrics they'd draped on him in mockery. He tried to empty his mind, but still he was unable to hear the prisoner's thoughts.

"You do not hear me," the captive man snarled at Lucius. "I am not human. If you do not allow me to find shelter before the moon peaks, I will tear this court apart limb from limb."

Lucius roared laughter that dripped with derision, his assemblage following suit. "Oh sir, you do not have the slightest idea what sort of court this is," he chortled. "You should have thought better than to try to break into our fortress."

Morrigan bolted upright from her chair. "Lucius."

"Tell us more about what you think will happen at this court," he continued to taunt the man crouched before him, seemingly unaware of her speaking. "Tell us more about how we will meet our doom at your hands."

"Lucius," she repeated, louder.

The court fell silent, all eyes upon her. David noticed her face was stricken with fear, causing him to rise up from his chair in concern.

"That man is not human," she cautioned, her expression frozen in bewilderment as she stared.

Lucius's face flushed with embarrassment, gesturing for David to remove her from the room. He complied, unnerved to see her wearing such an uncharacteristic expression.

No sooner did he reach her, did the man before them begin to scream in such a manner that the two knights holding him backed away in alarm. He gripped his skull as if something tried to burrow its way out, his rigid fingers pulling away tufts of his silver hair. His already substantial limbs appeared to grow larger, bursting through the confines of his clothing, his entire body convulsing as it slowly stretched itself beyond human proportion.

Before Lucius could react, there was a loud pop and a clank, and the iron chains that were wrapped around the man ruptured and fell, shattering as they hit the stone floor. Within moments, what stood before them was no longer a man, but a mammoth sized wolf, its wide, maniacal eyes glistening as its enormous mouth opened to reveal teeth dripping with saliva. The creature was so large, it dwarfed the *nemorti* who stared up at him in blatant consternation, its head grazing the wood beams that decorated the ceiling. It ripped away the tattered remains of his makeshift costume, letting out a roar so loud, it thundered throughout the chamber.

The room promptly erupted into chaos, *nemorti* forced to employ their unrefined power as the wolf began tearing its way through them. They were no match for its incredible strength, torn limbs and dismembered heads soaring across the room as rotten blood showered the hall in a fetid spray.

"Lucius, resolve this!" David cried out, as he shielded the weakened Morrigan from flying appendages and broken furnishings.

He caught sight of his sire, whose wide eyes betrayed his bewilderment as he stood, motionless, staring at hands that produced no fire, only tiny sparks that interrupted the tendrils of smoke diffusing from them like the cinders of an extinguished fire. His knights grabbed him by his arms, hoisting him out of the room for his own protection before he had time to object. David watched as they slammed shut the heavy arched doors against Lucius's protestations, leaving whatever was left of the court to the mercy of the voracious beast.

David pulled Morrigan behind an upturned table, contemplating his next move. He hadn't been in battle for many years, but he knew his body was still strong, even in the absence of his powers. He surmised that he could hold the beast off long enough for Lucius to convince his knight to let him back in to retrieve his beloved Morgana. His eyes caught sight of the hearty flames still alive in the fireplace, wondering how he might use them to his advantage.

Two small hands cupped his face, directing it downward.

Morrigan's eyes sparkled even though her lips were dry and bloodless. "Daghda, you must take me. It is the only way that my dormant powers can be used."

David stared at her blankly before realizing the implications behind her words. He shook his head vehemently. "No."

Her lips turned upward, momentarily softening her expression. "I know your love for me is deep, but that is why you must honor my request. How many more times must I beg you to free me from this life? Lucius does not have the strength to do it. It must be you. If you do not take my powers through my blood, the wolf will be your end as well."

Shrieks, howls, and the horrible sounds of tearing flesh created a lurid harmony around them.

"How do you know it will work?" David pointed out in desperation, searching her eyes for any bend in her resolve.

"I was once a very powerful god, my love, with many allies. I have known this was my gift to give you for some time now, one that I planned on offering you as my time on this earth came to a close. I didn't realize it would happen so soon, but although I played along in Lucius's presence, I know there is no cure that can rid me of Delicia."

"You cannot ask this of me," David repeated.

"I am not asking, I am demanding, and you would do well not to ignore me," she warned, though her face was still soft. "I am done with this life, with this abominable body. Drink of my blood and use my power until I one day return. Follow the wolf until you find a woman named Hekate. She holds all the answers that you seek."

"You want me to follow the wolf?" he repeated, his tone incredulous. "This is madness."

"I promise more shall be revealed to you, but our time is running out. Drink from me, Daghda, please."

Although bedlam ensued all around them, the world grew still. He tried to comprehend her words, to truly understand their meaning, but flashes of Gaia on her deathbed danced morosely before his eyes, distracting him. He could barely distinguish the memory from the present, holding Morrigan in his arms as he had once held her, with the resolute knowledge that this moment would be their last. "Why must every woman I love end up dying?" he whispered, ashamed of his vulnerability.

"Oh, you shall see me again, my sweet, broken David," she promised as her cold hands caressed the sides of his lightly whiskered face. "The bond between the Daghda and the Morrigan transcends all time. I will always find you." Her last words were singed with resolve as she lifted herself up to press their mouths together, her lips tasting of smoke and rain soaked earth. And then, she fell back, and in one ruthless gesture, tore the large vein in her neck with her taloned fingernails, pulling David against her.

The scent released into the air proved irresistible to him, her decayed but powerful blood a tantalizing elixir spilling down the smooth planes of her pale skin. David tried to resist, but her grasp on him was firm, and before he could stop himself, he drank.

Her secrets spilled into him as her body crumpled into his, visions of the archaic war goddess with her crow skull diadem and wild, matted hair, the violent sexual romps between Morgana and Lucius, covered in each other's inky black ichor. David felt her fingers through his hair, pressing him harder against her flesh. He heard the immobilized Delicia screaming for him to stop, her own memories invading the Morrigan's as she tried desperately to break free. He saw her life in flashes, the fawn-haired cherub raised by a monster, laughing as her father beat his slaves into submission, the genesis of her ritualistic bloodletting, the rise of her power in Rome.

And then, strangely enough, he saw Gaia, her radiant smile in the solstice sun and her olive eyes twinkling around the freckled bridge of her nose. Images of the three women danced together, the lines between them blurring until Delicia dissolved into nothingness, leaving Morrigan and Gaia linked together, as if they were one. He wasn't given a moment more to consider these visions when an effusion of power released out of Morrigan and burrowed into him, crows shrieking disapproval inside his skull as they clawed irately at his insides. The sensation threw him back from her now unconscious body, his muscles trembling and his skin rippling with intensity. "Find the woman Hekate," her voice echoed in his head.

The table that had been shielding them was suddenly upended, revealing the massive, snarling beast, its hoary fur drenched in the blood of dozens of slaughtered creatures. It roared at David, its rank breath hot on his face as it advanced, positioning its open jaws around his head, its claws stretched wide.

David's body surrendered to the shuddering energy that was pulsating throughout it, his bones and tendons suddenly snapping and popping as his muscles expanded, pain threatening his consciousness. It was the antithesis of his avian transformation, the restrictive pressure he once felt replaced by the sensation of expansion, as if he was being pulled apart from all angles. He howled, defenseless against it, at the mercy of the excruciating metamorphosis. Fortunately, the agony passed, and soon he was standing near eye level with the beast, wolf to wolf.

Startled, the creature stepped back, and David discovered that at last, he could hear its thoughts.

"I warned the tyrant I would murder them all," it said telepathically.

"What are you?" David asked him in the same manner of communication.

"I am the *vargr* Fenrir, killer of gods, son of Loki, who fused me to Baldur, son of Odin, the All-Father. I am *varcolac*!" the wolf declared with an air of pride.

David didn't waste any time, his body humming with the essence of the Morrigan. "Can you take me to a woman named Hekate?"

The wolf looked surprised but nodded. "I can."

The sound of Lucius screeching orders behind the barricaded doors reaffirmed the warning. David heard clanging metal as the nemorti brigade scrambled to honor their prince's request. It occurred to him that it would be in his best interest if he was not present when Lucius discovered the lifeless body of Morgana. He couldn't bear to look back at it himself.

The *varcolac* abruptly leapt from where they stood, crashing through the only window in the hall. The shattered pane of sooted glass created a nightmarish mosaic on a floor already marred by the remains of dismembered creatures. The shards and pools of spilt blood sparkled in the freely exposed moonlight.

David leapt up after him, pleasantly surprised by his newfound canine agility. He followed the *varcolac* closely, appreciating how well his four legs worked together to propel him across the castle grounds. They also aided him as the two creatures scaled the castle walls, oblivious to the ineffective wooden arrows whizzing past them as *nemorti* guards scrambled to protect their fortress.

They landed easily in the surrounding green and within moments, were concealed by the vast coniferous woodland that enclosed the castle. The tightly packed spruces and firs obscured the radiant moonlit sky as the two wolves wove through their sturdy trunks, tearing up a floor dense with moss and layers of dried needles. David's vaporous breath betrayed the frosty, pre-winter air, even though his coat of thick auburn fur prevented him from feeling its chill. Although the *varcolac* exceeded him in size, David was able to keep its pace, wondering how much farther down the mountain it would take them.

As soon as the depth of their descent ensured there would be no interruption from the stronghold above, the *varcolac* paused to snatch a wayward hare, killing it instantly in its oversized paw.

"Haven't you eaten enough?" David thought before he could help himself.

The wolf grinned, exposing a mouth of ridged fangs unevenly crammed together. "I killed for you." It threw the hare at him, which David caught and devoured before its blood had a chance to cool. He hadn't realized how hungry he was and was grateful for the unexpected renewal of energy.

They continued deeper into the woods at a modified pace until the varcolac finally paused. David stiffened as well, his supernatural senses picking up aromas foreign to those of the Carpathian Mountains.

A ring of torches roared to life around them. The *varcolac* bellowed in protest as a net barbed with silver ensnared him without warning. The beast cowered to the ground in easy defeat, wincing as the metal brushed against him. David realized that exactly twelve spears made of the same metal were aimed directly where he stood.

He shifted back into his human-like form, holding his arms up in surrender. "Hold your fire - I am no beast."

"That is for us to decide," a voice responded pleasantly, its syllables clinking together like melodious bells.

Behind each strategically pointed weapon stood a faceless knight clad in metal armor, situated between six men seated on thrones carved out of tree stumps. Each of them wore a different animal mask, their bodies entirely concealed by somber robes topped with corresponding furs or feathers The neutered beast at their feet let out a whimper at the barbs holding him in place. Apparently, the enchanted metal Lucius had once warned him about affected all the unnatural creatures on earth.

"Do not worry about your friend," the man assured him from behind the mask of an eagle. "He knows this is the only way to restrain him."

The curious sensation of repetition prickled David's skin as it occurred to him that five of the men seated around him were wearing masks in the likenesses of those he once met in a dream, many years ago: the angel, the lion, the eagle, and the bull. Flanking them was a figure wearing the mask of Anubis, the Egyptian god of the Underworld, and one dressed like a Sphinx, cloven hooves popping out from underneath the hem of his robes. "Libraean," he whispered in astonished recognition.

"We will lower our weapons once we have your word that you will not harm the humans among us," a low rumble came from the direction of the lion-masked man.

"You have my word," David replied easily. "Your creature fed me on our journey here."

"He is not ours," the bull informed him, the hollow eyes of his mask offering an unsettling visual as he spoke. "He is borrowed, like you. A gift from the Norse goddess Frigg, who sent her beloved child to further our cause. Yet one of her own brethren cursed him, the chaos god they call Loki. Danulf is now part man, part wolf, powerless to the metamorphosis as the goddess moon rises replete in her dark skies."

"You are getting ahead of yourself, Taurus," a familiar voice interjected. Even from behind the mask of the Sphinx, Libraean's one blue eye appraised him as he spoke. "David has fulfilled his destiny. His empathy has been restored. He will not harm a human among us."

"Very well." The eagle nodded, lifting a considerable wing. The encircling knights lowered their weapons at his command.

David felt a tug at his chest as the being's umber feathers caught the glow of the torchlight as it moved, reminiscent of Morrigan's oil slicked crows. "I must speak with a woman named Hekate," he said. "I was told that if I followed the wolf, I would find her."

"Do not worry, David," a seraphic voice soothed him. Its owner's mask appeared human, but lacked distinct features, glowing an iridescent white against the muted woodland colors that surrounded them. "Our Morrigan never stays away for too long. She always finds a way to be with the one who she eternally loves. You will meet Hekate when it is time."

"Who are you? Why have I been brought here?" David demanded, feeling his frustration rise.

"Davius," Libraean's voice from behind the Sphinx mask implored. David blinked at his former name being used, as if just speaking it tugged at a time long passed. "Please listen to what we must tell you. There is much more for you to learn, but our time here is limited. The veil between realms cannot stay thin for too long. You have my word that you will speak with Hekate soon - and now you have learned you can trust it."

David respected his point and allowed them to continue.

The angelic being spoke first. "We are the protectors of earthly affairs. All the gods and goddesses created in the collective minds of men answer to us, for we are the keepers of earth's magic, a council formed out of her precious elements in the absence of the First Protector. We shift in image however we must so that men from all religions will hear us. Yet we are eternal, unchanged, and our duties remain forever the same."

"The earth we now stand upon is the physical manifestation of the first magic, the Great She that existed at the beginning of time," Taurus, the bull, continued. "Not only are we tasked with keeping it safe, but we work to maintain the earth's precious balance, as Libraean once explained to you, for without it, this world would cease to be."

"The dark god Lucius upsets this balance," the lion said. "He has broken the sacred laws by which our realms follow, upsetting our natural order. His mere presence on this earth is an aberration, and now he threatens to destroy mankind, the very thing this world depends upon. He must be stopped. You are the only one who can do this, for you are the only creature that matches him in strength and power, but with a soul of a benevolent god."

"So I am constantly told." David sighed. "Though I do not recall any of it."

"There is still more you will learn, more will remember," the eagle reminded him. "But it is not time. A great war is approaching, and Lucius has already begun to prepare. Unbeknownst to you, he has been teaching his *nemorti* how to fight, training them while you embark on your travels or remain isolated in your study."

"Your omniscience is unnerving as always," David remarked.

"David, he plans to strike soon," Taurus interjected, ignoring the comment. "He intends to turn the world into blood drinkers, ridding the earth of the plague that is humanity while positioning himself as the reigning supreme. For a myriad of reasons, we cannot allow this to be."

Wind picked up in the air, rustling the dome of leaves overhead. David crossed his arms across his chest. "I still do not understand what you are asking of me."

A figure emerged from behind the circle of masked men, his face visible in the torchlight. David was surprised to discover he was a *nemorti*, but his body boasted the strength and resilience that emulated that of a true immortal. His skin was a tawny brown, his eyes a rich cocoa, rimmed with eyelashes so dark it looked as if he'd lined them with kohl. His hair was so unkempt that it stood away from his forehead, his absence of upper facial hair drawing attention to a wide mouth that tapered into a narrow chin and a pointed crop of chin hair. He wore the common clothing of peasantry, his embroidered linen shirt open at the neck, despite the chill in the air. "We need you on our side or it will prove to be a fight too great to win," he asserted, his voice thick with Wallachian dialect.

"And who are you?" David raised an untrusting eyebrow.

"Forgive me," the man mock-bowed. "My name is Dragos. I am part of the resistance that has risen up against the Imposter Prince. We number the hundreds, creatures and humans alike. Our plan is to aid in the restoration of balance, allowing blood drinkers and humans to live freely amongst each other without interference in each other's affairs."

David snorted. "How can that be, if we must feed upon humans to survive?"

"I have just shown you," a low voice broke in. The wolf had been restored to his human self, the formerly imprisoned jester staring at him from beneath his barbed net. His silvery beard was still streaked with *nemorti* blood, what was left of his clothing hanging off him in shreds. The knights wordlessly released him from the web. "Most of the blood drinkers in our army feed off animals, like humans do," he continued, sweeping the dirt from his trousers as he stood. "Others feed off the sick and dying, some take samples without the act resulting in death, all from willing participants."

David was taken aback by his brawn. He was taller than David's own substantial height, his chest wide and muscular with broad legs like elder tree trunks. His ribboned clothes revealed a full body of tattoos David hadn't noticed before, their markings and color similar to those drawn on the goddess Morrigan.

"Danulf is quite right," Dragos chimed in as he threw the man a fur lined cloak that he'd retrieved for him whilst he spoke. "Blood drinkers do not need to kill men to survive. It is a preference of the Imposter, who grows more corrupt with each life he takes."

"Surely, we do not need to explain all of this to the infamous monster with a conscience," Danulf quipped, throwing a half smile at David before he secured the cloak around his body and laced up boots that had also been procured for him. As he bent forwards, David realized the back of his hair was quite long, braided into ropes that had grown matted over time.

Dragos ignored the remark and continued with his attestation. "I have not fed upon any human besides my sire, Vlad Tepes, for years, yet I am endowed with the strength of ten men. Human blood is an unnecessary luxury, nothing more."

"Lucius created you?" David did not hide his surprise.

"Yes, I was created to be another *nemorti* slave, but instead, I serve as a spy for the Insurgence," he explained with an air of high self-regard.

"We digress from our purpose," the angelic man reminded them softly.

"You want me to be a part of your war," David stated for them.

"Correct," Dragos replied. "Danulf and I wish to take you to our stronghold, where you can see our army for yourself. That was our original purpose in Danulf infiltrating the castle, though we had not anticipated he would fail to reach you until after the full moon."

"I had a plan," Danulf growled defensively.

Dragos disregarded him once more. "Now that things are back in order, we have much to discuss with you."

The bull lifted his hand to arrest the speedy arrangements. "Before you depart, David, we will need your word."

David found he was in no hurry to respond, letting the conversation rest as he recalled the events that led up to the current moment. The Council allowed him his moment of reflection, the crackling flames the only sound in the barren winter woods. He thought of Morrigan's lifeless body abandoned by him on the stone floor of the castle, the image a dagger dragging over his chest. He remembered the vision of her and Gaia, his two lost loves, standing hand in hand, like sisters. "First, I must ask this question of you, since you are collectively all-knowing of the happenings in this world," he said. "Are Gaia and the Morrigan the same soul?"

He was met with silence, the Council still.

It was Libraean who finally spoke, lifting his Sphinx mask away from his head to expose the same face David had met so many eons ago, framed by dirty blonde waves. He set the golden facade down on his chair and approached him, painted with an earnest expression supplemented by a kindly singular eye. "There are things we cannot tell you, David, things you must wait to learn. That story is not ours to impart - our only purpose is to steer you towards what we believe is the best path. While we control the balance, the creatures on earth are free to choose their destiny. The divine beings that work amongst us have their own choices too. Our job is simple - restore, guide, protect."

David sighed, but accepted his words. He turned to look at the rest of the Council. "I want her back," he stipulated firmly.

The eagle let out a sound of exasperation. "Why must it always be this way with them?"

"Enough, Scorpius," the lion grumbled forcefully. "Your compliance in this matter will take you to Hekate. It is she who holds the key to the Morrigan's return."

"Then I wish to see her first before any talk of war."

Taurus the Bull snorted with disdain, the sentiment echoed by Dragos. "Our world falls apart, yet he thinks only of love."

"Our world would be nothing without it." Anubis, the man wearing the jackal mask, finally broke his silence. He stood, his cloak falling away to reveal a sculpted, human chest of smooth ebony skin bearing a gold-plated choker set with brilliant lapis lazuli. David's breath caught in his throat for the eyes that looked back at him were strangely familiar. The jackal seemed to grin as if pleased at David's moment of fuzzy recollection.

"I come from a time when the love between two beings shaped an entire civilization, when the broken heart of a goddess altered life forever."

"I remember," Libraean murmured.

"He shall visit the sorceress Hekate and have his questions answered," Anubis dictated. "It is the only way we can ensure his absolute assistance. What say you, Aquariolus?"

"I agree," the angel chimed.

Scorpius and Taurus looked visibly frustrated but nodded.

"Leo?"

"I have no quarrel against these terms," the lion replied, gruffly.

"Then the Council has spoken," Libraean declared.

Dragos looked unhappy but remained silent.

"You shall take him to see the witch," Scorpius craned his head towards Danulf, who had been standing silently, his bulbous arms folded before him. "Dragos, you may return to your stronghold until they arrive."

Both nodded their agreement.

The Council abruptly vanished, taking their mysterious knights with them. Libraean was the only member left, which revealed his bondage to the earthly plane still hadn't been resolved, and he shifted back into his boar guise before turning back to look at David. His expression was mournful, his good eye filled with regret. I did not know everything when last we spoke, he lamented. I am sorry I cannot divulge more to you, but I can promise, you will not regret following the path we have asked you to follow. I will see you again soon, and we can speak freely. He glanced at the other two physical beings left standing, offering a silent farewell before disappearing into the throng of mountainous woodland.

Dragos whistled, and a horse emerged from behind a slew of shadowy trees. "Do not dawdle," he warned Danulf as he hoisted himself up onto its back. "They anxiously await his arrival."

Danulf scowled, but nodded, watching as Dragos gave the mare a swift kick and followed after Libraean. Danulf looked back at David. "I will be grateful to take my final leave of that fellow," he remarked. He looked up at the sky, squinting to see through the crisscrossed ceiling of branches. "I'm afraid an overcast has obscured the moon past any helpfulness. We are going to have to embark on this journey by foot."

"We had best get started then," David suggested.

Danulf extended a sturdy, scarred arm. "I know we haven't met formally, as is the custom. You can call me Dan if you like."

David took his hand. "I prefer David over 'monster with a conscience'," he quipped.

"I bet," Danulf snorted. He gestured forward into the woods. "Shall we?"

Light spilled over the mountain, the thinly frosted evergreens glistening as a few robust birds began their morning melodies. What was a mere couple of hours as supernatural wolves felt like days on two legs. David was impressed by Danulf's resilience, for although he was part creature, the man who accompanied him now was undoubtedly human. His own bones were growing tired as dawn crept into the skies. "We should rest," he suggested, breaking what had been hours of silence.

Danulf looked surprised. "I assumed you were in a hurry to speak with our volva."

David noted his unusual use of the archaic Norse term for female shaman but decided not to comment. "While my body doesn't require much rest, it is helpful in times of overexertion," he explained to him. "I'm sure a reprieve might do the same for you."

Danulf looked thoughtful. "Perhaps the moon will show her face tomorrow evening and cut our journey by half."

Satisfied by this, the two searched for shelter. It was Danulf who discovered a suitable copse, the fallen trees and wayward branches creating a natural thicket that was nestled against several mountainous boulders. It was most likely used by wildlife at one point, but its lack of scent assured it hadn't been in quite some time.

The two burrowed inside just as a flurry of snow drifted down from the skies. Danulf shivered, adjusting his cloak so that it draped over his chest, folding up his long legs so they were nearby.

"Shall we make a fire?" David asked, attempting to empathize with human frailty.

Danulf did not smile. "I have traveled the better portion of my life in much worse conditions than a gentle snowfall."

"Still, I would rest better knowing I will not be waking up to a corpse," David insisted pleasantly, as he stood to gather up kindling. The act of building a fire felt peculiar to him, one that hadn't been required of him for years, partly since he was a creature and partly because he now belonged to the noble class. Watching the flames grow gifted him a sense of contentment, teasing him with a brief remembrance of what life was like as a human. He suddenly ached for the feral boy running barefoot in the green, with dirt in his gingery, unkempt hair and stories of Druid magic on his lips.

He returned to his corner of the thicket as the warmth filled the copse enough that Danulf could remove his furs and use them as a pillow to rest his head upon.

They sat in comfortable silence for several moments before David attempted conversation. "As a wolf, you alluded to me that you were a Norseman."

Danulf gave a single nod. "My people were who they now call Vikings. I am a human, but I have been alive for several centuries, the last of my clan."

David was shocked. "How can that be?"

"As our quartet of elusive friends explained, I was born human with the soul of a reincarnated god. That god was named Baldr, the beloved son of Odin, who is the All-Father of my people, and his wife, Frigg."

"Yes, I have read tales of the Northern men and their pagan religion. I grew up in the old ways myself, as part of a Druid tribe. Baldr was murdered by Odin's brother, correct?"

"Yes," Danulf's austere expression brightened for the first time since they'd met, openly pleased to meet someone knowledgeable of his culture, a fellow pagan in a rapidly Christianizing world. "After a *volva* foreshadowed Baldr's death to Frigg, the goddess searched the world to ensure that no object on earth would harm her child. They all agreed, except for a single branch of mistletoe that she had forgotten to include in her travels. Learning of this loophole, the diabolical god, Loki, tricked Bladr's blind brother, Hodr, into using a dart made from mistletoe for a game between brethren. He threw it at his brother during their play, accidentally killing him." He shifted, stretching his legs out before him. They exceeded the length of the gnarled woodland cove, catching snowflakes on the tips of his exposed boots.

"Desperate to bring him back," he continued, "Frigg petitioned the Council and it was agreed that since Baldr was killed by a god, he would eventually reincarnate human, as are the laws of the earth. However, a dark god named Lucius had cursed the land years before, preventing any god from reincarnating as a human unless he explicitly allowed it. Odin forced Loki to have Lucius lift the curse, yet Loki knew he could only do so by trickery. He asked Lucius to bring back his own son, Fenrir the *vargr*, or great wolf, and the dark god agreed, eager to potentially have Fenrir's servitude in this realm. Then Loki fused the souls of Fenrir and Baldr together with his magics, waiting for the day a human would be born to house them.

"Meanwhile, the Council discovered that the two souls were braided, one now belonging to Lucius. They made Frigg promise Baldr to them in order to combat the Lucius and Loki alliance. She agreed, and so here I am, half-human, half-*vargr*, parts of me promised to opposing sides. Fenrir has given me immortality, yet I have no extra strength in my human form, nor any powers, unless it is within the three night phase of the full moon."

David considered his story. "Do you recall anything from either past life?"

"No," Danulf admitted. "These things were revealed to me many years ago while I was still a young man. I grew up a strong warrior, as my father hoped I would be, until one day when the wolf emerged, slaughtering my entire village...including my kin." He grew quiet, staring blankly into the flames. A drift of snow blew in, causing them to flicker.

"I lost my clan as a child, too," David offered. "It is a special sort of suffering one must bear to lose an entire family."

"That it is," Danulf agreed, breaking from his trance. "And it was I who murdered them. Afterward, I did the only thing I could do - I ran. I became a frightened hermit, hidden away in the hills, content to spend the rest of my life traveling under their protection, lest the wolf come out to slaughter more innocent people. It was a *volva* who told me my true nature, binding me with one of her spells. She is the one who taught me to hide away during the full moon. I stayed far away from humans, but I inevitably grew mad with the isolation, shadowing villages but never venturing close enough to interact with their towns-people. Years went on in this way. As they passed, I realized I'd stopped aging, though my hair had turned a brilliant gray. The Age of Vikings had long ended, leaving me behind to live out my days as the last of my kind. Then one day, Libraean and the Council approached me, telling me that if I chose to align myself with their cause, they would help me be rid of the wolf for good. And that brings us current."

"Amazing," David commented. "I was told something similar, that I am also a reincarnated god, yet I remember nothing, even though I have become a supernatural being."

Danulf peered at him, his deep blue eyes catching the flicker of the flames. "What does it feel like, to be what you are?"

David sighed, considering how to respond. "At first, I felt invincible, a strength unlike any I have ever known coursing through my veins. I lived to hunt, my body the perfect construct of a predator - fast, spry, cunning, ferocious. I was rid of any human inclinations for empathy and compassion, until, like you, I was approached by Libraean and the Council, and through a series of actions, my humanity slowly returned. Now I'm an outlier, an outcast with the heart of a human and the body of a killing machine. I cannot say that I enjoy it much."

"I know the feeling," Danulf sympathized bitterly, drawing his fur around his ears as the fire started to dwindle. They returned to comfortable silence, the icy breeze bringing with it various aromas of pine.

"I never knew Lucius forbade gods from reincarnating without his consent," David reflected.

"Apparently your friend is quite the trickster in his own right. I honestly understand very little of this secret war between gods," Danulf confessed. "What was the line - 'there is more you will learn, more you will remember'?"

David couldn't help but laugh. It was another abandoned pleasure he realized he'd long forgotten.

Danulf smiled behind his thicket of beard before resuming his signature stoicism. "I'm sorry you lost your lover," he said, after a pause.

David looked away. "She was not my lover in this life but claims that we were in lives long passed. I cannot help but believe it, for I do care deeply for her in a way that seems to transcend common love. She gifted me her power before she died, which is how I was able to turn into a wolf."

"A shape-shifting goddess." Danulf nodded, his eyes sparkling with intrigue.

"She prefers wolves and crows."

"Ah, much like the All-Father. Crows are the wisest of birds, though they are mainly seen as harbingers of death. Yet their power runs much deeper than that. If you are kind to one crow, they will remember your face, passing the knowledge to their kin. The same if you cross them."

"That sounds like her," David remarked with a hint of melancholy.

"Do not fret, we shall get her back. There is no more powerful witch in all the land than my sister, Hekate."

"Sister?"

"Not by blood," he explained. "After the Council told me where I was needed, I made the long trek down to this region. I may be half immortal wolf, but the traveling took its toll on me. I lost track of the phases of the moon, fell asleep one night, and forgot to secure myself against the transformation. I cannot recall exactly what happened, but I was caught in a fight with a mountain beast and left broken, bloodied, and barely conscious. Young human Dragos found me and brought me to Hekate. That is when I discovered they were orphaned twins, dedicated to protecting and healing all of earth's creatures, even the deadly ones like me. And healed me she did, tending to my wounds until I was like new. I have lived with them ever since, in service to she who selflessly restored me to health. In fact, it was Hekate who gave me my name, adding a name common to her people, *Dan-* to my moniker, *Ulf…* which, I assume you can guess the meaning."

"The wolf," David said. "So her powers are great?"

"Her story is not mine to tell. I will let you decide for yourself."

"I hope for all of our sakes she is," David sighed. "Lucius is one highly skilled warlord, not one who can be easily defeated."

Danulf gave him a wide grin, revealing an assortment of silver capped teeth beneath the shelf of his peppered whiskers. "That's where you come in."

The snow continued to fall throughout their short respite, Danulf floating in and out of consciousness while David kept vigil over their simple camp. The cold, crisp air brought him comfort, as tiny flakes stubbornly broke through their shelter, landing on his arms and legs and remaining intact without internal heat to melt them away. He'd never experienced snow as a human, and he wondered if he would enjoy the experience nearly as much if warm blood coursed through his veins.

The stillness around him allowed his mind to settle, pangs of painful longing for the Morrigan breaking through, pulling at his chest as her loss became more real. He closed his eyes to reimagine the vision he had of her and Gaia as one, trying to interpret its meaning. It had to mean something, of all the secrets for her blood to spill, it was the most vivid. He hoped Hekate had answers, as he was assured, for he was beginning to grow weary of otherworldly beings demanding compliance without disclosure.

Suddenly, an unfamiliar scent reached his nostrils and his eyelids snapped open. Danulf snored next to him behind the remnants of their fire, oblivious to the world around him. The complete absence of light let David know the sun had fully descended behind the clouds, the soft hum of crepuscular animals foreshadowing the snowstorm's completion. He realized the moon's rays would soon be upon them, pulling his companion back to his previous feral state. He decided to quietly scan the darkness a few moments longer before waking him, unnerved that he was unable to place the unusual smell.

And that was when he saw it.

A monstrous creature lumbered towards him, one that looked like a giant, charred rat. Beady black eyes bulged from patchy, seared flesh above a mouth filled with jagged teeth, pus oozing from the cracks in its skin. It wiggled its elongated claws as it sped up its pace, thundering forward on its hind legs so that the entire forest shook with impact.

"Dan," he hissed urgently as he kept fixated on the monster, his reflexes stiffening his muscles in preparation for an attack.

The rat snarled as it grew closer, the revolting stench reaching its magnitude, gagging David. He hadn't been so repulsed by a creature since... "Nirus," he whispered.

The rat opened its mouth, freeing a fat, lolling tongue that lapped around a jaw that had long been broken. David immediately recalled his wolf guise, lifting himself on his hind legs as he braced himself for the assault. Yet the rat dodged him completely, aiming instead for his sleeping companion.

David cried out, but in an instant, the rat was on top of Danulf, clawing his flesh to ribbons with unnatural speed. David leapt forward, grabbing the neck of the vile creature with his own piercing jaws. He flung it across the forest floor like easy prey, bounding to where it landed and pinning it to the ground.

How are you still alive? David demanded of the weakened lump brought to submission below him.

The Great Lucius brought me back to life - he saved me! Nirus the Rat squeaked in response.

A bolt of fury livened David. He glanced back at the unconscious, heavily wounded Danulf, noticing the traveling sack laying at his feet. Shifting back into his standard form, he tore it open, revealing the silver barbed tent that had been kept in Danulf's close possession.

Nirus squeaked in frantic recognition as David braced himself for the impending onslaught of pain, wrapping the painful webbing around his fist before pummeling what was left of the rat's face. The creature died just as pitiful as it had once before, David now committed to the completion of the task. He tore the creature from limb to limb, until the wretch that was formally Nirus was truly deceased, pieces of dead rodent scattering the frosted forest floor. He stopped to catch his breath, letting the tangled net fall from his grievously burned hand. He winced as his body attempted to regenerate his skin, his fingers severely debilitated by the caustic metal, before remembering his wounded friend. He rushed to his side.

It was hard to distinguish Danulf's features through the copious ichor that coated them, his wounds oozing out what was left of his life. His chest still rose and fell with labored breath, but it was shallow and strained.

David was at a loss. Even with supernatural speed, it would take too long to reach town, and even then, who could he turn to for help? Danulf hadn't revealed Hekate's whereabouts before the attack and the otherworldly beings who visited him earlier seemed to have returned to the ether from whence they came.

A deep crimson pool spread out beneath him, defiling the blanket of white. The woods were soundless, save for the gentle tap of trickling snowflakes on their skin, as David watched the man below him slowly die. His mind was a mess of tangled, conflicting thoughts, knowing he'd seen countless men die, many by his own hand, and that watching one more shouldn't matter to him. Yet, he was unable to shake the feeling that this one should be saved.

He crouched down to where Danulf lay, turning him onto his back. The angry gashes that tore him open were slowing their steady hemorrhage, his chest no longer rising. David could tell he was moments away from death. He tried to steady his trembling voice as he spoke, "I can save you the only way I know how, but you must tell me that you approve - I cannot forcefully do to you what has been done to me."

Danulf did not respond, but David felt his finger twitch, brushing ever so slightly against David's folded leg. It would have to do.

"Forgive me," David whispered above to whoever was listening, and released the veins on his wrist so that black liquid poured from them onto Danulf's battered face. The syrupy trickle found its way to his open mouth, choking him before he swallowed. David swooped down to fasten his mouth onto one of his open wounds.

The taste of human blood jolted him as Danulf's memories assaulted his consciousness, visions of Viking war ships and battle axes drenched in gore. The earth shattering screams of Fenrir pierced his ears, but it was not the first time an attached soul protested its demise, and he ignored them, drinking harder.

The hoot of an owl finally jarred him out of his feeding haze, and he threw himself off Danulf, landing next to him on the snow, breathless and exhilarated from consuming human blood. He pulled himself to his feet, watching as the Norseman began to writhe in pain as the transformation took hold. Guilt and remorse quickly followed any lingering delectation as he observed Danulf's agonizing rebirth. "Please forgive me," he repeated, unable to tear his eyes away.

And then, mercifully, the excruciating process ceased. The lacerations that had ribboned Danulf's tattooed skin sealed, as color crept back into his lips and brightened his wild, silver hair. He gasped as he bolted upright, his sapphire eyes wide with new life. He cursed in shock.

David watched in silence as his friend took in his surroundings through new eyes, wiggling nimble fingers and stretching limbs that now surged with immeasurable power. He knew the gift would be strong in another reincarnated god, but he feared the wolf attached to Danulf, and he wasn't looking forward to discovering how it would fare with immortal power.

But before he could speak, what felt like a whip lashed his back, forcing him to his knees. They were surrounded by *nemorti*, all bearing Lucius's black and red dragon insignia. He caught Danulf's eyes for a fleeting moment before the daunting realization hit him - the moon was finally exposed again in the night sky.

The soldiers had noticed as well. "Hurry, before the beast turns!" one of them cried out.

David tried to transform back into his own canine form, but he was soon trapped under a net much like the one used earlier on Danulf, heavy silver planks burning holes into his skin. He growled in frustration as they hoisted him up onto one of their horses, fleeing as fast as they were able.

He watched as Danulf was left to the agony of a double metamorphosis, powerless to help him. As the horses increased their speed to a rapid gallop, he realized the whiplike sensation he'd felt earlier was actually a spear, one that had settled painfully between his ribs. He tried to remove it, but the net that held him was so cruelly constructed that any move he made encouraged a jolt of searing pain. He was growing lightheaded from the loss of blood, and though he knew it would take more than that to kill him, he was not immune to a loss of consciousness. He fought against it regardless, knowing he would need every ounce of strength he had to deal with Lucius. Yet the amount of blood he lost in Danulf's transformation and his current wounds proved to be too much. He groaned, and before long, gave in to the merciful darkness.

"How can you ever forgive me?" a woman's voice broke through oblivion.

"You have not done wrong by me, sister," a benevolent voice replied. "How could I ever hold ill will against the other part of my soul?"

Two women materialized, one seated on a throne of polished gold, layers of jade and lapis lazuli crawling up each arm. The other was crouched down before her, contorted by her despair as she looked up with doleful eyes. Both women were aesthetically stunning, their skin the color of the earth, their hair waterfalls of obsidian splendor. Paint darkened their eyes and rouged their lips, their limbs and chests dressed in sparkling gold jewelry and precious gems. Their skin seemed too smooth to be human, their bodies too hard, as if they had been exquisitely carved out of marble. Their faces mirrored each other in perfect symmetry, yet one kept the hair beneath her jewel encrusted crown in billowing waves around her emerald eyes, the other cropped short with eyes that rivaled the summer sky.

The green-eyed sister stood, pulling the other to her feet. "How could I understand this love that you speak of? I do not feel such things. My love is for humanity, Osiris my counterpart. He is my partner in the creation of humans, but I do not possess him as my own."

The blue-eyed sister wiped away a befallen tear. "It was when the humans started to create life amongst themselves without your aid. That is when I felt it - a yearning, a longing for him. The acts I perform with Set fill me with pleasure, but they pale in comparison to real love. My heart began to beat only for the man who was meant for my sister."

"No," the other corrected her firmly. "We are the broken She, and they are the broken He. No one among us possesses the other. Your prolonged time spent amongst the humans is turning you into one, but you must trust that I have not been affected in this way. I still see things clear."

"You speak these words to me, yet I still feel ashamed, Isis," the blue-eyed sister's voice dropped to a sullen whisper.

Isis took her hands, forcing her to look into her eyes. "We are the First," she reminded her. "We are everything. When they fall away, there will be nothing left but you and I again, as one. Nothing, no He, no god, no man will ever come between us."

The blue-eyed sister responded by a swift kiss. "Thank you."

The green-eyed Isis smiled as her hands moved down to rest on her sister's stomach. "The most important thing we must do now is to figure out what to do with the child. No god has ever created life in this way, like the humans do. My intuition tells me that you have created another god, and if Set were to find out..."

"He cannot find out. He will kill Osiris's son."

The green-eyed sister turned away, as if swept up by a wave of sadness. "I have an idea, but the thought itself destroys me."

The blue-eyed sister nodded with immediate understanding, another tear escaping from her eye. She spoke for her, "You will take him and raise him as your own, under your protection. No one can ever know he was created of me and Osiris."

It was now the green-eyed woman's turn to weep, gathering her sister into her arms. The twins held each other, in sorrowful silence.

"It is the only way," they whispered, in unison.

David jolted awake, the dream vanishing immediately as it was replaced by terror. It didn't take him long to discover he was shackled to the outer wall of the castle in the yard Lucius used to put deceitful nemorti subjects to death. The enclosure was empty of spectators this morning, however, David facing the harrowing rise of the sun alone.

He pulled at his chains, although he had the sinking sensation Lucius made sure they were sturdy enough to withstand his strength. Lucius also had the foresight to keep Davius drained of blood, ferocious hunger now biting his stomach as he hung weakly from his bounds. The scent of daybreak was reaching a suffocating peak, his instincts screaming at him to find shelter, yet he found he could not shape-shift as he had done before.

From behind an adjacent row of stones, Lucius emerged, several guards trailing him at a distance. He had abandoned his signature gold and crimson costume for robes of violet, a flowing midnight cloak catching the wind as he walked. He carried a parasol made with darkly dyed animal skin, equally dark tinted glasses shading the sun from his eyes. David knew that behind the opaque lenses, fiery coals of hatred smoldered in his direction. Lucius's jaw was tight, his lips pressed into a line as he stood silently before him, enjoying the sight of David's weakness.

"I did not want to kill her," David croaked through parched lips.

Lucius waved his hand dismissively. "It doesn't matter. You may have freed the spirit of the Morrigan, but her vessel still lives. Delicia is immobilized by unconsciousness, but I will retrieve Morrigan's soul and animate them once again."

"Then why?" David asked. "Why have you sentenced me to death?" He struggled to speak, realizing the spear had been carelessly removed from his back, leaving his lung punctured in such a way that each word proved excruciating to create.

Lucius removed his glasses, keeping the parasol positioned to prevent a single wayward ray of sunlight from reaching his exposed skin. His face was obscured by its shadow, yet his eyes still burned, an image that brought back the memory of their first meeting, so many centuries ago. "Our arrangement is no longer working, Davius," he explained, surprising him by using his former name. "Somewhere along the way, our priorities shifted in opposing directions, driving a wedge between us."

"Your priority to destroy humanity?" David scoffed.

Lucius looked surprised. "Whatever gave you that impression?" He paced, twirling the handle of his parasol with a casualness incongruous to the severity of what currently transpired. "I want to save humans, Davius. I want to protect them from destroying themselves. They are deeply stupid animals unable to advance in this world without direction. I was given life on this earthly realm unlike any god before me. I can create others in my image simply by sharing my blood. It is my destiny to promote the evolution of mankind - with or without your assistance."

"Your displays of hubris never cease to surprise me," David deadpanned.

"I have never been anything other than who I am now," Lucius pointed out. "I told you from the start that I desired power above all else. It was you who chose to see the different sides of me, to ignore what was laid out right before you. How many battles did you fight to advance my cause, how many times did you assist me in my endeavors?"

David was silent.

Lucius edged closer to him. "The only one who has changed is you. You and your newfound conscience have become my greatest obstacle, but you have gifted me with an easy way to remove you. The court believes you murdered Morgana and their hatred for you grows with each hour she lies comatose in her tower. They have agreed to let you burn under the sun's rays so that you will suffer before we execute you properly, in front of them all, by beheading." He grinned with satisfaction, revealing the tapered point of his smooth ivory teeth.

David heard his words but struggled to accept them. He had long felt the animosity steadily growing between them, but a part of him had always hoped there would be a way to repair their former bond, a sliver of brotherhood still lingering between them. "You once told me immortality robs us of our emotions, but I beg to differ," he said. "We never truly lose them, otherwise how could we feel rage or love? We become distracted by the killing and the carnage, but we still are not beasts. I know there is still goodness left in you, despite what you've become. Do you really think you could put your own brother to death, the one who has spent centuries at your side?"

Lucius did not respond, his expression impassive, his eyes still cold.

David shook his head in disbelief. "Then what is it truly, Lucius? Is it because my existence threatens you? You enjoy having creatures look up to you, following you around as submissive minions, but the moment I evolved into something more, something strong enough to challenge your ultimate authority, that was when you decided I was your enemy."

"Whatever you want to tell yourself." Lucius chuckled. "Do not fear, your blood is so old, you should bear the sun easily. It's only a day of hanging out here, then a swift and merciful execution. At least I have not sentenced you to death by impaling."

"Even if you kill me, Lucius, she still will never love you."

"What did you say?" Lucius's expression darkened as heat began to rise visibly from his skin.

David met his eyes with an unwavering severity. "You will never possess her, no matter what scheme you devise. I freed her from her prison, and she is not coming back. Your powers were taken from you, just as mine were, and what you don't know is that there are forces working behind the scenes who will ensure you never have magic powerful enough to bring her back. But even then, even if you found a way to do so and managed to bring her to life, she will never love you in return."

Lucius's collected demeanor nearly crumbled, his knuckles whitening around the stem of the parasol. "You speak of things of which you have no idea," he spat. "I am the power in this world, I have made it that way. Isis may have been the only one strong enough to bring me to life initially, but her daughters are mine too, meaning any magic left on this earth belongs to me. Hekate will bring back the Morrigan and restore Morgana, and neither you nor her has any say in the matter."

David's eyes nearly betrayed his recognition as he silently pieced things together. Hekate was exactly what he was promised, now confirmed to be the most powerful witch on earth.

Lucius gave him a sardonic smirk. "I cannot say the same about your Gaia, however," he continued his derisive taunt. "Whatever ties she may have had, she was born and died unquestionably human. At first, it caused me great pain arranging her death, knowing you would be shattered, especially when I discovered she would never reincarnate. Yet you proved to be such a disappointment, I'm glad you will never be reunited again. Why should you deserve a happy reunion when you consistently ruin mine?"

The fury that gripped David was unlike any he had ever known, his insides beginning to shake. "Somewhere deep inside, I have always known it was you who killed her," he snarled.

"I didn't need to, I simply arranged things to my liking and let life take its natural course. Don't take it so personally - your lover needed to die so that you would come to me willingly. I assumed Libraean's flaw lay in the fact that I turned him against his will, so I wanted you to choose this path of your own volition. Unfortunately for us both, my theory proved incorrect. I also hoped that by avenging her death, you would forget the girl for good and recommit yourself to our cause. But the act proved to be your undoing. Just like Libraean, you are a complete and utter failure."

"You would allow a woman with a child inside of her to die?"

"Nonsense. That was another inaccurate story told to you by that poor sap, Libraean, his gullible mind warped by his obsession with that angel lover of his. You cannot believe one word of what those creatures and their God impart, they are masterful liars. I never corrected you because it suited my agenda. Your thirst for vengeance was thoroughly enjoyable to me and it brought the Morrigan into my life."

"You are so consumed by selfishness that it will one day be your undoing."

Lucius bellowed with laughter, nearly losing the grip on his parasol. He paused before offering a retort, suddenly understanding what David was doing. "Ah, very clever to engage me in conversation so that I may perish along with you. Unfortunately, it will take much more than a little sunlight to harm me. I am a god after all." He placed his sunglasses back on the bridge of his long, narrow nose, before nodding curtly. "Goodbye, brother."

He headed back down the pathway to the castle before he paused. Without turning around, he added, "And even if you are right - if there was some part of me that still feels emotion, who misses the days of camaraderie and conversation - you threw it all away the moment you took her from me." Then he disappeared behind the castle walls in a swoop of rippling fabric, the sun so close that smoke drifted off his cloak as he abandoned him in the yard.

David tried to break free of his bounds once more, pulling at the double wound chains with all the effort he could muster. The way they stung his skin let him know they were silver, the answer to why he was unable to shift out of his human form. He looked up towards the sky in desperation, only to observe that it was devastatingly clear of any clouds that might yield a winter storm. He yearned for his magical gifts of yore, trying to will the wind as he had once before. But there was nothing, only the still air and the unwavering copper sunrise.

He slackened in defeat, wondering what it would be like to feel the sun's rays against his skin, a sensation lost to his early days in Ancient Rome. His swollen lips uplifted slightly as he recalled his life before immortality, one that was filled with vivid colors and the warmth of summer. Perhaps he might see it again as Hēlios melted his body away. Would he feel like Icarus in that horrific moment when he realized he had flown too close, his wings dripping melted wax into the sea? Would it be as terrifying as it was to the poor souls trapped inside the Wickerman, sacrificed to gods they'd never heard of nor seen?

Rivulets of oily black sweat poured down from his forehead as his body succumbed to instinctual quaking, acutely aware that death was near. He relented any further struggle against his bounds, weakened by the impending dawn, the chains biting at his flesh from his weight as he hung against the Traitor's Wall.

I began my life in chains and now it will end that way, he thought bitterly, his vision blurring as delirium crept in. He squinted back up at the sky, hoping to at least catch a glimpse of celestial blue spotted with bright white before his eyes melted away.

The pressure at his wrists unexpectedly brought forth the memory of a man he'd met long ago, years before the fall of Rome. His followers referred to him as the Christ, believing he was the son of the Hebrew god, Yahweh, and the long-promised savior of the Jewish people. Lucius had written him off as just another overzealous prophet, but David had been intrigued. He'd wondered if he was a reincarnated god like himself, finding his interest piqued when he overheard tales of miraculous healing.

Eventually the man's followers turned on him, as it happens when a man threatens to shift the balance of power. He was given to the Romans to hang on a cross, a common method for putting thieves and murderers to death. David was curious why they judged him so harshly, keeping to the shadows as he made his way to his public execution under the dome of gray sky.

Women sobbed at his feet as the man hung slackly against the wooden monstrosity, a crown of gnarled thorns stabbing the flesh of his forehead while cruel nails tore his hands and feet. His skin was ripped and flayed, cascades of blood streaming down his half-naked form. A rumbling storm had settled upon the land as the sounds of wailing reached a fevered pitch, provoking the sky to bellow in response. David wondered if the man also bore the same power as he, *Potestatem Caeli*, the way the wind howled to reflect his affliction. Soon the swollen clouds above burst, spilling onto the mass of spectators below.

The fully darkened skies allowed David to leave his shelter, drenching him as he edged closer to where the man hung. Why didn't he use his powers to escape, he wondered, to show his people the truth of his power?

It was in that reflective moment that David understood why he had become so fascinated by the man. He represented everything David wanted to be - compassionate and kind, filled with a true, altruistic empathy that David would never feel again for the rest of his immortal life. He suddenly yearned to help the man, to lift him down from his cross so that his grieving wife and mother could have him back in their arms, so he could continue his work on earth. He moved in closer, weaving through the crowd as he debated how it could be arranged.

You do not have to save me, Davius, this was my choice, my gift to them, a voice abruptly invaded his mind.

David stopped in his tracks, connecting eyes with the man. They were a soft ebony that swirled with emotion.

"Death is not a gift, it is giving up," he argued.

If you only knew who you once were and from where you came. His voice seemed warm and kind although the man hung limply, gaunt and mere moments from death. You have fallen away from who you are meant to be, but it is never too late to remember.

"Is your god the one my friend Libraean spoke of, the god of light?" David asked him.

My Father was not a benevolent god, but He has decided to become one, relinquishing much of His power to me. My death will create a new following, pulling them away from archaic religious practices into a new way of life. He will not abandon His people, for He loves them most of all, and I will look after the others.

"So you plan on converting your following, tearing them away from their prior beliefs? Is that not the antithesis of what you preached in the streets?"

I simply wanted to inspire, hoping that others would learn kindness and compassion by my example. I do not want to be hailed as a god, though my Father insists it shall be that way.

David peered at the dying man. "It is hard for me not to aid you with any power," he admitted.

That is another gift for me to give. There are levels of divinity that inter- act in the ethereal realms, some working together, some trapped in conflict. They have been watching the devolution of the dark god Lucius and your willingness to transcend your curse, determined to follow your own path. We know you cannot feel true compassion or empathy for humans, but I want to change that.

"Wait ..."

The skies shuddered as lightning cracked down from above. And then, for the first time, David heard the thoughts of the entire crowd surrounding him, a frenzied uproar of voices that seized control of his mind. He fell to his knees as the power of telepathy surged through him, frantically trying to push through the near deafening cacophony before the Christ's voice cut through them all. *My Father and I will take care of things on our end. We realize the fight between your parthenon is your own. But this is our gift to you, our aid in the Great Fight ahead. Use it wisely.*

And then, with a final crack of thunder in the sky, the man took his last breath, and died.

"What does that mean?" David cried out, but it was too late to receive a response. He watched as the boundaries between realms fractured above them, angels descending from bright, heavenly skies to collect the soul of their king.

"Davius," a voice broke through the memory.

Was it an angel? Coming to collect him, to take him to the heavenly realms? Or was it a daemon who arrived, prepared to drag his soul to the depths of Tartarus, where the abandoned gods and sinners go?

"Davius."

His nose filled with jasmine.

"Gaia?"

The sun had now fully risen, reaching its crescendo, flooding the death yard with malignant light. The pain was unbearable, his skin bubbling as he choked on the smoke that rose from his blistering skin.

A male voice reached his ears, one that tried to hide its alarm behind a facade of dry annoyance. "I see they did not hold back on you."

David could not reply, his consciousness wavering.

He heard Danulf grunt as he pulled the chains from the wall with impossible strength, reminding David of what had transpired hours before his capture. He tried to speak, but his mouth was desiccated from the heat.

"Come, we have only minutes before true daylight and not even this cloak will shield us." David felt himself being hoisted up on his friend's shoulders and draped in fabric. Although it provided merciful shelter from the scorching sun, as soon as Danulf broke into a run, David found he could no longer fight off death, and he capitulated willingly to its call.

CHAPTER SEVEN

❧ The Gods ❧

"He shivers," a voice broke through the void. "They are tremors, signaling his return to consciousness. He is through the worst of it." The other voice was just as strong, but female, almost familiar...Was it Gaia? Had he crossed over?

A wave of heat washed over him in response, wrenching him back to life. Pain seared throughout his entire body and he immediately succumbed to unrestrained screaming.

The female voice shouted to be audible over his eruptions of agony. "Dragos, bring me more of my honey and milk serum from the cabinet and more belladonna from underneath the table," she instructed. "Dan, please fetch the meat and blood. Now that he is conscious, he will be famished after he adjusts to the pain."

David continued to shriek as his body involuntarily thrashed, his supernatural powers of healing ineffective against the intensity of his wounds. He had felt nothing before like the torment he now endured, oblivion pulling him back towards its sanctuary.

"Stay with me, David, it will end soon," the woman soothed. His vision was blurred, but he could see her silhouette as she approached him, pushing him back towards the bed. He caught her scent as she shifted, realizing she was human.

He was now delirious with pain, unable to fight the overwhelming desire to devour her, his survival instincts dominating his rational mind.

He twisted in her grasp, baring his fangs, until she finally jumped on top of him, using the weight of her body to keep him still.

"David, listen to me," she ordered. "You almost burned to death, and had we not intervened, you would have. Drinking my blood will not help you with the pain, but I can if you let me."

David forced himself to focus on her words. "Yes!" he croaked between charred lips.

"I know your powers have been stagnant for centuries, but they are still inside of you. They are connected to your humanity, the part of you that still thrives. You must find them again."

He didn't have time to ask how she could have possibly known these things. "How?" he managed. His throat, tongue, and chest all labored painfully with the effort.

"Be still. Imagine yourself back in your homeland. Feel the wind and the rustling of the forest," her voice dropped to a soothing whisper. "Remember from where you came."

After so many years, the memories of his past surfaced, enticing him like a lost lover. The emerald hills rolled against the crisp, cloudless sky, as birds flocked around the branches of ancient trees, while wolves roamed the forest floor and fish leapt from anarchic waters. The lines between realms began to blur, the nimble fingers of unconsciousness cementing their hold.

"Now see me in the forest," her voice instructed him. "Allow me to heal you."

He opened his eyes to see a falcon perched on the branch of an unusual looking tree, one he'd never seen before. It held his gaze with rich black eyes as he approached her with caution. He glanced down to see that he was his former self again, life coursing through young, supple hands.

She crooned at him, commanding his attention to return to her, whipping up the air with her giant wings. The breeze shifted something within him, lifting the small hairs of his flesh as it glided across his skin.

His eyes flew open.

The pain was gone.

The woman straddling him offered a smile. "Well done, David."

He was finally able to make out her features, his eyesight shuddering as it came back into focus. Long mahogany hair framed an oval face with skin the color of warm earth. Bright green eyes that rivaled his own burst brilliantly against it in contrast, rimmed by heavy lashes. She wore a linen shirt, damp with sweat, open at the neckline to reveal dozens of beaded necklaces, some that looped down to her waist. Her red skirt was drawn up around her knees, revealing bare legs unrestricted by stockings or shoes. Thin hoop earrings hung brazenly from her ears.

He looked past her to take in their surroundings. It appeared they were in a commodious cellar, the dirt walls haphazardly covered in rows of uneven stone. Tree roots interrupted their shoddy pattern, a few tendrils sweeping the impossibly clean wood floor. Several modest torches smoldered against the walls next to bundles of drying herbs, bringing warmth and pleasant aromas into the dark atmosphere. He noted a large cabinet overflowing with glass bottles, all filled and neatly labeled, hanging over a desk covered with chopped herbs and apothecary tools. His bed was the only other furniture in the room, the stiff linen stuffed with bits of straw and wool.

He returned his gaze back towards the woman removing herself from astride him, whose difficulty in doing so came from her condition. A full, pregnant belly swelled beneath her skirt as her naked feet hit the ground.

"Who are you?" he finally asked.

"Oh, forgive me," she said as she waddled towards the desk stool, which she picked up to place near his bedside. "There was no time for introductions. I am Hekate, the matriarch of the Pădurii clan until my daughter is born. This is my home, where I care for humans and creatures in secrecy. You were lucky to be found when you were. You were moments away from certain death."

"Hekate," David sighed, grateful to have finally reached his destination. "I have been searching for you."

She smiled, lighting up the features of her smooth, oval face. Her human warmth emanated from her, smelling strongly of sweet rose attempting to mask an undernote of black henbane. "And I have been waiting for you. We have much to discuss. But first, we must care for your physical self."

A man appeared from behind her, David grateful to discover it was Danulf, confirming that he was the one who delivered David from his untimely fate. His skin now bore the ashen cast common to blood drinkers, blending against his brilliant grey beard and hair, but highlighting his deep blue eyes. Relief was instantly replaced with regret as David replayed their last encounter. "I am so sorry, my friend."

"Bah," Danulf shrugged his massive shoulders before handing Hekate a large carafe. David could smell the sheep's blood from where he lay. "You saved my life, and now I have saved yours," he made it simple. "We are even. Now I can boast that I am the only creature in history to be both nemorti and varcolac."

David chuckled, wincing at the effort. He opened his mouth to thank Danulf for rescuing him when another man descended the staircase to enter the sick room.

"I see you are finally awake," Dragos said as he handed several bottled tinctures to Hekate. His friendly expression contorted with disgust as he grew closer. "Ye gods, is that what happens to us in the sunlight?"

"Dragos," Hekate chided him as she took the procured medicine to her desk.

"My apologies, sister," he said emptily, his eyes affixed to the wounded creature before him.

"The two of you may leave us now," Hekate commanded gently.

Danulf nodded his farewell, guiding an indignant Dragos away by the shoulders before he could vocalize his protestations. "We will have plenty of time to talk of war," Danulf's voice echoed up the staircase. "Let the man heal."

Hekate watched them go, turning back to face him. "I'm sorry to say this, but my brother is quite right - you look terrible. Even as strong a creature that you are, the sun managed to scorch away several layers of your skin. Thankfully, I am proficient in the art of healing blood drinkers. You need an agent to stimulate your natural healing process before the skin will repair itself. Fortunately, I've perfected a salve to do just that, which I want to apply thoroughly before layering you in bandages. I will, however, need you to remain completely still throughout the process and it will be extremely painful. So I am going to give you a concoction of belladonna, opium, and blood, which will render you unconscious. I would like to meet you in the astral plane so we can speak while your body convalesces. Do you remember how to do it?"

"I've only traveled unintentionally in my dreams," David admitted, recalling his meetings with the Council.

"No matter." Hekate added a pinch of the dried belladonna to the carafe of blood, swirling it around as she approached him. "When you fade away, look for a great tree that will be unusual to you, similar to the tree you found my familiar in a few moments ago. That is where you will find my projection."

David nodded as she brought the finished mixture to his lips. He could smell the opium and the sweet syrup of baneful berries, mixed with something foreign. Hemlock? he wondered as he swallowed. The herbal concoction was suddenly overwhelmed by the taste of human blood. David's eyes popped open in recognition as a flood of Hekate's memories inundated his consciousness. He tried to hold onto them, but they slipped through his fingers as intoxication prevailed, the last thing he saw before tumbling into oblivion was a falcon soaring through the skies, tailed closely behind by a crow.

He landed, his bare feet sinking into wet, slippery earth. He was under a canopy of strange trees, shaded from the sun, who could only trickle through the crevasses of the broad leaves that fanned out above. Insects buzzed around him as the calls of wild birds reverberated throughout the tropical foliage. He heard rushing water, realizing that he stood in the vegetative area of a great riverbank, and the mud that stuck to his feet was actually clay. It occurred to him that he was walking unharmed in the daylight, and he looked down to observe hands and feet that were once again flushed with life. Thrilled, he exited the cluster of plants into an open plain, letting the sun beat down on him freely. His skin welcomed it as tall, dry grass brushed up against his legs. He could now see the massive river that stretched out farther than the eye could, the same birds he heard singing hovering above giant, bulbous creatures that meandered happily along its muddy banks. Ahead of him was a magnificent tree, its large silhouette obscuring a sky streaked with the orange brushstrokes of early sunset. The wind seemed to whisper its name to him, acadia.

He moved closer, noticing a woman seated at its base, her long bronze legs tucked beneath a sheer white dress, rivers of hair billowing out behind her. On her arm, she held a stately falcon, who watched him carefully. When he was close enough to see her face, he saw that her eyes were a brilliant green. He remembered the sisters. "I have seen you before," he realized aloud.

She smiled as she gestured for him to come closer. "Please sit," she invited.

He found a patch of clean dirt to sit upon, unable to take his eyes away from her, thoroughly confused by what he was seeing.

"Do not doubt your instincts," she said. "You have known me far longer than you can imagine."

"Are you Hekate, the woman who is tending to my physical body?" David asked.

"She is my most recent manifestation," she replied cryptically. "I am also one of the sisters from your dream." She looked up at the branches stretching out above them like the arms of fervent worshipers. "I thought of bringing you to the woods of Gaul, to appeal to Davius, the Druid boy of the forest. But I wanted you first to remember your life with me."

David was speechless, hoping his expression would suffice in imploring her to continue.

"Do you know where we are?"

"No," he admitted.

"The great fertile Nile in Egypt, where human life began," she explained proudly, the gold tones in her skin shimmering in the sunlight.

"I have to admit, I know little about the land. Its written history is hard to find, though I do own several ancient scrolls," David explained. "The language always gave me trouble, but Lucius has told me stories."

She laughed, her voice harmonizing with the warbling birds. "Yes, he also hails from this land, though there are parts even he does not remember. I took his memories from him when he cursed me, but they come trickling back to him from time to time. But perhaps I should start from the beginning."

Thoroughly intrigued, David stretched out on his patch of earth, resting on his arm as he nodded for her to continue.

Egypt, The Beginning

"At the beginning, there was nothingness, only a swirling mass of chaos and *heka*, the most ancient magic. When chaos reached its peak, *heka* blossomed, manifesting itself into the first He of the skies and the first She of the earth. He formed the constellations and the planets, the clouds and the sun, while She became the dirt, the mountains, the rivers. Eventually, She also created life - animals, plants, and insects - all fragments of Her Divine Essence. And then one day, She was corporeal, in the form of twins, the first demigods to walk the earth - Heka and Lilith. They were identical in appearance except that one had green eyes that mirrored the forests, while the other's were sky blue.

"The twin goddesses loved their earth and all that flourished within its vast, fertile womb. The sisters were content alone until one day the earth created the first human life, made in their image. Confused, they looked to the skies, wondering if it came from the Great He they had left behind, but they found no answers. They did learn, however, that the Great He of the Sky had also fragmented into a set of two, a pair of brothers, a god of Light and a god of Darkness. The sisters decided to bring the brothers to earth to join them in physical form. Light breathed souls into the humans, that differentiated them from animals and plants. And so, humanity began.

"The sisters realized that with male gods and humans now roaming the earth, their *heka* required protection, and it was decided that Heka would bear it all, continuing to birth humanity, while Lilith would serve as her protector. As Heka watched her human children grow and evolve, she realized they needed direction and guidance, to be taught how to set laws to keep peace between them and how to grow food to survive.

She asked Light to help her, for he shared her innate desire to guide and foster human evolution. The two made the perfect pair and they guided the humans into an enlightened existence unfathomable prior. But what they failed to notice during this time of innovation and expansion, was the deep resentment the other brother, Darkness, was beginning to harbor towards Light. Where Light cherished harmony, Darkness wanted dominion over mankind. He thought humans were foolish and weak, unable to understand why they were allowed to control the earth that Heka and Lilith created. He believed they were meant to serve the gods, for it was the gods who came before all else, to whom they owed their very lives. But he was outnumbered - Light and Heka saw humans as extensions of themselves and Lilith believed humans existed to cultivate and protect her beloved earth, therefore worthy of her loving protection and care.

"Eventually, the humans began to revere the quartet as sacred divinity; Heka became Isis, the mother of mankind, and Lilith became Nephthys, goddess of death. They named the god of Light, Osiris, and the god of Darkness, Set. Isis and Osiris were the mother and father of humanity, husband and wife, while Nephthys was paired with Set. They decided that Set and Nephthys would be their deities of death. Nephthys accepted her role, realizing souls required protection as they navigated the Realms of Existence. At this time, there were only three: the astral plane, where deceased souls awaited reincarnation, the earth, and the Underworld, where souls returned to rest. It was Nephthys's duty to choose which souls would reincarnate on earth and those who would descend into the Underworld under Set's guardianship, guiding them safely to their destinations. She also worked on earth; unlike her sister, Nephthys assimilated into the physical world of the humans, becoming an integral part of their everyday affairs. She gave council to those who needed it, presided over disagreements, and allowed the dead to speak to their loved ones before their final departure.

"Set, however, was displeased with his role, one he viewed as inferior. He had no qualms about presiding over death and destruction, but he wanted to be adored like his brother and his brother's wife, not feared. Humans abhorred the notion of dying, for they did not understand it and they projected those detestable feelings onto the Underworld's ruling deity. Set also loved war, which only deepened their fear of him - if one crossed him on the battlefield, they were doomed. Set's only consolation was the lust he developed for Nephthys, which grew stronger as the years passed.

He was unable to create life as his brother could, but he discovered that with his body he could create inexplicable pleasure when intertwined with Nephthys. She adored this part of their relationship, which kept her loyal to him for many years. Eventually, she would be the one who taught the act to humans and unlike the gods, humans could create life in this way. After that pivotal moment, Osiris and Isis no longer had the exclusive responsibility of constructing bodies and souls and could stand back and let the humans procreate on their own.

"And so life continued on, the four gods living for many years in peace, coming to the aid of the humans when called. Set seethed quietly in his resentment, leaving his brother and wife alone, for he enjoyed his life with Nephthys. They had their own palace in the Underworld, but they often worked on earth, even joining Osiris and Isis on occasion in their palace made of precious gold, surrounded by trees and luscious gardens brimming with flowers. Humans erected elaborate sculptures in their likeness which they visited each morning with fresh milk, honey, and bread as offerings.

"Then one fateful day, Nephthys, dirty after a long day on earth, decided to sneak a bath in the Nile. Over time, she had become further drawn into the human experience, donning the disguise of a kite so she could interact with them whenever she felt called to. Bathing in the clear waters was one of her favorite pastimes, learned by watching the young women do the same."

"Wait, I know this story…" David murmured, although he had not intended to interrupt.

Hekate's face was stone. "On this particular morning, Osiris had left the palace to take a walk amongst the marshy flora of the Nile Valley. He loved to be amongst the greenest part of the desert, listening to the gurgling waters and breathing in the sweet morning air. He caught sight of his sister-in-law bathing, joyously untamed and feral in his favorite place, and he fell in love with her. He had glimpsed her before in passing, of course, but never had he witnessed her raw, unrestrained beauty in such a way. These feelings were foreign to the young god; he could comprehend love for his companion Isis, brotherly love for Set, and agape love for mankind. Yet this feeling was different, a yearning for her to be his, the desire to take her into his arms. As he tried to reconcile these feelings, she noticed him watching her, her eyes meeting his in a moment that sealed their fates forever - for she fell for him as well."

David shivered, the world around them responding with a sharp shift of wind. Hekate's long white dress fluttered around her like the falcon's wings. He forced himself to focus on her words.

"Years of longing passed as Osiris tried to distract himself with his affairs. But soon he was writing poetry to her, inscribing on sheets of papyrus which he hid in a tamarisk tree near the part of the river where she swam. She discovered them and wrote back, the two beginning a daily correspondence where they could pour out their devotion to each other secretly in verse. They both hoped it would be enough to sustain them until late one evening, Osiris stumbled upon her in her waters again, after a heated argument with Set, and this time, he could not resist approaching her. She took him into her arms without hesitation, teaching him how to make love, an experience unlike anything he had ever felt. Their love was so powerful, they created the impossible - divine life within her womb. She would eventually birth the first gods to ever come from the coupling of divine beings - a set of twins, named Horus and Anubis."

David sat upright, gripped by the urge to flee. "Why are you telling me this story? What does this mean?" The branches of the acadia tree thrashed as the turbulent air around them raised in intensity.

Hekate stood, her falcon giving a disapproving squawk. "You must hear what I have to say, David. The story is far from over."

She grabbed both of his hands, and instantly, they stood in the tomb of an ancient pyramid. David took a sharp inhale. The room seemed to glow, for its walls were made of gold, covered in scores of hieroglyphics. Piles of the precious metal clustered every inch of space, interrupted only by colorful jewels and the painted sarcophagus situated at the center.

"Nephthys worried that Set would discover their affair," Hekate continued, turning his attention back to her. "She feared it would ruin the harmonious life they had built, convinced that Set would attack Osiris and murder her children. So she approached her sister, confessing everything."

"I had a vision of the sisters in my dreams," David told her.

"It never ceases to amaze me how powerful your mind is," she briefly appraised before she continued, not offering David a moment to grow bashful. "Isis held no ill will towards her sister, nor her husband, for she did not understand romantic love," she explained. "Instead, she shared her sister's apprehension of their family's fate. They decided that Isis would take the boys under her wing and proclaim to the world that the children belonged to her and Osiris. Although it pained him, Osiris agreed to the masquerade, also understanding that he would have to stay far away from Nephthys for the story to be believed. He agreed to it only because he believed it would protect her and their children.

"After the twins were born, Nephthys disguised herself and went into exile. Although she tried to distract herself by becoming involved once again in the affairs of men, she eventually fell into a deep despair. She longed for her children and for Osiris, and eventually her melancholy consumed her. She attempted to end her own life, hoping that in doing so, her soul would float about the astral plane in peace. It was her grown son, Anubis, who stopped her, knowing all along that she was his real mother and had been searching the realms to find her. Finally being reunited with one of her sons proved vitally restorative for Nephthys, a beginning in lifting her from her dismal state. Still concerned for her wellbeing, Anubis covertly petitioned Osiris to let him guard the entrance to the Underworld, hoping to keep his mother from death's alluring pull while protecting her from Set, should she ever be forced back into the Underworld. Osiris quickly agreed.

"Meanwhile, with her sister in mourning, Isis was left unguarded. She was strong and formidable in her own right, but being the only creature bearing the world's precious *heka* left her vulnerable. The weight of it grew heavy, consuming her like despair consumed her sister, isolating her from humans and gods alike. She remained stowed away in their earthly palace, distancing herself from Osiris and their new sons, who only reminded her of her lost sister. They had no choice, but to leave her in peace." A rueful look passed across her face. "It was Set who finally reached her," she continued after a pause. "He had discovered the letters between Nephthys and Osiris admitting their love, and it inflamed his already standing jealousy and contempt for his brother. He believed Osiris tricked her into falling in love with him and that Nephthys's exile was his fault. He was incensed that she had left him as well, spending every moment he could searching for her."

David watched the hieroglyphics that were etched along the walls of the tomb swirl themselves to life, images moving as if he was witnessing the transpired events in the present. He gasped as he recognized Lucius, his skin still pale in comparison to the green eyed, bronze goddess seated not far from where he stood. He watched Lucius storm into her throne room, completely shirtless save for thick gold jewelry around his neck and arms. On his crown was a jackal headdress, similar to the one worn by Anubis, except that it did not obscure his angular face nor his burning topaz eyes. His original body was still very tall and narrow, but his arms were defined by muscle, his hands so long and narrow, they appeared to be clawed.

Isis had been draped listlessly over her throne, her eyes curious as she watched him approach her.

"Osiris has been consorting with my wife," he hissed as soon as he reached her. "I found physical evidence of their adoration." He tossed their letters at her, the ripped papyrus trickling down to the marble floor like feathers.

"I cannot control what Osiris does," Isis responded, apathetically.

Lucius made a sound of disgust. "You are both fools. Humans couple and are bound by invisible ties - you are gods and you cannot manage to honor the same commitment? Nephthys was my wife, my companion in this world, and because of my vile brother, she is now missing. His betrayal is unforgivable. You should feel the same as I."

Isis frowned, her jade eyes catching the candlelight, their brilliance overshadowing the actual jewel that lay at her throat. "I feel nothing."

Lucius paused from his rant, realizing her dismal state. "You are the Creatrix, the Divine Mother of mankind, loved by all. How could you possibly be morose?"

She met his eyes. "I am no longer needed. The humans sustain themselves. Osiris sees to the worldly affairs with our children. My sister has fled our homeland. What else should I feel?"

"Rage," Lucius replied with a snarl. "You should feel rage at what he has done to us all."

"And yet, I do not," Isis sighed. "Leave me alone now."

Lucius turned to retreat in exasperation, before he paused. He reached up to remove his beastial diadem, sending his long atrous locks down around his shoulders. He approached her, climbing the stairs to Isis's throne with careful steps, as one might approach a feral cat. She apprehended him with widened eyes as he slipped his fingers around her neck, cupping her face as he kissed her. She allowed him to continue for a moment before pulling away in surprise. "What are you doing?" she whispered, though her expression had warmed from his kiss.

"What our mates do with each other. It is only fair that you might partake in such pleasure. Why should you sit here alone in misery as a result of what they have done?"

Isis considered his point for only a moment before she met his eyes, her jaw set in determination, an expression common in her sister. With one easy movement, she released the clasp that held up her dress, letting it fall around her feet. "Then show me," she agreed.

Lucius scooped her into his arms.

"Hoping to heal his broken heart and create his own children, he seduced Isis," Hekate's narrative voice shattered the vision. David observed that her once impassive face now betrayed wistfulness as she retold her story. "They made the physical act of love, but it was not the fruitful coupling Set had secretly yearned for, and it was not what Isis had hoped it would be either. She was no closer to understanding romantic passion than she was before. But what neither Isis nor Set had anticipated, was that in Isis giving of her body, she gave Set a part of her soul, infusing him with *heka*."

"*Manibus Ignem.*"

"His hands of fire," Hekate nodded. "And perhaps most importantly, it fine-tuned his intelligence, twisting it into the art of deceit. Set used his newly honed guile to finally enact his vengeance on his brother, tricking him into diving into the Nile to save who he thought was a drowning Nephthys, only to have Set hold him under until he died. His vengeance still not satisfied, Set then separated Osiris's body into forty-two pieces and scattered them all across the land so that no amount of magic could ever resurrect them.

"Nephthys felt Osiris's death in her bones, jarring her out of her melancholia. She flew back to Egypt, horrified to learn of her beloved's murder at the hands of her husband. Determined to reverse the deed, she transformed into a raven colored kite, scouring the ends of the earth to collect each piece of Osiris's dismembered corpse, bringing them to her sister who she begged for assistance. Equally furious that Set has murdered her companion, Isis complied."

David's eyes were pulled towards the sarcophagus, which had now opened to reveal a corpse wrapped entirely in strips of linen bandages. Emotion caught in his throat as he saw Nephthys folded over its edge, stubborn tears escaping down her cheeks though she fought them away. Isis stood at its head, murmuring silently with her hands stretched out above it. Heavy incense choked the air, swirling around them as energy pulsated beneath Isis's palms. He recognized Anubis, who stood next to his mother protectively, a hand placed on her shoulder. With his head cast downwards under his headdress, the eyes looking upwards appeared wicked, beads of shining glass set in the narrow face of a jackal.

"It is not working," Nephthys cried out in volatile frustration, slapping her hands on the rim of the sarcophagus.

Isis dropped her hands, matching her sister's vexation. "I am the goddess of life and you are the goddess of death. Our son, the god of funeral rites, stands beside us. I do not understand what more we need."

"Blood," came a soft reply from the shadows.

The three gods looked up to see a man moving towards them with an unusual crop of golden hair, bright against his complexion. Nephthys let out a gasp in instant recognition of her other son.

His stoic expression melted at the sight of her, disarmed immediately she ran up to throw her arms around him. Again, David felt a strong pang of emotion, watching mother finally reunited with son. She held him tightly for a moment until they both were able to collect themselves, pulling herself away so he could speak.

Horus's face was stern but handsome, with the same herculean build as his twin brother and the same cerulean blue eyes they inherited from their mother. The only difference between them was their hair, his a golden flax that contrasted against the coal black hair of the jackal crowned Anubis. "Blood," he repeated, "is the only part of him that is missing, the substance that sustains life on earth. We all share the same blood, but none so powerful as our uncle, Set, for it is identical to that which once flowed through the veins of our father."

Anubis looked at him. "You are right. They also shared the same soul once, before they split into separate beings."

Horus nodded. "Set's blood is the key that will bring Osiris back to life."

The flesh on David's skin prickled as he watched Nephthys rise to her feet with new resolve, wearing a look evocative of the Morrigan, the two sharing the same wild, cropped hair, the same fierce blue eyes. "I will do it," she declared.

Horus looked admirably at his mother. "It can only be you, for you are the only one Set trusts. You must bring him here before we can resume the ritual."

The vision shifted, lifting away like a curtain to reveal a similar arrangement, with Set now suspended by cords that bound his arms so he could not bring forth his flames.

"You may bring Osiris back, but he will never be the same," he mocked them as the two sisters raised their hands over opposing sides of the body. Anubis waited nearby, anointing the bandages with precious oils, a rite that would eventually become Egyptian custom.

A knife glinted in Horus's hand as he nervously tightened his grip, his attention affixed to his uncle as he waited for the signal to attack.

"You will never be able to truly stop me," Set continued to taunt. "I am the most powerful god among you all, now infused with both masculine and feminine power. I have killed my counterpart, for darkness always presides over the light - night always consumes the day. Do you not see how the humans now cower before us? How their land is barren and dry at my hands, and how they beg for my mercy?" He laughed. "There will never be anyone who can surpass my power. Even if you do manage to bring my nefarious brother back."

The sisters ignored him, chanting over the mummified body of Osiris. The air in the room began to stir as they pooled together their opposing energies until it funneled into a palpable force with an intensity so strong, it threatened to consume the chamber and its occupants.

Horus advanced to cut Set free from his bounds, prepared to place his body on top of Osiris for the bloodletting to occur. Unfortunately, Set had anticipated his move. As soon as Horus cut the cord, Set kicked his legs out from beneath him, shoved him to the ground and with one brutal sweep, pucked out one of his eyes.

Nephthys wavered in horror, but both sisters held fast to their chant, knowing it couldn't be broken. Anubis, however, leapt to his brother's defense. But Set's hands were already ablaze, smirking as he turned one fist towards each brother, prepared to immolate them in unison. Nephthys, unable to hold back any longer, finally broke out of her trance. "Set, no, they are my children!" she shrieked.

Set faltered for a moment, his eyes wide in surprise. It was all Horus needed to pounce, slicing the thin flesh of Set's throat from ear to ear. The brothers then grabbed him, lifting his body over their father until his gurgling blood coated the corpses's bandages in visceral red. Set crumpled to the ground, dead, as the mummified corpse lifted itself up from its sarcophagus.

Nephthys flew to her resurrected lover's side, ripping away his bindings. But the face she revealed was not Osiris, but one that was ghostly pale, with coal black eyes and a set of shocking fangs where his teeth should have been. The creature she uncovered grabbed her and without a moment of hesitation, sunk its teeth into the tender flesh of her neck. She gasped, but did not fight him, her mournful eyes closing as she submitted willingly to what she knew would be the end to her suffering on earth - it was clear Osiris would never return.

Isis realized what was happening and extracted the sword from a shocked and frozen Horus, plunging it into Osiris's heart from the back. The two lovers collapsed into his tomb together. Isis rushed to the sarcophagus only to learn she had been too late, both her sister and her husband were dead, lying together in a mess of blood and tangled limbs. She whipped around to see that Horus had also expired from his wounds, his yellow hair radiating out from his handsome face like the sun, his expression peaceful beyond the horrific gore of his removed eye. She almost collapsed then but made the gruesome discovery of Horus's detached eye lying not far from where he lay. She forced herself to retrieve it, placing it gently back into his skull so that he would be whole when he arrived at the Underworld. Then she draped her body over his and succumbed to her building lamentation.

The ground trembled with her pain, collapsing the towers of gold treasures that lined the tomb. Isis was despondent as they crashed to the floor, rooted to the floor where she lay with Horus, even as the earthquake split the land in two, the volatile chasm swallowing everything around her.

David found himself back in the underground apothecary, the torches extinguished and Hekate nowhere to be found. He was grateful to discover that his pain had lessened considerably, but he was still unable to move. Although he was motionless, he could feel his body working furiously to repair itself, twitching as the sensation of being pricked by needles rolled over his skin. He turned his mind to other thoughts, piecing together everything Hekate had told him before he'd slipped out of his trance and into a restorative slumber.

He replayed the events in his mind, wondering what the story of ancient gods had to do with him. Lucius's origin did not surprise him, but the rest were obscure, figures in a hazy dream one forgets until they revisit it.

A wave of fresh pain hit, and he groaned, realizing the concoctions she'd given him were wearing off. He wondered where she went, what time or what day it was, the brick and mud walls offering no answers. He sighed, trying to recall Morrigan's image in his mind for comfort, but seeing Lucius's cold expression instead, right before he left him to die, hearing his final words, "you took her from me…"

David sighed. He still believed there was some part of his old friend left, hidden beneath his monstrous facade, but he was now assured what needed to be done. Beyond his detriment to humanity, David knew they could no longer exist together on the earthly plane.

"Good evening, David." Hekate's voice arrived before she did, carefully descending the stairs. He could smell the animal blood she held, his hunger instantly ignited.

He wasted no time in slurping down its contents, embarrassed by his fervor though she'd politely looked away. He could taste the medicinal herbs she'd added, but he enjoyed its warmth, the boost in nourishment immediately setting to work on his limbs. He was drowsy again in moments, staring at her through drooping eyes.

"I'll see you soon," she murmured, settling down next to him on the bed.

David found her again underneath the unusual tree, her legs tucked neatly beneath her. She smiled in greeting, gesturing for him to take his place next to her. "Hello, David. Where was I?"

"The ancient ones," he reminded her as he complied.

"Yes, Isis's fate," she nodded. "As the great chasm threatened to take her down with her dead family, a falcon appeared to save her. Although she thanked her familiar, she no longer had a desire to stay on earth. She freed her consciousness to the astral plane and transformed her body and *heka* into a graceful acadia tree, so she could exist, undisturbed."

David followed her gaze to the majestic tree behind her. "Anubis," she continued, "seized Set's soul as it lifted away from his body, dragging it down to a realm called Tartarus, the lowest point of the Underworld, where traitorous, banished creatures dwelled. Since that time, other gods have used it as a place to send their most despicable entities, which added a fourth realm to our world. Set, with all his intelligence and cunning, eventually became its ruler, lying in patient wait for the day he could enact his revenge against those who deceived him."

"Why do you tell me this tale?" David couldn't help but interrupt, now fixated on the tree as his mind spun at the parallels being laid out before him.

"None of the Ancient Ones can fully remember their lives as Egyptian deities, but this is our history. Your history. I am the only one among us who truly remembers."

"You are Isis."

"I am her, reincarnated."

David stared in awe. "Is there more?"

She nodded. "The second part of this story lies within your own memories, but they are buried deep within your unconscious mind where even I cannot reach. I would like to try, however, by telling you what I have been told and what I have witnessed, in the hopes they will return to you."

"Yes, please continue," David urged.

"Osiris and Nephthys ascended to the Upperworld, a place above the earth where they could exist peacefully. It soon evolved into a collective realm for all the gods, similar to the territories we create on our earth, with each pantheon in its respective space. It became the fifth and final otherworldly realm.

"Anubis eventually realized Isis had left the *heka* vulnerable. It began trickling out of the Acadia Tree and was absorbed by the other plants through their networks. Anubis feared that eventually the *heka* would dissipate entirely and the Acadia would perish, so he created a council of ethereal beings, manifested out of the four elemental properties of earth, who would protect the tree and its power from harm. The Council also became responsible for maintaining order on earth in the gods' absence, ensuring *ma'at*, or perfect balance, since the departure of the Ancient Ones disturbed it.

"Ironically, the humans would begin to call Set's Underworld the Kingdom of Osiris, believing he was the one who would greet them when they died. But it was Anubis who took over the Underworld, or Duat, as we called it, aided by several other gods the humans would eventually create.

"The story could have ended here, but Nephthys grew restless, missing the earth she'd grown attached to. She discovered that gods could visit earth in the form of apparitions, and she found herself drawn to the lush hills and waters of Ireland, far away from her homeland and its painful memories. She was so in love with the land that she whispered stories to the ancient Druids, telling them tales of a god and goddess so strong and noble, they would protect the Celtic people for centuries. The Druids believed her, siphoning heka out of their trees and bringing Osiris and Nephthys back in the form of demigods. They called them the Daghda and the Morrigan."

David shut his eyes, overcome with emotion. "Go on," he whispered.

Her voice seemed to detach, tumbling over the hills that he now saw himself surrounded by. "Morrigan knew Set would never find them in different bodies; humans were creating new gods at an alarming rate, the ancients powerless to stop them. But although it was a time of divine expansion, it was also a time of peaceful co-existence, all deities complicit in an unspoken agreement to maintain the proper balance and continue fostering the evolution of man. What Morrigan did not anticipate, however, was that their reincarnation meant the complete dissolution of their former lives, their memories scattered to the wind. Fortunately, they still maintained their love for each other, and Morrigan bore a painful longing for children she could not recall. Save for that, Osiris and Nephthys were no more.

"Regardless of their absent memories, Daghda and Morrigan lived contentedly among the Celtic tribes, joined by a pantheon of gods who became their brethren. Daghda was named patriarch of their family, the Tuatha De Danann. Morrigan was never again able to conceive, but the earth had given her the power to shape-shift, which produced a strong, maternal connection to the animals she invoked, particularly the wolf, the horse, and the crow. She thought of them, and the Celtic warriors she protected, as her brood.

"In the meantime, Set had been waiting patiently in Tartarus for the moment he could strike. The instant that Morrigan and Daghda reen-tered the physical world, a crack appeared in the fabric that separated the realms allowing Set to rise to the surface in non-corporeal form. He made a deal to switch places with a snake *daemon* called Typhon, who had offered aid to the Council throughout the years with their less pleasant affairs. He used Typhon's body to make his way to Egypt, where he found a madman who worshiped at the foot of an acadia tree, raving to all who listened that the tree whispered secrets to him. The Council knew about the man, but believed he was harmless and paid him no mind. But Set knew better, for the man had discovered the body and dormant magic of Isis. Set possessed the handsome young tree-worshipper and pulled Isis out of hiding. He then convinced her to come to his home so that he could care for her, and Isis, not knowing he was anything other than a human, agreed.

"After several days together, she fell for his charms and allowed him to lay with her. When she awoke, the apparition of Set was by her side. He informed her that he had cursed her womb, and that from that point on she would birth one daughter, who would birth one daughter, and so forth, each new child taking her power until she withered and died. They would be his daughters to call upon when he needed them. Devastated, Isis tried to enact revenge, but Set was not yet physical and could not be harmed. He told her he would lift the curse if she brought him to life."

"He said a powerful sorceress brought him to earth as a beast."

Hekate nodded. "So wicked was his soul that it could only be housed by an abominable creature. Isis discovered the only way she could give him human form would be to use the body of the young man Set had once possessed. She had to pull out the poor man's soul completely before sending Set's soul permanently back inside. She never forgave herself for this act, for her actions went against everything she represented - she was a goddess who created life, not destroyed it. Heartbroken, she withdrew immediately to the empty, mountainous hills of what would one day be Transylvania to birth her first daughter and wait patiently for death."

"Why do you call her she, if you are her, reincarnated?"

"I have detached memories like yourself, but I have long practiced their retrieval. I can see the timeline as if I am standing witness, but my true perspective is in the eyes of the mortal woman, Hekate. Just like you are David, above all else. I am the first time Isis has truly reincarnated, for it took our family generations before a vessel was created that was strong enough to house both her soul and her *heka*."

"You are one of the daughters then."

"I am. Lucius never lifted the curse. In fact, with his rebirth came the additional curse that no other god would ever be able to reincarnate on earth again unless he explicitly allowed it. He created his own network of *daemons* and creatures to serve him, including other blood drinkers like himself."

A thought occurred to David. "What about your brother, Dragos?"

"Having a twin was what ensured my body would be strong enough to house Isis. He absorbed any human weakness that would prevent my body from serving as a sound vessel, but please don't ever tell him I referred to him as weak." She gave a playful smile before continuing. "Morrigan did not remember her sister on earth until well after she and Daghda returned to the Upperworld, once the Christian religion replaced the religions of old. As soon as they ascended, their full memories returned, and Morrigan discovered that her sister was not only trapped on earth but was now joined by their nemesis.

"Morrigan called upon all the gods and goddesses in the Upperrealms to inform them of her sister's tragedy and Lucius's new reign on earth. Not one among them provided her with a solution, and Lucius had made it impossible for any of them to return there even if they were willing to help. Although she was furious that they had allowed her sister to be harmed, she petitioned the Council to help her find a discrepancy in the curse so she could go back."

"Wait," David interrupted her, softly. "I remember."

It was as if a piece of him had returned.

He could see her clearly, holding her head in her hands, crumpled against the ancient oak tree. They were in the Upperrealms, an enchanted forest of swirling colors and vivid greens, surrounded by midnight skies that housed shooting stars and spinning planets.

David was unable to comfort her, his own heart broken.

"You cannot ask this of me." Tears streamed down Morrigan's face. "We just settled in here."

"It is the only way," he said, sinking into the moss beside her.

"I will tear him apart," she muttered.

"I do not doubt that you shall," he told her with a sad smile.

Morrigan stood, her sorrow replaced by indignation. The skies around her responded to the shift, lightning crackling throughout the darkening, thunderous sky. "We created the damned place, how can we be ousted from it? Just like the old religion that has been warped beyond recognition, the Roman gods our replacement. It is as if we are no longer wanted."

"The world has grown much bigger than us," David agreed. "Look how many gods now exist, we are but two."

"I know." She sighed. "As I know the earth follows its own rules, like the mothers who created her."

David rose to his feet, pulling her hips against him so she was close enough to be kissed. "Humans do not have to remember who we are, but it is still our duty to protect them. That is why we must make this decision. We cannot let him destroy everything they have built."

Her stony exterior collapsed once more, overwhelmed by grief. "You cannot ask this of me. I cannot live here without you!" Her words pulled rain down from the sky.

David pulled her back to him, holding her tight as he buried his face in her hair. "Do I have to tell you the story of Daghda and Morrigan, of Osiris and Nephthys, the most ancient of gods who find each other, always?" he murmured into her ear.

She closed her eyes, nuzzling into his neck. "Please tell me," she whispered.

David, a voice called from outside their realm. David, it is time to wake up.

He shut his eyes, memorizing her body against his, her skin, and the scent of her hair. "There are two souls who will continue to find each other until the end of time, the first lovers, whose love for one another transcends all bounds," he began as he folded her hand around the handle of his knife. She let out a sob as she realized what he was doing. They were now drenched in frigid rain that had created a river where they stood. He gripped her tighter. "They circle the realms, restless and incomplete until they find each other...but find each other, they always will."

"Remember me..."

And with a battle cry laced with despair, she sunk the knife into his chest, the realm screeching her pain as he dropped to the ground, picturing her face over and over in his mind, determined never to forget her eyes.

Quickly, I am losing him, the strange voice interrupted. The earth shook as wind roared around him, the Otherrealms furious with his departure. And then, he died, all the worlds around him fading to black, the sound of crows echoing in his mind.

LONDON, 1857

THE RAIN HAD RESUMED ITS ONSLAUGHT upon the earth, a crack of distant thunder awakening David from his dreams.

The window was open, the frigid breeze agitating the curtains into a frenzy. He lifted himself from the chair to close it, catching a glimpse of his disheveled reflection in the glass. He ran his fingers through his tangled copper curls, straightening a wrinkled dress shirt that had lost both its ascot and waistcoat. How long had he slumbered? He wondered absently as he fished around the darkened parlor for a smoke. He retrieved one, lighting it before turning the match onto a nearby candle as the tiny flame threatened his fingertips. The newly illuminated room was empty, a pile of unsettled blankets left in a heap on his sofa.

He remembered his companion.

He grabbed the candle, rushing into the hallway. "Jacob?" he called.

"In here, sir."

David followed the voice upstairs to the guest bedroom where he found Jacob bent over his companion, who lay motionless beneath the stiff blankets of the formerly neglected bed. Several crumpled and bloodied napkins scattered the floor near her bedside.

"What happened to her? Was it…" David trailed off before giving himself away, almost revealing his true nature to his manservant. David often suspected Jacob had already figured it out, skeptical that he never saw the bottles of blood kept in the secret cellar in the kitchen nor questioned the perpetually foodless pantry. Tonight, however, was not the time for unnecessary divulgements.

If Jacob noticed the err, he didn't show it, his weathered face appearing grim in the dim light. "She took a turn for the worse last night, sir.

I found you both sound asleep in the parlor, yet when I went to retrieve her dishes, I noticed her skin had taken on a shade of blue. I was able to revive her and relocate her to the bed, but I'm afraid her moments on this earth are fleeting. I'm sorry to give you such horrid news, sir."

David sighed, glad to learn her state was not a result of his own doing but saddened to learn her time was near. "Thank you, Jacob. You have exceeded yourself in altruism. I thank you deeply."

Jacob brushed off the compliment, rising to his feet. "You should sit with her now, sir. I would suggest calling for the doctor, but there is no point in it. The girl needs companionship now, or a priest."

At the suggestion, she coughed, releasing a spray of blood from her mouth as she fought for air. Jacob hurried to catch the expulsion with a fresh handkerchief, dabbing her chin as she quieted. "No priest," she whispered through cracked lips.

Jacob nodded.

"Thank you, Jacob," David dismissed him kindly. "I will stay with her now. I just needed a bit of rest."

"Yes, sir." Jacob bowed his head, slipping out of the room with the soiled handkerchiefs in his arms. "I'll be up with provisions in an hour, if she is able to eat."

His companion offered David a weak smile. "Good Morning," she croaked. "I think it's safe to assume you didn't anticipate bringing a whore into your home to die."

David grabbed a half-empty glass of water from the bedside table. "I have long learned not to question the events that unfold in my life." He tipped the glass towards her parched lips as she swallowed carefully.

She leaned back with a sigh, running a moistened tongue over her dry lips. "I suppose that means you've cut me off from the stronger stuff."

"Anything you want is yours," he responded earnestly, setting the glass back on the table.

"Good, then I want you to sit with me," she said, patting the open space next to her on the bed.

David slipped out of his house shoes and crawled into the place she directed him, propping himself up against the collection of pillows, which released a thin cloud of dust into the air. The scent of death was stronger on her now, hanging like a drowning captain to his floundering ship.

"I was once told there is an art to dying, but I'm afraid I've missed the instruction," she continued to lightly jest. She rolled herself onto her side so she could look at him, shadows hollowing her face beyond recognition, remnants of dried crimson lingering at the cracks of her mouth. Her dark hair was matted in the back where she had been resting.

David smoothed it back before resting his hand on hers. "Well, lucky for you, not only have I died myself several times, but I have had two women pass in my arms. You could say I'm a professional at this sort of thing."

She smiled. "Then the heavens must have known what they were doing when they threw us together. You had best hurry along with your story. I refuse to go until the end."

David frowned. "You couldn't possibly want to listen to me drone on about myself during your final hours."

"Quite the contrary," she said sleepily. "Your voice is soothing. Besides, how could I ever cross over without knowing how it ends? You'll doom me to haunt this house forever."

David couldn't help but smile. "All right then."

"Would you mind holding a third dying woman in your arms?" she asked.

David scooped her up without a word, so that her head rested against his chest and both his arms were draped around her.

"Now, where was I?"

"The part where you finally remembered her," she murmured. "The memory of when she killed you."

"Ah, yes," he said softly, resting his cheek on her hair.

WALLACHIA, 1462

"You're awake."

David's freshly opened eyes caught the silhouette of Hekate folded at her desk. She looked tired, even in the dim, forgiving candlelight, dark circles gathered around her eyes. "Glad to see it. You took a turn for the worse in the early hours of night, but fortunately, Dragos and I were able to keep you alive. You've been healing quite well since."

David sat up, pleased to learn that his body could now move without excruciating pain. He looked down at his arms and hands, wrapped in bandages similar to the mummy in his vision. "I remember," he said after he looked back up. "I remember my life with Morrigan. I don't recall our lives before that, however, no matter how I try."

"I know," Hekate sighed wistfully as she rose to her feet, her rotund girth swelling out her skirt.

A pang of guilt struck him, replaying their story in his mind. "Please forgive me for any pain I caused you in our former lives."

She reached his bedside, sitting down at the edge and patting an unbandaged part of his arm. "The memories from that life come from magical means, and I cannot sufficiently recall the feelings that go along with them. I can only watch it unfold like you can, through Hekate's eyes."

"That does not absolve me of the guilt I feel," David sighed.

"Do not lament over that which you could not control," Hekate corrected him. "This existence we are trapped in has its own set of rules. I know now that I loved you like a brother and understand that you loved me like a sister. I have long accepted your passion belongs to her."

"Our love is what led to Set manipulating and using you," David insisted.

"Set is responsible for his own actions," she argued. "He let jealousy embitter him and fuel his decisions. As for me, I was curious to feel the touch of a man, not once, but twice. A part of me knew that mortal was Set in disguise, and I could have spurned his advances, but I was lonely. I chose my path, just as Set chose his. I take full responsibility for my own mistakes and you should let me have it."

She rose and moved towards the wall to lift a low burning torch, using it to set the others ablaze. The light caught on her assortment of apothecary bottles, revealing several unsavory ingredients amongst her herbs and tinctures, including a capsule of disembodied eyes and a bottle of wormy rodent tails. They looked sinister in the flickering shadows.

"We were young, inexperienced gods," she said as the dank room attempted to grow warm. "We had no book of rules, no parents to teach us."

"And now here we are."

"Yes, here we are," she parroted with a sigh. "And still our world is threatened by the decisions we have made."

"So you are now pregnant with Lucius's child? How is it possible? Has he ever come to collect the women in your bloodline?" He paused. "Forgive me for asking so many questions. I suppose I'm just surprised I never heard of you before tonight."

"It's quite all right," she assured him. "Isis successfully hid us away for many years - her daughter, her granddaughter, and so on, over the centuries. We do not know the exact magic behind it, but on the night of our eighteenth birthdays, we become with child, always a daughter. The absurdity of our curse is also what makes it so dangerous, for you can imagine what sort of problems arise for pregnant, husbandless women alone in the world. Some of us tried to make children with other men and failed, others were virgins when they gave birth. Eventually, Isis was forced to hide us away from even the most remote mountain tribes, creating a clan of women which she called the Pădurii. She appeared to anyone who ventured near our home as a frightening old hag. After she died, the eldest woman of each generation took on the same guise until it eventually earned us the name Muma Pădurii, a witch feared by men for centuries. Save for Isis, who died in the ancient times, most of us are semimortal, meaning we live longer than humans but not forever. It has ensured a large enough clan to care for each other as the years pass."

"And Lucius never found you?"

"Isis's magic has protected us throughout the centuries. Even now, as his last remaining children live in his own village, he cannot detect our presence."

"Where is your mother?" David wondered. "And the rest of your clan? How did Isis eventually die?"

Hekate paused as her green eyes shifted. The air around them seemed to grow heavy. "There are some secrets that must be kept," she said quietly. "But I can tell you, my mother died while giving birth to me, moments after bringing my brother into the world."

"Forgive me, I did not mean to pry."

"I told you, David, it is quite all right. I have taken it upon myself to deliver your history to you and I shall. There are just things too painful to discuss, particularly when it comes to Hekate's story. Those emotions I do feel."

"I understand."

"To answer the question of how Isis died," she continued, "we honestly don't know. Our history has been passed down through oral tradition, and somewhere along the way, the exact way she died became unknown even to the oldest among us."

"And now she is reincarnated in you."

Hekate smiled as she resumed her seat at her desk. "Yes. But enough talk of my past. There is a bit more I must tell you, and then I will leave you to rest."

Since they were underground, David could not see the time of day, but assumed by the damp aroma of the dirt surrounding them that it had reached nightfall. "You need your rest as well," he pointed out, gesturing towards her stomach. He felt a painful tug at his heart, reminded of Gaia and the child she never bore.

Hekate's hand found her belly as she shook her head. "I must tell you all of it, so that you understand what is at stake."

David leaned back in the sick bed, allowing her to resume.

She brushed back a stray lock of her burnt chestnut hair, the movement disturbing her long metal earrings and layers of necklaces, who clinked together in dissension. "There was one other god who managed to reincarnate right before Lucius arrived and halted the reincarnations. This creature was Horus, his memories lost just like each reincarnated god before and after him. Even though Isis returned his plucked out eye, it cursed him to roam the astral plane in death and when he did return to earth, he would be nothing like the beautiful man he once was, but a beast with deformities. His mortal life was spent roaming the world in confusion and isolation until the day he stumbled upon Lucius.

"It was only moments after Lucius had risen and was promptly abandoned by Isis, consumed by a thirst I'm sure you remember. With no one to guide him, he fell prey to his carnal instincts, tearing through dozens of animals in untamed savagery, including a boar. It transformed before he could strike, revealing he was actually a human being, one with a deeply crooked spine, the hooves of a boar, the wings of a bird, and the horns of a stag."

"Libraean is Horus." David was amazed.

"The two creatures fought until Lucius drained Horus, leaving him for dead. Yet Horus had accidentally consumed some of Lucius's blood during their battle and was reanimated as a blood drinker. I believe Libraean revealed to you what transpired after that."

"He told me that his human conscience returned over time and a frustrated Lucius abandoned him," David relayed. "He longed for death and tied himself to a tree to await incineration by sunlight. An angel saved him before he burned."

"Yes," she confirmed. "The angel, Gabriel, fell in love with him and decided to enlist him into serving their cause. He told him their version of the beginning: that their "God of Light" cast out a rebellious angel named Lucifer and his traitorous minions from the heavenly realms, who were now Lucius and his daemons. Libraean believed this version of truth for many years, ignorant of his true history. His love for Gabriel kept him loyal to their cause for many years. It was not until the end of the Ancient Era, when Anubis petitioned the Christ to allow us to speak with him, did he learn of his true past. Its revelation shattered the bond between Libraean and Gabriel, and he now works with us, alongside the Council."

David was quiet for a moment, his heart heavy for the tragic being, who was, incredibly enough, once his son. He struggled to grasp the notion that the two beings he had seen in the astral plane, the jackal headed Anubis and the Sphinx, Libraean, were actually both his children - his and Morrigan's. The ache to be reunited with her surfaced again, but he swallowed it, intent on hearing the rest of Hekate's story. "What does Lucius know about our past?" he asked her.

"Since his reincarnation was unnatural, he remembers more than the rest of you, but it is still choppy," she replied. "He recalls bits of Egypt and Tartarus, but he has no idea who Morrigan or Daghda truly were. He'd forgotten Horus completely, even when they were companions."

"His love for Morrigan never died," David murmured in reflection.

For the first time, David saw a flash of emotion cross over Hekate's eyes. "Interesting," she commented with an impartial air.

He had little time to explore her eyes further, to try and pull out the thoughts he was blocked from, for they were interrupted by the sound of a man bounding down the stairs.

"Enough, Hekate," Dragos demanded. "He needs to come with us."

Hekate rose to her feet, putting her hands on her hips. "Look at him, Dragos, he is still covered in bandages. You want the Insurgence to appear weak?"

Dragos turned towards David and frowned, mirroring his twin sister's stance. The way his brows furrowed confirmed the source of his paternity, sending a shudder up David's spine.

"When will he be healed?" he asked her, frustration gnawing at his words.

Hekate softened her voice as she presented her appeal. "You must have patience brother. We almost lost him."

Dragos approached the bedside, David observing eyes like polished hematite. He peered into them, hoping to catch a flutter of thought, but discovered he was shielded from them, just like his sister and Danulf. He was beginning to wonder if it was intentional amongst creatures to shield their thoughts by magical means.

"I apologize, Great David," Dragos said half-heartedly.

David rose in alarm, the words pulling a distant memory from his past. He saw the grotesque *daemons* of Tartarus dancing in the inky pools of his eyes. "What did you say?"

Hekate inserted herself between them. "Your coming has been prophesied for decades, David," she explained quickly, "passed down from the first oracle who made her home here. The Dacian tribes have referred to you by that name for longer than you know, the man who would someday deliver them from the Dark Times."

David heard her words but could not shake the sensation of foreboding that had settled over him. He continued to keep his gaze locked on the scowling Dragos.

Hekate turned to her brother, her voice matching the tension of her body. "Please, Dragos, leave us. I will send for you when it is time."

Dragos threw up his hands in exasperation but retreated from her sick room.

She turned back to David. "My brother is not the most patient of men," she attempted to explain.

"No matter," David assured her.

The torches crackled in the silence of the cellar. Hekate offered him a tired smile as she gently squeezed his bandaged hand. "Rest now, David. We are done with the stories."

She rose to extinguish the fire around them, submerging the room in delicious darkness. David closed his eyes, realizing how heavy his eyelids had been. Within moments, he fell into a dreamless sleep.

CHAPTER EIGHT

❧ The Night War ❧

"COME," A GRUFF VOICE JOLTED HIM AWAKE. "You have laid in bed for days now and much happens in your absence. It's time to go."

David's eyes snapped open to see Danulf hovering above him, wearing his signature scowl with a torch in his hand. "Hekate is gathering herbs from her night garden," he explained. "I decided to steal you away while I had the chance. She warned me against explaining things to you too soon, worrying about your health. Apparently, you had it rough learning the destiny bit. But I think you are good on your feet. We are talking about the first god that ever was, are we not?"

"Dragos calls me the Great David," he kept up the playful banter as he pushed off his blankets. He noticed several of his bandages had been removed, with a few left behind to protect, what he assumed, were more extensive wounds. David was surprised how efficiently he'd been healed thus far.

"Well, I definitely will not be calling you that," Danulf snorted in reply. He lent his hand, pulling David up from the bed.

It took him a moment to adjust to being upright and he steadied his stance as Danulf observed. When the room ceased its nauseating spin, he gave him a nod. "I am ready."

They climbed the stairwell, out through a trapdoor that Danulf hid with a straw mat after they exited. David looked around the first floor to observe a house that appeared to belong to cunning folk, provisions and medicines on display for purchase, several chairs and tables set out to mend wounds and care for ailments. He surmised that the hidden floor from which they had emerged was intended for their less standard patients.

A strong breeze whistled through the cracks in the door, sharpening David's senses. "There it is," Danulf noticed. "I knew you longed for fresh air."

He threw open the front door to reveal the accumulation of yet another snowstorm, the wind whistling as it drifted across the frozen ground. David relished for a moment the crisp, biting air before following Danulf down the street.

The town was desolate in the evening snowfall, save for muted lamp-light that flickered ahead out of a frosted window. It happened to be the town's ale house, the only establishment still open in the late hour. Danulf trudged towards it, gesturing for David to follow, his boots leaving generous footprints in the snow.

David could hear the audible bustle behind its walls as they approached, as well as the fleeting thoughts of the mortals inside. He raised an eye-brow as Danulf prepared to enter, surprised that he would expose them to humans so casually.

"Are you ready?" Danulf asked him, noticing his bewildered expression.

David bobbed his head in reply.

Danulf opened the front door to bring a visual to the noise, the modest room brimming with chattering men of all shapes and sizes, clustered around dozens of tables arranged in front of the bar. They grew still in silent unison as they entered, the barkeep eyeing them suspiciously before brightening. "Comrades!" he erupted in a thick Wallachian dialect. "Let me fetch you some ale."

The tavern patrons retrieved their glasses, lifting them in salute as David walked awkwardly through, discomfited by the gesture. Their thoughts trickled into his mind like the slow drip of water, disclosing that many of them knew who he was and were convinced he was the one who would save them from Lucius's terrible reign.

"They do not have time for ale," Dragos appeared from behind the gathering of men, dressed in formal livery, his hair pushed flat underneath a fur cap. A sheathed saber lay at his waist. "They are needed in the cellars."

The barkeep nodded. "Carry on, gentlemen," he instructed the rest of the patrons, who resumed their boisterous chatter.

"It took you long enough," Dragos remarked as they entered the back room where kegs of ale were stowed.

"Your sister is a formidable obstacle," Danulf muttered. They both began to move around the heavy containers until they revealed yet another door that led underground.

As soon as Danulf lifted it open, David was accosted by the sour smell of offal. The room they entered was dim, save for a weak lantern on a table that revealed rows of fermenting ale in barrels, alternating evenly with vats of animal blood.

"This room serves as our butchery," Dragos explained as David observed a long butcher's block at the far end of the room, stained with crimson and cluttered by knives. Several wooden boxes of animal meat were stacked against the wall, chilled by layers of ice. "We drain the animals, preserving their meat for the rest of the town. The smell of wild game conceals the creature presence here."

"*Nemorti* live in town?" David was surprised.

"Some of the men in the tavern are human and some are creatures, for we do not use the word *nemorti* like you. Our creatures are free. The humans have offered us an alliance, also of their own free will, for they understand what is at stake - that the Imposter Prince intends to wipe out humanity and force us all into servitude. They assist us in our daylight affairs. A few of the sick and dying even offer us their blood, helpful to satisfy the bloodlust that our newly created creatures suffer from in their first days."

"You create blood drinkers?" David repeated incredulously.

"We do not create them ourselves, the Imposter has his Hunters for that. They are not only responsible for kidnapping innocent townspeople for food, but they have been turning new recruits at an alarming rate. Do you pay attention to anything that transpires in your own home?" he chided, shaking his head in disbelief. "We are the ones who steal them out of the castle, so that they might find freedom here. Many are quite young when we discover them."

David ignored the denunciation. "Forgive me, but if Lucius is planning for war, then his army is vast," he pointed out. "Dan may have killed half his court, but his knights range in the thousands. The men in the tavern are militia, half of them lacking the strength to take on one immortal, let alone dozens. Even starving nemorti can kill quite well."

"That is why we brought you here," Danulf interrupted their exchange. He led David away from the butchery down a corridor that opened into a meeting room. At its center was a substantial table, mimicking the high table preferred by royalty. A man was already seated behind it, his hand cradling the white marble orb that topped his staff. All around him, Turkish soldiers stood in full armor, their pointed iron helmets shining in the torchlight.

The man looked up to face him, causing David to startle with recognition. Radu cel Frumos was a near identical version of his imposter brother Lucius, with the same radiant black hair and striking eyes, but was far more delicate, his graceful mannerisms accentuated by the silk caftan draped around his slender frame. "The eldest son of Vlad Dracul, the true heir to the Wallachian throne," David murmured aloud, before he could stop himself. "I thought Lucius had murdered you."

"You are correct, I am the true heir to my father's throne. I wish to take back what is mine and was told that you are the ones to aid me in achieving this." Although he was visually charming, his voice was cold and clear, without a hint of pleasantry. "Let us sit."

Dragos nodded to Danulf and David. Once they were all seated, he turned his attention towards Radu. "My people have been victims of senseless torture and death for as long as the Imposter Dracula has sat on the throne. He has created his own army of creatures, whom he calls *nemorti*, immortal creatures that he keeps starved and submissive. He intends to use them first to wipe our territory clean of humanity, then continue to ravage the rest of Europe until no human is left standing. He will then force his newly minted creatures into servitude. The Wallachian people are no strangers to mythical creatures, but the delicate balance that we have painstakingly preserved over the centuries has been destroyed. Half of our town is now walking death. We propose that if we combine our forces in battle, the immortal Wallachians and the Ottoman Turks, we can usurp Dracula, and not only restore this precious balance, but restore the rightful heir on the Wallachian throne."

Radu was quiet as he considered his request, pursing his lips together as he thought. "Can the fiend even be killed?" he asked. "And how do you propose my men fight these creatures of darkness, these *nemorti*, as you call them?"

Dragos gestured towards David. "We have recruited the second oldest one on this earth, the only one who matches the Imposter in power."

Radu raised a delicate eyebrow. "He is covered in bandages," he said flatly.

"My name is David, and I am the first true immortal blood drinker,"

David found words tumbling from his mouth unrestrained. He wasn't sure if it was exhaustion, Hekate's revelations, or the tension that thickened the room, but he had grown past his point of patience. "I am over one thousand years old. I have lived to see the Roman Empire fall, Jesus Christ murdered, the Crusades launch and end. I have outlived some of the greatest minds and worst men on earth. The one you know as Dracula, I know as Lucius, a dark god incarnate, who proceeds my age by hundreds of years. It has been told to me by those who hold the magic in this world, that he is my brother and I am the only one strong enough to kill him. I intend to do so, with or without your help. I have no time for, nor do I care about, the power struggles between men, but if I have the opportunity to be helpful while I complete my task, then so be it."

The room was silent, Dragos's face drawn up into blatant mortification.

Yet, remarkably, Radu nodded. "I understand. Forgive me for not seeing the true warrior behind the mask. How many men does this Lucius have?"

"At least a thousand," Dragos responded without hesitation.

Radu looked at Danulf. "You say you have a thousand men in your army, as well. How many are creatures?"

"Only half."

"Are you planning to make the rest *nemorti*?"

Dragos interjected. "Our main purpose for this war is to establish the rule that creatures and mortals must coexist, neither one having dominion over the other," he explained. "We will not be turning any humans, since that would go against our purpose."

"But we do understand that they have their weaknesses," Danulf spoke up. "Our plan to keep the human army behind the others, armed and waiting with silver tipped weaponry. We discovered that this metal could kill creatures as efficiently as the naked sun."

David was aghast at the open revelation of their most precious secret but was able to arrest any display of emotion.

Radu again presented a contemplative visage. He crossed a pair of bony hands before him, his fingers unusually barren of jewels for someone of royal stature, a stark divergence from Lucius. The longer David observed him, the more he understood his handle, Radu the Fair, for although he could easily pass as Lucius's twin, his youth brought an undeniable softness to his features.

Finally, he spoke. "I was the one who led the attack on Wallachia for Sultan Mehmet, armed with troops in the hundreds, after the Imposter attempted to sneak into our camp to assassinate him. It was I who saw the dead Turkish soldiers he surrounded his castle with, the stench of decaying bodies in the summer sun unbearable. My men became so distraught by the sight of their people butchered in such a manner that they refused to fight, retreating to our camp and withdrawing from the army. I will never forget the sight of it for as long as I shall live.

"It is the reason why I am alone now, with the Sultan's blessing, but not his janissaries. He has not spoken it aloud, but he believes the Imposter is true evil and will not venture into his land again. I have a few Turkish soldiers with me now, but they are of moderate value to him. Many of my men I have recruited on my own, allies I made during my time spent in the Ottoman Empire as a youth. Some I have collected from across the Danubian plains. In total, I have two thousand trained soldiers, yet none of them are creatures. I will have to offer them the same positions that you intend on assigning your humans, relying on your immortal army to take the forefront."

Danulf nodded. "We should strike on the offensive by raiding the castle as it sleeps - right at nightfall. Although it cannot fully kill them, a creature must steer far from fire, which we can use to our advantage. Your flesh and blood army can attack the castle using incendiary weapons to push them back, allowing our creatures to enter."

"Yes, that would work," the prince agreed. He sat back in his chair, contemplating the proposal in its entirety. "We will align our causes."

Dragos clapped his hands together in unrestricted delight. "We are honored to make this alliance," he said, standing to offer Radu his hand.

Radu's eyes looked past him to settle on David, extending his hand towards him instead. David took it without hesitation. "We will meet again soon," Radu told him. "I wish to destroy the Imposter as soon as possible, before he realizes what transpires under his own nose."

Dragos quickly recovered from the insult, deciding to act as if it had not occurred. "My general, Danulf, would like to further discuss our strategies with your general."

Danulf, who had been enjoying the exchange playing out before him, rose to his feet. "Allow me to speak with your general. We are hoping to go to war within a fortnight."

David was surprised. "So soon?"

Dragos interrupted before Danulf could respond. "As much as we try to remain underground, the Imposter has shadows planted throughout the village. As soon as word reaches him that you are still alive, he will come searching for you. And when he finds out that you are part of an insurgence revolting against him, it will be immediate war."

David nodded, understanding his point.

"As you wish," Radu inserted. "I will take your general to mine." He stood, gesturing for Danulf to follow.

"And I will escort you back to our safehold," Dragos instructed David, with a look that dared him to argue. David watched Danulf leave with Radu and his soldiers, realizing that his skin still throbbed, and his bones still ached for rest. He acquiesced to the notion of returning to his bed, following Dragos out of the tavern.

The snowstorm had ceased, leaving the skies clear enough to see a sliver of moon peeking out from behind the rugged mountain tops. The air was cold, but not enough to maintain more than a thin layer of snow on the ground that dissipated with each footstep.

David had time to observe Dragos, who moved with the determination of a warrior yearning for battle. He was dressed in dark colors that blended with his skin tone, offering natural camouflage, with various weaponry strapped to his legs and waist. His long facial hair seemed even longer with the height of his tall fur cap. David tried to pick up his thoughts but could only hear the chaotic buzz of insects. He absently wondered if he'd lost his telepathic gift forever, another power removed.

They reached the threshold, greeting a visibly displeased Hekate. Her curvaceous frame took over the doorway, her hand perched at her hip. She glared out from underneath the hood of her cloak.

"It was Danulf that brought him to me, though I support his actions," Dragos explained before she could speak.

Her sharp virid eyes narrowed, and although they differed in color, they burned in a way that revealed they were undoubtedly her father's. David wondered how Lucius would react to his children if he met them, if he would be pleased by his lookalike son or proud of his beautiful daughter's cunning, and if his heart would break when he learned of their abhorrence towards him.

"While you were away, one of the soldiers came to my door," Hekate told him. "Apparently there was a scuffle between the camp and the Sagittaureans, and now one of theirs is wounded. They are demanding our assistance, but you know how they feel about me."

Dragos cursed under his breath. "The last thing we need right now is their animosity."

"Where is Danulf?" she asked.

"He should be reaching the camp shortly with the others," he replied. "Hopefully, he can keep the peace until we get there."

"We?"

"I am taking David with me."

Hekate went to protest.

"Hekate, he is almost entirely healed," Dragos cut her off. "I am going to need his power if they become combative."

Hekate frowned, but begrudgingly nodded. "Come, get my bag."

"Where are we going?" David broke in.

"The Sagittaureans live in the most remote part of the mountains," Hekate explained hurriedly as she threw bundles of herbs and tinctures into a leather satchel. "They are quite content to leave us alone, provided we do the same. The Ottomans, however, unknowingly made camp on a portion of their land, and it took much convincing on our part to get them to accept their presence there. It seems as though they have decided to renege on our agreement." She lined the bag with fresh bandages before placing it in Dragos's arms.

"They are also notoriously obstinate, and they detest women," he added, securing the straps of the bag across his chest, its bulkiness, plus his costume of weaponry, giving him an intimidating facade.

Hekate inspected David and sighed. She removed her cloak, draping it over his shoulders to conceal his bandaged arms. "Please be careful."

David gave her a gentle hug around her swollen stomach, watching the apples of her face redden from the gesture. "I will," he assured her.

"Come, we should hurry," Dragos called from the door. David followed, the two reentering the frozen terrain.

"Are you able to move at our speed or shall we travel by horseback?" Dragos asked with an impartial expression.

"I can run," David told him, though he wasn't convinced his response was not motivated by pride.

Dragos did not argue, seeming to disappear instantly from the white-washed town into the forest of evergreens. David darted after him, wincing only slightly as his body balked at the sudden movement. Dragos stopped when they reached the far edge of the mountains where the woods were so thick that only pine needles cluttered its floor, free of the snow that had gathered on the tips of its conifers. David fought collapse, realizing the overexertion had not been in his best interest, when the stomps of agitated horses interrupted, jolting him enough that his preservation instincts overcame his moment of weakness.

"We come peacefully, at your request," Dragos called out into the darkness. Even with heightened senses, David struggled to see.

"One of your kind has wounded our man. I would like to have a limb in payment," came a haughty male voice.

"I can only offer you my healing services," Dragos replied coolly.

"Of course," another one snorted.

"Let them help, and if they cannot, we will take a limb ourselves," another suggested.

From the murky black stepped forward several horses, except that they were not simply horses, but the torsos of men connected to bodies of equine limbs and hair. David tried to conceal his surprise, for he had assumed centaurs were creatures of legend. Furthermore, they were prominent in Greek tales, and the revelation that they stalked the inhospitable forest of the Carpathian Mountains proved additionally surprising.

The centaur in the middle was larger than his counterparts, his chest covered in patches of auburn hair that resumed at the waist to cover four strong legs secured by ample hooves. He crossed his arms, his muscles tight. "Who is this you have brought along with you? He reeks like another *strigoi*."

"He is like me, along to help mend the wounded," Dragos calmly replied.

From behind the three creatures appeared several others, smaller in frame, holding bulky crossbows with arrows drawn and aimed at them.

"Rid yourself of all weaponry before we proceed," instructed the leader.

Dragos nodded, removing his saber from his waist and bending to unstrap the knives from his thighs and ankles.

"And you?" The centaur studied David suspiciously, its dark eyes sweeping over him before resting on the bloodied bandages that peeked through Hekate's cloak.

"I have brought nothing," David stammered in reply.

"You came to the Sagittaureans weaponless?" the creature scoffed.

"I know him, Sagittari, he lives in the castle with the Imposter *Strigoi*," the centaur to the right of him said.

"Ah, so you brought one with power so you would not need your weapons," the leader snorted, turning a reproachful gaze towards Dragos.

"If you do not want our help, we will return to where we came." Dragos's signature irritation was surfacing.

"I mean you no harm," David attempted.

The centaurs burst into laughter. "Oh, you cannot harm us, *strigoi*. I am simply pointing out the obvious truth which your friend attempts to hide. He has brought you here in case we turn on you. He has no powers of his own and is no match for our herd."

Dragos fumed but did not speak.

"You may enter to help our fallen brother, then you must promptly leave," Sagittari decided.

Dragos nodded, leaving his weapons behind and following them deeper into their woods. David followed suit, curious how the events would unfold. Now that the initial shock had worn off, he could feel his exhaustion gnawing at him steadily, reminding him that he needed rest.

He distracted himself by studying the centaurs, poised but brawny creatures, moving with a grace that went against their size and temperament. The horde dissipated gradually as they descended into their territory, the archers moving to defend the boundaries against any other intrusions.

Sagittari paused before the mouth of a cave, gesturing them forward. Through the light of a meager fire, David saw the wounded centaur, lying amidst a heap of straw. Its back leg was bent at a dangerous angle, its flesh ribboned over its joints. He was unconscious, his human half covered by a thin blanket that he shivered under regardless.

"You need to set the bone, then apply a salve to heal the surface wounds," David blurted out, ancient memories of his time as a stable boy drifting up from the recesses of his mind.

Both Dragos and the centaurs turned to stare at him in surprise.

"I have never set an animal's bone before," Dragos admitted in a rare display of diffidence. "Hekate included the necessary tools for wound care, but I am afraid that was all she anticipated."

"May I?" David asked the centaurs carefully.

Sagittari maintained his hostile expression but nodded.

David approached the wounded centaur, studying the broken leg. Thankfully, the fractured bone had not pierced through the skin and had remained partially attached to the knee bone. "We will need to find pieces of wood and size them to his leg. Two should work," he said. "I will then need a plank to strap the leg to, along with the sturdiest rope you can muster. Pieces of leather would also be suitable."

Sagittari glanced at the centaurs flanking him, gesturing for them to retrieve the requested items. They disappeared seamlessly into the bleak, shapeless woods.

Dragos opened up Hekate's bag to set out the bandages and tinctures, producing one of her salves and a bottle of hemlock and opium. "He will need this for the pain," he explained.

Sagittari nodded, and Dragos bent to put the concoction to his lips. The fallen centaur looked young, with wavy chestnut hair that was long enough to wind itself through the bed of straw. He resisted the taste at first, but eventually relaxed enough to allow Dragos to pour the liquid down his throat. Within moments, he began to emit a low rumbling snore.

"He is my son," the elder centaur abruptly offered, his face still impassive and his arms still crossed before him.

"I am sorry," David extended.

Sagittari shook his head. "I do not need you to be. It is a great honor for a Sagittaurean warrior to die in battle. It would be selfish of me to feel sorrow at his passing. Yet my eldest son left our herd long ago and I have attached myself to this one."

"Mourning is a gift many do not receive," David murmured as he bent to study the leg. "It means that we have been able to truly love another in our lifetime."

The centaur was again taken aback by him. "You are not like the other *strigoi*."

"He is the Great Promised One," Dragos flatlined.

They were interrupted by the sound of stomping hooves, the centaurs returning with arms full of wooden planks and branches. David went to work immediately, throwing off Hekate's cloak and rolling up his sleeves without any regard for his appearance. Memories floated back to him as he worked, recalling conversations held between him and Eridus many years ago. It was common practice to slaughter horses with broken appendages, but David had assured him that he could fix the bone within two months' time. Eridus had protested, unable to see the point in feeding an animal that could no longer provide them with transportation, but David pressed until he gave in. The fallen horse he'd worked on had to be sedated, just as the creature now before him, still whimpering through unconsciousness as he wrapped a makeshift tourniquet at the thigh.

Dragos assisted in securing the leg as David grabbed the knee and pushed the leg bone back into place. He worked quickly, strapping the amended leg firmly to the plank of wood while Dragos applied the salve heavily. He then wound the plank and the sticks with rope, ensuring that the set leg would remain firmly in place.

When he stepped away, he realized he was drenched in sweat, black oil dripping from his forehead. He wiped it away, embarrassed by the blatant display of his blood drinking nature, realizing gratefully that neither him nor Dragos had been affected by the amount that had been spilled.

"*Strigoi* who heal. I am amazed," Sagittari commented.

"He has a long stretch of healing ahead," David warned him as he gingerly unrolled his sleeves back over his bandaged arms. "But if he forces himself to rest, he will be able to walk again."

"We appreciate your assistance. This absolves our vendetta against your kind. However, let this serve as my final warning - if one more human comes near our borders, we will kill them without hesitation."

"Understood." Dragos nodded. He seemed to know better than to attempt to shake the centaur's hand, bowing curtly in his direction instead. They followed him out of the cave, back into the black forest. Sagittari's eyes met David's. "I can tell you are a traveler. If you ever happen upon my eldest son, tell him he is still welcome here. His name is Chiron."

David startled with recognition as the centaur abruptly broke into a gallop and disappeared into the darkness. He had named the most infamous centaur in Greek myth, the one who came to teach humans the art of medicine.

"Come," Dragos said. "We should check in with the camp."

"Would you mind if we walked?" David asked, hoping the act of healing a living being had softened Dragos's generally brusque disposition.

He snorted in contempt, swiftly dismissing Davis's speculation. "I suppose."

They walked for a while before the forest brightened, cracks appearing in its ceiling of needled branches and pinecones, offering the ground its sparse light. "It is daylight, but we are protected in here," Dragos told him. "Our arrival should time perfectly with nightfall, for we still have far to travel."

David nodded, not bothering to ask if they could use the time to rest. "I never knew centaurs inhabited the Carpathian Mountains."

"They place autonomy and privacy above all else. The Greek centaur myths that have been passed down among generations are based on Chiron, the great intellect who fled his herd in defiance and found his way down to the Mediterranean centuries ago."

"They are immortal?"

"Of course they are," Dragos scoffed. "You really don't know much of anything, do you?"

David swallowed a flare of anger. "I ask questions so that I do know. Ignorant is the man that thinks he knows all."

Dragos laughed. "Now you sound like my father."

David was surprised. "I thought you never met Lucius. Hekate said you have spent your lives hiding from him."

"Stories have been passed down to us by those who remembered him," he explained. "I am the first son to ever be born of the Pădurii, so of course it revived all talk of our patriarch."

"He was once a decent man," David admitted. "Though very vain and slightly mad."

Dragos paused his trot. "You know, you do not have to kill him."

"Is that not the entire point of the Insurgence?" David sputtered, thoroughly bemused.

Dragos merely shrugged. "It is our fight, not yours. It was Hekate's idea to recruit you. Danulf and I were steadfast against it until she convinced us that you were the key."

David was silent as they continued their stride forward. Soon, the conifers gave way, signaling the end of the southern forest and the place where the Ottomans had made their camp. Dragos was correct in his prediction, the sun had set, its intense rays settled below the mountain tops, the only hint of its departure a lingering red haze, blurred by perpetual fog.

The camp was much larger than David had expected, positioned near a small stream which had yet to freeze over. Fires were already lit in preparation of evening chill, the entire army covered in cloaks and hats of varied animal furs, save for the man that approached them.

Danulf's scowl appeared more fierce than usual, his beard and matted hair dusted with frost. His hoodless cloak looked flimsy compared to the humans around him, the acres of tattoos scrawled down his arms exposed. "How did it go?" he asked bluntly.

"I was able to mend the fallen centaur," Dragos replied. "They will not attack again, provided the Ottomans stay out of their territory."

Danulf sighed. "That is going to be hard to do. Four men lie wounded from their arrows, and eventually someone will decide to avenge the act. This war needs to happen before tensions reach their peak." He looked at David. "You look like death."

Dragos cut in before he could respond. "I am taking him back to our apothecary."

"Are you certain he is well enough to travel there?" Danulf asked, continuing to study him. His scrutinous gaze made it harder for David to convince himself that he wasn't near collapse.

"Shall we take horses then?" Dragos asked.

"Nah, you and I will fly with him," Danulf decided. "I need to return to the stronghold as well. The two of us together can manage him."

David went to protest, but each of them grabbed an arm. In moments, they were at the village gates, the impact of their landing sending a nearby snowdrift into collapse. David stabilized himself as Danulf ducked into the tavern, leaving Dragos and him alone once more. They headed towards the apothecary, the ground beneath them crunching with their footsteps.

"So I assume my sister informed you of your entire history?" Dragos cut through the quiet, his voice thin.

"Yes," David replied, as the house came into view. Its windows lacked the glow of lamplight, apparent that Hekate had finally allowed herself the sleep that she desperately needed.

"You are taking it remarkably well," Dragos commented. "I cannot imagine that I would be so calm knowing that my two lovers were sisters, one who tricked you into believing she was an innocent mortal."

"What do you mean?" David asked, confused.

Dragos raised an eyebrow, widening the almond shape of his eye. "That Gaia was actually Isis reincarnated, but stripped of her magic."

David almost faltered but maintained a calm facade as his heart hammered against his chest. He hoped Dragos's supernatural senses wouldn't catch its climb. "I believe she did what she thought was best," he said lightly, as if he already knew what Dragos unintentionally revealed.

Dragos snorted in response. "Isis would never admit her love for Lucius, but they once became very close. After the death of the Ancient Ones, Isis visited him in the Underworld, avoiding Anubis's watchful eye by pretending to be Persephone, the Greek god Hades's queen, living with him during the winter months and returning to her mother each spring. When in reality, she was an Egyptian goddess trapped in her tree, visiting him when she knew the seasons changed. An incredible ruse, if you ask me. Don't you think it strange that the same dark god who supposedly took her unwillingly was the same god she visited so often?"

David was speechless.

"Well, you might miss your old friend Lucius," Dragos said as they reached the apothecary and he pulled open the door. "But tricking you into falling in love with Isis in human form so he could be with Morrigan was despicable, on both their parts."

David walked through the opened door, prepared to demand answers from Hekate, when he realized the room was in shambles. Lucius's promise to him at the Death Wall suddenly returned - he was planning to force Hekate to bring back the Morrigan. *And I will let him*, came a brief, selfish whisper.

"She was taken." Dragos cursed, grabbing David's arm and heading out the door. "Now it's only a matter of time before he discovers that you are alive and strikes."

Dragos evoked once more their unnatural speed, carrying the still weak David so they would reach the tavern in seconds. He threw open the door to see the men were already gathered in visible agitation.

"Dragos," Danulf appeared from behind the swell of bodies. "There is a traitor among us. Lucius knows we have David and he plans to attack us to retrieve him within the hour."

David felt his world spin.

Danulf noticed, grabbing his arm. "You need blood."

He pulled David down into the cellar, leaving Dragos to speak with the general. David was helpless to resist, feeling as though all the strength he had managed to gather the last few hours had been drained from him. His mind was a whirlwind of incoherent thought.

He slumped onto the straw littered floor as Danulf pulled open a cupboard that housed a variety of lopsided decanters. He grabbed one labeled, "oxblood", removing its cork with his teeth, spitting it against the wall, and jamming the opening between David's lips. A stream of sour, tepid liquid found its way down his throat. David tried to hold on to consciousness, knowing it would only take a few moments before the nourishment revived him, but he couldn't halt the sensation of falling.

"This is the worst time for this," he heard Danulf curse as David watched the floor tremble and crack open between them, revealing the flames of a volatile inferno that rose up from the crevice as if determined to consume him. Dozens of skeletal hands beat them to it, crawling forward until they attached to his skin and clothing, twisting around strands of his hair. It was no use fighting them off, for as soon as they captured their prey, they descended, dragging him into the raging abyss in one seamless, brutal swallow.

THE UNDERWORLD

D AVID WAS BECOMING MORE ACCUSTOMED to traveling through the realms, yet when he opened his eyes to reveal the tenebrous domain of the Underworld, he immediately sprang to his feet in panic.

"Do not fret, you are only a visitor."

David turned to see Anubis before him. They stood upon the only plateau in the rocky, cavernous world, crags jutting up all around them from an unforgiving river that loudly vocalized its vexations.

The plateau's high elevation was enough to alarm David, who tried to maintain his footing as he beheld the creature standing in front of him. Anubis was purely anthropomorphic in his kingdom, lacking any obvious human appendages, but standing on hind legs, his claws wrapped around a slender staff. His jackal head cocked to the side as he curiously observed David's apprehension. "Shall we move somewhere that is more comfortable for you? You loved the rushing waters in your first life."

David shook his head stubbornly. "I will be fine," he assured him, though his voice wavered. "I have recently discovered that traveling realms takes a toll on me, but I am learning to adjust. It seems this is a part of my life now."

The jackal nodded although his eyes remained marked with concern. "I would not have summoned you, had there not been urgency," he explained. "As you now know, I am the head of the Council, as well as the guardian of the Underworld. Since we last spoke, Lucius has prevented any further interference by the Council. Libraean and I are the only ones now who can reach you."

"How can this be?" David was perplexed. "I thought the Council was responsible for harboring and protecting the heka for Isis, existing above the rule of gods? How is Lucius able to control them?"

"This is why I brought you down here to speak with you. The mortal witch, Hekate, is as she told you, a part of Isis reincarnated, but she is above all, Lucius's daughter. This affects her decisions greatly."

"Before I fell unconscious, Dragos told me Isis was once Lucius's companion - that there was no animosity between them, that all of this was planned."

"This is true," Anubis confirmed. "The Underworld exists much like the Upperrealms, chambers of space created by each religion - except many of them are so similar in concept, they tend to bleed together, the lines between them often quite blurred. We never thought a banished god would find a way to rise up from Tartarus, yet Set found a way by claiming to be the Greek god, Hades. He fooled us all, taking on the role with such precision that all the Underworld guardians believed him. I had no reason to question it, assuming the Greek Underworld simply bled into ours."

"So the rest of what Dragos told me is also true."

"See for yourself," Anubis suggested.

They were both instantly in a chamber of the Underworld, the inside of Hades's palace, a near identical version of what was described in mythological texts. David was immediately accosted by memories of the Ancient World and his brief stay in Greece as he admired the smoky marble that created every arch and statue, Lucius's take on classic Doric columns, and the massive fountains that either spurted out sapphire liquid or struggled to contain plumes of vehement fire.

Lucius sat at his throne, a gargantuan chair carved out of a solid block of obsidian. His hair was much shorter, kept in waves. His bone structure appeared even more angular when free of facial hair, but when he looked up from the scrying pool that he had been studying with keen interest, his golden eyes were undoubtedly the same.

David also recognized Isis by her emerald eyes, though she now had waves of sunflower hair flowing from her rounded face. Her dress was the color of Lilies of the Nile, sweeping across the polished floor as she paced it. "If you go back to earth, your memories will be erased," she said with emotion that revealed they were in the midst of an argument. "That is how the two of them were able to live in bliss, roaming the earth without a care in the world, oblivious to their true history."

"Yet, if I return, I can wrest you from that cursed acadia tree that you've been trapped in for good," Lucius pointed out. "You will finally be free to come and go as you please instead of waiting until autumn to visit me." He rose from his throne, descending the stone steps to where she stood. His tall frame towered over her as he spoke. "I have always tried to convince our counterparts that humans need direction, to be dominated by their gods. Now you can understand my point. You and I should be roaming the earth, as King and Queen of them all, with full control of *heka* - your *heka*," he reminded her. "You are the one who gave birth to them, the true mother of them all! Why should you live like a prisoner in your own home?"

Isis stared at him, her mouth twitching as she considered his proposal. "How?" she finally asked. "How can we do this?"

Lucius lit up with excitement. "When the Druids brought the souls of Osiris and Nephthys to earth to act as their own deities, they created a tear in the fabric that separates the realms. When it is time, I can use that tear to rise to the earth, concealing myself just as I do here. Then I will find the Acadia Tree and pull you out of it. Once you are restored to a physical being, then you can return the favor to me." He grinned, visibly proud of his idea.

Yet Isis looked doubtful, still not convinced. "Bearing the *heka* in its entirety was a terrible burden to bear. I do not think I can do it again."

Lucius frowned. "Is there any way to ease the burden?"

"I cannot risk it being vulnerable again, especially with the way humans act now," she sighed.

Lucius brightened. "I have an idea." He gripped her hands, his words brimming with fervor as he stared into her eyes. "We will create new life on earth that will belong to you and me. Our children will help you bear the *heka*, ensuring that only you or I can access it while relieving you of its burden."

"You cannot bear sons, Set," Isis gently reminded him.

"You leave that part to me," he assured her. "I will make it happen. I promise you."

"How do you intend on pulling me out of the tree?"

"You gave me some of your power long ago," he told her. "It never left."

"But how do we know your plan will work?" Isis continued to press him, although her pursed lips had finally lifted.

"We do not know anything for certain," he shrugged. "But I do know that anything we try is infinitely better than wasting away down here."

David saw flashes of a history he'd already learned, similar to how he had observed his own death and botched resurrection. He watched Lucius possess the body of the young tree worshipper, pulling Isis from her wooden prison and giving her a child which she channeled her *heka* into. He saw Isis in the cave that bore Lucius, her arms outstretched as she chanted, the four elements swirling around her, fire radiating out of her palms as she manifested a giant black *daemon* out of nothingness. He watched them use the body of the poor tree worshiper once more, funneling the hideous creature into it to give Lucius human form. He saw a ravenous, newly transformed Lucius search for the human Isis in hunger, only to realize she'd already disappeared, apparently remembering the tragic reanimation of Osiris. He watched Lucius tear his way through any animal he could find until he met Libraean. He witnessed their confrontation, Libraean's death, his painful rebirth.

"Once Lucius had quenched the raging beast inside, he left Libraean behind in search of Isis," Anubis's deep voice broke through. "The transformation had taken away most of his memory, leaving him unable to recall the deities of the Morrigan and Daghda, but still remembering Isis, Nephthys, and his brother. He was unable to find her, nor any of their daughters, until many years later in the Dacian Kingdom, the territory that is now Transylvania. It was there that he finally stumbled upon the oldest daughter and the rest of the Pădurii tribe, none of whom wanted anything to do with him. But before the eldest sent him away, she explained that since Isis gave her *heka* to her daughters through each new birth, she was unable to maintain her immortality. Before she withered away, she decided to inhabit the Acadia Tree once more, hoping none of her daughters would ever be strong enough to bear the *heka* in its entirety, as she was once forced to. Centuries later, however, that strength occurred in a set of twins - the brother taking the human aspects, allowing the sister to inherit the *heka*."

"Dragos and Hekate."

"Correct," Anubis nodded. "Both of whom are reincarnated gods - Ares, the Greek god of war made immortal, and the ancient Isis, reborn and brimming with power."

"They could both be in league with Lucius," David realized. "I don't know why I never put that together - I need to return to earth."

Anubis put up a hand to halt him. "And you shall. Do not worry, time can stop here and it will not move forward until you return. There is one final part that I must share with you, one that you were shielded from when uncovering the rest of your past."

David nodded, attempting to quiet his impatience.

"Once Lucius heard what happened to Isis, he tried to pull her out of the tree a second time, but found he no longer had enough power to do so. So he scoured the earth searching for the magic that could. He eventually found the Druids, the only sorcerers known to man who could bring a god to life. He convinced a handful of priests and priestesses to embark on a harrowing overseas journey to the Acadia Tree, where they chanted before it for days.

"Finally, their work produced results, but they brought forth only a frail human girl who Lucius was adamant was not Isis. Furious, he left her with the Druids, whose boat, on route back to their homeland, was overtaken by Romans."

"Gaia," David said her name softly, the cockles of his heart, long dormant, emitting the slightest of flickers.

Anubis's eyes confirmed. "Little did he know, she actually was Isis, but just a piece of her soul that was completely stripped of magic. Lucius had no idea that she would survive or that you would find each other and fall in love. Yet once he discovered it, he realized it could be the key to your undoing. He wanted you to become an immortal willingly, so that you would never think to abandon him like Libraean did, and by allowing her death, it would hasten the process.

"My purpose in telling you this is because you need to know that your love for Gaia was real, not a plan put together by Isis and Lucius. She was a human, a pure, innocent soul, and when she died, that soul returned here to rest."

Consolation settled over David, his words offering him the closure he hadn't realized he needed. "Thank you," he said softly.

"I felt you needed the truth in its entirety before you entered into battle," Anubis elaborated. "Do not believe anything Ares tells you, he exalts conflict and thrives off chaos. The twins have assisted in Council matters and with this burgeoning war, but I have also doubted their intentions."

"I sensed as much, but I have not been myself since injured," David confessed.

"Do not worry, I also brought you here to offer you the last bit of *heka* available to us, in the hopes that you will use it to kill Set for good. Before your father died, he left you all the earthly power remaining in the realm, putting it in the hands of the Council to give in pieces as you became ready."

"My father." The words seemed strange to say out loud, the memory of him so distant, David struggled to make it clear.

"Not long after Lucius created Gaia, far away in the land of Gaul, you were brought back in your mother's womb. Your father recognized you immediately upon birth, seeing the imprints of both your godly lives. He remembered a promise he made to the Morrigan, years prior, to deliver you to Lucius. She foresaw your arrival in your mother's womb and knew if given to Lucius, he would turn you into a creature like him, making you equals on this earth. So your father invoked him, convincing Lucius that he was simply desperate for power. My mother has always understood that dealing with Set requires a mental game of chess and she plays it well."

David smiled sadly.

"Rest assured, once he is back in Tartarus, I will make sure he remains there," Anubis promised. He propped his staff up against one of the nearby rocks before continuing. "You may have noticed that your powers faded over time, as mankind has slowly abandoned their belief in and desire for magic, affecting their entire realm. But your power is still with you, simply awaiting your retrieval."

"And Lucius's power?"

"That I do not know for certain, but I would guess Hekate has helped revive her father's manipulation of flame, as well."

"Does she have the power to bring back the Morrigan, as he hopes?" David asked.

Anubis shrugged, the gesture appearing odd coming from a usually grim-faced animal. "That I do not know. But I would prefer if my mother was not forced to inhabit a body she does not want to. I have no doubt that if that were the case, you would take care of it."

David frowned, reminded of his confliction. He longed to be reunited with her again, especially now that he could remember most of their past, able to put history to what had always been a perplexing desire. Yet Anubis was right, bringing her back as Morgana was not the way.

"You remember her as your mother," he commented with a smile.

Anubis nodded, his ears relaxing backwards, softening his narrow canine face. "I have never forgotten her. Horus and I were robbed of her presence, yet our father kept her alive in our hearts. We watched her from afar and we watch over her still."

"It pains me that I cannot remember you, nor my life as it existed before."

Anubis placed a comforting hand on his shoulder. "My father, the revered Osiris of Egypt, has long since passed. He has borne many heroes since then, including the Great David, soon to be known as the Great Dragon Slayer."

David placed his own hand on his. "Thank you, Anubis. Truly."

"Thank me by delivering Set, so this business can be finished."

David nodded his head once in firm resolve. "I will."

No sooner had the words slipped from his mouth did he hear a voice, spinning around to apprehend its owner. His tension softened when he realized it was Libraean.

The Underworld had improved his appearance, revealing a glimpse of the god Horus who David had seen in his visions. He stood straight next to his brother, matching his height, waves of golden hair sweeping his collarbones. His white eye glowed an iridescent opal, while his other radiated a cerulean hue that matched his mother's. Although his forehead was still studded with interrupted horns, bare human feet moved agilely across the plane where they stood. His pearly wings were whole, folded neatly behind his back.

Libraean embraced David before he could speak. "I am so glad we could meet again," he said, his voice tight with emotion. "They told me everything, everything about our past and how we almost lost you again." He pulled away from him, and for the first time, David was struck by the wave of familiarity one feels when they can't quite place where before they'd met a soul.

"Have you passed on?" David wondered.

"I am also a visitor to this realm," he replied. "Anubis brought me here so that we can offer you the last bit of power that we have left to give."

"Is your mother here?" David thought to ask them.

Anubis shook his head. "We cannot find her in any of the realms. We can only surmise that she is hiding somewhere in the astral plane, waiting for the right time to reveal herself."

David nodded, silently hoping Lucius and Hekate would also be unable to locate her whereabouts.

"We will find her," Libraean assured him.

Anubis withdrew to the edge of the cliff, reaching his clawed hands over the raging waters below. They rose at his command, funneling upwards before accumulating into a perfect sphere. Anubis guided the sphere back towards them, cupping the swirling ball of waves. Libraean lifted it from his brother's possession with great care, the energy from his hands brightening the orb until it transformed into a shimmering mass of luminosity.

He then approached David, its blinding light bathing his face in its incandescence as he grew closer to where he stood. He waited until they were inches apart before he blew into the orb, transferring its light onto David. He was struck with a foreign sensation, a calm serenity that settled over him like a heavy blanket, the chill of his bones instantly soothed. He sighed with relief, instantly renewed.

"Until we meet again," Anubis said, directing his attention back towards them.

The apparitions of the two brothers were rapidly fading. David reached out to say goodbye, but the world was shifting again, leaving him with a vision of them holding hands, but as two young boys, one light, one dark, lifting up their opposite hands to wave farewell to their father.

WALLACHIA, 1462

WHEN DAVID AWOKE, he was back in the cellar of the tavern, Danulf's broad frame towering over him, his arms crossed. "That was much quicker than I thought," he remarked.

David stood, pulling off his remaining bandages to reveal skin that had completely healed. "Apparently, I needed more power."

"Good. These fainting spells of yours are a pain."

David chuckled, only to remember what he had learned in the Underworld. "Dan, there is something I need to tell you about Dragos."

"It can wait," Danulf dismissed, bounding up the stairs. David promptly followed.

Radu had arrived and was now seated at a table near the bar surrounded by Ottoman soldiers, including a well-dressed Turk who was pacing the floor in apprehension. David assumed he was the general, his uniform woven with fine silk, a sleek turban wrapped around his head. Both stopped to stare as he entered.

"My men have discovered a traitor among us, a shadow, who divulged our plans to the Imposter Prince," Radu told him. "He now plans to attack the village and our camp in the wee hours of morning, while we slumber."

"Lucius has also taken a woman named Hekate, sister to Dragos and our quiet ally," David informed him in return. "He plans to coerce her into using her powers to revive the comatose Lady Morgana." He decided to omit the idea that she could potentially be in league with Lucius until he knew for certain. "It might have been she who revealed our plans under duress," he continued. "Trying to convince her to use her magic, however, might prove more difficult for Lucius. I believe this offers us some time. But the moment he discovers I am still alive, there will be no stopping him."

"We attack tonight," Radu decided, shooting a glance at his general who nodded once his accord.

"Tonight," David echoed after receiving similar approval from both Danulf and a visibly agitated Dragos.

The room burst into uproar, men scrambling to action. David lost Danulf in the shuffle but could still hear his sonorous voice barking out commands. Most of the men retreated underground as Radu and his foot soldiers left to return to their camp and rouse their army. David turned to leave himself when a fist wrapped around his arm. "And where are you off to?" Dragos asked.

David scowled, brushing his hand off in an easy motion, letting the act serve as a warning. "To collect your sister," he lied, unwilling to reveal his true intentions in light of the new information he'd received. "I wage my wars better alone."

"Then you should dress for battle," Dragos pointed out. "You never know what will greet you when you leave the castle."

David considered his suggestion and reluctantly agreed.

Dragos led him down into the annexed portion of the cellar that served as their armory, fully stocked and swarming with men and creatures. David could hear their frantic, excited thoughts as they gathered their armaments, pulling on pieces of armor and mail. Danulf shouted above the racket, apparently at perfect ease instructing soldiers in battle preparation. He looked oddly misplaced amongst the iron clad Wallachians, the nomadic Norseman with his light eyes and hair, dressed in a plain tunic and slacks with axes strapped to each hip, maps of tattoos covering his skin. David smiled, surmising that had they met decades earlier, they would have proven quite the formidable duo of warriors.

David turned towards the wall, appraising the collection of weaponry. He noticed that every saber, spear, and knife had been dipped in silver metal. He reached for a dagger when a tattooed arm halted him.

"Radu asked me to give you this," Danulf said as he pulled an arched saber from its sheath. "I know it may not be your weapon of choice, but anything that can help you murder that fiend, the better." He handed it to David, who examined its blade. Curiously enough, its entire body was made of silver, its handle a pretentious gold carved in the emblem of the Dragon.

"It was the sword of his father, Vladimir Dracul," Danulf continued. "He thought it would be fitting if you used his father's sword to kill the one who murdered him."

David accepted the weapon, admiring the feel of it in his hands and the way it sung as it sliced through the air. "If you get a chance, please give him my thanks."

"Hurry, it is time!" Dragos's voice interrupted them as it bellowed throughout the cavernous hold.

In an instant, the shuffling and voices of a hundred men rising out from the armory drowned out all else, their rising trepidation palpable in the air. They met the night, a clanging metal rabble, joining the Turkish Cavalry which had just arrived. The knights appeared polished and clean in comparison to the hodge-podge Wallachian militia, sitting regally on their glossy Turkoman horses, both protected by smooth, glinting armor. They waited patiently underneath the arches of decorative woodwork that lined the main road of the village.

David considered approaching one of the horses, impressed by their temperament, but for as calm as the animals were beneath their riders, he could smell their apprehension. He'd long accepted that no matter what his change of heart, animals would never let him forget that he was, first and foremost, a predator.

The normally desolate town was soon overcrowded by anxious bodies, the wives and elderly villagers coming forward to offer final goodbyes and well wishes. He watched as children kissed their fathers and women hugged their husbands, reminding David of what waited for him at the keep. Although he had struggled to feel a part of the collection of men, in that moment, he found himself worried that he, too, may never see the one he loved again.

The families of the soldiers did not linger long, barricading themselves back inside their homes, preparing for the worst. The mismatched aggregate lumbered forward with Radu at the forefront, boldly leading them on his horse, ornamented by his embellished armor, a white feather protruding from his solid, pointed helmet. The smell of exhilaration soon overwhelmed the piney aroma of the late November air, the rocky hills leading up to the castle clear of snow but not of its polar temperature. David trudged behind, waiting for the precise moment when he could slip away.

In the distance, the great fortress loomed menacingly, its sharp towers stabbing the evening skies. It was not long before they reached Lucius's gruesome Forest of the Dead, its occupants grotesquely preserved from decomposition by the biting cold. They stared at them, frozen in their last expressions of suffering.

David could hear Radu's unsettled thoughts as he approached them, almost able to taste the rage that settled around him.

"Do not let it upset you, Prince!" one of his men called before David had a chance to speak. "He puts them there for that reason - we will not let him run us away again."

"I shall impale his head upon a stick and parade him for all to see," the prince promised.

They arrived at a citadel that was completely dark and still. The bridge that laid over the moat, a manmade bifurcation of the Arges River, had been drawn up in preparatory defense, the waters treacherous from the earlier precipitation. Although they were unseen, David sensed the nemorti guards that lined the castle borders, awaiting command.

At the Turkish general's orders, the archers moved to the front of the men, holding up the oiled ends of their incendiary arrows for the torchmen to light. In one fluid movement, they aimed towards the flammable sections of the castle and sent them soaring, hoping to catch its weaker parts ablaze. A second wave followed, this time with silver tipped longbows, these soaring with enough force and precision to pierce several of the nemorti soldiers that quietly guarded the perimeter.

"Again," the general commanded, this time at the javelin throwers who prepared their weapons to also be lit and tossed overhead.

"Enough!"

The castle came to life, conflagrant posts revealing Lucius in full, glistening armor, flanked by hundreds of poised archers aiming down at them from overhead. As David presumed, they had been lying in patient wait for their arrival.

"I see you have come to try to take the upper hand," Lucius jeered. "Look around you, fools. See the men wasting away on the spikes. Do you wish to join them?"

David silent, concealed by the throng of bodies and weaponry.

"You shall pay for your treason and your lies!" Radu cried out, unable to help himself.

"Is that you, Radu the Fair?" Lucius could not contain his laughter. "I'm not surprised that your exaggerated self-worth has brought you back to these gates. Or is it in the hopes of pleasing your Sultan lover? He had enough sense not to test me further. But I suppose we could add more Turkish soldiers to my Forest. Perhaps I will be adding more Wallachians as well, since after I kill all these traitorous men, I will rid the town of its women and children."

"You fiend," Radu said with disgust.

"Go home to your sultan and spare the Turkish bloodshed. I will deal with my traitorous subjects myself."

"I will reclaim what is mine!" Radu maintained.

"Then perhaps you should have reconsidered attacking a fire god with his own element," Lucius laughed, waving his hands through the air. In an instant, every flame they had went out, plunging the army into absolute darkness. The cavalry horses whinnied in alarm, echoing the panic that gripped the human army.

David was dismayed to learn Lucius had managed to revive his powers, knowing that he had to move quickly, for the armed men would not stand for long. He found Danulf rows ahead and sent him the clearest message he could muster, hoping their once telepathic channel was still open. *I must go now before it's too late.*

"Oh, sweet Radu, do not retreat quite yet," Lucius called down, good naturedly. "If I set you all ablaze - which, rest assured, I can do quite easily - where would the fun be? I must give historians a good tale to write in their books. Come in, let us have a proper fight."

On his command, the chains holding back the drawbridge released, lowering with clamorous exertion before landing with an echoing thud. All was quiet before hundreds of armored *nemorti* appeared from the shadows.

"Attack!" the general cried.

Go, now. He heard Danulf's voice clear in his head.

The battle had begun.

Pandemonium ensued. A maelstrom of violence consumed the outer courtyard of the castle, the groans of dying men reverberating off its stone walls, the smell of mortal and immortal blood thick in the air.

David's eyes burned, a gruesome concoction of blood and sweat dripping down his body. He'd removed most of his armor, annoyed by the way it limited his movement, as he remembered the dormant warrior inside and unleashed him without restraint. He tore through Lucius's *nemorti* with ease, his muscles singing in recognition as they responded effortlessly to the call. It proved hard to remain grounded, nearly losing himself to an exhilaration he hadn't felt in years. It helped that the *nemorti* provoked no guilt in him, for their deaths were necessary for the good of all.

David wiped his brow as he paused to reassess his surroundings, bringing back a smear of jet black on his hand. He was not far from the castle, the bulk of the soldiers on the ground, ensuring that he could enter the Hunters' gates without resistance.

The clank of metal cracking against metal rang in his ears as he pushed towards it, dodging swords slicing off appendages and axes severing heads. The *nemorti* who died by silver weapons were lucky to explode into clouds of dust, while the rest groaned pitifully on the ground, their bodies unable to replenish their loss of blood nor regrow their severed limbs. He took pity on those directly in his path, beheading them swiftly with his sword so they could rest in peace.

He hadn't seen Danulf nor Radu since the battle began, the horde becoming harder to push through even as he cleaned up the fallen bodies. He began to speculate whether he could leap to the towers without drawing attention to himself when a *nemorti* blocked his path, hissing with its teeth exposed. David plunged his sword into its heart without hesitation, pulling the blade out in a spray of ink. The dead creature's dust sprinkled the human remains beneath him as David took a moment to ascertain who had suffered the greatest loss of men. He struggled to differentiate between the blood drinkers who fought at their side and those loyal to Lucius, the copious amount of spilled blood obscuring any discerning marks.

He turned his attention back upwards, catching the familiar sight of Prince Radu, who had been tossed from his horse and was now cornered by a group of *nemorti*. David ran forward and impaled them swiftly with his sword. Radu nodded his thanks, adjusted his helmet, and disappeared once more into the battling assemblage.

David narrowly avoided another collision as he continued to press on, taking out several more creatures along the way. He caught an advancing spear out of the corner of his eye, grabbing the pointed end with his fist and inverting it to the owner's demise.

Finally, he saw Danulf up ahead, spinning his axes to connect with the necks of dozens of *nemorti*, who tried to arrest his barbaric but artful killing. He caught David's eye as he took out the two creatures flanking him in a perfect sweep of murderous ambidextrousness. "I thought you were headed towards the castle," he called out over the clamor of swords.

"I'm headed there now," David responded, cleaning his sword of creature gore with a flick of his wrist.

"We are losing men quickly. We need to find a better way to kill them," Danulf warned as he took a moment to catch his breath. He had also chosen to fight free of iron, grime and blood covering his bare, tattooed chest.

David felt a cold drop on his shoulder and looked up to see storm clouds had collected above them. Fat droplets of icy rain expelled from their glutted reserves, turning the earth to mud. The soldiers slipped and swerved as they struggled to keep their footing. Danulf was right; the rain washed away enough gore for David to see that the majority of those still standing wore Lucius's dragon on their armored chests. If he was correct in his assumptions, they were down at least a hundred men.

He looked up at the castle, still unable to push himself through. The grim faces of the dead preserved on iron spikes stared blankly back at him. He had an idea. Gathering his strength, he lifted one of the stakes out of the ground, letting it fall flat onto the muddy earth. He whispered an old Druid verse of reverence before gingerly removing the corpse from its picket. Danulf appeared from behind him, grunting his approval. He shouted at the men closest to them to follow suit.

Soon, their army had dismantled most of the castle's barricade and began driving the clean pikes into the necks of Lucius's warriors, some two or three at a time, the force popping their heads from their bodies or immobilizing them until they could be killed by silver tipped blades. Danulf disappeared once more as the scuffle intensified. David gripped his own spike tightly in both hands and charged, driving through bodies until at last, he reached the edge of the moat. The churning waters that funneled out of the Arges reminded him of the Underworld, the freezing rain feeding it as it pummeled around the bend of the castle and down the mountainous ravine. The moat had been one of Lucius's more clever ideas, for no human enemy could possibly hope to cross such a death trap.

He secured his sword behind his back and took a deep breath, picturing Anubis and Libraean standing before him. "Whatever power you have given me, I call upon it now," he told the heavens, and then he took a deep breath, and dove into the choppy abyss.

CHAPTER NINE

❧ THE DRAGON SLAYER ❧

ALTHOUGH THE BLOOD IN HIS VEINS ran cold, the water swirling around him was so frigid it still hit like pin pricks against his skin. He was glad to discover he was strong enough to fight the current, battling against the river demons as he kicked himself forward towards the castle wall.

He struggled to keep his head above the waves, the deluge of icy water from above making it difficult to see. The water stank of refuse, the pungent odor choking him as he continued to propel himself forward until he nearly collided headfirst into the wall. Fortunately, the stones that made up the castle were unevenly laid, making it easy for him to grip and hoist himself up out of the thrashing channel. He scaled the tower without difficulty, grateful that the splattering rain had not yet turned to ice. He found the closest window and threw himself into it, landing on the castle floor with a thud, broken glass following closely behind him.

He paused to catch his breath, picking the embedded particles out of his skin. The keep was eerily quiet in comparison to the war raging outside, the steady drip of condensation the only sound echoing throughout its halls.

"Hekate? Morrigan?" David's voice shattered the silence as he stood. He shook the water from his hair, the droplets that dampened his skin catching the musty castle air. He checked to make sure Radu's sword was still in place, relieved to discover that it had stayed with him through his watery journey and hasty ascent.

Outside the castle, the battle racket raised in intensity, letting him know that his idea to use the upended spikes had proven itself worthwhile. He quickened his pace, still unsure how much longer he had before Lucius discovered he was still alive, climbing the winding staircase to Morgana's quarters two steps at a time.

The keep was neglected in her mental absence, roses withered in their vases, a thin film of dust settled on her hanging collection of avian bones. He followed the path to her bedchambers, his anxiety building at what he might find. His senses had instinctively heightened in response, but his nose picked up nothing unusual, only the scent of Morgana, her telltale clash of rustic cedarwood and lavender still lingering throughout the halls.

He reached her door, steadying his nerves as he opened it.

A woman in a stained nightdress stood at the open window, the frosty evening air lifting her tattered clothing and threatening to extinguish the low burning candles that surrounded her.

The room was painted red, a pool of it darkening the center of the bed. Soaked linens lay in heaps on the floor, and David found himself once again piecing together what tragic event had transpired in Morgana's bedroom. The acetic bite of human blood dominated the air, but there was something more, something distinctly pungent. He inhaled sharply, realizing it was henbane. He knew instantly - Hekate was dead.

Morgana turned from the window, her face a malnourished mask of sunken eyes and dry lips. David did not hesitate, rushing to where she stood and gathering her against his chest. "I am too late," he managed in a confusing blend of disappointment and relief.

Morgana was relaxed in his arms, the dual entity apparently being controlled by her stronger half. But when he pulled her away to peer into her eyes, they were tarnished brown without a hint of Morrigan's telltale blue.

"Hekate was unable to complete the task," she explained, observing his bewilderment. "Delicia's mind has long gone, her body an empty shell. I possessed it to care for my niece as she unexpectedly gave birth. You can rest assured that you now speak to the Morrigan."

David felt relieved now without the nag of guilt, grateful she was still in control. Before he could help himself, he grabbed her face, kissing her ardently on the mouth. He was disheartened to discover she tasted of decay, a hint that her time with him would be brief.

"Ah, so you remember me now?"

He choked back his rising emotions. "I remember you."

She smiled weakly and laid her head to his heart. "I cannot stay long," she murmured as she wrapped her arms around his waist.

"What happened here? Has Hekate passed?" David asked, caressing her hair.

"Here," she lifted away from him, placing her hands where her head had laid. "I can show you."

In a heartbeat, David was able to see them together in the room as if he'd leapt backwards in time. Hekate, alive and still with child, sat behind a cauldron of noxious liquid, herbs strewn about the floor around her, situated amongst sleepily burning candles that dripped pools of wax on the stone.

The cluster of crows she'd just summoned fell away, leaving a scowling Morrigan behind. Her hair was cropped, its waves unkempt behind the corvid diadem that interrupted her icy eyes. The muscles of her tattooed arms bulged with tension as she gripped her spear with unabashed irritation. "You dare," she hissed.

Hekate stood, looking relieved despite the war goddess's mood. "It should not have to take that much for you to come to your own sister."

"You are not my sister," Morrigan scoffed. "My sister died a very long time ago. She was my twin - I felt it the instant she was gone. You are simply the result of a poorly hatched plan by her and Lucius."

"Come now. Why be so cross with me?"

"After my death, I was able to see your true nature and all that you have done. You deceived the Council, convincing them you were on the side of righteousness while you and your brother murdered your entire bloodline, including your own mother, to ensure absolute power."

Hekate shrugged. "I have my reasons."

Morrigan snorted. "Oh yes, I am sure you feel very resolved in your selfish motives."

"Oh, as if you are absolved of selfishness," Hekate retorted as she gathered up her ingredients, tenderly placing the delicate herbs back into her apothecary box and snapping closed the lid. "Did you forget how you left me behind while you frolicked about the earth with Osiris while Set, your true husband, rotted away in the Underworld?"

"Stop acting as if you are her," Morrigan demanded. "If you were truly my sister, you would remember his crimes and why we banished him there."

Hekate put her hands on her hips. "Whether you wish to accept it or not, I am her reincarnation. You might have forgotten me during my abandonment, but that does not change the true nature of my soul."

"I did not abandon my sister!" Morrigan sputtered. "She chose to stay on earth. How could I have possibly foreseen that my memories would be taken from me when I rose to earth?"

"Even if it was not intentional, Nephthys, it was abandonment just the same. First Protector, indeed," she said with a snort. "And furthermore, Set is not the creature you believe him to be. He regrets murdering his brother - it was a crime of passion. You were the one who betrayed him, leaving him behind. In fact, running away seems to be a common theme for you."

"So that is your intention - to force me to be with Lucius? That plan has never worked for anyone."

"Sister, you must understand that it is your and Osiris's love that has shattered the balance of earth," Hekate softened her tone. "In order to restore it, you must return to Set, the one who loves you above any other."

"I am not your sister," Morrigan asserted, her voice reaching a poisonous intensity. "Might I remind you that Isis became Set's consort, the reason that you are even alive holding his descendant in your very womb?"

Hekate sighed, running a hand over the swell of her stomach. "Yes, this is true. It was my idea that we have children together, planting the seeds in his mind so he could feel as though he figured it out on his own. It was the only way to ensure my *heka* would remain safe - dispersed amongst my daughters. But believe me when I tell you, I have long accepted that Set loves you, just as I once accepted that Osiris felt the same. Unlike you, I do not require adoration from any male, nor do I need another being to fulfill me."

"If your intention is to upset me, it will not work. You are simply affirming what I already know - that you are not my sister. She understood and respected my love for Osiris when we lived in Egypt, she even watched over my sons. In fact, I should tear you apart for desecrating her memory."

"Had I known that the love between you both would threaten our realms, I would not have accepted it," Hekate maintained.

"No one could not have stopped it. Even we could not."

"Nephthys, Osiris knows his history now. I told him everything. He does not search for you; you mean nothing to him. He loved a mortal girl named Gaia and his love died along with her. You must abandon this need for his affection - you are a goddess above all else! Osiris and I will remain on earth, as it should be, to fix all that has been broken, while you and Set return to the Underworld, taking your proper place as the guardians of death."

Morrigan laughed at her. "Anubis would never let that happen. He guards the gates against my forced return."

"Oh, do not fret, I have thought of everything. I plan to put you back into the body of Delicia, then formally end your life. Anubis will think you are her. As for Set, I let him believe that David was dead, then I brought him back to life in secrecy. David will end his life, since that is the only way that we can ensure he is delivered to the Underworld for Anubis to guard. Hopefully, there you will reconcile."

"If you wanted what was best for Set, why take him away from the earth that Isis brought him back to?"

Hekate sighed, a look of dismay settling over her features. "This earth does not serve him well. The longer he stays here, the more tormented he becomes. He started this life a seeker of wisdom and truth, not some power-hungry warlord. What he has become is disgraceful. Humans are not meant to live so long in one body. It has poisoned him. I've worked alone to orchestrate this plan, not even Hekate's twin is aware."

Morrigan shook her head in disbelief. "You speak to me from a high pedestal, yet you betray him. And she who you consider to be your sister."

"Nonsense. I am taking control of that which is mine. *Heka* is mine, giving life is my gift. I am the mother of this world, and as such, I must restore its *ma'at* and put its shattered pieces together again. This is why I had to consume all power, so that none of you would be able to prevent my doing so." Her face was smug, satisfied by her plan, when unexpectedly, the expression crashed. Fear flashed across her eyes as they widened, water trickling to the ground from between her thighs. "Oh no...it is not yet time..." she groaned. She reached her hand between her skirts, lifting it up to reveal a coating of bright red.

Morrigan rushed to her side only to be blindsided by Delicia, revived by the scent of such powerful blood. She tore at Hekate's throat before Morrigan could pull her off. Frantic, Morrigan's apparition quickly resumed its place inside its former vessel, halting the attack, but Hekate already lay in an unconscious heap on the ground.

David found himself breathless as the vision faded, realizing his hold on Morrigan had tightened. He let go to face her. "Did Hekate survive? And what became of her child?"

"Hekate is dead, Isis's bloodline is no longer," she assured him.

Before David could press her further, she leaned forward to kiss him, filling his mouth with her taste. "I will miss you so much," she sighed as she pulled away. "I am starting to believe that this is just my life - an endless yearning for that which I cannot have."

"Wait -" he began, before he sensed Lucius behind him.

He turned to see his nemesis covered in shining armor, the black panels shielding his entire body save for his head, an ornate dragon carved into his breastplate. He nearly dropped his sword and helmet in surprise, beholding Morgana standing before him. "It worked?" he said, hopefully. "She brought you back?"

Morrigan narrowed her eyes. "Your plan failed. I possessed her body of my own accord, one final time, so that I can speak to you both before I return to the Otherrealms."

"Both?" Lucius realized David was in the room. "You!" he growled in recognition, but before he could lunge, Morrigan waved her hand, freezing them both in place.

David searched her eyes frantically, realizing that not only couldn't he move, but he also could not speak.

"I am sorry it has come to this, my love," she explained to him sadly. "But I have no time to bear witness to another one of your fights. When Hekate died, I absorbed her power for myself, which I intend on taking with me." She shifted towards the window, her bare feet gliding on the floor.

David tried to summon any power he had to move, but it was of no avail. The invisible chains the Morrigan had wrapped them in held firm.

"After I died, I entered our Upperworld and my every memory was restored. My days as Nephthys drifted back, my long, happy years as the Morrigan, my most recent days in this rotting prison of flesh. And as I paused to examine my life, to fully understand it, I realized there had always been two constants." She faced them. "The two of you. I realized that I cannot have one of you without the other, and that all this - eons of chaos and pain, battles and strife - all come down to one great flaw. Me."

David felt his insides screaming.

"I am the reason the two halves of the Great He cannot reconcile, I am the reason the scales of earth have tipped into instability, I am the reason my sister's soul has been fragmented and lost forever. I tell you this not to invoke pity, it is just the simple, clear truth of what is. I am tired of being fought over, tired of this world."

She approached Lucius, placing her hands on his chest as she looked into his eyes. "My Set, I can never love you the way you need me to, but your fire will always burn in my veins. Even so, know that you will never possess me. No matter how you try to manipulate the world around you, I will never be yours. You must abandon this game, for if you force me to play, I will always win." She placed her lips against his cheek and pulled her hands away, pulling along with them tendrils of fire. She was robbing him of his powers.

She placed her hands on David in a similar way, and he immediately felt the extraction of energy. "You may keep what was given to you by our sons, but I will need back my crows." She smiled sadly, pulling wisps of black smoke from the hole she'd opened in his chest. Then she cupped her hands around his face, kissing him, long and firm. When she pulled away, Delicia's eyes had turned to a sparkling blue, boring into his. "Horus will look after you," Morrigan said. "Do not search for me. I must take my leave of you again, this time for good." Although her words were resolute, he watched tears well around her eyes, threatening to spill. "I love you more than I ever thought was possible, and yet, I know we were never meant to be."

He could hear the winter wind screaming outside, knowing it was he who stirred its squalls. It nearly drowned out the sounds of men, battling beyond the river that ran below the tower.

Morrigan drew back to the window as if responding to its call. The frayed, blood stained dress she wore fluttered around her. Her raven hair followed suit, its waves rippling in the crisp air. She turned her head slowly to look at them one last time. "Do not come after me."

And with that, she jumped.

It only took a few moments before their invisible bounds dissipated, David racing to the window to observe Delicia's body smashed on the rocks that carved out the river below. Both Delicia's and Morrigan's souls were free.

He fell to his knees in disbelief, as the pouring rain left with her.

She was truly gone.

From the corner of his eye, he noticed Lucius had also collapsed to the floor, holding his head in his hands in similar torment. When he looked up, the whites of his eyes were like coal, his cheeks streaked with inky black tears. David found himself trapped in a moment of compassion for him. He had never seen him look so distraught, his arrogance melted away by heartbreak, his gleaming golden eyes snuffed out by the tragic curse that was immortal weeping. It occurred to David in that moment, she was just as much his weakness as she was David's. "We do not have to fight this war," he said quietly.

Lucius did not respond, his head falling back into his hands as he gripped fistfuls of ebony hair. David felt a sudden, unusual shift in the air. He rose to his feet.

"She took all the power…" Lucius managed.

"She does not want us to fight," David continued as he approached him. "We can put this feud of ours to rest, to honor her memory."

"Hear me!" Lucius screeched, catching David off guard, his overwrought expression, painted in black, terrifying. "She took the power that kept me a man!"

David scrambled backward, realizing what he meant.

Warmth steadily rose around them as David flattened himself against the wall. He had never witnessed a transformation like the one that now befell the unfortunate soul before him, staring in perfect horror as Lucius's armor fell to pieces, his skin bubbling and popping as it melted away to reveal leathery black scales, his skeleton distorting its shape and bursting cruelly from its confines. Smoldering heat strangled the room as gnarled wings ruptured from his back, stretching up towards the heavens, scraping the ceiling as it lengthened beyond human proportion.

The floor beneath them trembled as it struggled to maintain the immense weight of the creature rapidly expanding within its hold, the beams loosening as crumbling limestone rained down from above. A wayward stone landed on David's shoulder, breaking him free of his paralysis. He edged towards the open window as he watched he who was once a man of refinement and splendor fall victim to a merciless metamorphosis.

It looked directly at him, opening its jaws to scream, David face to face with the abominable creature from his dreams. The recognition jolted him, causing him to fall backwards out of the window just as the *daemonic* dragon let fly its torrent of fiery breath.

David hoisted himself out the rubble, his head pounding and dust in his lungs.

Somehow the tower had managed to fall in the same direction of the extended drawbridge, saving him from a fate like his lover, tossing him onto solid ground. In the distance, the war held on, corpses cluttering the menagerie of gargoyles Lucius once filled his courtyard with. They were in their element among the contorted bodies beneath them, their exaggerated grins and bulging eyes even more menacing amongst the gore.

The human calvary and infantry had long since retreated, the battle now creature versus creature clashing together in a growling culmination of metal and bared teeth. There was no holding back between the combating creatures, who swooped and dived as each tried to gain the upper hand against their equal.

David crouched down to search the crumbled stone for his sword, his freshly bruised and battered body provoking a wince. He knew it wouldn't be too much longer before the beast rose from the collapsed tower, if it had survived the fall.

Without warning, a sword whizzed past him, narrowly missing his extended arm. He ducked forward, missing another forceful blow, Dragos striking without reserve. David groaned, his body still working to mend itself from the fall. "I suppose this means you are the traitor. I should have known."

Dragos did not respond, his eyes cold behind his armored helmet. He took another purposeful swing, this time, the blade nicking the exposed part of David's arm. "I warned you to wear armor," he said, matching David's smug tone.

The beads of black rising from his skin brought David back to life. He leapt to the top of the highest pile of wreckage and swooped down to knock Dragos from where he stood. His helmet dislodged from the impact as he hit the ground, revealing eyes and a grin wild with exhilaration. He laughed, thoroughly enjoying the confrontation.

Weaponless, David reached around the fledgling blood drinker's throat, but was unable to impede his joyful laughter. He gripped tighter, his entire being tensed with exertion as he tried to stop it, when Dragos abruptly slammed his fist into David's unprotected chest, grinding what felt like razor blades into his skin.

David fell back with a gasp, realizing the gloves that covered the creature's hands were welded with silver, silver spikes extending out from between each finger. The wound he'd left behind was considerable, David heaving for breath as blood gushed from the torn flesh. Dragos retrieved both his sword and helmet without rush, knowing he'd incapacitated David well beyond immediate repair.

David grew dizzy as he tried to stop his rapidly seeping wound, searching frantically around him for a weapon that could hold off his opponent before he had the chance to make it worse.

Dragos came closer, flippantly twirling his sword. "Do not despair, Great David. I only meant to slow you down. Lucius would never forgive me if I stole his kill. In fact, I am in charge of someone else who I was hoping would be near.." His taunting proved prophetic, for mere seconds after he'd trailed off, Danulf emerged, his dual axes slicing through the air without mercy. They connected with their intended target, Dragos swept off his feet in one swift blow.

David could now stand, the hole in his chest mended enough that he no longer poured blood onto the wet earth. Noticing he was weaponless, Danulf tossed him one of his axes. David caught it easily, enjoying the feel of the leather wrapped handle and the heaviness of the blade. From memories long forgotten, he recalled a similar feel to his hammer, a weapon that would one day be referred to as the Club of Daghda. He met Danulf's eyes as Dragos struggled to his feet. "Dan, he was the shadow for Lucius."

"That explains a lot."

Dragos stood but did not attack, instead sticking two fingers in his mouth, pulling out a shrill whistle. From all ends of the courtyard, the surviving *nemorti* paused in mid-battle to turn towards the sound. Dragos casually moved out of the way as hundreds of *nemorti* hurtled towards them, their weapons at hand.

Danulf and David braced themselves with axes raised. "Are you ready for this?" Danulf called.

"No, but at this moment, I am too exhausted to be afraid."

"Bah, we are pagan gods from the lands of old. We are the ones to fear." Danulf took a few practice swings.

"Still, I would feel better if we had your wolf half right about now."

"That would help," he agreed. "But don't forget, I am not only a *varcolac* and a blood drinker," he said as the mob drew closer, "but I am also a Viking." The final word passed through grinning lips while the first wave lunged.

The rest of the swarm followed suit, and after some time, David and Danulf fell into an unintended synchronicity of movement, their quick but savage butchery unfolding in thundering unison. The *nemorti* fell pitiably to the ground in droves as the two primordial warriors invoked their innate brute strength to slaughter them all, one by one.

It wasn't long before David looked up to see his warring partner completely drenched in blood, finishing off the last pitiable soldier with a celebratory battle cry. Danulf then turned towards him with a triumphant smile, his bright blue eyes and metallic teeth glowing eerily against the oily black that covered his face. "Good fight!"

David shared the sentiment with a nod, then paused to assess his surroundings. Not only was Dragos nowhere to be found but neither was the dragon Lucius. He frowned, taking a moment to rest his over-exerted limbs as he surveyed the courtyard.

"I do not see him anywhere, either," Danulf muttered as if he read his thoughts. "In fact, the whole damned army has deserted us." He was right, it seemed the only bodies left were those that littered the ground. "I should go after the traitor," he suggested.

David nodded. "And I should find Lucius."

"Do not lose my axe. I will be coming back for it after I kill him."

The two took leave of each other without prolonged ado, grabbing each other's forearms, as in the ancient practice, before going their separate directions. The courtyard was quiet save for the pitiful moans of dying creatures. The sleet from earlier had ceased at some point during the battle, leaving the sky cloudless and bitter cold. The remaining pieces of a once magnificent fortress interrupted the exposed moonlight with its jagged frame, casting irregular beams over on the grim scene below.

Exhaustion pried emotion out of him, grief settling over him like a gentle snowfall. Even if Lucius was still alive, he was no longer the man he'd once known, memories of their happier moments in life slowly drifting by in his mind. Like many of their homes throughout the centuries, the castle was a source of pride and joy for Lucius, the Wallachian fortress the one he cherished most. Watching it crumble slowly into the Arges marked the end to life as David had known it for many years.

His morbid reflection was interrupted by trembling earth, accompanied by sounds much like the forewarning of an avalanche. David struggled for balance as he watched the dragon uncoil from the stormy waters of the river, plumes of steam rising along with it. Its golden eyes held on to David's as it unfurled its massive wings, shaking the water from its scales. When it had risen to its feet, it was taller than the castle it had destroyed, tightening the muscles of its arms and legs as it opened its mouth to shriek its hateful flames.

David rolled out of the way just in time, his refuge a pile of discarded limestone. A flicker of metal caught his eye, revealing Radu's sword lodged between the rocks. He retrieved it as the shaking ground escalated in fervor, the creature finding its footing on land. A wave of memory inconveniently smacked him, interrupting his action. He was underwater, struggling against the firm fingers around his throat, holding him under. Black patches took his vision, save for the maniacal gold eyes burning above the surface, his own brother sending him to the arms of death without a shadow of remorse. He was reliving the moment Set killed Osiris.

It cleared as quickly as it came, and David realized he'd created a storm of violent wind, circling them as it pulled fallen rocks into its funnel. He greeted the dragon with new resolve, calm as it faltered, distracted by the building storm. He tightened his grip on Radu's sword, ready for battle, until the dragon let out another fiery stream, right into the winds itself.

David gasped as it became a swirling wall of fire, the wind and fire feeding each other as it spun. He fell to his knees, choking on the stifling heat as the dragon advanced. Fear taunted him, but he shut his eyes, trying not to recall the agony of burning alive as he gripped his weapon close. "Let the power I was given come forth," he whispered, hoping someone would hear him.

A swarm of crows shrieked their reply. He rose to his feet as an onslaught of rain fell from the sky, extinguishing the tornado of flames with a hiss. He shivered as the frigid water hit his skin, pulling his lips into a smile. She was still out there, watching over him.

The moment was jolted by a sudden rush of energy, followed by the painful sensation of his back being sliced into two. He realized wings had sprouted out from his shoulder blades, his body humming with a power he'd never felt before. He envisioned Anubis and Libraean watching him leave the Underworld, grateful for their gift and renewed by the feeling of his family surrounding him as his new wings unfurled.

The monstrous creature called his attention back in its direction as it loudly made its way onto the dry land, undeterred by the rain. This time, when it opened its mouth, David leapt into the sky in flight, missing the scorching stream and landing right on top of its viscous back. It struggled to throw him off as the battlefield below them transformed into a duel of flame and water, angry river tides dragging the smouldering vestiges of war into her abyss.

David felt as if his body was not his own, vibrating with the souls of every creature that ever was or had ever been, his mind an orchestra of lions' roars, bear growls, and eagle calls. He felt them all - animal, bird, angel - gripping Radu's sword with him as the dragon frantically tried to shake him off. With one unified thrust, they drove the metal straight between the shoulder blades that wielded its massive leathery wings.

The dragon howled in agony, finally able to toss David from its back. But David's wings caught him, allowing him to hover in the air not far from where the creature thrashed, powerless to remove the lethal metal from between its back bones. The mountains crumbled with its panicked movement, taking along more chunks of the castle as they fell into the raging waters below.

David watched as the earth cracked open, not far from where the dragon struggled and fumed. Sulfuric heat rose from the widening split, swallowing up the corpses and debris as it inched closer to the dragon's taloned feet. Soon the blistering steam was joined by hundreds of skeletal creatures crawling out from the depths, as a horrific rendition of Anubis leapt out over them all. He landed squarely on the scorched earth in his divine manifestation, the vicious, jet black jackal with glowing eyes, pointed teeth, and savagely curved claws. He stood vigil amidst the flames as the *daemons* of Tartarus scuttled forward to collect their master, their nails popping into its scaly black flesh as they dragged him backwards.

The dragon that was once his beloved companion howled its wrath as it fought fruitlessly against them, severely weakened by the caustic silver searing between its shoulder blades. David flew to the apex of what was left of the castle, captivated by the struggle unfolding before him, watching as the hideous creature that had once struck such terror in his young soul fell helplessly to its death, the all-powerful earth claiming its prize.

Anubis caught David's eyes before he jumped in after it, restoring after many eons, the dark gods of the Underworld back to their proper places.

And then, all was still.

The ground smoothly sealed itself as David floated to the ground. He felt the borrowed power trickle out of him as he landed, the heavy rain giving way to a calm snowfall that drifted sleepily down from the sky. It extinguished the last stubborn flames, the scores of *nemorti* and their megalomaniac creator gone for good.

David promptly collapsed, overwhelmed by fatigue. A single crow fluttered down to where he lay, carrying Morrigan's diadem in its mouth. It dropped it before him, scolding him with a squawk. "All right, I will keep moving," he replied weakly, pulling himself up to his feet.

The crow followed him as he shuffled through the charred remains towards the village. Out of the corner of his eye, he caught two bodies folded atop each other, both of which had narrowly avoided incineration and were now collecting snow. He nearly cried out when he recognized the tattooed flesh of his friend, his wounds so deep, there was no question that he'd died in battle. He pulled his broad body off a dismembered Dragos, setting him down flat on a nearby snowbank. His face looked peaceful, white flakes building on his silver beard and eyebrows, giving him the look of a slumbering snow god. David removed the axe he had kept at his side and joined it with its mate, crossing his friend's arms, an axe in each fist.

He fell to one knee. "May the Valkyries find you in this strange land and carry you swiftly to Valhalla," he entreated in a low voice.

The crow cawed for him to move on.

He rose once more to his feet, his limbs throbbing as fatigue continued to weigh him down. He reached the edge of the village and froze, finding himself unable to continue forward. While he knew the humans would be grateful to him, perhaps even honoring him as Radu finally took the throne and restored them to a peaceful existence, he feared that all it would do was remind him of that which he'd lost, cementing the grim, unsettling truth that he was now entirely alone.

The thought of an eternity of solitude finally drove him to collapse, his exhaustion victorious, rendering him unable to move from the pile of snow where he'd fallen, despite the crow's protestations. He stared up at the white and black speckled sky, sighing as the flakes kissed his cheeks and got trapped in his eyelashes.

The crow sounded far away now, its pitch revealing an urgency he could not address. David closed his eyes, picturing Morrigan's face, watching her dance amongst circling flocks of crows.

"It's not time to give up quite yet," a gentle voice brought him back.

He opened his eyes to see Libraean standing above him. As grateful as he was to see him, he found he had no energy to speak.

"Do not worry, David," he assured him. "I promised I would look after you, and I intend to do just that." With a grunt, he hoisted David onto his shoulders, careful not to stab him with his blunted wings. David made a mental note to thank him, thinking of Morrigan's brilliant eyes, Lucius's goblet, and Danulf's banter, teasing him for passing out yet again, before he gave in to blissful, well-earned rest.

CHAPTER TEN

❧ THE BEGINNING ❧

LONDON, 1857

DAVID WATCHED THE LAST OF THE RAIN trickle down the windowpane, signaling that the storm had finally passed, the only sound left the hum of early autumn crickets and the croaks of distant bullfrogs. Old Man Jacob had cracked the window earlier in the evening after leaving a tray of soup and bourbon, muttering something about old superstitions and stories of souls being trapped behind closed entryways. The tray remained untouched, for his companion never left his arms, her breathing so shallow that the only way he knew she still lived was by the lingering warmth of her skin against the chill of his own.

The completion of his tale left him with a hollowness he had not felt for many years. He had learned to live on after that fateful evening, when he had lost everything he'd come to know, enduring the tedious existence of immortality. He had hoped early on that his memories would fade, and they would trickle away for a time, but then he would catch the scent of a certain wood burning, or hear the faraway call of a crow, or even taste a certain flavor in wine, and he would tumble back into his past. Not long after such a moment occurred, he would be lost to melancholy, unable to leave his study for days, stagnant and staring off into the distant unknown as if he no longer lived in his body. He never remained imprisoned by these lapses for too long, however, for the instinctual drive to feed eventually shook him from his stupor.

Only once had David considered taking his own life, as he lingered out on the hills of his acreage as the sun began to rise. He no longer feared its rays as he once had, the unease replaced by curiosity, wondering what would happen to his soul if his immortal body ceased to be. He knew she would not be waiting for him in the Upperrealms they had once called home, but maybe he could wait there for her, to see if she would arrive? He contemplated the idea as his shirt began to grow damp, his trouser legs sopping up the morning dew.

Yet what if she had already come back as a human, or worse yet, he came back to earth again with no recollection of who or what he was? Neither he nor Libraean had heard word from the Council, Anubis, or any other unearthly creature since the Night War - what if there was no one left who remembered him? His mind then drifted to Libraean, who was patiently waiting out his own life underground.

Although he could never disclose it to him, David often wondered if it was more difficult to have him so close in proximity, serving as a constant reminder of what was. Some days, he considered taking his leave of him, that maybe in doing so, the long years would finally rob him of his memories for good, giving him the chance to disappear into the world a different man with a different name. But he couldn't will himself to abandon Libraean as had been done to him before, and although he couldn't recall feelings of paternal love for the creature, he'd grown to care for him deeply. It did help that Libraean preferred solitude, politely declining David's standing offer to reside with him in the manor, even though the accommodations were far more comfortable than in the vaults. But to leave him to die alone, the last creature left on earth, that David simply could not do.

He had flown home before the sun could go any higher, tumbling through the open window of his parlor and draping himself across the floor under the shadows, waiting for the old familiar despondency to creep back in.

David's memories were interrupted by the loud squawk of a crow, which had landed right at the windowsill. It blended seamlessly against the evening sky, its glistening eyes the only thing distinguishing it from the darkness. It was too late in the evening for crows, but David knew this was no ordinary corvid. He smiled to himself, appreciating the coincidence. "I was just talking about you," he told the statuesque bird.

But the crow looked grim, clicking its talons impatiently on the pane. It was one of the largest crows David had ever seen, so much so that he initially mistook him as a raven, until he realized that it was the same crow who found him on the battlefield, so many years ago. He was weathered but strong, ruffled plumage at the back of his neck as if he'd once been caught in a fight but won. The crow visited him so often after that initial meeting, that David soon figured out he had been sent to keep vigil over him in her absence. He'd taken to calling him Grip, his weekly visits bringing David comfort during some of his bleakest periods.

"Are you here because you anticipate my impending sorrow, or have you taken on the role of harbinger of death?" David asked him, as his fingers found his dying companion's hair.

It cawed in reply, the guttural sound echoing throughout the guest room.

"I suppose I will miss her company, though it was brief," David admitted. "It brought me solace to have someone near who knows what I am. Besides Libraean, of course."

The crow lifted its plumed wings and in a sweep of black, flew across the room to land on the bust of Athena that David kept on the fireplace, one of the few items he'd salvaged from the Ancient World. The bird looked even more ominous next to the polished white marble, the image evocative of the dual entities that were Morgana - the patron goddess of Delicia, commanded by the Morrigan's crow. The bird stared at him patiently, his claws wrapped around the narrow shoulder of the forgotten war goddess as it squawked once more.

His companion shifted, though she was still unconscious, turning her head towards the sound. A thin line of red trickled down from the corner of her lips as they parted, letting out a soft, curious murmur, "My crows…"

David's mouth went dry.

"What did you say?"

The crow boldly darted towards them, landing right on the narrow dip of her side. David's eyes widened as dozens more of his kind entered the room, a flurry of onyx feathers soaring in through the open window and settling around the guest room, flapping their wings as they settled into their positions.

David's entire being was now rigid with shock, staring at the congregation that flocked around him. Grip turned to face him from his womanly perch, opening its mouth once more to scold him. He relocated to the bedpost when David finally heeded his instruction, gently rolling his companion onto her back.

Her face was serene, already settling itself into the blank expression common in the deceased. He almost didn't dare speak her name, reluctant even to hope. "Morrigan?" he whispered, choking on the syllables.

She could not respond, but the frustrated crows that invaded their room called out a response for her.

"Goddamn it, no!" he cursed, leaping up from the bed and darting across the room with unnatural speed, leaving the corvidian mass behind him. He reached the vaults in seconds to greet a visibly shaken Libraean, who had been peacefully reclined across his couch with a book. He fumbled for his glasses.

"It...it is your mother," David panted, so panicked that he spoke plainly. "Please come, she is dying."

Libraean bolted to his feet, the movement sending the glasses which had been resting on his lap to the ground. He scooped them up and shoved them back on his now colorless face, grabbing his overcoat with shaking hands and following him up the stairwell of the vault.

Although Libraean moved at a significantly slower pace, they both reached the guest room within moments, David throwing open the door with such urgent force that it nearly fell from its hinges.

The crows fluttered in surprise, but remained fixed in their respective places, dozens of beady black eyes observing their arrival. Libraean gasped at the sight of them.

His companion had not moved, draped across the bed like a beautiful, broken doll, her arms bent awkwardly where David had left her.

"My gods," Libraean whispered, as he limped around the birds to the bedside. He felt for her pulse, his eyes swimming with sadness. "David, I'm quite sure she has already passed."

"Nonsense, I would see her spirit rise," he argued, climbing onto the bed to take her back into his arms.

"Ah, yes, your clairvoyance," Libraean remembered.

Her lips had parted, the slightest bit of steam rising from her mouth against the chill wind drifting through the open window. The more David studied her, observing her raven hair and bony face, picturing her blue eyes grayed by sickness, the more he was convinced. How hadn't he seen it before? "We must do something," he pleaded.

"I know you've been waiting for her for centuries, but there is nothing that can be done," Libraean sighed, gazing wistfully at her as he spoke.

"Not true," David disagreed. "I can turn her into one like me."

"Do you hear yourself?" Libraean sputtered. "You should know most of all what happens to a mind forced to live and kill for centuries. You and I are outliers, taking this damned curse along with us when we die - putting an end to this madness! You cannot make another blood drinker. You would be cursing her again, like you and Lucius did so many years ago. She would never forgive you."

David felt tears, dormant for decades, surface. "If she has come back, then it means something has gone wrong," he insisted as he swallowed them. He added, softly, "She would not come back just for me."

"Don't say that…"

"You know it is true. We have not seen Lucius in years, neither have we received correspondence from the Council nor any other gods. Something may have happened - we cannot be certain that Lucius is still contained."

Libraean was quiet.

"And I miss her, Libraean," he whispered as a stubborn tear finally escaped his stony facade. "More than you know." He wiped at his face in annoyance.

Libraean looked down at where she lay. "Then I will do it," he decided.

"Absolutely not -"

"It is the only way I will allow it," Libraean cut him off. "My soul has been unblemished for millenniums, my sins long been absolved. Perhaps my blood will ensure that she keeps her goodness throughout it all."

"But you haven't been a true blood drinker for centuries," David protested.

"I may have been forgiven and allowed to age, but Lucius's blood still runs through my veins, however it has been transmuted since I first turned."

David was torn, his conscience battling his selfish desire. "But you have worked so long for absolution, how can you simply throw it away?" he continued his dispute.

"This will just serve as another gift from me to mankind. Lucius can never again be allowed to rise, and if she has returned to warn us, then we must allow her to."

David slipped out from beneath her, allowing her body to settle back into the starched pillows. He took his place next to where Libraean stood. "I will not stop you," he gave in quietly.

Libraean did not lunge, but slipped down beside her on the bed, lifting her up and cradling her in his arms. He kissed her softly on her forehead, and whispered, "Forgive me", provoking the old memory of David's first turn to nip painfully at his mind. He focused on Libraean, watching as he lifted her limp wrist to his mouth and bit her so gently that she barely stirred.

David could not tear his eyes from the scene before him, for he had never witnessed an immortal drink with such careful reserve. Libraean did not succumb to the bestial thrall that human blood invoked and stopped himself easily, pulling up the sleeve of his right arm and allowing the vein he subsequently severed to linger right above her lips. He let it drain for a moment before setting her back down in the bed. He wrapped a nearby handkerchief around his wound to stop the bleeding, then stood up to cover her back up in blankets.

They stood, motionless, in wait. The crows around them had quieted, emitting nothing more than a gentle rolling purr. After several minutes had passed, Libraean sighed. "We are too late."

David rested his hand on his back. "Thank you for trying."

Suddenly they were interrupted by a loud clattering.

They looked up to see Old Man Jacob in the doorway, his expression incredulous, shards of broken glass from the water carafe he was holding now glittering around his feet. David felt Libraean stiffen under his hand. "What are you doing here?" he asked, his face completely white.

"Please forgive me," Jacob stammered as he walked towards them, with the careful trepidation one has when approaching a wild dog. The glass crunched under his shoes. "I had to watch over you, to make sure you were all right. I - I have left the flock."

"It does not matter," Libraean retorted, an unusual ferocity in his voice. "Your actions are unforgivable."

David was perplexed, looking back and forth between his manservant and his friend. He was well aware that they had never met, but he hadn't anticipated this sort of reaction. "I don't understand."

Libraean turned towards him, his pained expression offering a glimpse of the man he once was. "David, this is Gabriel, the angel who deceived me long ago. Apparently, he is now a human."

David was speechless.

284

Jacob stopped his approach a few feet from them, wringing his gnarled hands with apprehension. "Please forgive me, sir," he addressed David. "I could not leave him behind. I gave it all away so I wouldn't have to. I didn't intend on revealing myself to him or you, I simply wanted to watch over you, to protect you from harm. It was the very least I could do, after my…" He trailed off, overwhelmed with emotion.

David put up his hand to stop him. "You do not have to apologize to me, Jacob. You have been unquestionably loyal and devoted to me for years. And, if anyone understands the complexities of love, it is me."

Libraean scoffed. "You don't lie to the ones you love," he muttered.

"Sometimes you do," a soft voice came from the bed.

David spun around to see her, sitting up calmly, her black hair flowing down around her. He flew to her side, pulling her into his arms. She no longer reeked of death, the transformation completed quietly under their notice. He pulled her away to stare into eyes that had been restored to a vivid shade of blue. "Is it you?" he whispered, hopefully.

"I cannot seem to recall, but I've just been told the most beautiful story that is helping me remember," she smiled.

He kissed her, assaulted with the aroma of bonfire smoke and crisp fallen leaves. His heart felt as if it would burst from joy, as he pressed his cheek to hers. "I will always help you remember."

They were interrupted once more, this time from a pounding that echoed throughout the manor, that came from the front door. A few of the crows loudly expressed their irritation.

Jacob moved to resume his role of caretaker when David rose to stop him. "Amend your situation with Libraean. No matter his protestations, he has missed you as well."

He turned back towards his eternal companion, who was sitting patiently on the bed amongst her crows. "I will return. Please do not go anywhere," he said, only half in jest.

"I won't," she promised.

He descended the staircase, wondering who the late-night visitor might be. It seemed irrelevant, his thoughts being pulled towards the woman sitting in his guest room. A sharp crack of thunder let him know the storm had resumed as he reached the tall, stained oak doors, hoisting them open with unintended gusto.

Standing in the doorway, pummeled by the sudden downpour of rain was none other than Danulf.

The third shock of the evening drained any bit of color from David's face, his jaw slack as he watched his dead friend step through the doorway and remove his elegant tophat to reveal a recently trimmed crop of silver hair. He was dressed the part of a perfect gentleman, save for aged ink that peeked around his cuffed sleeves. A new scar had settled down his cheek, but it didn't take David long to realize that he was still very much a blood drinker.

"Hello, Dragon Slayer," Danulf greeted him, rain trickling off the ends of his coat. "Sorry to barge in on you like this, but you were extremely difficult to find. I hate to be the bearer of bad news, but you're going to have to come with me.

"Our old friend, Lucius, has returned."

LIMINALITY

❧

THE ANCIENT ONES TRILOGY

Volume II

COMING 2021

Morrigan stood at the window, watching the howling storm toss the trees in the distant woods. The old house creaked and groaned in vexation, as the wind rudely threw anything it could find at its windows and walls. The woods were almost entirely barren, the last remnants of brown leaves swirling around the cemetery below. A distant intuition suddenly whispered that tonight was Samhain, the Celtic celebration of the night between the autumn equinox and winter solstice, the night she'd first made love to David, centuries ago.

She closed her eyes against pain so strong it seemed to rot her from the inside, a suffocating, overwhelming sorrow that demanded her submission. She had obeyed at its onslaught, refusing to leave the parlor when she realized that her clearest memories were there, David and her sitting near its fireplace as she lay dying, telling her the tale of their forbidden love affair. Even if her memories hadn't returned, she had fallen for him then, entranced by the careful way he pronounced each word, as if he fought a hundred different accents to mimic the proper English tongue. She admired the way his forest colored eyes would dim as he recalled moments of tragedy, then burst into a vivid green as he spoke of the mysterious goddess he called the Morrigan.

She tried to picture where he was now, hoping that wherever he'd retreated over the past few days offered him solace. She had to trust that the decisions she'd made in her recent past were sound, even though every part of her present being ached to be reunited with David.

Tonight, she decided to retrieve her old diadem of corvid bones from the top of his bookcase, remarkably well preserved for its age, and put it on, trying to recall every moment lost. It had worked, visions of him and her swept up in battle dancing dreamily in her distant mind as she stared out into the dying autumnal forest.

The door opened behind her, but she did not turn, assuming it was Jacob bringing her a fresh bottle of blood. He was such a kind soul amid the deadly creatures who had overtaken the house, she wondered why he'd chosen to remain amongst them.

"Why so solemn?"

She whipped around, for the voice that spoke was not Jacob's.

Lucius stood in the doorway, his long frame leaning against the wood as he examined her with his arms crossed. She blanched at the sight of him. "You shouldn't be here," she said, lifting the diadem away from her head.

"Why are you taking that off? It looked lovely on you, as if you were some exotic priestess from a distant land." He smiled as he sauntered into the room.

"You need to leave," she repeated, her voice forceful though she was delicate in replacing the diadem in its box. She looked back up with him with a scowl, placing her hands on her hips. "I understand that you do not remember me, but believe me when I tell you I can tear a man's spine from his body, even without a weapon."

His smile didn't falter, undeterred by her words. "Oh, I believe you," he said. "I witnessed that side of you quite vividly. And, normally, I would respect your wishes to be left alone. However, I'm not here for my own pleasure, rather, sent on business."

Morrigan's recently unearthed memories had made his true appearance clear in her mind, and she briefly marveled at how similar his new body was to the god she'd once known. He was still pale, tall, and thin, with cheeks that hollowed and mischievous golden eyes. This creature was more youthful, however, with his wavy, cropped black hair and long sideburns that grazed the cut of his jaw. She could smell him from where she stood, the aroma of extinguished bonfires spiced by cloves overwhelming her senses. "I don't think you understand how important it is that you leave. We have history, you and I."

"Is that right?" His lips danced with amusement as he walked right up to where she stood, seating himself right on top of David's desk. His movement knocked over the quill box as loose sheets of parchment crunched beneath him. "I cannot begin to imagine what kind of history would exist between you and I that would make you want me to leave so badly." His words were softened by his accent, the syllables ending in a gentle purr.

Morrigan growled in frustration, the windstorm outside suddenly bringing with it a smattering of rain. Crows screeched in the distance.

Without flinching, Lucius snapped his fingers and the dwindling flames in the fireplace roared to life with such intensity that they nearly escaped their confines of stone. "Two can play at that game," he teased.

Morrigan crossed her arms. "For someone who doesn't remember who I am, you certainly spar with me just the same."

He waved his hand so that the flames quieted. "And that brings me to why I am here. The wolf and the halfling are concerned with your wellbeing and have tasked me to pull you out of your melancholy. Apparently, they'd like to tap back into that lovely mind of yours."

Morrigan frowned. "Nothing good can come from my memories. They did not serve their intended purpose and now my lover has abandoned me. I cannot stand to be in this house another minute, let alone go through that again."

"Excellent," Lucius stood, clapping his hands together. "I feel similarly in sentiment. Let us take our leave of this drafty old place."

"I cannot go with you," Morrigan sputtered, horrified at the thought. "You are the cause of my problems."

Lucius shrugged. "Then allow me to be your solution."

She barely had time to register his movement before he darted forward, tumbling out the parlor window. She flew to the edge, looking down to see him smiling back up at her. "Why do you look so surprised?" he laughed. "You mean to tell me that you've never used our abilities before?"

Not to be outdone, nor admit to him that she hadn't, she jumped down to join him, landing on the moist earth with a soft thud. She stood, surprised at how easily her body had just moved. She glanced back up at the window, realizing she'd jumped down two stories as if it was nothing.

"Ah, my dear, you have much to learn. Come, I have something to show you," he extended his hand out to her.

She realized, much later, when they'd reached the heart of the city, that she hadn't even hesitated to take it.

Discover more from this author at
www.quillandcrowpublishinghouse.com

.

Printed in Great Britain
by Amazon

81261259R00171